Fairy tales, myths, and le... imagination for generations, even as many of them offered explanations for things the human mind otherwise would have a hard time comprehending. But as readers of science fiction and fantasy are well aware, often what is considered as magic at one point may only be science we have not yet learned to understand.

Now, in fourteen original stories, some of science fiction's and fantasy's most innovative minds take up the challenge of retelling both classic and some lesser known fairy tales in a science fiction context, including such wonderful reading experiences as:

"The Goldilocks Problem"—This world was too hot, this world was too cold, and this world. . . .

"Ailoura"—Robbed of his patrimony by his stepbrothers, could a young man regain what was rightfully his with the aid of a genetically enhanced felinoid?

"Dancing in the Ashes"—She'd fled to a medieval realm through a one-way transporter. But would she find the prince of her dreams or end up as the lowest of servants in a society that had no concept of upward mobility?

More Star-Spanning Anthologies Brought to You by DAW:

SOL'S CHILDREN *Edited by Jean Rabe and Martin H. Greenberg.* This original collection explores the entire Sol System, from the planets and their moons to the Asteroid Belt to the interstellar visitors that periodically pass through our section of space. So fasten your safety harness, rev up those rocket engines, and get ready for the trip of a lifetime with sixteen memorable stories by such stellar navigators of the imagination as Timothy Zahn, Jack C. Haldeman II, Kristine Kathryn Rusch, Mike Resnick, Roland Green, and Michael Stackpole.

MARS PROBES *Edited by Peter Crowther; with an Introduction by Patrick Moore.* In this fine volume you'll find seventeen imagination-grabbing tales ranging from the incredible discovery made by a native Martian species which may change the entire course of their future . . . to a reporter hunting down the crew of the very first mission to land on Mars . . . to a "rescue" mission to recover an astronaut "kidnapped" by Martians . . . to a Ray Bradbury Mars story never before published in the United States.

OCEANS OF SPACE *Edited by Brian M. Thomsen and Martin H. Greenberg.* From an alien tribal leader displaced from his rule for failing to stop the takeover of his world by humans . . . to a biologist creating new forms of humans able to thrive in environments different from our own . . . to a ghostwriter spinning adventure yarns in a distant star system, only to find himself living them . . . here are sixteen original tales of the humans and aliens ready and willing to explore the unknown for the pure thrill of discovery or in search of glory and fortune beyond most people's dreams. . . .

ONCE UPON A GALAXY

Edited by
Will McCarthy,
Martin H. Greenberg,
and John Helfers

DAW BOOKS, INC.

DONALD A. WOLLHEIM, FOUNDER

375 Hudson Street, New York, NY 10014

ELIZABETH R. WOLLHEIM
SHEILA E. GILBERT
PUBLISHERS

www.dawbooks.com

First Printing, September 2002
1   2   3   4   5   6   7   8   9

DAW TRADEMARK REGISTERED
U.S. PAT. OFF. AND FOREIGN COUNTRIES
—MARCA REGISTRADA
HECHO EN U.S.A.

PRINTED IN THE U.S.A.

ACKNOWLEDGMENTS

CONTENTS

INTRODUCTION

by Wil McCarthy

WHO can imagine a childhood without fairy tales? Frog princes and enchanted ladies, an intertwining of magic and moral instruction. These stories entertain, diverting children from the tedium of a rainy day or winter's night by the fireplace. But they're much more than that.

Collectively, fairy tales are among our most formative influences, adding a visceral heft and sting to the purely verbal warnings of authority: beware of strangers. Fear the forest and its creatures. Be kind. Be clever. Don't be fooled by appearances. And above all, *don't forget*. And indeed, we haven't; the words and morals of every fairy tale echo down through the decades of our lives, teaching and re-teaching the same lessons in a context that evolves around us, while the tales themselves remain unchanged.

Every bookworm knows it: you are what you read.

This is all well and fine, but even as a child I was sometimes bothered by the fact that fairy tales, without exception, hinge on a supernatural occurrence. I had waited and waited for a supernatural occurrence in my own life, some little sparkle of magic, but it never quite seemed to happen. And in a way, this seemed to undermine the authority of fairy tales, to relegate them to some other, slightly parallel universe where things like that could really happen.

But in January of 1985, during the Christmas break of my first year at aerospace engineering school, I picked up a copy of *Isaac Asimov's Science Fiction Magazine,* and read a story which literally changed my life. It was "The Spinning Kingdom," by Thomas C. Wylde, a story which was unambiguously a fairy tale, despite being set on a generation starship, and hinging not on magic but on the vagaries of

9

angular momentum. The idea hit me like a thunderbolt; I
saved that magazine for years, and then finally sliced out
the story with a razor blade and threw the magazine itself
away. "Someday," I said, "I'll read this story to my own
children, and their lives will be subtly shaped by a morality
play that could actually happen."

Now, at the dawn of the twenty-first century, I do have
children of my own, and I do read to them from those
tattered and browning pages, held together with an ancient
paper clip. And though I'm a science fiction writer myself,
that strong link remains to the fairy tales of childhood.
They travel with me, coloring my choice of language, of
subject matter. My latest novel, *The Collapsium,* is about a
hero and a queen and a villain . . . and the quantum-
mechanical effects of miniature black holes.

To me, the marriage of science fiction and fairy tale is a
natural bonding, a coming together of soulmates, and it is
with great pleasure that I've joined longtime anthologists
Martin H. Greenberg and John Helfers in compiling this
collection of original stories—including Wylde's long-
awaited sequel to "The Spinning Kingdom." Hopefully,
you'll find something in these pages that will, in some small
way, shape your own life. At the very least, we'll hope to
entertain you on a rainy winter's night. Best wishes. . . .

SPINNING KINGDOMS, TWO

by *Thomas Wylde*

The author of four novels and a score of short stories, Thomas Wylde sees this tale as "a kind of reverse-image companion" to the original "Spinning Kingsom" story he published in *Asimov's* seventeen years ago. Wylde is a middle-aged git living in the hills of Los Angeles, along a road where rainstorms sometimes wash down corpses from a defunct cemetery. He once fixed radar units at an army air defense site on the Jersey coast, which made it convenient to get to Woodstock, with ticket number 13 in his pocket.

Lately he has been intermittently at work on a multi-volume novel, for which he professes to have low hopes: "I positively excel," he says, "at sloth."

THERE was once a wooded kingdom that rested in the bosom of a spinning cylinder on a journey between the natural planets in search of a new home. This kingdom had no King at all, but was ruled by a Queen of surpassing beauty and wisdom. Now the Queen had a son who, having reached a marriageable age, was about to take of himself a bride. Samantha was her name—the only daughter of the Queen's most senior adviser, Brickelstaff.

The banns were published, and throughout the kingdom echoed happy rejoicing for this coming union. Euphoric voices all, save one: Brickelstaff himself, the father of the bride. He paced his chambers in nervous agitation, and spoke his mind to Hampton, his factotum, saying, "This is the final insult!"

Hampton kept silent. He knew of his boss' secret hatred

for the Queen and wished not to inflame the angry man's passion any further.

"The Queen is beloved!" Brickelstaff announced. He then came close and whispered, "I cannot tell you how that galls me!"

Again, Hampton remained silent.

The adviser resumed his perambulations, and soon came to a decision. "The marriage will not occur."

"But they love one another," Hampton said, surprising both of them by this outburst. As Brickelstaff turned his awful glare upon him, Hampton ducked his head. "Forgive me, sir, but their love is plain for all to see."

"Nevertheless," said Brickelstaff, and though he loved his daughter, and had denied her naught her whole life through, his mind was made up. "I will find a way. The time has come to take my revenge."

As the day of the marriage drew nigh, the kingdom over-flowed with festive celebrations and contests of skill.

The prince himself climbed greased poles and tossed rings of braided bark and bobbed for bright red apples with the best of them, often winning, to be sure, but also laughing off his defeats with a grace befitting his station. Samantha, his intended, was likewise caught up in breathless displays of agility and mock prowess, proving herself worthy of the Prince time after time. When, on occasion they were thrown together, the two grinned and capered in delirium, their hands entwined in not-so-secret caresses.

The Prince also made merry with his cohorts, who plied him with strong beer and weak taunts. Together they competed in the Castle of Cards contest, though by the time the Prince's construction neared shaky completion, he was panting and sighing and his ears so roared with intoxication that he took himself off for a solitary walk in the woods.

He found a grass-covered hillock and lay down to rest. Above him the curving walls of his world rose up and over, miles away. The deep waters of Lake Penelope, which glistened overhead in the arc lights, seemed for a dizzy moment about to fall on him. "Please stay where you are," he muttered. "At least until after the marriage. After that, I don't care what happens."

"A fine sentiment," said a voice, high and raspy.

The Prince looked over to behold a red-furred fox.

"Are you talking to me?"

"Someday you will be King," said the fox, and he made his whiskers bristle. "I do hope by then your attitude will have aligned itself with the welfare of the world in which we all dwell."

The Prince exhaled an alcoholic sigh. "I will not apologize for my happiness."

The fox laughed. "Just teasing, Prince. Though I am but a clockwork creature with a heart of sand, I think I understand the ways of human happiness."

The Prince grinned. "She loves me."

"In that case, far be it for me to intrude with those niggling doubts I happen to be privy to."

The Prince sat up. "Whose doubts? *Her* doubts? Are you saying Samantha has doubts? Doubts about *me?*"

"They are but infinitesimal quibbles," said the fox, waving his bushy red tail to and fro. "I see now I should not have said anything. Please forgive me."

"I demand to know."

The fox shrugged. "You could, of course, unlock my heart with occult commands. I am quite helpless, as you know."

"So be it," said the Prince, and uttered the override code to the fox. In moments he knew the unhappy facts, but before he could despair at the imperfection of Samantha's love, the fox provided him with a perfect solution.

So armed, the Prince rushed back to the contest grounds and swatted aside his ill-shaped creation, scattering cards over the cobblestone path. "I shall retire to my rooms," he said, "where I might complete my entry in peace."

Then, with a mysterious wink, he hurried off.

"He's drunk," his friends concluded, and resumed the bachelor party in earnest, toasting their now absent guest of honor with heroic gusto.

The Prince returned within the hour, carrying his Castle of Cards on a wooden slab, which he lowered to the judging table with exaggerated care. Even Samantha found annoying his well-lubricated smirk.

"What are you up to, Sly Boots?" she asked.

"You'll see," said he. "I think you'll find I have an excellent sense of humor after all."

"I never said you didn't."

With that his smile faltered a bit, but he shrugged.

"So you say now. Just watch . . ."

The fat, beribboned judge approached the table, which was covered with enough card castles to house all the people of all the worlds, spinning and otherwise. Of a sudden, the ground began to quiver, thence to shake with authority, at which the fragile constructions flew to pieces in a fluttering blizzard of cards. All but one: for the Prince's Castle still stood amid the pasteboard ruin—with the aid of an unlawful application of adhesive.

"Whoops," said the Prince.

After a moment's suspenseful pause, everyone began to laugh, even those whose labored creations were naught but piles of bad poker hands thrown together in heaps.

The laughter died, however, when the shaking did not stop, but rather grew to a fever pitch. All about them windows cracked, and chimneys sent down a rain of dusty bricks. The shelves of village shops forthwith buckled, releasing their bounty into the aisles. The Prince frowned, uncomprehending. Then the shaking did indeed stop, and that was the worst of all, for the gravity of the kingdom began steadily to rise. . . .

Before it was over, the spin-gravity on the cylinder floor had reached two gees, and people were crawling like beasts of burden toward the end cap walls to climb to their relief. In the control room, it was found the fuel gauges all read zero: the spin-rockets had exhausted their reserves in urging the kingdom to its faster pace.

The Queen summoned her chief adviser, Brickelstaff. His clever hands dipped and probed among the controls, then he stood back, shaking his head. "Your Highness, there is no solution here."

"How could this have happened?" asked the Queen.

"Perhaps the security disks will tell us."

Indeed they did. Throughout the hour before the incident, the only one to have touched the controls was the Prince. He was sent for, and arrived with such a hangdog look that the Queen knew at once his guilt.

"Why have you done this?" she demanded of her son.

He could but mumble it was a joke gone wrong.

"A joke!" cried Brickelstaff. "Our world in disarray.

Four people fell to their deaths, and two others died of heart attacks. This is the fullness of your *joke.*"

There would be no need of a formal trial. Brickelstaff advocated the death penalty, and the Queen assented, holding back tears. This was no time to show leniency to favorites, even to her own dear son upon the eve of his marriage.

Throughout the kingdom, celebration turned to mourning.

Brickelstaff called for his factotum, Hampton, who took charge of the prisoner, leading him out into the forest to perform the execution.

They had not gone far when Samantha caught up to them, struggling against the heavy gravity. "Please don't kill my beloved!" she cried, then handed up all her jewels. "Take these, and spare his life if you can find a way."

But Hampton refused the glittering items, saying, "Keep your pretty things, Samantha."

She took back the jewels with reluctance, then broke down and wept. "What shall I do?"

"You have bruised my heart with your heavy tears," said Hampton. "I shall spare the life of the Prince. Instead, I will place him in a deep sleep, from which he will awaken only at the trumps announcing the End of Time."

Samantha bowed her head. "You have my undying thanks."

She wiped the tears from her face, and used them to anoint the Prince in wordless prayer. She turned again to Hampton, who was eager to be off. "Don't tell me where you hide my beloved. Such knowledge might corrupt my heart and give hope to my enemies. It is enough to know that he remains safe in the world, though hidden away from me."

"I so promise," Hampton said, then led the remorseful Prince away to work his sleeping spell.

Samantha returned to her cottage in the woods. She placed her jewelry back in the wooden case, then took the box to the fire and dropped it in. She went to her wardrobe and donned the only black dress she owned, then carried all the others—including her unused wedding gown—to the fire.

"That's that," she said, and collapsed by the hearth to await the End of Time.

*   *   *

Meanwhile, in hopes of correcting the kingdom's woes, the Queen met with anyone who might provide a solution. It was suggested rocket fuel could be replenished by the fermenting of grains, or that hydrogen might be teased from the waters of Lake Penelope, or perhaps even that chunks of rock could be accelerated away by means of some electrical apparatus, causing the cylinder to slow its spin. All plans, she was assured by Brickelstaff, that might succeed in the fullness of time, should that interval stretch into a few patient centuries. A more timely solution was sought.

One young engineer took the Queen on a flying tour of her unfortunate kingdom. They donned gas-powered reaction suits and pushed off from the central axis, where the spin-gravity was nil. Here many of her subjects had set up a nebulous encampment, floating in pressurized plastic bags that drifted about like clouds.

The young engineer first guided the Queen close to the cylinder's inner surface, where the buildings and trees roared past with dizzying speed, just below them.

"As you can see," said he, "the kingdom's spin-gravity only affects things that partake of that motion. We are free to float above it all."

Still, the wind tugged at their clothes, trying to force them to the unforgiving ground. "Let us away from here," said the Queen.

They flew on squirts of gas back to the axis line and alighted on the north end cap, near the spiral stairway that led to the surface. "Please come with me, Your Highness," said the young man, starting down the path.

Initially they could glide headfirst along the curving steel banister, but soon they gained a certain weight and were forced to walk. Halfway down, they paused. "This feels a familiar heaviness," said the Queen.

"We are now at one gee," said the engineer. "Imagine if we were to relocate the surface here."

The Queen looked out along the length of her world, attempting to see in her mind's eye the solution. "It would be smaller, of course."

"Exactly half as big," said the young engineer, "but our population is small. At worst, the tedious expanse of our forest wilderness would need to be reduced."

The Queen thought to make the best of it. "You may set to work at once."

As construction began, the Queen discussed the solution with her chief adviser, Brickelstaff. " 'Tis true," she said, "we lose half our ground, but the half that remains will be of a proper gravity. This is fitting, is it not?"

"Perhaps," he replied. "But have you not noticed that since the . . . incident . . . the gold in your treasury has doubled in value, as it now weighs twice as much."

The Queen frowned, and shook her head free of this thought. "I care not for such ephemeralities. The comfort and health of my people is uppermost in my mind."

"Of course," said Brickelstaff.

"They can't live in the clouds forever, you know. They would grow weak and puny, unable to tolerate the transition to a planet's unrelenting gravity."

"Naturally," Brickelstaff said, taking care to keep the contempt he felt from his voice. *This woman,* he thought, *is too good to be true.*

The work continued. In time there were thousands of pillars erected, and composite mesh was stretched across to form the new surface. Soon, material of the land below was hauled up to fill it out. Workers toiled all day in the new kingdom, then slept in tents or on the bare ground. Those citizens not involved in the reconstruction floated in the clouds, observing the progress in hopeful comfort.

"It is going well," said the Queen, on her inspection tour, but something nagged at her. She questioned the young engineer, saying: "Are you certain you have located the correct level for my new lands? I seem *heavier* than when I was last here. Should we not be closer to the axis?"

The young man blushed, for he knew of this unwelcome weight. "It is not the placement, I'm afraid. The more of the kingdom's mass we shift to our new home, the faster the cylinder spins—the way a skater revs to a blur by drawing her arms closer to her body. In truth, this will only get much worse as we near the completion of our task."

The Queen sighed. "Unacceptable," she pronounced. She ordered the pillars of the world destroyed, and the new surface dropped back down to its former place. The kingdom's spin slowed, reversing the recent trend, but stopped again at two gees

"An unforgivable waste of time," said the engineer, "but I have fashioned a new notion from the ruins of the last one. Suppose we were to expand our world, rather than contract it. Moving the mass of the kingdom farther from the center would naturally slow the cylinder's spin."

"True," said Brickelstaff, who was listening in to this consultation, "but increasing the radius of the world also increases its spin-gravity. Plus, we don't have enough material to build the airtight basement level that must be in place before the mass of the current kingdom could be transferred. I'm afraid your new proposal is as fruitless as the first."

The young engineer bowed and slunk away in defeat.

"I have an idea of my own," Brickelstaff told the Queen. "If you would indulge me."

"If it will solve this weighty problem," she said, "I would indulge the Devil himself."

Brickelstaff secretly bridled at this innocent expression, but outwardly he smiled. "I have discovered some extra rocket fuel your son sought to hide. Although the quantity is not sufficient to slow the entire kingdom to its natural gravity, I have calculated it may suffice for a world half as massy. It would mean splitting your lands in two again, but this time in a different manner."

Brickelstaff explained his plan. He would erect a double end wall halfway down the length of the kingdom, dividing the world into two, equally truncated versions. When folks and goods had been migrated to one half, the kingdoms would be separated by explosive power. The populated cylinder could then be slowed to a proper gravity by use of the remaining rocket fuel. "Our new world would be shorter by half," said he, "but the sky would be just as tall as before, so it would not seem so cramped."

"I see your point," said the Queen, who needed no further convincing. "Pray begin at once."

"Your command," said Brickelstaff, who went sneeringly away to complete his revenge. For it was his evil plan to abandon the Queen alone in the discarded kingdom, condemned to tread the lonely paths at twice her weight to the end of her weary days. "Let's just see how beloved you'll be," he muttered, "when there's no one there to do the honors. . . ."

*   *   *

Samantha saw her father's work begun, and despaired. She believed—she *needed* to believe—that the Prince was safely hidden somewhere in the kingdom, still with her in some sense. But when the kingdom split in two, would the Prince be in the populated half, or the other? "I cannot bear the thought," she said to herself, "that my beloved might be cast off in an empty world, all alone, forever."

She went at once to Hampton, her father's factotum, and pleaded to know where he had placed the Prince's sleeping form. He refused her request, saying: "You made me promise not to tell you."

"But you can see how matters have changed."

"A promise is a promise," said he, in obvious sorrow.

So Samantha laced up her boots and strode off to find the Prince herself. She had not gone far before she stood at the head of a well-worn path and looked about her.

Villages and towns, woods and meadows, streams and lakes, all in profusion, spread outward in every direction. To the north and south, the distant end caps put up their boundaries, but west and east the kingdom stretched on without limit, curving upward to become the distant sky itself. Now a shiny new thing captured her eye. It circled the kingdom: the swiftly rising double wall that split the world in two, layer by layer, built by construction drones in a frenzy of work. Time was running out.

"I shall need help in my task," she concluded.

She stepped into a meadow of nodding flowers and spoke to a bee at work upon a yellow petal, saying: "Please rest a moment, Mr. Bee. I would speak to you of an urgent need."

"You must know," said the bee, "I am a very busy creature." He scraped some pollen from his tiny plastic legs and placed it in a sack hanging from his belt. "Nevertheless, go ahead and tell me what you want."

Samantha knelt down beside the bee. "You and your fellow creatures fly about the kingdom without restriction. You go everywhere and see everything. Please help me search the world for my beloved, who has been placed in a sleeping trance and hidden away from me."

The bee flexed his wings, motors idling on low power. "It would be a hardship to add this search to our naturally programmed duties, but we will do your bidding if you will perform a service for us in return."

"Only name it," said Samantha, "and it shall be done."

So the bee put Samantha to work, righting the hives that had been knocked over by recent events, and which the bees could in no way lift on their own. Samantha sweated and grunted and lifted up the heavy devices, placing them on power-activated pedestals that allowed the bees to recharge their batteries and perform maintenance on themselves. She also aligned antennae that received daily instructions as to what crops needed pollinating, and so forth, allowing the bees to perform their useful tasks in the living kingdom.

"Is that the last of them?" Samantha asked, slumping to the ground in exhaustion.

The bee, who had guided her about the landscape for this mission, replied: "More than enough."

True to his word, the bee then flew off and communed with his brethren. The industrious creatures commenced their search, swooping low between the flowers, skimming just above the leaves of grass, swerving around trees, then rising high into the sky, scanning in all directions. They invaded houses and shops and castles alike, avoiding with ease the occasional rolled-up magazine. The bees even dropped from the air to scuttle about on the dusty floors of deserted cabins, wriggling under doors to examine closets and to root about in cellars and attic spaces. The bees sniffed and prodded and ran sophisticated olfactory routines, tuned to the Prince's scent by samples Samantha had provided them. Though the kingdom was large, their numbers were vast, and in no time they had made a thorough inspection of both halves, finding nothing.

"We owe you one," the bee said, when he had finished his unwelcome news. "Count on us, when the time comes. . . ."

Samantha sighed, then rose from beneath the branches of an apple tree. "I am certain you did your best," she said, "but now I must continue my search elsewhere."

She came to a small pond and knelt by the edge of lapping waters. She spied a fish nibbling at the grass just beneath the surface. "Please, Mr. Fish, leave off your work for a moment, that I might entreat of you a favor."

The fish poked his head above water. "What is it you want? It is not all play for us fish, you know."

"Forgive me," Samantha said, trying not to cry, lest her acrid tears drop into the water and affront the fish. "You and your finny kind swim hither and about in the waters of the world. You go everywhere and see everything. Please help me search for my beloved, who has been placed in a sleeping trance and hidden away from me."

"Just a minute," said the fish, and he swam off to meet with several others in his school. When he returned, he agreed that he and his fellows would scour the waters of the world in search of the Prince. "But first you must agree to perform a certain task for us in return."

"Name it," said Samantha, "and it shall be done."

The fish put her to work, realigning effluent pipes and sluiceways that had been knocked about by recent events. Now the fish could gain access to neglected waterways and perform their duties of purification. It was hard work, both wet and filthy, but Samantha labored to the bitter end, and complained not a smidgen, though her black mourning dress grew heavy with thick, ill-scented mud. She rinsed it clean in a stream that was now full flowing once again.

"Have I performed to your satisfaction?" she asked.

"You take to water like . . . well, like one of us," the fish said. "You have our thanks."

Fulfilling their promise, fish spread out through the waters of the world, searching every lake and stream, every creek and river, every reservoir and pond, every sewer and treatment plant in the kingdom, finding—alas—neither hide nor hair nor chemical scent of the Prince.

"Please accept our condolences," said the fish, when he returned with the sad news. His lithe body thrummed with electric motors. "We went everywhere the water went, where fin and tail could take us."

Samantha nodded, and tried to speak, but only sobbed, and lost control of a tear, which dimpled the water beside the fish. His own unblinking eyes became clouded, and he said, "Though we have but hearts of sand, please believe we know the pain of loss."

"I am certain you did your best," Samantha said, "but now I must continue my search elsewhere."

She arose in her still damp dress and went into the forest. Her tread was slow and painful, for the weight of the world was upon her. The wall that cut the kingdom in half was nearing completion, closing up like the silver iris of a giant eye. "Surely," she said to herself, "I have lost him forever."

Up scampered a red-furred fox, who perched before her on a slender stump, his head quizzically cocked. "Are you the one looking for the Prince?"

"How did you know?"

The fox shrugged his little shoulders. "I climb a tree for a peach, and the bees are all abuzz about it. *Bzzz-bzzz-bzzz.* I crouch by a stream to slake my thirst, and it's all the fish are talking about." The fox made fishy sounds with his mouth: *glop-glop-glop-glop.*

"Can *you* help me?" Samantha asked, most exasperated.

The fox leaned back and put his paws behind his neck. "Tell the truth, I thought you'd never ask."

The fox trotted along beside her, chattering away. "I've never actually met the Prince, you understand, but he seems a likable lad, from what I've read."

He had agreed to search the depths of the world—the burrows and holes and caves and depressions of the earth, sniffing out the Prince.

"Excellent," said Samantha. "Now it is time to strike our bargain. What is it you want of me in exchange for your valuable services?"

The fox became quiet and thoughtful, then said: "I think someone has been inside my head, Samantha. My memory is faulty, clouded with unformed images that tug at the corner of my eye. I want you to find out who's been in there, turning over the soil, planting things in my head."

"I wouldn't know where to start."

"Go to the security records," he said. "Search the surveillance disks to see who has been interfering in my natural life. In the meantime, I'll gather up my fellow foxes, and we will find your wayward Prince."

"Very well."

Samantha went back to her cottage and jacked into the net, using powerful access codes she had pilfered from her father. She performed an image-match search for the fox, keyed to his particular shade of red fur, which was unique. There were dozens of hits. Here was the fox: scampering through the forest, digging in the dirt, sniffing the air, knocking over a trash can and running away—scenes captured by various cameras dotted about the kingdom. More than once the image jerked forward in time, as though edited in haste by an unknown hand. "Most curious," said Samantha.

The search priority provided a graded selection of shots, beginning with the best matches, trailing off to those of least confidence—blurry patches of fur slinking through a backyard, lit by a distant porch light, that sort of thing. The last image in the series was a puzzler, for there was no sign of the fox at all. What *was* there formed a knife that pierced Samantha's unready heart.

"Why have you shown me this?" she asked the screen.

The hateful image was just this: her beloved Prince, lurching about in the control room, his foolish hands upon the spin-rocket panel—the very scene that had doomed him before the Queen. The search-match confidence here was less than two percent. "All right," she said, with sudden anger. "Find me the fox in this scene."

The computer zoomed in to the control panel, where Samantha found reflected in a glass-covered dial the very image of the fox, who was standing out of the way of the security camera. "Astonishing," she said. Though there was no sound, she could tell the fox was talking to the Prince, egging him on, no doubt, to perform his unfortunate actions.

Still, this was the final image, and the fox's question had yet to be answered. "Search this scene again," Samantha said. "Find me someone else in the control room."

At once, the computer zoomed in on the fox's eyes, and showed reflected there the image of a man who was standing even farther in the shadows: her father, Brickelstaff.

Samantha sat stunned for a moment, then said, "Burn a copy of this sequence for me."

She was on the way to the Queen to show her the disk when she ran into the fox.

"Good news," he said, grinning to exhibit his many sharp teeth. "We've located your slumbering Prince."

The fox led Samantha into the woods and to a hole in the dirt, surrounded by mounds of debris excavated by several hunchbacked mechanical diggers, which still prowled the periphery with growling impatience. A glass coffin had been hauled forth from the hole, and within lay the Prince in uncanny stillness.

"Is he alive?" she asked Hampton, as he rose from the stump of a nearby oak tree.

"Of course."

She gazed fondly through the glass, and brushed some dirt away. "I thought you said you wouldn't help me."

"I said I wouldn't tell you where he was hidden," Hampton said. "I never said I wouldn't help you."

Samantha produced the security disk from her apron. "Here is your nemesis," she told the fox. "Your boss," she told Hampton. "My father," she said to herself.

The fox snarled, but Hampton declined to comment.

At this moment, harsh tocsins sounded throughout the twin kingdoms. Samantha looked up and saw clouds full of people drifting through the air lock in the middle of the double wall. Time was up. She said, "We are all of us on the wrong side of the world."

Hampton pointed his clicker and chirped the glass coffin, which flew open with a sigh. He then retrieved the sleep button he had plugged into the back of the Prince's neck. The young man's eyes popped open as if on springs.

"Samantha!" he cried out, for she was the first thing he saw. She took his hand, and helped him climb out of his slippery chamber.

Hampton said, "I am perhaps overstepping my authority, in releasing the spell, but I would be willing to bet the spin-rocket controls were rigged to cause the accident, however manipulated by the Prince in his cups."

"And I think we all know," said Samantha, "who so rigged the controls to his evil ends."

"Who?" asked the Prince, blinking in the glare of the overhead arc lights. He then noted the red-furrred fox sitting on his haunches nearby. "Ah, yes," said the Prince. "It is all coming back."

The fox shorted. "Not me, you dolt!"

Samantha explained everything to the Prince on their way to see the Queen. It was time to put an end to a certain nefarious plan.

Brickelstaff sat at his new control panel, watching on security monitors the progress of the evacuation from the

Queen's half of the cylinder. He had just spied the rejuve-
nated Prince enter the throne room—oh, how his mind
reeled in confusion!—when he looked beyond the screen
to find his factotum, Hampton, in the room with him.
"What means this?" Brickelstaff demanded, pointing to
the monitor.

"Things fall apart," Hampton replied, and extended his
arm, meaning to slap one barely-used sleep button on the
old man's neck. But Brickelstaff saw it coming, and flinched
away in time. He fired a neural-pulse weapon, turning
Hampton's heart of sand into a lump of inert glass.

"Next time," said Brickelstaff, "you'll be getting a double
helping of Loyalty in your makeup." He looked again at
the monitor, where the Queen embraced her resurrected
son, alone—as far as he could see—in the barren half of
the kingdom. "A better time will never come," Brickelstaff
said, and reached for the switch that would detonate the
explosive bolts holding the two worlds together.

Before he could toggle the switch, however, a bee flew
up and stung him on the forehead, inoculating him with
the self-same sleep potion in Hampton's button. Brickelstaff froze solid, his hand still pointing at the untouched
switch, now harmless.

"A bee never forgets a debt, asshole," the mechanical
insect proclaimed, with—let's face it—quite a bit of unnecessary attitude. The bee then flew out the window and
across half the world to pass through the still open air lock
and find Samantha to tell her they were even.

Ah, victory!

The order was given, the migration reversed, and the
Queen herself took charge of the transfer of spin-rocket
fuel into her half of the cylinder. The plan to bifurcate the
kingdom would continue, for Brickelstaff had spoken the
truth in part: there was only fuel sufficient to slow the spin
of a cylinder but half the original kingdom's mass. This
time, it was decided to keep the half with the castle.

Things had progressed very far, and the new migration
was complete (except for the slumbering Brickelstaff, who
would be moved last, as befitting his crime), when it was
discovered the fuel tanks on the Queen's half of the cylinder were breached—more sabotage!—and the fuel they

pumped into them was spilling willy-nilly into the vacuum of space. The operation was halted at once, whence began the debate on which would be easier: repairing the tanks and continuing the fuel transfer, or performing the tedious migration yet another time, forget about the castle.

In that instant, and through no fault of the well-intentioned bee, the sleep potion injected into Brickelstaff unaccountably failed. He awoke with a start, and his arm perforce continued its once-halted motion, throwing the switch that separated the halves of the world.

The explosive bolts blew with a sharp, reverberating report, and the air locks slammed shut, as they are wont to do in these circumstances. Now floated there in space: spinning kingdoms, two. The worlds drifted apart, and for a moment nothing at all happened. Then folks commenced to breathe again, like a motor starting up, and voices rang out in consternation and in fright.

Brickelstaff might well have joined them. His monitors displayed scene after vacant scene—a deserted world for him alone. "Wait . . . wait . . ." he said, over and over, as the naked meaning of this disaster descended upon him. "Wait . . . oh, wait . . ." Then he saw that his own beloved daughter Samantha was there with the Queen and her son in a crushing world without fuel and no way to supply it. *He* had the fuel, and it was his to burn, with whatever effect, in his own empty world.

It came to him that the Queen was speaking to him through the ether. "Now that we know who is responsible," said she, "is it possible to know why?"

Brickelstaff lashed out, saying: "You rejected me! And all because I was a commoner!"

"That was fifteen years ago," replied the Queen. "And I rejected you because you were self-serving and vindictive, as I think you have again demonstrated so very nicely."

Brickelstaff could say nothing to that, could only look upon the face of his abandoned daughter and think of the life he had just condemned her to endure.

"Brace yourselves," was all he said.

He angled his spin-rockets and fired them off in perfectly-timed pulses. The spinning cylinder wobbled in wild precessing gyrations that became so violent he thought his gullet would unclamp and discharge a month of rancid dinners. Then his world flipped all the way over, and he did strive with his rockets to dampen the oscillations.

Now the kingdoms lined up again, but this time spinning in opposite directions. Brickelstaff fired his center-line maneuvering rockets, bringing the end caps of the two worlds together. He burned recklessly through his precious allotment of fuel, keeping the cylinders in tight contact. The metal surfaces slipped and scraped and ground together with a hideous shriek, the twin cylinders shivering in heated protest. Yet both worlds began to slow their spin, braking upon one another.

In the Queen's half, the new southern end cap growled and bellowed and grew red hot. Water from the lakes and streams left its confining banks, urged by the northbound thrust from the other cylinder, and sloshed against the tortured metal. A cloud of glowing mist arose, and the water boiled away in hurricanoes of swirling steam. The kingdom continued to slow, its spin-gravity dropping. . . .

At one gee, precisely, the shrill grinding stopped—Brickelstaff had pulled his world away.

The Queen looked about the castle, eyes wide. Samantha clung to her Prince. She felt suddenly light as air, and her sigh was as a million gasps of relief.

When the sultry fog dissipated, the southern end cap was inspected, and found to be in good shape, thanks to the cooling effect of the displaced water. The fish came out of their hiding places and splashed crazily about, and the bees buzzed all through the world, looking for someone to right their hives again, but not worrying about it overmuch. A certain red-furred fox emerged from a deep burrow and sniffed the air with obvious approval.

Yes, all was well in this foreshortened kingdom, and the folks came down from the clouds and resumed their happy lives, as best they could. In due time, the Queen presided over the belated marriage of her son and his persistent bride, and many excellent times were had.

As for Brickelstaff, he fared less well.

The shattering heat that scoured his end cap had not been soothed by healing waters, as occurred in the Queen's cylinder. Consequently, the weakened metal was worn through in numerous places—tiny holes that slowly released the life-sustaining air of his world. And the sound of that air escaping into space at supersonic velocity was like the keening of a thousand banshees, a lonely wail that haunted Brickelstaff on his excursions about this hollow kingdom, all the way to the premature end of his unhappy days.

OF WOOD AND STONE

by Ronnie Seagren

Ronnie Seagren is the mild-mannered wife and mother of a household in Colorado. A longtime denizen of that state's most famous writers' workshop, she publishes infrequent but excellent fiction which straddles the lines between magic realism, mainstream fiction, and SF. She has just completed her first novel, *Seventh Daughter*, a fantasy adventure involving the 1937 solar eclipse in Peru.

An avid nature photographer, Ronnie is deeply concerned about the environment and the conservation of natural resources, especially our forests. "Of Wood and Stone" grew out of that concern and the recognition that paper is a permanent part of our lives—from gum wrappers to the daily newspaper. The computer revolution that was supposed to make ours a "paperless society" has in many ways actually increased paper waste.

BUSHES rustled, and Kevin Ferguson jumped. Tripping over an unseen root, he stumbled into the scratchy embrace of a scrub oak. He glanced over his shoulder. He couldn't see the house, only the trees shining silver in the moonlight. Trees. Their leaves rustled, whispering of secrets and mysteries. Murmurs of guilt and betrayal.

If only I can find the gate, he thought. But which way? He dared not use the tunnel. That was Halbert's domain.

He should've paid more attention. He should've watched the trail instead of the scenery. But he'd been too entranced by the delicious wildness, the green that had held him bespelled.

The green . . .

*   *   *

. . . *Green.* Two days earlier, Kevin had stood before the wall and knew that there was *green* behind it. It spilled over the top and oozed between the massive stone blocks. The wall, twenty feet high and spanning the width of the canyon, held back the surging tide of *green.*

Kevin sniffed at the warm, spicy aroma. So unlike artificial scents that claimed to be "wood glen" and "deep forest," he was uncertain whether to label it pleasant or foul or simply different. He stood in the shadow of the wall as if that cascade of green spilling down could wash away the memory of the devastation he'd seen, the brutal tragedy.

From Denver to Grand Junction and south to Telluride, acres of standing deadwood mottled the slopes of the Rocky Mountains, dry, spongy wood stained the distinctive, dusty purple of Sunspot Blight. Isolated, doomed patches of healthy forest only served to emphasize the futile struggle. *And this is just the beginning,* Kevin had thought. *We have a lot of penance to do before our sins and errors can be forgiven.*

Triggered by solar activity and the ever growing holes in the ozone, Sunspot Blight had first appeared in 2011, infecting thirty percent of North America's trees before scientists could even isolate the cause—a simple fungus, once considered harmless. Some blamed air pollution; others claimed it had escaped from a genetics lab.

The plant manager at Pandora Mill had brought Kevin this far, and then abandoned him. He cast him an expression of both suspicion and sympathy with a cursory "Good luck!" that seemed more threat than affirmation. How far from Telluride? In all the twists and turns of the rutted Jeep trail he'd lost any sense of direction and distance, but thought it couldn't have been more than two, maybe three miles.

Kevin's chest already hurt from the effort of breathing in the thinning air, and he wondered how people could still live at this altitude. The air was warm, and he considered removing his suit coat, but his shirt wasn't rated for UV protection. He tugged at his hat and pushed his sunshades up tight against the bridge of his nose as he gazed up into an intense, eye-watering blue unseen east of the Mississippi River in fifty years. He stared at it, wishing he could tattoo the color into his memory.

"You come to gawk, or have you some business here?"

Kevin spun around, staggering a step as the motion made him dizzy. He blinked until his eyes readjusted to the dusty shadow beneath the wall. A section of the wall had disappeared, revealing a twelve-foot-wide, arch-shaped hole. A small sign and a web of red light beams warned of a laser gate. Had he chanced to lean against that particular section, he would've fallen through the holographic illusion into the field of the laser net. He shuddered.

Behind the gate, a man glowered at Kevin from the shadow of a wide-brimmed leather hat. Dressed in jeans and a plaid work shirt worn open over a bright yellow T-shirt, he appeared stout and at least a head shorter than Kevin, who was himself a mere six foot three. A gardener, Kevin decided, noting the man's heavy work gloves, or maybe a janitor. He didn't offer a name, and Kevin didn't bother to ask. In his line of work, such questions made people nervous.

Setting his face in a deliberate scowl, he announced, "I'm Kevin Ferguson with the IRS, and I'm here to see Dr. Steinhaus."

"Which one?" the short man asked in a voice as sonorous and deep as someone twice his height. He paused, watching Kevin closely before adding, "There are two, you know. Husband and wife."

Kevin leaned into a stance he intended as pure intimidation. "Both. It's a joint return."

"Ah, yes. To be expected, I suppose." He waddled toward a gatekeeper's shack to the left of the arch. "Hang on while I open a passage," he called over his shoulder. He entered the shack, then reappeared a moment later to beckon Kevin forward. When Kevin hesitated, the man flapped his own arm across the barrier to prove it was safe. Still, Kevin held his breath as he stepped through. When an alarm buzzed, Kevin jumped a good three feet. He spun around to watch the archway shimmer back to the holographic solidity of the stone wall.

"Metal detector," the little man explained, striding toward Kevin with a large basket. "Part of our security, I'm afraid."

The man didn't look at all afraid. His stance—arms folded, feet planted firmly—indicated rock-solid stubbornness. Kevin frowned and began emptying his pockets.

"You'll not be needing any of this," his guide announced, dumping keys, coins, and wallet into the basket. He took Kevin's cell phone and camera, even his watch.

"No need for it," he said simply. Kevin rubbed his wrist like a slave freed from chains, even as he stammered a protest. The man eyed Kevin's bag and briefcase as if he might be harboring vipers. "Has this a metal frame?" he asked, pulling the briefcase from Kevin's hand and fumbling at the catches.

"Hey, that's government property!" Kevin protested. The man ignored him, rifling through papers. He pulled out Kevin's PPC—the pocket-sized desktop computer that was so essential for the complex equations involved in calculating taxes.

"I need that. I can't run an audit without it."

The man's glance brushed a stroke from the computer across Kevin's conservative denim suit to meet his eyes. "Surely the sum of you is greater than this," he said, sniffing at the device. "Solar or battery powered?"

"Battery."

"Hmm. Would need charging, then." He unfolded the command board, flicked on the holo-display, and powered up the drive. Fat, stubby fingers waltzed across command icons.

"Hey, you can't do that!"

But the man only glared at him, then proceeded to scan the directories. Not a gardener, then, Kevin decided. He reassessed the man's build—torso like a tank, arms and legs well-muscled. Big, beefy hands. Security guard, perhaps. The tough, scrappy sort, good in a brawl, dangerous in a dark alley.

"We like to keep things simple up here. You might find it a bit primitive, compared to Washington." He proceeded to gut Kevin's overnight bag as well, confiscating several toiletries, his electric razor and blow dryer.

He'd been warned to expect certain eccentricities, and to put up with them. Steinhaus was Steinhaus, after all. But just how far could he let this go? He glanced around him at the wall, at the trees and barren rock. The isolation of the place enclosed him like a bubble. He suddenly felt very vulnerable.

"Not to worry," the man assured him. "We have every-

thing you need. You'll get all this back when you leave."
His escort carried his loot into the shack.

Kevin followed, peering over the man's shoulder. "Quite
a system," he said, nodding at a control panel and monitor
bank and automatically calculating a rough estimate of its
value. "Must take a lot of power."

" 'Totally solarly,' " the man responded, quoting a popular advertising phrase. His nod indicated an array of PV
cells installed along the top of the wall. "Once charged up,
the lasers require only a small amount of power to stay
active. Those red beams are no more than an elaborate
electronic eye, about as dangerous as a flashlight. The lasers
fire only under specific parameters." He rummaged around
for a sack for the disposed contents of Kevin's briefcase
and travel bag. "Can't be frying harmless rabbits and curious chipmunks, now can we?" He handed the bag to Kevin.

"But if you can power this, why can't I have my computer?"

"It's not so much the *what* as the *where.* This is a sanctu-
ary. We will tolerate your presence because the government
says we must, but not your gadgets. Besides, the house isn't
wired. You'll just have to make do the old-fashioned way."
He glared at him as if that were a challenge.

"But how am I supposed to do my calculations? On an
abacus?"

The man raised an eyebrow. "You know how to use
one?" Kevin started to laugh, then cut it short when he
couldn't tell if the man was joking or not. Outside, the man
started hiking up the hillside. Kevin hesitated, already breathing heavily. Did everything here have to be so vertical?
he wondered.

His escort stopped. "This way, Mr. Ferguson." He gestured toward a battery-powered utility cart with a green-
striped awning parked among the trees. Kevin watched him
swagger toward the cart. *Underlings,* he thought with scornful contempt. *Always trying to impress you with power they
don't really have.*

Kevin folded himself into the passenger seat and settled
the bag on his lap, hugging it to him as if it were the last
vestige of civilization. The cart lurched forward, and he
clutched at the frame for support. The driver chuckled.

They followed a narrow dirt road through a grove of

pine. Kevin inhaled the pungent aroma—true pine, he realized, and not anything like the artificial stuff people sprayed on their plastic Christmas trees. He decided it was a pleasant scent after all, and breathed deeply, as if to capture every molecule.

This is real, he thought, peering into the unkempt undergrowth and hoping for a glimpse of a deer or even a squirrel. True wilderness. Neither the planned and cultivated plantings of the new East Coast forests, nor the VR hike he'd taken through Yosemite. He could get lost here, both figuratively and literally. He could wander in and through and around and never choose to be found. He leaned out of the cart to peer up at green treetops.

The driver cast him a baleful glance. Measuring him, sizing him up. Much had changed since the tax riots of '09; the IRS had lost a lot of its power. But people still reacted to him with fear and suspicion. Kevin was tired of being cast as the villain.

"I'm not an ogre, you know," he said with a deep sigh. "Don't judge me by the job. I'm as human as you are."

The driver grinned. "No doubt, Mr. Ferguson. Ogres are much uglier." Kevin allowed himself a brief smile in return.

His escort steered abruptly to the right. "Shortcut!" he proclaimed as Kevin clutched the frame to keep from being thrown from the cart. They entered an old mine adit, a tunnel barely wide enough for the cart to pass. Kevin removed his sunglasses, but the darkness remained, as thick as a veil across his eyes. He could see nothing but the twin gleaming of his driver's eyes.

In the dark, time and distance were lost parameters, but finally the cart jerked to a stop and the man got out. A door opened, sounding heavy as it scraped the stone floor, and pale light illuminated a narrow passage. They emerged into the dappled shadings of an aspen grove, the round, light green leaves twinkling as they shivered in the breeze.

"This be *Caer Cully*. 'Castle of Trees,' or Tree House, if you prefer." Beyond the trees, a large house seemed to grow from the granite that formed its foundation. Trees— tall spruce and incongruous oak shaded and concealed the roof. Kevin thought it looked more like a cottage transplanted from the English countryside than a proper Colorado cabin.

As they came around to the front, Kevin kept his gaze on the trail at his feet and thought only of breathing. "Wouldn't it have been more economical to build someplace less remote?" he asked. *Someplace with oxygen.*

"We like our privacy. Besides we were already here. Our people were among the original settlers around these parts."

Kevin looked up suddenly.

"You're, uh—" The view beyond the house captured his attention before he could complete the thought. Wave upon wave of green and darker green, a puzzlework of pine and spruce and aspen, complemented by a blue, blue sky like a perfect chord.

"You here to work or stare at the scenery?" His guide nudged his shoulder.

Kevin felt the tingle of heat rising up his throat and across his face. *Guilty,* he admitted to himself. He'd been sent to do an audit, but he came for the trees.

But aloud, he could only murmur, "No Blight."

"Of course not," his escort replied. "It wouldn't dare. Loren wouldn't allow it. She takes good care of her things."

Now and for the first time, Kevin looked at his companion, peering behind the mask of his own assumptions. He saw a face like a wad of crumpled paper, the skin as pale as putty. Wrinkles of mirth gathered around brown eyes and a thick-lipped mouth. A darkness beyond the mere shadow of his hat smeared his face like ash. Not at all what Kevin had expected of the Nobel Prize–winning scientist hailed as "The Man Who Saved Trees."

"You're Halbert Steinhaus, then." He tried to sound calm, even reproachful, at the same time feeling his heartbeat gather momentum. How could he not have known?

"Of course. What'd you think I was—the gardener?" The man giggled. He actually giggled and slapped his thigh like some country hick. "Had you going, didn't I?"

"Goodness, Hal! He's a government agent. You shouldn't be teasing him like that."

The new voice was a rich, throaty alto. Kevin turned and returned the gaze of wide, dark-lashed eyes that embodied the essence of green. His gaze fell slave to hers, and he tumbled instantly in love.

She approached Halbert, her posture relaxed and famil-

iar. Soft waves of autumn red hair framed a narrow face
with high cheekbones. Her skin was a golden tan. *Lord, no
one tans anymore,* thought Kevin. Not with the high risk
of skin cancer. "You'll have to forgive my husband," she
continued, rubbing the man's back and playfully tipping
his hat forward. "He just can't resist a practical joke now
and then."

"Oh," Halbert Steinhaus said, somewhat petulantly. "But
I didn't lie to him, love. Did I, Mr. Ferguson? I merely
allowed you to persist in an incorrect assumption. People
often pass judgment based on biased observations. I do
apologize." His mirth made it seem less than sincere. "If
you had asked my name, of course I would've told you. *If
you had asked.*"

"Of course," Kevin responded, acknowledging the joke
with a false smile for the woman's benefit. What had happened to his sense of humor, he wondered. Surely, it was
around somewhere, like a set of keys temporarily misplaced.

"My wife, Loren, by the way, though you haven't asked.
Kevin Ferguson, my dear. Of the IRS."

She was taller than her husband, a graceful, slender figure dressed in dark green slacks and a softly ruffled, white
blouse. Her smile greeted him with genuine warmth as she
extended her hand, her touch so charged with energy, he was
surprised that his own hand was not scorched, that he continued to breathe. Not since high school had he felt this
way—Mary Jo Cooper, he thought, surprised that he even
remembered the name.

Loren Steinhaus ushered him into the house. Kevin's
hand brushed against the wooden door as he entered, and
the coarse texture sent a shiver across his shoulders. Inside,
he gasped at walls, floors, and furnishings, all made of
wood.

People simply didn't waste wood like this anymore. The
Earth couldn't afford it. Synthwood, made from recycled
plastics, the wood grain imprinted on its surface, was now
the height of decorating fashion, made so by economic and
ecologic necessity. But synthwood was brittle and dull, with
neither the texture nor the scent of real wood. Kevin inhaled the subtle aroma now and felt a twinge of guilt at
enjoying it so.

The Steinhauses brought him to a room halfway down a wide hallway. It was furnished with bed, dresser, desk, and chairs, all in real oak. Thick, green carpet matched drapes framing the window and a view of meadow and forest beyond.

Kevin reached out to tentatively stroke the wood of the desk. It felt *alive,* almost as if it breathed. No synthwood could ever match this. He yanked his hand away when he realized Loren Steinhaus was watching him, but she only smiled and nodded, as if to encourage him.

They deserved such extravagance, he decided. After all, if it wasn't for Steinhaus, there might not be any such wood to waste. The world's forests had been fast approaching extinction before the Steinhaus Process introduced a cheap alternative to chopping down trees for foolscap and toilet paper.

"Our room is just across the hall, and the bathroom is at the end," Loren told him. "If there's anything you need, just ask.

"Not as nice as a motel, I suppose," Halbert said, "but we can't be ferrying you up and down the mountain every day."

Halbert picked up a lump of unpolished onyx, like a mountain in miniature, with a delicate, four-inch sprig mounted at its apex. "When we introduced the Process, every nation on Earth wanted to gift us with samples of their finest wood. This twig is from the last baobab tree in existence."

He touched a short, beefy finger to the tip of the smallest twig, gently, thoughtfully. For a moment, he was quiet and pensive. "We persuaded most that living specimens would be more appropriate."

Kevin nodded. Everyone knew of the Steinhaus Arboretum in New York, where these specimens were nurtured; these days, it outranked Disneyland in popularity.

He stared at Halbert, trying to decide if he was what he'd expected. Newscasts described a shy, dedicated scientist, but pictures of him were rare and of poor quality. Using the anonymity of the Internet, Halbert Steinhaus had managed to pull off the greatest revolution of the century, convincing a failing lumber industry to plant trees instead of cutting them down and to retool their mills to literally "grow" paper. Minions of lawyers had bulldogged through government red tape. He'd then retreated into seclusion before the news media caught on that a potential celebrity had escaped their scrutiny.

Halbert abruptly slammed the paperweight down, making Kevin wince. His tone abruptly hardened. "You'll have to work on your own, of course. Loren and I have more important things to do." He held up his hand, forefinger and thumb half an inch apart. "We're this close to finding a cure for the Blight. I did my taxes once, and that's enough. Now it's your problem."

"Look, I'm not your enemy—"

Halbert grunted and stalked out of the room. Loren set her hand upon Kevin's arm. "You have him at a disadvantage. He's more a night person, and hungry, besides. Your arrival delayed lunch. You'll join us, of course."

"I should contact my supervisor first," Kevin said quickly, "to let him know I've arrived."

"Ah, but we have no 'net here."

"No 'net? What about a phone?"

Loren shook her head. "However, we can send a message, if you like. Rest assured, it'll get through."

Kevin was not at all assured. He imagined a messenger pigeon landing on his supervisor's desk.

Lunch was served on a shaded veranda at a carved granite table that could've grown like a mushroom from the patio's stone base. A well-tended garden segued into an alpine meadow where the bloom of wildflowers hovered like purple and yellow mists. A creek chuckled nearby, its path marked by cottonwood saplings. Beyond, pine and aspen made a mosaic of green on green, and distant mountains were dusted with a blue haze.

They ate vegetables, bread, and fruit served with polite but strained conversation. Kevin noted the glances each Steinhaus passed to the other, as if to confirm or question the wisdom of each statement, the truth of each answer. Typical, he thought with a private smile. His job demanded the ability to read people as well as figures, to capture the compulsive glance as easily as a hidden asset. He idly turned his fork to examine the imprint on the back. Sterling silver.

"Loren is allergic to certain metals," Halbert explained

quickly, as if Kevin had posed a question. "While medication alleviates the worst of the symptoms, avoiding contact is still the best course. Now you understand why it was necessary to confiscate certain of your belongings. And you'll not find a single nail in the entire house."

"It wounds the wood," Lore murmured. Her long, delicate fingers caressed the stone table as if tracing an invisible pattern. Halbert smiled broadly, watching him intently as if challenging him to see how it was done.

"Good thing I'm not a building inspector, then," Kevin responded with an uncomfortable laugh, which Halbert and Loren politely echoed.

"So, how do you do this audit thing?" Halbert asked, waving his fork in a circle. "Where do you start?"

Kevin set down his fork precisely across the top edge of his plate and shifted into a more businesslike posture. "Well, to start, I'll need all financial records for the past ten years—and a tour of your facilities."

The Steinhauses exchanged nervous glances.

Kevin explained, "If I'm to properly analyze your records, I need to have some idea of what's involved—expenses, equipment value and depreciation, running costs."

Halbert frowned, but nodded slowly. Kevin understood his reluctance. The Process had been in production for eight years commercially, and so far no one else could duplicate it.

"You needn't be concerned about security," he assured them. "I'm not asking to see secret formulas; I wouldn't understand them if I did. I'm only interested in dollars and cents."

They seemed appeased, and Kevin relaxed. While not strictly true, how could he pass up an opportunity to gain access to inner workings ever other government agency had chosen to ignore for the sake of the trees and the environment? He would be the envy of the office when he returned, not to mention the local chapter of his nature club.

Loren led the way along a well-worn trail. They crossed the creek over a stone bridge not more than fifteen feet from the brink of a waterfall. She paused to allow Kevin to take in the view. "Power lines used to cross the valley, but we had them removed. It spoiled the scenery."

Kevin was more interested in the way sunlight glowed in her hair as if it were aflame. A gust of wind tugged at his hat, and Loren laughed as he clutched at it.

"Why aren't you wearing a hat?" he asked. "Aren't you afraid of cancer and all that?"

"Such an odd attitude," she answered as if pondering a new concept. "Though I do worry about Halbert. He breaks out in a terrible rash."

"Is that why he's not coming with us?"

"Oh, he'll meet us there. He has his own ways, but I thought you might enjoy this." And she waved her hand at a view that seemed to have escaped from a fairy tale. "You like the green, don't you? You hunger for it."

Kevin had to swallow hard before he could answer. "I could watch these trees forever," he admitted.

Beyond the bridge, the path curved around a brow of barren stone to a long, low building, its facade carved from the mountain's own dark granite. Styled like some medieval monastery, it appeared both earthly and ethereal. Intricate stonework edged the roof, and gargoyles perched like sentries at each corner. He smiled at the whimsy of it and shook his head at the absurdity, then merely stared open-mouthed. Loren laughed lightly at his reaction.

"Hal comes from a long line of stonemasons, Mr. Ferguson; it's an inherited trait. He does this for a hobby."

"When he's not busy saving the world?" Kevin asked with deadpan irony, just to hear her laugh again.

"Something like that."

Halbert waited inside, in a laboratory that was contrarily modern—white walls and harsh lights, gleaming copper and glass. *So much for primitive conditions.*

If Halbert was annoyed by Kevin's intrusion, he was equally proud of his work. He showed Kevin around the facilities as if lecturing a grade school field trip. Kevin recognized an assortment of instruments from high school science classes. But others— A gene splicer, perhaps? And a DNA scanning electron microscope. A mini-Cray on an antique desk. *Probably doesn't have Taxman 23.6 in the software, though,* Kevin thought sourly.

Halbert stopped at a glass case to remove a small petri dish, holding it as he would a holy relic. "This is what you really wanted to see. The first viable cloned cellulose fibers." He gazed thoughtfully at the contents. Kevin leaned forward to peer into the dish, but there really wasn't much to see—just some yellowish matter streaking the nutrient base.

"Of course, it required improvement," Loren continued. She sat on a stool and twiddled with an elaborate glass structure. "These first cells were crude, noncohesive. It took two years before we were able to produce anything of use, and another nine months to develop a commercially feasible process. The hard part was producing cells with self-degenerating lignin, which allows us to bypass the old pulping process."

"You're a team, then?" Kevin glanced from one to the other. "You developed it together?"

"Of course!" Halbert Steinhaus again became boisterous and effusive. "I'm only an engineer; Loren's specialty is genetics. She figured out how to do it. I made it work."

"But the patent's in your name," Kevin protested. He'd read that somewhere, he was sure of it. "Isn't it?"

"Patent? We don't have a patent. The Process is too new and too complicated. There are occasional, ah, glitches." A warning glance from Loren.

"But someone else could steal your Process and claim it for their own. They could put you out of business."

The two exchanged glances that shared a secret. Loren spoke. "If someone else were to tamper with our Process, even a minor mistake might mean global disaster. That's why we must maintain such tight control."

"All the more reason. Patent it before someone else does."

Halbert interrupted. "It's not likely, Mr. Ferguson. Sometimes even we don't understand what we're doing." He pulled back his plaid shirt so that Kevin could see the yellow T-shirt underneath. Its design showed two scientists standing before a complex equation. In parentheses in the middle it read, ". . . and then a miracle occurs."

Instinct told him the two were hiding something, but this was beyond his jurisdiction as well as his understanding. Perhaps they only feared what he might say—and to whom. He decided to shift the focus of the conversation.

"So with the work going on in polymer research, plastic paper, and all that, why did you take this approach? Isn't paper becoming obsolete, anyway?"

Kevin could've sworn he heard a low sound, close to a growl, from Halbert, but Loren spoke first.

"Not until people are willing to give up gum wrappers and daily newspapers they barely read. Not until they're weaned from hard copy bank statements and paperback books. Not till corporate computers all speak the same language and people lose the need to hold information in their hands to make it real."

Halbert took up the diatribe as the two of them flanked Kevin and escorted him across the lab to a long corridor. "Petroleum won't last forever either. I can tell you, there's no hive of elves in the middle of the Earth producing the stuff. It's a limited resource, man! Eventually, it'll run out. On the other hand, our Process uses organic waste broken down into essential compounds—pure and simple, everyday, filling the landfills to overflowing, trash.

"We've eliminated the middleman, so to speak, producing wood pulp direct. No more spending thirty years to grow a tree for the sole purpose of cutting it down. I'm oversimplifying, of course, but the idea is, no more sacrificing forests for toilet paper."

"Consider the savings, Mr. Ferguson," Loren added. "In terms of manpower, energy resources. Chemical pulping wastes half the wood and requires thousands of gallons of water, tons of kaolin. It involves toxic chemicals like sulfur dioxide and magnesium bisulfite. Then there's pollution and waste disposal.

"Eventually, we'll be able to manufacture virtually any grade of paper, from fine tissue to the strongest cardboard. We're also working on vat-grown wood virtually indistinguishable from the real thing. Someday, there won't be a single reason to kill a tree." She paused, face flushed to a rosy glow.

"That's what they said about the whales," Kevin muttered. "Didn't stop us from hunting them to extinction, did it?"

Loren's expression wilted. She dropped her hand from Halbert's grasp and nervously pulled at her fingers.

Kevin felt her despair like a chill wind. "I'm sorry. I

didn't mean to sound cynical. I really liked whales. I spent summer vacations in college on whale watches. When the last one died, I felt so—so helpless, as if I should've stopped it somehow." Loren reached out and squeezed his hand. Kevin thought he would melt but for the relief of her smile. Even Halbert's expression softened.

"You're all right, you know. I felt the same way about the warthog. But not to worry; we've learned our lesson. It won't happen again." He clapped Kevin's shoulder. "We won't let it."

Kevin's stomach soured as they entered a long, narrow gallery overlooking the production facility. He felt like Judas in the garden. His boss had ordered him to take Steinhaus down, to go for every penny. He could do it, no doubt, but the prospect made his stomach churn. He knew the government wanted control of the Steinhaus Process, and he was but the first assault. But Steinhaus had become a worldwide hero in the last three years. He was Kevin's personal hero as well.

This portion of the building apparently extended into the mountain, for the chamber seemed part Gothic cathedral with classic, pointed arches, and part natural cavern. A work in progress, perhaps. Pillars buttressing the roof were crude columns, but the stone railing on the balcony where they stood was fashioned into a vine-covered fence, and the curved stairway at the far end imitated the trunk of a tree. The artistry and detail were amazing, even to the veining in the leaves.

Twenty feet below, stone troughs fed into eight large cisterns covered with copper lids. The air was humid and thick with the smell of growth and greenery. Kevin scrubbed at the scent clinging to his face. Halbert handed him a filter mask and a grin.

"Not the most pleasant aroma, to be sure, but this is where it happens. We use cells from living trees to create what we call the seed batch, genetically altered cells that reproduce up to ten thousandfold. A three-inch core from a single tree can produce as much as an entire forest in only a tenth the time. Once the cells germinate and are viable, we pipe them down to the Pandora Mill—our main facility in Telluride. From there, it's trucked to the paper mills." He pointed to the far end of the chamber where pipes from the vats converged into a large conduit that pierced the mountainside.

"That goes all the way to Telluride?"

"It's not so far on a direct line. A portion of the tunnel was left over from the gold mine era. We laser-bored the rest."

Kevin shook his head. "How do you do it?" he murmured, an innocent statement of pure awe. But Halbert and Loren exchanged a *what do we say about that?* kind of look, shaded with fear.

"Pure magic!" Halbert responded, then laughed while Loren glanced at him reproachfully. "Or so it might seem. You know what they say—one man's science is a lesser man's magic. Oh, not to say you're lesser, to be sure. But as you said, you're not a scientist. The things you accountants do with numbers are no less magical to me."

Halbert peered over the balcony and sniffed at the air. "If you'll excuse me, I smell some work to attend to. Loren will see you back. You must be anxious to get started."

Kevin raised his head and opened his eyes, and until he did so, did not realize he'd fallen asleep. He gazed unfocused at the onyx paperweight, the baobab twig like a miniature tree. He reached for it, then reflexively withdrew, afraid of breaking the delicate twig. Adopting a rigid, *let's get down to business* posture, he attacked the rat's nest the Steinhauses had presented as tax records. Scraps of paper, incomplete ledgers, cryptic, undated notes. How could an engineer be so thoroughly disorganized, Kevin wondered.

His supervisor insisted he would find evidence of fraud and evasion. Since it was a private company, its records were not public, and the experts could only guess, but certainly, the Process had to be making millions—billions—yet Steinhaus continued to claim losses and income far below expectations. "Keep it tight," he'd been advised. "We need irrefutable proof or we'll have the whole world on our backs." Kevin knew the truth, however. He was the scapegoat. If he failed, he would no doubt be out of a job. If he succeeded, he'd be a national pariah. Others would follow. Like piranha, they'd feed until there was nothing left. "Do your job," his supervisor had told him. "No sentiment, no mistakes."

No hope, Kevin added, squinting at a receipt written on a tissue in Halbert's illegible scrawl. *Asset or debit; personal or business? Was that a two or a seven?*

He uttered a cry of futility and pushed away from the desk. Stretching, he moved over to the window. When this was over, he decided, he'd find a view just like this. He'd sit and stare until his eyes were filled to bursting with green and blue.

Movement in the garden caught his attention. Loren worked in one of the flower beds. Halbert was nowhere in sight. Kevin found his heartbeat increasing, his palms beginning to sweat. He scooped up a stack of papers—the pile mentally labeled "What the __ is this?" The missing word depended on his degree of frustration. He'd planned to ask Halbert about them later on, but now would do as well, and Loren better. He grabbed his hat and sunshades, leaving his suit coat discarded on the bed.

By the time he'd reached the garden, Loren had moved on. Kevin found her at the edge of the meadow beneath a twisted oak. A single shaft of sunlight lit her face as golden dust motes danced in a slow spiral. Struck with sudden, adolescent temerity, he hesitated. Stopping just a few meters away, he waited for her to notice.

Loren circled around the trunk, peering up into its cool green canopy. "And how are you today, Sam?" she said, but Kevin could not see anyone hidden among the branches.

Loren caressed the rough bark of the trunk. "It's all right, Sam. I understand." Kevin shook his head. He'd heard of people talking to trees, but naming them? He thought to edge away, sure that his presence would embarrass the woman, but Loren began to sing. The words were foreign and the melody almost alien in structure and tone. Nonetheless, the song evoked images of green things growing. Rich, dark soil and sparkling water. Sunlight. His mind drifted, absorbed in the music of her song, the scent of green. . . .

Green.

"Mr. Ferguson, are you all right?"

A voice in his ear, a cool touch on his arm.

Kevin blinked. Loren stood beside him, her hand steadying him, her face expressing both surprise and concern.

"What happened?" he asked, feeling more than a little dazed. "I remember light and—"

"The sun," Loren explained quickly. "Sunlight through the leaves can play tricks. Perhaps you should sit down for a bit."

He let her guide him to the veranda where they'd eaten lunch. His senses seemed numb. He could barely feel the rough stone beneath his fingers as she sat him at the table. A discordant whine made his teeth itch.

Loren lifted his hand and pressed it around a chilled glass, then sat down beside him.

"Drink," she said. "It's lemonade." Kevin obeyed.

"I apologize. I've never reacted like that before."

"The altitude, I should think. And too much sun."

Kevin nodded. He drank more of the lemonade, licking at the taste lingering on his lips. Something nagged at the back of his mind, a feeling that he'd forgotten something.

"Was there something you wanted, Mr. Ferguson?" Loren prompted, nodding at the papers he still clutched like a lifeline.

"Please, call me Kevin. I had some—um—questions." He fumbled through the papers and pulled out several receipts. "For instance, these items here."

"Oh. Those."

Oh, but Kevin knew that reaction well; it usually signaled a desperate attempt to dismiss as meaningless something of importance. He leaned forward, sensing a mystery, and caught instead the scent of the woman, a very earthy, green smell that called to mind tall trees and delicate flowers.

"Ah." He plucked at his thoughts as if gathering those flowers. "Perhaps you could explain?"

"Certainly." Loren's fingertips drummed against the table. *Tick-tick-tick-tick.* "We've both mentioned allergies and certain sensitivities. The medications we need to counteract them are both rare and perishable."

"And apparently expensive." Kevin nodded at the receipts. He frowned.

"They're prescribed by our family doctor in Denver; we're no band of drug smugglers, if that's what you're thinking." Her smile made a jest of her words.

Kevin shrugged away any such thought—he'd leave that to some other agency. He watched her fingers. *Tick-tick-tick.*

"So it's a medical expense, then. That would be personal, not business."

"Oh, but it's necessary to my work. You've seen the lab, all that—metal." Her mouth circled the word as if even the sound of it was painful. "I couldn't even walk through the door if it wasn't for my medicine. Even then, I must limit my exposure. That's why Halbert does most of the work." *Tick-tick.*

"So why do you do it?" Kevin reached out to touch her hand, to still the *tick-tick*ing of her fingernails.

"For the trees, of course." She returned his grasp, clutching his hand so tightly her nails pricked his skin. "I'd do anything to save the trees. You understand, don't you? You hunger for the green. You need it." The glow in her eyes lit her face. Her voice was husky with desperate passion, the scent of her deep forest, fresh soil, and green. The world seemed to tip, and Kevin leaned forward to keep his balance. Her face was so close. Without quite meaning to, his lips brushed hers. Their touch was an electric charge, so aching sweet, he wanted—needed—more. He reached for her.

She broke free from his grasp with a small cry. Kevin fell against the back of the bench, and his breath rushed out of him. The rest of the world returned as if a moment before, it had not existed. Loren was watching him. A faint trace of a smile lingered, as if she were privately pleased, but her gaze was like a warning. Beware!

Kevin stammered an apology, a flushed heat spreading across his face. "I don't know why I did that."

Loren merely nodded. He stared at her, trying to convince himself it hadn't happened. But his mouth burned as if touched by fire, and he was uncomfortably aware of other, more intimate reactions. He dared not let her gaze ensnare him.

Fumbling with the papers, he coughed self-consciously. "I'd better get back to work," he mumbled, backing up in full retreat. He turned in time to catch a hint of movement at one of the windows, perhaps a curtain falling into place.

* * *

Kevin pounded his temples with the palms of his hands. *I want my PPC!* he mentally screamed, then repeated it aloud just for effect. Doing this kind of work by hand was simply barbaric. No matter how he juggled the figures, they refused to make sense. Debits mysteriously disappeared, and assets followed torturous paths from one account to another. Personal accounts merged with business records in a hopelessly tangled knot. Halbert Steinhaus was either the most incompetent fool ever created or a con artist of stellar proportions.

Worst of all, it appeared the Steinhaus Process was a miserable economic failure. The Steinhauses had taken out incredibly massive loans to finance the Process, running up debts well into seven figures. Expenses trampled profits into the dust. The grand scheme to save the world's trees was all a sham, a house of cards in imminent danger of collapse.

Yet bills were paid; payrolls met. Whenever money was needed, it was there—simply, inexplicably there. How did they do it? What secrets did they hide? He was too experienced to ignore the signs. Money didn't just appear in accounts; it had to have a source. If that source was hidden, it was usually illegal. It looked as if his boss was going to be right. And where did that leave him? National hero or dastardly villain?

Or victim? If he was right, he was vulnerable, isolated here with two passionate, desperate people. *I'd do anything to save the trees.* Was that why they'd taken his phone and computer—to keep him out of touch?

Head cupped between his hands, Kevin stared at the figures until his vision danced. *Is that how you do it, Halbert?* Stare cross-eyed until the assets double and the problems vanish? He closed his eyes, but that did no good, for then he saw Loren's face, eyes wide, mouth open—in surprise or expectation? Her cry echoed like a song trapped in his mind.

I hate this job! he thought, and realized it was true, and had been for some time. He glared at the baobob twig as if it were at fault, and then slapped the desk with both hands as he stood. Papers fluttered to the floor. *Please, let me be wrong,* he thought. *Let there be something I'm missing.*

Too tired to continue, too keyed up to sleep, he ventured into the hall. The rest of the house was dark and still. Had it been that long since dinner? Muted creaks and groans followed him down the hall. At the far end, he found a library, book-laden shelves towering over him like trees in a forest. A huge desk, old and very ornate, crouched like a beast before tall windows. Moonlight drifted through the window to light leather-bound spines. He scanned the titles, looking for something to read. The diversity of subjects surprised him. Folklore and history, fantasy, biology, and chemistry. Physics and mythology side by side, as if the two were related. He bent to read the faded gold lettering on a particularly ancient tome.

"I doubt you could read it." Halbert's sudden voice caused him to jump. "It's not in English, you know, not even the same alphabet." Halbert advanced into the room and caressed the binding gently. "It's been in my family for many generations. I should hate to see anything happen to it."

"Oh, I wouldn't—"

"I know, Mr. Ferguson. You're not the sort of man to take what does not belong to you. But sometimes—well, you are a tax collector, are you not?"

"Auditor. Only an auditor. I have no intention of taking anything at all."

"Oh?" The man's tone implied skepticism. *Even my wife?* Kevin imagined him thinking. But then how could he suspect anything? There was nothing to suspect. An innocent kiss, no more. The result of too much sun. An accident. He'd convinced himself of that. Then why did he feel so guilty?

"I do have some questions, though," Kevin said, trying to sidestep an issue that, for all he knew, could be purely imaginary. "To be blunt, your books don't balance. Your debits far outweigh the credits." He hesitated, realizing that in his panic, he'd blundered into a subject potentially far more dangerous. If Steinhaus had something to hide, Kevin could be risking his life. But like topping the first hill of a roller coaster, he had no choice but to finish the ride. "You owe billions, not counting personal debts. Furthermore, as a personal business, you can't claim a loss more than three years out of five; after that, it becomes a hobby, no longer deductible. There has to be at least a marginal profit, even if it means not claiming all of your deductions."

"You mean it's okay to cheat myself, but not the IRS?"

"I wouldn't put it that way."

"Of course not."

"But the Process is an economic failure; it's all a charade. How long can you keep it going?"

"As long as it takes," he answered with a diffident shrug.

Kevin wanted to scream with frustration. He had to take a deep breath before he could continue. "But how *can* you? The interest alone—"

"Oh, I have my resources, Mr. Ferguson." Halbert walked over to the desk and pulled open a drawer. "My family has many, uh, hidden assets." His hand dipped into the drawer, and Kevin tensed. *Gun*, his mind screamed. *Duck, run, hide, do something!* But he could only stand and watch.

Halbert produced nothing more than a leather bag, the kind used to keep marbles. But rather than aggies and cats-eyes, he poured out nuggets of gold and uncut gems. They clattered across the desktop, some as big as walnuts. One pudgy finger nudged the stones, turning them so that the light danced across their facets. "Whenever I need a little money, I just dig up a few of these."

"But— But—" Kevin stammered. "You can't do that!"

"Why not? It's my gold and my business." The expression on Halbert's face was as guileless and stubborn as a child's. "I own most of the mines in the area, you know."

"But that's a source of income; you have to claim it."

"It is?" Halbert seemed truly surprised. "But I didn't earn it; I just found it. Besides, if I own the land, isn't it already mine?"

Kevin simply raised his hands, let them fall, blowing out his exasperation between pursed lips. "It doesn't work that way," he responded in subdued defeat.

Halbert frowned. He began scooping the nuggets back into the bag. He held out a gold nugget. "Want one?" he asked as if he as offering him a piece of candy.

Kevin shook his head. "That could be considered bribery," he warned, and watched Halbert's eyes and mouth turn into perfect circles of "Oh!"

"I never did understand all this tax and finance business. I'm just a simple engineer, you know."

Anything but simple, Kevin thought. "Then hire an accountant. Someone to look after these matters." Kevin tried to be officious and brusque; instead he just sounded concerned.

"We had one once," Halbert responded, looking thoughtful. "Queer little fellow, always mumbling." He glanced sideways at Kevin. "Would you like the job?"

Kevin shook his head. He tried to hate the man, to convince himself Halbert deserved to be taken down. He failed. "It's going to take more than a bag full of gold to get you out of this mess."

Halbert hefted the bag as if calculating its value. "I'll go get more, then."

"Why not go corporate and sell shares? You could be a millionaire in no time."

Halbert looked at Kevin sadly, as if he were a child who refused to understand. "It's not about money, Mr. Ferguson. It's about the trees. If we did that, it would be like selling our own child. We have to keep it under our own control."

The government won't let you. It'll declare you a monopoly, Kevin thought, but aloud, he said, "You don't understand. Some corporation is bound to take over. All it would have to do is buy up your loans. You can bet they won't hesitate to raise prices."

"But they can't!" Halbert seemed genuinely distressed. "We'd lose half our customers, the ones that can afford it the least and need it the most. And the Process isn't stable yet. There are still glitches."

"But I don't understand how—"

"No. I guess you don't," Halbert said softly. "What is it they call your kind? Paper *pushers?* No insult intended, I assure you. But understand this. Personally, I prefer good, solid rock." He held up the bag of gold. "But for Loren, it's different. She *needs* the trees. I do this for my wife, Mr. Ferguson. I would do anything for my wife." The innocence and sadness were gone, and his tone became sword sharp and dark as storm. His pudgy fingers clutched the bag tight, tighter, until his fist shook. "*Anything,* Mr. Ferguson." Then, as abruptly as a summer storm, his mood changed, the sense of threat vanished, leaving only brusque impatience.

"Now, if you'll excuse me, I have work to do."

He put away the bag and ushered Kevin through the door and back to his room. "Please don't be wandering about. It could be dangerous," he warned. From his doorway, Kevin watched Halbert waddle down the hall, muttering and humming to himself, and descend a stairway at its end. Closing the door, Kevin undressed and crawled into bed.

Eventually, he settled into a fitful sleep where he wrestled with visions of numbers marching across the ceiling. They jeered at him, beating him with mathematical symbols, then chased him into a forest. Trees uprooted themselves to defend him in battle. The images persisted after he awoke, but he couldn't remember who won.

"I really don't understand how you let yourself be surrounded by numbers all day," Loren commented at breakfast, and Halbert was eager to agree.

"Perhaps a hike in the woods would do you some good," he suggested. "Have you ever seen a ghost town? There's a place called Tomboy down in the basin—"

"I'm here to do a job, not stare at the scenery," Kevin responded curtly, tossing Halbert's own words back at him. "I'm not paid to go sightseeing." Besides, the last thing he wanted to do was to wander off into the wilderness with a psychotic munchkin who seemed all too aware Kevin was interested in his wife.

Loren was humming softly, but he avoided her gaze. Just sitting near her made his skin feel hot and itchy. He was actually grateful for Halbert's presence, for he created a buffer, a numbing antidote to the allure of his own wife.

At the same time, Kevin found he hated the man, truly hated him for what he possessed. His life had purpose, meaning; he didn't waste it toting up other people's successes and failures. Most of all, he had Loren. Kevin felt feverish just thinking about the two of them together. Such a woman deserved better, he thought, not some shrunken parody of a man. What claim could such an ugly little man hold on such beauty? How could she bear to allow his touch, his . . . He glared at Halbert from beneath his brows as he drank his coffee.

Yet Halbert apparently failed to notice his ill humor.

"Just as well, I suppose. We need to finish testing the polyphasic T-cells. Keyed for the right enzyme, they'll inhibit the fungi's ability to feed. Won't kill the Blight—not directly—but it'll starve to death, so to speak. . . ."

Fool, was all Kevin could think. *Fool, fool, fool.*

"You should've gone with him, you know."

Kevin glanced up briefly as Loren entered his room and took a seat on the opposite side of the desk, crossing her legs and leaning back, her arms resting casually on the arms of the chair. She wore a royal blue jumpsuit that was particularly appealing.

"He only wanted you to relax. A rare gesture for him."

Kevin pretended to ignore her. He started entering numbers on a ledger sheet, hoping the scratch of the pencil would drown out her voice.

"I think Hal wanted you to see the mines. Just so you don't think we're international jewel thieves or something."

Kevin looked up. Loren was smiling.

"You shouldn't make jokes like that in front of the IRS. Some of us haven't much of a sense of humor." He thought he sounded threatening, but Loren seemed to miss the message. She leaned forward, one elbow resting on the edge of the desk, and stroked the baobob twig as if it were a pet.

"And you? Do you have a sense of humor? Imagination? What do you dream about?"

"Dream?" Kevin responded as if the word were foreign to him. He set down his pencil precisely at the top of the ledger sheet and placed his hands flat on the desk. He thought about last night's dream. Unexpected resentment expanded like a balloon in his chest until it threatened to burst. "I dream about columns of numbers that add up to nonsense, and stacks of ledgers ten stories high. I dream of dancing calculators and monsters made of adding machine tape. On a good day, I don't dream at all." He looked down at his hands. They trembled.

"How sad," Loren said and looked as if she truly meant it. She rose and moved around behind him. He tensed, feeling like a rabbit caught by a hound, uncertain whether to stay put or bolt for cover. Her fingers brushed across his shoulders, shocking him into immobility. But all she did was knead the tight muscles that held his neck rigid. "You really should dream of more pleasant things," she whispered.

This is wrong, he thought. *This is dangerous.* But his body betrayed him. His eyes closed; his muscles relaxed, yielding to her work.

"You should dream of green. Tall trees and sweet grass."

His head bobbed to the rhythm she set, and his mind gradually yielded to the images she suggested.

"Scent of pine. Birdsong. Golden sunlight slanting through dark pines." Kevin leaned back against the chair as if it were a tree trunk. He nudged off his shoes, curling his toes in a carpet that felt like grass. Loren's voice became a pleasant murmur, melding with the trill of a brook and the serenade of birdsong. Adrift in a warm haze, he felt sunshine on his face, warm and pure. A soft breeze scented with pine and wild primrose caressed his cheek. Nearby, a doe grazed; even without opening his eyes, he felt her presence. He held still, so that she might come closer. Closer—

Somewhere a door slammed, and he jerked awake. For a moment the dream persisted, as if the house had been the illusion and the grove reality. But then he blinked, and the grove vanished. So had Loren. Shaking his head to clear the last fading wisps of dream, he picked up his pencil and viciously attacked the numbers before him. The sooner he finished, the better, he decided.

Voices intruded.

". . . batch 338. Blight contamination." Loren's voice was full of frustration and despair. "I already shut down the main flow valve and notified Pandora."

Halbert's response faded with distance. Kevin hurried to the door and caught a flicker of movement in the stairway at the end of the hall. He followed. At the bottom, a long tunnel led toward the lab facility. It was dimly lit by overhead lights he could not see. Ahead, the dark silhouettes of Halbert and Loren lured him on. Too preoccupied to look back, their voices echoed off the rock.

"What about the T-cells?"

"They're not ready yet. We could lose the whole batch."

"We can't afford to. Ferguson's right. We're on the brink of financial disaster. Losing this batch could push us over."

The tunnel ended at a corridor lit only by the light slanting through a doorway twenty feet away. Kevin slipped inside and found himself in the vat chamber. The stairway to the gallery was only few steps away. Kevin hurried up the stairs, his stockinged feet noiseless on the solid stone. His vantage point provided a view of the entire room but kept him hidden behind the ornately carved railing. The smell was still overpowering. He had to hold a handkerchief over his mouth and nose to breathe without retching. Crouching behind a buttressing pillar, he peered through a gap in the railing.

They came into view from a room off to the right. Kevin watched as Halbert wrestled with a heavy lid almost directly below. A new smell wafted up, sickly sweet like rotting vegetables. The yellow sludge in the cistern was streaked with a dirty purple.

"We'll have to dump it," Loren said.

"It would take a week to clean out the system and sterilize it. We're behind schedule as it is."

"Then I'll have to fix it."

Halbert's face darkened, his fists clenched. "You shouldn't have to. I hate what it does to you."

"I can handle it. There's no time for anything else." Loren leaned out over the cistern and waved her hand in a broad circle as if stirring the mixture. Eddies seemed to form in her wake, spreading out over the rest of the surface. The purple streaks curled in upon themselves and drifted toward the center of the vat, gathering into a single clot.

She began to sing.

Something clung to her fingers like filings on a magnet. It spilled into the vat, sparkling like diamond dust, too bright for this murky place. Her song filled Kevin's head with its harmonics. Sympathetic vibrations coursed through his bones and set up a resonance in his chest.

Surely his heart would burst. He could bear no more and opened his mouth to scream, but no sound came forth. Abruptly, the song ended. Kevin found himself clinging to the railing with sweating hands, gasping for breath. He pushed himself away, back against the wall.

When he dared to look again, he saw Halbert cradling his wife in his arms, murmuring softly and stroking damp hair from her face. The mixture in the vat continued to churn, but the purple clot and the smell of decay were fading. Of Loren's work, only a faint glow remained.

Halbert helped Loren to her feet, supporting her as they walked slowly toward the door below. Kevin realized he was in imminent danger of discovery. He could not reach the tunnel before them, could not hope to run its length unseen, for it was too long and too straight for him to reach the far end before they entered the near. He crouched back into the shadowed corner behind the buttress, willing himself invisible and praying they would not take this route.

He caught just a glimpse of them as they passed through the doorway below, Loren supported by her husband and he murmuring to her. Loren glanced in his direction. Kevin feared she'd seen him, but she said nothing. She merely closed her eyes and shook her head as if too weary for his presence to register.

He waited until after they'd passed into the stairwell and the door had closed, then counted to thirty, just to be safe, before he dared relax. He slumped against the railing, his chest suddenly too small for the beat of his heart. What had he just seen? he wondered. *What* could cause such a reaction?

They could cure the Blight, he realized suddenly. With a wave of her hand, Loren could eradicate that evil scourge. How could they keep such a secret? Why didn't they share it?

His thoughts then turned down an ugly alley. Had the Steinhauses created the Blight? Such a thing made sense. In a way, the Blight had ensured Halbert's success. With civilization facing ecologic meltdown, the EPA had virtually tripped over itself in waiving requirements and issuing licenses. Even the Fundamentalist Party had given its blessing, in spite of its stand on genetic engineering and cloning. No one had looked too closely at how the Process worked, or even *if* it worked. Perhaps they all suspected the truth and feared to face it.

Still, the question remained, how did Loren do it? What had he just witnessed? Aliens, perhaps, performing magic—

Not magic! This was after all, the twenty-first century. What had Halbert said about one man's science?

He was an accountant, not a scientist. What did he

know? More than likely, Loren had merely sprinkled something into the mixture. Fungicide? And her singing had been just that. Singing. Only his infatuation with her gave it power.

He dared not use the tunnel to return to the house, for fear one or the other would return. Instead, he found the door leading outside and started down the dirt trail. If discovered, he would say that he'd gone for a walk to get some fresh air. He had no reason to think they'd suspect he'd spied upon them.

Except that he'd forgotten his shoes. He looked down at his feet and considered which would be less conspicuous. With a sigh, he pulled off his socks and stuffed them under a rock, then rolled up his pants legs as if he'd been wading.

He picked his way gingerly down the path, still feeling shaken and not entirely certain of his perception of reality. What would happen if this secret got out? Halbert's reputation would be ruined. The whole precariously balanced system would collapse. They'd be forced to surrender to some conglomerate, one that would raise prices, holding the forests for ransom.

And what could he do about it?

He'd passed the bridge and thought he might make it back unseen. But as he rounded a cluster of juniper and pinion pine, a hand suddenly grasped his arm fiercely.

"Mr. Ferguson, you gave us a fright!" Halbert bellowed. "I thought I warned you not to go wandering about on your own. Much too dangerous. Any number of, um, accidents could occur."

"I just needed some air."

"Ah, yes. Well, don't we all." Halbert glanced at Kevin's bare feet, then up at his head. "You forgot your hat," he added flatly, but said no more. He steered Kevin toward the house.

"But I tell you, this valley's far from tame, and it's protected in ways hard to describe. My poor Loren was worried. She's deactivated the safeguards until we're safely back."

"Sorry," Kevin mumbled, wondering what kind of safeguards this remote and hidden place might require. He envisioned Loren sitting before a computer monitor—or was it a witch's cauldron?

"No harm, though, but come along. The sunlight's making my skin itch, and Loren's not feeling well. She needs to rest."

Kevin took up his work as if it were a shield, armor against his fear. As long as he worked, he figured, and feigned confusion and ignorance, he'd be safe.

But he could not concentrate. Sunlight through the window, filtered through the surrounding trees, cast patterns of shadow across his work, and rustling leaves answered the chatter of squirrels and chipmunks. Loren's presence was like a bright light at the edge of his vision. He fought back with the only weapon he had: numbers. He took to chanting the figures out loud as he worked, as if they were a mantra, a talisman. But the more he tried to concentrate, the less sense the figures made, numbers swimming before him like the dance of dust motes.

He should flee, he thought, and turn the matter over to—

To whom? he thought, fingering the baobob twig. And what evidence did he have? Certainly nothing substantial. Besides, if he turned the Steinhauses in, it would be like the whales all over again. What could he do?

He allowed himself a thin, tight smile. He could do his job. If he completed the audit properly, the IRS would end up owing them money—not a lot of money, but enough to pay off a portion of the debts and keep the wolves from the door. And he had a friend, a lawyer who specialized in corporate law. If he lost his job over it? Suddenly that seemed more reward than punishment. He wondered if Halbert had been serious about his job offer. If he did all that, they might forgive him his curiosity. With fresh determination and a fervent sense of mission, he renewed his attack on the recalcitrant numbers.

He refused dinner.

"Loren's still asleep, and I'm a poor excuse of a cook, I'm afraid," Halbert told him through the closed door. "Just sandwiches. I'll leave a tray out here in the hall."

Kevin listened to the small creakings and shiftings, like whispers and murmurs. An old house, he told himself, built with no nails. Of course it would creak. Yet as the windows filled with darkness and evening's shadow slid across the room like a predator, the whispers became more tangible. The harder Kevin tried to ignore them, the more his ears strained to catch their meaning. He listened as if eavesdropping on a conversation.

He finished sometime past midnight. Carefully sorting the papers, he set them in the center of the desk. Smiling, he leaned back in his chair and contemplated the neat stack, feeling quite satisfied with himself. But his stomach growled for attention, and he remembered the tray left outside the door. Yet he hesitated, listening to the house creak like a warning.

Ridiculous. This was the twenty-first century, an age much too rational for spooks, spells, and haunted houses. Science had chased such nonsense into the dark corners of the mind, harmless shades useful only for a good, sweating nightmare.

Time to start behaving like a modern adult instead of some quaking medieval peasant. He stepped resolutely to the door, determined to face the ogres and sirens of his fancy.

The hall was deserted. Whatever spirits his fancy had conjured hid their presence well. He retrieved the dinner tray from a hall table and slipped back, nudging the door closed with his elbow. It didn't quite latch and swung open again.

As he ate, he studied the twisted branches of the baobob twig, and tried to picture the original whole. He smiled to think he now played some small part in its preservation.

"Are you done, then?"

Kevin jerked his gaze up. Loren stood in the doorway, hair tousled from sleep. Her long white robe hung open, revealing a pale green gown with a deep V-neckline. The thin, silky fabric clung to her, highlighting her curves. Kevin worked his tongue around a mouth suddenly gone dry.

"Uh, yeah. I just need to file this with the regional office." He tapped his finger on the amended 1040 topping his stack of paper. He went on to explain his solution and describe how they could protect their work.

She nodded and moved into the room. Kevin stood, fingers braced against the desk. "I can leave in the morning."

"But we can't let you leave."

"Why? My work's finished; there's no reason to stay."

"You spied on us. You saw something you shouldn't."

Kevin worked his jaw, but no sound came forth. He didn't know what he could say if it did.

"What're you thinking now? What do you think you saw?"

"I saw you cure the Blight as if by magic."

"Magic?" she responded with arched brows. "You do have an imagination after all. It was nothing more than an old family recipe, one my grandmother taught me. In fact, it was the inspiration for our T-cell research."

"But you can *cure* the Blight!"

She appeared to weigh the truth against a lie. "Only on a small scale. It's all I can do to keep it out of the valley."

"So patent it, release the Process so others can—"

"It's not something I can write out in a formula." She smiled. "Or a spell. Isn't that what you're thinking?"

Kevin could only shrug. Loren picked up the onyx paperweight, fingering the twig.

"You believe, don't you?"

"Loren, it doesn't matter what I believe. I can help you. If I don't return, they'll send someone else to do my work—someone less sympathetic. They'll destroy you. I have to go."

She smiled, leaning across the desk. Kevin backed against the window and sidled along the wall.

"Would it be so terrible to stay?" She moved around the desk. Kevin found himself trapped in the corner.

"I don't think my boss would approve. Nor your husband." He tried to make that sound like a threat.

"And you?" She smiled, moving closer. "I know what you want. The trees, the land. You want the *green*."

"No!" Kevin yelled and heard the lie in his own word. *Yes!* His mind screamed back. *Stay. With the trees and the blue, blue sky and that incredible green. Stay with her.*

Then he was holding her, though he wasn't sure whether it was his motion or hers that brought them together. He kissed her. She twisted her head back—in submission or resistance? Kevin didn't care. He took her down, the carpet rustling like fallen leaves beneath them. His kisses moved along the line of her chin, down her throat. She inhaled deeply, her chest rising against him, and he buried his face between her breasts, tasting her clean, earthy essence.

Pain like a high-pitched twang struck the side of his head.

His vision blurred into a miasma of color. Loren pushed away, twisting from his grasp. He rolled to his knees.

"Loren, please," he cried out. A black, humming numbness circled him. He sank into it still reaching out for her.

Kevin became aware first of voices somewhere, arguing. He thought it had something to do with him. He decided to wake up, and only then did he open his eyes.

Smudges of light and color ran like watercolors in the rain. He focused on what might've been a distant mountain, and it resolved into a onyx paperweight. He touched his hand to the throbbing pain on the side of his head. Sticky blood matted his hair and something was tangled there. He pulled free the baobob twig. Rubbing the blood from his fingertips, he stared at it as if it were a broken promise.

"Loren," he cried out, his voice barely a hoarse croak. He pulled himself to his feet, bracing himself against the desk. The voices that had wakened him now lured him into the corridor. He crossed the hall to lean against the closed door.

"He did what?" Halbert's voice shrieked with murderous rage.

"It doesn't matter. That's not the problem."

Halbert grumbled incoherently.

"Hal, he knows what we are, though he doesn't believe it yet. In this day and age, who would? But if he tells anyone, they might start asking difficult questions."

"And whose fault is that? And what do we do about it?"

A long pause. Loren must've made some gesture.

"You can't do that!" Halbert squawked. "He's government, Loren—the IRS! They'll come looking for him."

"But he's so unhappy, so hungry for the green. He wants to stay, he really does."

Part of Halbert's response was muffled as his footsteps retreated across the room and back. ". . . my mother was right. I should've married my own kind."

"But you didn't." Loren's voice deepened to a warm, sultry purr that made Kevin ache with fever. "You married me, and I wed you. You're the only one I truly love."

Halbert grunted petulantly. "Sometimes I half believe you only married me for company when no one else is available."

"Kevin doesn't want me; he wants the green. No matter what, you're the only one that gets this." Loren's words were followed by a wicked little laugh, her voice melting to silken desire. "We'll deal with Kevin in the morning. I have something else in mind for now, Dear One."

"Mmm, do that again."

The sounds that followed were unmistakably intimate. Kevin backed away, holding his breath. Something snapped, the sound to his ears like the crack of a baseball bat. He stared in horror at the twig crushed in his hand, at the silence beyond the closed door. An eternity seemed to pass before he realized Loren and Halbert were too preoccupied to have heard or noticed.

. . . Kevin sat upon a boulder, a sulking, waist-high block of granite. He ached with fatigue, bruised and scratched from stumbling through the dark of the forest. It seemed every rock had contrived to trip him up, every bush had snagged his legs and arms. *Something* had pursued him, an intangible threat, a shadow, a whisper. A wraith of moonlight and mist.

Now with the dawn came sanity. Sunlight touched the wall, golden light mellowing the dark stone. He wondered how he could open the laser gate. No doubt the controls would be coded and the shack, itself, protected. But if he could get past the wall, he could hike into Telluride. He'd be safe there.

The rustle of leaves advanced across the valley as a fresh wind approached. A wave front of nodding flowers swept the hillside. The wind eddied around the stone to ruffle his hair. He shivered.

"Kevin." The whisper of leaves rustling. He peered into the misty shadows beneath the trees.

"Kevin."

He stood and turned, but only the wind plucked at his shirt. He turned again, and Loren stood in front of him.

"I've been looking for you." Her throaty voice made him tremble. "So has Halbert. We were worried about you."

"I bet." Kevin's mouth was too dry for anything but bitter sarcasm. He sidled around the boulder, keeping it between them.

"Are you afraid of me, Kevin?"

He forced a laugh, flat and unconvincing. "Why would I be afraid of you?"

"Oh, but you should be. You should've gone to Halbert. He might've been merciful. He might even have protected you."

"Halbert wants to kill me."

"He wouldn't hurt you. He wouldn't hurt a fly."

"Flies don't fall in love." The bleak confession had no effect on Loren. She seemed to have expected it. Kevin slid into the custody of her gaze. His fingers clawed at the boulder's rough surface, clinging to its harsh reality.

"Loren, I'm sorry for what happened. I don't know why I did that. I'm not really like that. Honest. I just sort of—"

Loren began to smile, and all emotion washed out of Kevin like a spring thaw—all hope, all passion, "—lost control."

"What are you thinking, Kevin? Who do you suppose we are?"

"I wouldn't know," Kevin answered with a shrug, as if his answer didn't matter. "My first guess would be aliens."

"Aliens?" Loren echoed and began to laugh. And the laughter that yesterday had so enchanted Kevin now terrified him. She stopped and glared at him with true anger. "I'm as human as you or anyone else. Throughout time, my people have protected this planet when yours would destroy it. My talent doesn't make me something else, any more than the color of my skin or the slant of my eyes."

"Your talent? Just what is your talent? Magic, illusion?" Kevin used anger as a wedge between him and the thrall she held him in. "*Witch*craft?"

She drew herself up, seeming to grow taller, even as he shrank beneath the fury of her gaze. "And what do you know of magic and illusion? The mind believes what it expects to see. You expect to see a house, and so it is. But what did you see in your dreams?"

Kevin opened his mouth, closed it, then tried again. "I saw trees," he admitted. Loren smiled thinly.

"I would not be bound by walls, Kevin. Walls create boundaries for the mind and spirit, as well as the body. They limit the possible. When people learned to build walls, they lost their connection with the forces and powers in nature, the energies of life. Such things became mystery, and mystery begat superstition. Stories grew, as stories will, until myth surpassed reality. *My* people are but the reality behind the myths, the nugget of truth at their core. Once, they were both honored and feared."

"But then came the so-called 'Age of Reason,' the age of science and technology, and there was no place for our arts. We were forced to choose, as with any species on this planet. Adapt or perish. My people chose survival over extinction, sacrificing our culture and our power, even our identity.

"Now few retain the ability to connect with the earth; our gene pool's too diluted. Nothing short of global catastrophe could bring back the old ways. We're simply not willing to let it go that far."

For just a moment, she gazed into the distance with a sad, lost look. Kevin thought to run. Before he could react, though, she gathered her thoughts like errant sheep. Cocking her head to one side, she circled around him, appraising him like a work of art. Kevin turned to follow her motion.

"Stand still," she admonished him, "or you'll grow twisted, like Sam." Then she began to sing.

Kevin opened his mouth to protest, but could not. A cold, prickling numbness oozed along his limbs. Bright, bright colors streaked the edges of his vision, but he saw only Loren, soft focused but for the green of her eyes. The crystal melody of her voice threaded his thoughts like pearls on a string.

"You want this, Kevin. You've dreamed of the *green*. Sleep now. Sleep, and dream true."

Kevin raised his arms to ward against her. They felt heavy, stiff. The bright colors whirled, closing down on her image, fading to black.

Kevin didn't so much awaken as he came to awareness. For a long time, he was content with that. Then he opened his eyes, or perhaps simply willed himself to see. The result was the same, and just as frightening. Leafy branches framed a view of the valley from perhaps twenty feet off the ground.

He couldn't remember climbing a tree, or why he would have. The thought of falling in his sleep gave him a shivering chill, one that made even the leaves around him tremble. But he seemed to be firmly tied down. One of Halbert's practical jokes, he decided. He hoped. He tried to wriggle free—cautiously, for he was uncertain of his perch as it was.

He became aware of a presence below and dared to gaze downward. Halbert sat on a boulder that shouldered against the base of the tree—a familiar boulder, in spite of the change of perspective. *But there wasn't a tree here before.* Halbert looked up slyly as the wind rustled the branches.

"So, awake at last!" he called, climbing off the boulder and staring up into the branches.

Kevin tried desperately to move, to scream, anything. His voice didn't seem to be working, but he thought he succeeded in moving one arm. He must have, for a branch to his right rustled.

"Careful now; you'll break a limb." Halbert giggled as if that were a joke. "Just relax. You'll get used to it. I must say, you picked a nice view."

Once more Kevin tried to scream. The only sound he heard was the creak of branches rubbing together.

"Too bad you didn't trust me," Halbert said. "I might've let you go. *Might* have." He giggled again, but then shook his head ruefully. "Too late now, though. Once my wife sets her mind to a thing, there's no undoing.

"Let me guess what you're thinking. 'This isn't possible. I can't be a tree.' Maybe so, but your mind believes you are, and so you'll stand. My mind believes you are, and so I see you. And as your mind believes, so will you become, though it takes some time. Your awareness will fade eventually, and then you won't mind so much. At least that's what my Loren tells me. I wouldn't know, personally. You'd have to ask Sam and the others. If you could."

"They're looking for you, of course. The Feds, I mean. Won't find you, though. Haven't the eyes for it." He chuckled. "They found your car in Leopard Creek, but no body, of course. Water runs high this time of year."

If this is another joke, Kevin thought, unable to speak the words. *It isn't funny. Let me go*! He struggled against whatever bound him, aching to cry out, to make that one small noise that would surely wake him from this nightmare.

"I do want to thank you for your help and advice. Oh, and the new T-cells worked, by the way," Halbert continued. "We'll have the Blight under control in no time.

"Ah, we make a fine pair, my Loren and me. We're a mixed match, to be sure, and people said it'd never work, but we complement one another. Sidhe and Dwarf. I work in stone, and she in wood. Myth, all myth. A different kind of science." He reached out and patted the trunk of Kevin's tree. "And the world can always do with one more tree."

THE GOLDILOCKS PROBLEM

by Gregory Benford

One of the best-known voices in modern science fiction, Gregory Benford is a professor of physics at the University of California at Irvine. His writings have garnered the Nebula, British Science Fiction, John W. Campbell, Ditmar, and *SF Chronicle* awards. As of this writing, he has penned some twenty-six novels, a hundred and thirteen short stories, dozens of assorted poems, essays, and articles, as well as *Deep Time,* an excellent nonfiction book about the artifacts which endure.

In an oddly magical twist, Benford is an identical twin. Whether he is the evil twin or the good one, he isn't saying.

ALPHA went first, as befitted the older god. Not that he was the brightest.

He (the older was always a he, though among gods the distinction was purely nostalgic) chose the world circling closer in to the young, brimming sun.

The contest began between the three of them, in peacock pride.

At first it was easy work. Alpha was of course a lesser god, like Beta and Gamma, and so had diminished powers. He could not create a whole planet from scratch, making elements in stars cook to the right ratio of masses. That had to come from Omega.

And to each of the planets the three were to cultivate Omega would finally come, to judge.

So Alpha took the inner planet, already simmering with its birth energies. He huffed and puffed and forced from its rocks outgassing water, carbon dioxide, and lava. The lava was for show, and because Alpha had to have something to watch in the long slow churn of time a world took to bake out.

Into the ever-denser air of Alpha's World (he always named them for himself) gushed torrents of thick vapor. And from the new sun lanced down fingers of golden glow, warming the gases.

The mass of Alpha's World was a given, set by Omega. Its compression fed huge energies, the exuberance of warm youth. This matched Alpha's own physical manifestation—a prickly plasma, swirling with sparks. His magnetic fingers worked incessantly, a playing phosphorescence.

Alpha loved the vortex storms that raged across his world, the vast tornadoes that eroded away the fresh, volcanic mountain chains. Huge slabs of rock rose and the heavy mantle of gnawing gas around them down.

At the very top of the cloud decks, the water vapor thickened until the miracle of life sprang forth—suddenly, in Alpha's quickened, aeon-leaping time sense. Molecule met molecule in organic embrace. Some liked their bonds, and made more. Soon whole organisms spawned in the lofting currents of the simmering atmosphere.

He yearned to see the vast decks of water condense into ponds, lakes, seas. And at first great banks of steam roiled across the face of his world, bringing a ferocious sting to the rocks. Cycles fed, circled, built.

But in the march of aeons, the spongy, ever-warmer air sopped up the vapor as it trembled into drops, fell, and was eaten anew by the ferocious thirst of carbon dioxide.

Alpha labored. He brought soft rains from low clouds, and gratifying ponds, shimmered beneath the crash and fizz of vast lightning. Alpha cupped pressures around these, to conjure up deeper lakes . . . but overhead, the blanket of gases sopped up the falling droplets, sucked away molecules from the lapping waves.

For as water was always abuilding, so was carbon dioxide. The two ancient enemies warred.

And just above the brimming tiny cells of new life, the jabbing rays of the sun forked into the sleepy water layers. The ultraviolet hammer fell upon those molecules, sputtering away the light hydrogen, leaving the hungry oxygen to wander.

Oxygen found slabs of rock, and was eaten. Slabby silicone digested it.

Hydrogen—always flighty, seldom sincere—frolicked away into the vacuum of space. Alpha watched it blow off, oblivious, and fumed . . . which added again to his world's smoldering fires. For carbon dioxide cloaked the skies now, its blanket keeping in the heat.

Alpha's few muddy lakes lasted longest. First his ponds evaporated into the thirsty thickness above. He wept as the last great lake dwindled, fumed—and vanished.

The rule of carbon now descended. Volcanoes still belched water, but the sun broke the young molecules on its ultraviolet anvil. Carbon and its oxides the star ignored. So banks of it built and built and built. Each new carbon dioxide trapped more heat from below, and Alpha's world began to bake out.

Furious, Alpha raged across his world. His intemperate outbursts only worsened the heat. The murky air caught more infrared and cooked the rocks to a smoldering incandescence. Runaway greenhouse. Lead melted and ran on through sulfurous valleys.

Chemistry laughed at Alpha's rages.

Beta was smug.

Her slow, cool energies condensed around the outer of the three rocky worlds. If Alpha's fate was forced by two facts—size of the planet, and distance from the newborn star—only one sufficed for Beta.

She manifested as lacy liquids, great calm masses. Her presence brought a slow, gracious dance to the play of molecules and time.

Wrapped in her condensing clouds, Beta's fresh globe of shifting rubble was much smaller than Alpha's. She thought this a fine fact, for then it would not belch forth so much gas, could not grow the coat of carbon oxides that trapped heat.

Or so she thought. She was busy with her mountains, thrusting up great peaks that roared forth their bounty. These she always loved, playing in the fiery streams of lava, percolating from them just the right recipe for an atmosphere that would, of course, be cool and serene.

At first, all worked well. Ponds formed, then lakes, and all joined into great basins of muddy wealth. The air above thickened into a useful cloak, trapping enough heat to keep the lakes from scumming over with ice.

This world's spin was the same as had been given to the others, moderate and forgiving. This rotational energy fed the slide of vast plates of rock, masses that rode over each other, butting and slamming and sliding with tectonic fury. Chunks the size of lesser worlds rammed each other, forcing out still more heat and gas and bubbling lesser liquids.

Rust-red ran the rivers. Energies sparked and danced over the scummy seas. Again, life kindled.

Molecule loved molecule and order built up its jigsaw chains.

Beta was beautiful in her ruddy, simmering splendor. Canyons yawned, rivers carved deep, moist deltas spread in ample sites for the brimming life. Crusts of algae lined the lakes, lapped at the shores. She kept carbon in its place, a light blanket suitable for infants. Even a little oxygen salted the soft layers of sheltering cloud.

Her world frothed with fervor, while inward, Alpha raged impotently.

But . . . mass began to tell. Again, fierce ultraviolet from the distant sun broke water into disloyal hydrogen, which rushed off into the welcoming vacuum. Oxygen wandered forlorn . . . and the pinks won over.

Rust grew like a fungus on her mountains. Volcanoes voiced their vapor wealth, but the fires below them ebbed. The sputter of Omega-born radioactives slowed. Heat leaked away from Beta's small, beautiful, doomed world. High above the once sheltering sky now skimmed clouds of carbon dioxide ice. They chilled the world further, reflecting the sun's radiance away.

River valleys dried out as the air thinned. Carbon—she did not have enough, now. Water sputtered away into space, and now Beta envied Alpha's rogue heats. She pined for her forlorn, shrinking seas. The life she had brought forth in beautiful, brimming births fell prey to the stinging ultraviolet that poured down, unhampered by the thinning water clouds.

Cringing algae retreated deeper into the rusty waters. Microbes fled into the hard rule of rock. Finally, dryness held sway. Seas shrank to lakes, then dwindled to mud plains dotted with scummy ponds . . . and then, parched valleys of windblown sand and dust.

Soon, too soon, Beta saw even the winds still as the air froze out. Now the glinting poles of water and carbon dioxide ice inherited the last fleeting remnants of the atmosphere. Only a skimpy skirt of gas now hid the barren hills from the sun's full glaring onslaught. Oxygen trickled away, locked up by the iron in the ridges, making a rusty globe.

Her world had been too small, not too cold. With enough mass, Beta knew, she could have held onto the atmosphere until the sun slowly warmed. A mere matter of a few billion years would have made the difference.

Her flinty anger froze into a glacial silence.

Gamma laughed.

Never nostalgic for the old ways and symbols, this small god chose no sex, preferring to be called by Beta and Alpha an it. Impersonal forces worked within the god's ample reach.

Gamma shifted constantly. It danced, slid, rained, and erupted—manifesting as matter, sounding all the grace notes of mass in its movements. No single mode captured Gamma's attention for long.

Gamma's World was lucky—not too near the sun, not too small in mass. But to fashion a suitable nest would take more than blind luck, the incidental collision of parameters. With enough mass Gamma's planet would retain the internal heat of its first compression, and the slow sputtering fires of radioactives throughout its mantle.

Again carbon dioxide graced the early airs, sang through belching volcanic chains, spun storms, and danced destruction on countless shores. For from the first, there were seas. Comets smashed into the ruddy brown methane, bringing a ponderous plenty of ices and precious organic molecules.

As with the earlier failures, these long chains kindled interesting marriages between groups of dancing molecules. Some learned to copy themselves and overwhelmed the others. Cells drew themselves apart, whispering thinly of pregnant promise.

Water worked its wonders, digging great basins for the oceans that grew with each hammering of iceteroids, each volcanic belch. Wind and water's rub opened fresh rock to the air, trapping carbon, so that its oxides got locked away.

Gamma coaxed, taught . . . dreamed. The sun waxed, learning its own nuclear pathways. Over billions of years it built its pyre higher. The riser worsened Alpha's inferno, but was not nearly enough to salvage Beta's icebox. But beneath Gamma's gaze, the middle world's warmer surface increased the weathering rates, plucking more carbon from the thick skin of air.

Not that no problems loomed. There is an ebb and sway to worlds, and they can go unbalanced. At times a large rock would come smashing in, cloaking all in cloud and dust. Temperatures plunged, the poles crept toward the equator.

Several times, the eating ice came close to blotting away all the absorbing ocean and land, smothering it beneath the bone-white shroud that would have doomed all the life that sang and grew within the seas.

But each time, the volcanoes saved Gamma's planet. They gorged themselves on deep stores, spewing these into chilly air, bringing the warmth of carbon dioxide and water to the dry, cold surface. Gamma labored, worried, breathed fire where it could.

The chilly rocks above lost their hunger for carbon, letting it build anew in the clear skies. Each time, so near victory, the crust of ice retreated. But it sat at the poles, awaiting its next opportunity. The catastrophe of whiteness always lurked.

Across the span of a hundred million years, new sea floor upthrust into mid-ocean ranges, spread like a crusty pancake, made fresh land. Then it would reach an edge, slow . . . and be sucked down into the lava below.

Such subduction drew into the mantle stores of carbon, then replenished them as the mass again returned to the surface, again in mid-ocean. This immense clock cycled carbon through the rock shell, a ticking so profound that Gamma itself could scarcely mark the time.

For now the very air had learned to edit the quickening sun above. Ozone built, a prickly skin of ferocious oxygen, cloaking the atmosphere on high. It soaked up the sun's sleeting ultraviolet, eating eager photons. This world became a milder place.

Below, life lifted its head. Slime stuck itself out from its crannies, and found the sunlight obliging. Free at last from the sledgehammer blows of piercing radiation, algae ventured across barren slabs of stone.

Such thin sheets exhaled gratefully. Gases mingled. The cloaking air obliged, and cadences surged between cloud and sea and land—the elemental dance.

Such stately rhythms graced the waltz of worlds, but only on Gamma's did the music play on.

Among the outer giant planets, life found purchase in the clouds of ammonia, or deep in the buried oceans of moons. But all snuffed out as energies ebbed, or currents carried microbes to their deaths in places cold and unforgiving.

This gravid gavotte of ice, from pole to the skirts of the equator, had effects that pleased Gamma. Life had grown to maturity in the oceans, and then ventured onto land.

The coming of the glaciers crushed much of it, but the survivors were hearty, rugged, different. Each time a pruning left behind new traits that life came to enjoy in its restless rummaging for new places to poke, eat, make more of itself.

Some simpler parts of life's armies came to regulate the atmosphere's own ebb and loft. Microbes gnawing in rock liberated carbon when needed, aiding the geological grace notes that sounded through millions of years. Plankton pruned the air, flinging sulfide forth to make clouds.

And so, while Beta and Alpha glowered from their dead spheres, Gamma rejoiced. Laughing, it slid from gas to mass to forking plasma—all states of Creation knew its surge and beat.

It was having such a good time, Omega's arrival surprised it.

Omega was pleased.

Alpha's heat and Beta's freeze it dismissed. Sad lessons, so often learned, but always forgotten in the slow sad sway of eternity.

Chuckling with deep bass plasma waves, it lingered over the crystalline air of Gamma's World. Skated through the shimmering aurora. Savored the saline seas, their bouquet of life. All of it was Just, and also Right, and so Just Right.

For Omega was not a god, but a Principle. Alpha, Beta, and Gamma hailed Omega's entrance, a wise searchlight probing forth.

Gods work within the Rule of Law. This universe had come forth like a blossom from the Meta-Universe, from which all lessons finally issued. Knowledge came from the percolation of experience through the sieve of Law.

Omega was the Principle which gave forth Law. Only Omega knew Purpose, for Law could not see the end aim of itself, any more than a mortal can fathom the point of Eternity.

Omega stroked Gamma, imparted fresh vision—and on the green face of Gamma's World, a slow kindling began. In what is to gods a mere tick of time—and to Gamma, a nothingness, for it stands outside of Time—crafty cognition brimmed, rose, thrust up its own puny peaks.

In an eye blink, intelligence spread across the lands. Leaped into the skies. Spanned between worlds—seeking, seeking.

These motes of fevered ferment sniffed the scorched plains of Alpha's World, and learned from its terrifying example. More particles of reason prodded Beta's world. They clambered down through ancient, volcanic vents and found there the valiant, trapped remnants of what had once enjoyed sunny seas.

Omega watched, and instructed the gods. Gamma sat on the Right side, and learned well.

Mortified, Beta watched as the motes spread soil upon her world's poles, implanted microbes, kindled long-slumbering fires in the feet of dead volcanoes. In a twinkling, gases sprang anew. Warmed her world. Began to flirt with fragrances organic and promising.

Alpha was over his pique, and so waxed glad to see his world start to cool. The motes had arranged shields, moved mountains, sucked the planet away from the still-waxing fires of the sun.

Omega showed Gamma what would become of even so fine a world as it had wrought. As the star burned still brighter, carbon would again come to rule the air. All the finely balanced rhythms of geology, sea and life and land—all would come to naught.

Except for the Principle. The new Mind that now played

out its dramas among the worlds had seen the lesson early. It moved Gamma's World, shrouded it too against the glare, and prolonged its life.

Not content, it stirred the inner gut of the star itself, to cool the fires, extending its life tenfold.

By this time, the Principle was enormously (how else?) gratified.

The motes of Gamma's World had seen the Just and the Right. Now that their reach enfolded all the worlds of the system, even the dead hulks orbiting far out, in primitive states—now that they had done the work of gods, the Principle became clear.

Life spread. Intelligence, crusty and crafty. Like a disease upon inert mass, it brought ferment.

First to the nearby stars, hesitant colonies, some doomed. With time, it learned, adapted, paid the price of blood and toil and death. Yet kept on. (What else to do?)

Then in a gathering rush, it spread—a spectacular stain across the great gyre of the galaxy. It penetrated to the Core, and read the meanings there. It learned tales of vast black portals into the Meta-Universe, of voyages into that shadowy realm. And of what lurked beyond, transcending the paltry limits of illusions like Space and Time.

All this, from creatures born on the plains of now-distant Gamma's World. They chittered and chattered and clutched each other. But on their two spindly legs they kept coming.

And so Omega came full course, and ate its tail, and told its tale. Life, ever clever, engulfed the realms of brute matter. And the Principle again burst like fresh light upon the cooling, forever expanding darknesses.

Alpha, Beta, and Gamma (coming first) greeted these motes of Gamma's World. Small they were, but promising. Here was fresh companionship—the point of it all.

They blended. And came to be called Zenith.

AILOURA

by Paul Di Filippo

Paul Di Filippo has been writing SF regularly since 1982, and is thus approaching his twentieth anniversary of speculating for fun and profit. A native Rhode Islander, he lives in Providence and conducts guided tours to H. P. Lovecraft's grave site upon request. He and his mate, Deborah Newton, have been together for twenty-five years, and recently celebrated that anniversary with a trip to Hong Kong, the most alien place they have yet visited, and yet a land which felt strangely like the home of another lifetime.

For those who didn't catch it, "Ailoura" is a clever retelling of "Puss in Boots."

THE small aircraft swiftly bisected the cloudless chartreuse sky. Invisible encrypted transmissions raced ahead of it. Clearance returned immediately from the distant, turreted manse—Stoessl House—looming in the otherwise empty riven landscape like some precipice-perching raptor. The ever-unsleeping family marchwarden obligingly shut down the manse's defenses, allowing an approach and landing. Within minutes, Geisen Stoessl had docked his small deltoid zipflyte on one of the tenth-floor platforms of Stoessl House, cantilevered over the flood-sculpted, candy-colored arroyos of the Subliminal Desert.

Geisen unseamed the canopy and leaped easily out onto the broad sintered terrace, unpeopled at this tragic, necessary, hopeful moment. Still clad in his dusty expeditionary clothes, goggles slung around his neck, Geisen resembled a living marble version of some young roughneck godling. Slim, wiry, and alert, with his laughter-creased, soil-powdered face now set in solemn lines absurdly counterpointed by a mask of clean skin around his recently shielded green eyes, Geisen paused a moment to brush from his protective suit the heaviest evidence of his recent wildcat digging in the Lustrous Wastes. Satisfied that he had made some small improvement in his appearance upon this weighty occasion, he advanced toward the portal leading inside. But before he could actuate the door, it opened from within.

Framed in the door stood a lanky, robe-draped bestient: Vicuna, his mother's most valued servant. Set squarely in Vicuna's wedge-shaped hirsute face, the haughty maid's broad velveteen nose wrinkled imperiously in disgust at Geisen's appearance, but the moreauvian refrained from voicing her disapproval of that matter in favor of other upbraidings.

"You arrive barely in time, Gep Stoessl. Your father approaches the limits of artificial maintenance, and is due to be reborn any minute. Your mother and brothers already anxiously occupy the Natal Chambers."

Following the inhumanly articulated servant into Stoessl House, Geisen answered, "I'm aware of all that, Vicuna. But traveling halfway around Chalk can't be accomplished in an instant."

"It was your choice to absent yourself during this crucial time."

"Why crucial? This will be Vomacht's third reincarnation. Presumably this one will go as smoothly as the first two."

"So one would hope."

Geisen tried to puzzle out the subtext of Vicuna's ambiguous comment, but could emerge with no clue regarding the current state of the generally complicated affairs within Stoessl House. He had obviously been away too long—too busy enjoying his own lonely but satisfying prospecting trips on behalf of the family enterprise—to be able to grasp the daily political machinations of his relatives.

Vicuna conducted Geisen to the nearest squeezer, and they promptly dropped down fifteen stories, far below the bedrock in which Stoessl House was rooted. On this secure level, the monitoring marchwarden hunkered down in its cozy low-Kelvin isolation, meaningful matrices of B-E condensates. Here also were the family's Natal Chambers. At these doors blazoned with sacred icons Vicuna left Geisen with a humid snort signifying that her distasteful attendance on the latecomer was complete.

Taking a fortifying breath, Geisen entered the rooms.

Roseate illumination symbolic of new creation softened all within: the complicated apparatus of rebirth as well as the sharp features of his mother, Woda, and the doughy countenances of his two brothers, Gitten and Grafton. Nearly invisible in the background, various bestient bodyguards hulked, inconspicuous yet vigilant.

Woda spoke first. "Well, how very generous of the prodigal to honor us with his unfortunately mandated presence."

Gitten snickered, and Grafton chimed in, pompously ironical. "Exquisitely gracious behavior, and so very typical of our little sibling, I'm sure."

Tethered to various life-support devices, Vomacht Stoessl—unconscious, naked and recumbent on a padded pallet alongside his mindless new body—said nothing. Both he and his clone had their heads wrapped in organic warty sheets of modified Stroonian brain parasite, an organism long ago co-opted for mankind's ambitious and ceaselessly searching program of life extension. Linked via a thick living interparasitical tendril to its younger doppelganger, the withered form of the current Vomacht, having reached the limits of rejuvenation, contrasted strongly with the virginal, soulless vessel.

During Vomacht Stoessl's first lifetime, from 239 to 357 PS, he had sired no children. His second span of existence (357 to 495 PS) saw the birth of Gitten and Grafton, separated by some sixty years and both sired on Woda. Toward the end of his third, current lifetime (495 to 675 PS), a mere thirty years ago, he had fathered Geisen upon a mystery woman whom Geisen had never known. Vanished and unwedded, his mother—or some other oversolicitous guardian—had denied Geisen her name or image. Still, Vomacht had generously attended to all the legalities granting Geisen full parity with his half brothers. Needless to say, little cordiality existed between the older members of the family and the young interloper.

Geisen made the proper obeisances at several altars before responding to the taunts of his stepmother and stepbrothers. "I did not dictate the terms governing Gep Stoessl's latest reincarnation. They came directly from him.

If any of you objected, you should have made your grievances known to him face-to-face. I myself am honored that he chose me to initiate the transference of his mind and soul. I regret only that I was not able to attend him during his final moments of awareness in this old body."

Gitten, the middle brother, tittered, and said, "The hand that cradles the rocks will now rock the cradle."

Geisen looked down at his dirty hands, hopelessly ingrained with the soils and stone dusts of Chalk. He resisted an impulse to hide them in his pockets. "There is nothing shameful about my fondness for fieldwork. Lolling about in luxury does not suit me. And I did not hear any of you complaining when the Eventyr Lode that I discovered came on-line and began to swell the family coffers."

Woda intervened with her traditional maternal acerbity. "Enough bickering. Let us acknowledge that no possible arrangement of this day's events would have pleased everyone. The quicker we perform this vital ritual, the quicker we can all return to our duties and pleasures, and the sooner Vomacht's firm hand will regrasp the controls of our business. Geisen, I believe you know what to do."

"I studied the proper *Books of Phowa* en route."

Grafton said, "Always the grind. Whenever do you enjoy yourself, little brother?"

Geisen advanced confidently to the mechanisms that reared at the head of the pallets. "In the proper time and place, Grafton. But I realize that to you, such words imply every minute of your life." The young man turned his attention to the controls before him, forestalling further tart banter.

The tethered and trained Stroonian life-forms had been previously starved to near hibernation in preparation for their sacred duty. A clear cylinder of pink nutrient fluid laced with instructive protein sequences hung from an ornate tripod. The fluid would flow through twin IV lines, once the parasites were hooked up, enlivening their quiescent metabolisms and directing their proper functioning.

Murmuring the requisite holy phrases, Geisen plugged an IV line into each enshrouding creature. He tapped the proper dosage rate into the separate flow-pumps. Then, solemnly capturing the eyes of the onlookers, he activated the pumps.

Almost immediately the parasites began to flex and labor, humping and contorting as they drove an infinity of fractally minuscule auto-anesthetizing tendrils into both full and vacant brains in preparation for the transfer of the vital engrams that comprised a human soul.

But within minutes, it was plain to the observers that something was very wrong. The original Vomacht Stoessl began to writhe in evident pain, ripping away from his life supports.

The all-observant marchwarden triggered alarms. Human and bestient technicians burst into the room. Grafton and Gitten and Woda rushed to the pumps to stop the process. But they were too late. In an instant, both membrane-wrapped skulls collapsed to degenerate chunky slush that plopped to the floor from beneath the suddenly destructive cauls.

The room fell silent. Grafton tilted one of the pumps at an angle so that all the witnesses could see the glowing red numerals.

"He quadrupled the proper volume of nutrient, driving the Stroonians hyperactive. This is murder!"

"Secure him from any escape!" Woda commanded.

Instantly Geisen's arms were pinioned by two burly bestient guards. He opened his mouth to protest, but the sight of his headless father choked off all words.

Gep Vomacht Stoessl's large private study was decorated with ancient relics of his birthworld, Lucerno: the empty, age-brittle coral armature of a deceased personal exoskeleton; a row of printed books bound in sloth-hide; a corroded aurochs-flaying knife large as a canoe paddle. In the wake of their owner's death, the talismans seemed drained of mana.

Geisen sighed, and slumped down hopelessly in the comfortable chair positioned on the far side of the antique desk that had originated on the Crafters' planet, Hulbrouck V. On the far side of the nacreous expanse sat his complacently smirking half brother, Grafton. Just days ago, Geisen knew, his father had hauled himself out of his sickbed for one last appearance at this favorite desk, where he had dictated the terms of his third recincarnation to the recording marchwarden. Geisen had played the affecting scene several times en route from the Lustrous Wastes, noting how, despite his enervated condition, his father spoke with his wonted authority, specifically requesting that Geisen administer the paternal rebirthing procedure.

And now that unique individual—distant and enigmatic as he had been to Geisen throughout the latter's relatively short life—the man who hd founded Stoessl House and its fortunes, the man to whom they all owed their luxurious independent lifestyles, was irretrievably gone from this plane of existence.

The human soul could exist only in organic substrates. Intelligent as they might be, condensate-dwelling entities such as the marchwarden exhibited a lesser existential complexity. Impossible to make any kind of static "backup" copy of the human essence, even in the proverbial bottled brain, since Stroonian transcription was fatal to the original. No, if destructive failure occurred during a rebirth, that individual was no more forever.

Grafton interpreted Geisen's sigh as indicative of a need to unburden himself of some secret. "Speak freely, little brother. Ease your soul of guilt. We are completely alone. Not even the marchwarden is listening."

Geisen sat up alertly. "How have you accomplished such a thing? The marchwarden is deemed to be incorruptible, and its duties include constant surveillance of the interior of our home."

Somewhat flustered, Grafton tried to dissemble. "Oh, no, you're quite mistaken. It was always possible to disable the marchwarden selectively. A standard menu option—"

Geisen leaped to his feet, causing Grafton to rear back. "I see it all now! This whole murder, and my seeming complicity, was planned from the start! My father's last testament—faked! The flow codes to the pumps—overriden! My role—stooge and dupe!"

Recovering himself, Grafton managed with soothing motions and noises to induce a fuming Geisen to be seated again. The older man came around to perch on a corner of the desk. He leaned over closer to Geisen and, in a smooth voice, made his own shockingly unrepentant confession.

"Very astute. Too bad for you that you did not see the trap early enough to avoid it. Yes, Vomacht's permanent death and your hand in it were all neatly arranged—by mother, Gitten, and myself. It had to be. You see, Vomacht had become irrationally surly and obnoxious toward us, his true and loving first family. He threatened to remove all our stipends and entitlements and authority, once he occupied his strong new body. But those demented codicils were edited from the version of his speech that you saw, as was his insane proclamation naming you sole factotum of the family business. All of Stoessl Strangelet Mining and its affiliates was to be made your fiefdom. Imagine! A young desert rat at the helm of our venerable corporation!"

Geisen strove to digest all this sudden information. Practical considerations warred with his emotions. Finally he could only ask, "What of Vomacht's desire for me to initiate his soul-transfer?"

"Ah, that was authentic. And it served as the perfect bait to draw you back, as well as the peg on which we could hang a murder plot and charge."

Geisen drew himself up proudly. "You realize that these accusations of deliberate homicide against me will not stand up a minute in court. With what you've told me, I'll certainly be able to dig up plenty of evidence to the contrary."

Smiling like a carrion lizard from the Cerise Ergstrand, Grafton countered, "Oh, will you, now? From your jail cell, without any outside help? Accused murderers cannot profit from the results of their actions. You will have no access to family funds other than your small personal accounts while incarcerated, nor any real partisans, due to your stubbornly asocial existence of many years. The might of the family, including testimony from the grieving widow, will be ranked against you. How do you rate your chances for exculpation under those circumstances?"

Reduced to grim silence, Geisen bunched his muscles prior to launching himself in a futile attack on his brother. But Grafton held up warning hand first.

"There is an agreeable alternative. We really do not care to bring this matter to court. There is, after all, still a chance of one percent or less that you might win the case. And legal matters are so tedious and time-consuming, interfering with more pleasurable pursuits. In fact, notice of Gep Stoessl's death has not yet been released to either the news media or to Chalk's authorities. And if we secure your cooperation, the aftermath of this tragic 'accident' will take a very different form than criminal charges. Upon getting your binding assent to a certain trivial document, you will be free to pursue your own life unencumbered by any obligations to Stoessl House or its residents."

Grafton handed his brother hard copy of several pages. Geisen perused it swiftly and intently, then looked up at Grafton with high astonishment.

"This document strips me of all my share of the family fortunes, and binds me from any future role in the estate. Basically, I am utterly disenfranchised and disinherited, cast out penniless."

"A fair enough summation. Oh, we might give you a small grubstake when you leave. Say—your zipflyte, a few hundred esscues, and a bestient servant or two. Just enough to pursue the kind of itinerant lifestyle you so evidently prefer."

Geisen pondered but a moment. "All attempts to brand me a patricide will be dropped?"

Grafton shrugged. "What would be the point of whipping a helpless, poverty-stricken nonentity?"

Geisen stood up. "Reactivate the marchwarden. I am ready to comply with your terms."

Gep Bloedwyn Vermeule, of Vermeule House, today wore her long blonde braids arranged in a complicated nest, piled high atop her charming young head and sown with delicate fairylights that blinked in time with various of her body rhythms. Entering the formal reception hall of Stoessl House, she marched confidently down the tiles between ranks of silent bestient guards, the long train dependent from her formfitting scarlet sandworm-fabric gown held an inch above the floor by tiny enwoven agravitic units. She came to a stop some meters away from the man who awaited her with a nervously expectant smile on his rugged face.

Geisen's voice quaked at first, despite his best resolve. "Bloedwyn, my sweetling, you look more alluring than an oasis to a parched man."

The pinlights in the girl's hair raced in chaotic patterns for a moment, then settled down to a stable configurations that somehow radiated a frostiness belied by her neutral facial expression. Her voice, chorded suggestively low and husky by fashionable implants, quavered not at all.

"Gep Stoessl, I hardly know how to approach you. So much has changed since we last trysted."

Throwing decorum to the wind, Geisen closed the gap between them and swept his betrothed up in his arms. The sensation Geisen enjoyed was rather like that derived from hugging a wooden effigy. Nonetheless, he persisted in his attempts to restore their old relations.

"Only superficial matters have changed, my dear! True, as you have no doubt heard by now, I am no longer a scion of Stoessl House. But my heart, mind, and soul remain devoted to you! Can I not assume the same constancy applies to your inner being?"

Bloedwyn slipped out of Geisen's embrace. "How could you assume anything, since I myself do not know how I feel? All these developments have been so sudden and mysterious! Your father's cruelly permanent death, your own capricious and senseless abandonment of your share of his estate— How can I make sense of any of it? What of all our wonderful dreams?"

Geisen gripped Bloedwyn's supple hide-mailed upper arms with perhaps too much fervor, judging from her wince. He released her, then spoke. "All our bright plans for the future will come to pass! Just give me some time to regain my footing in the world. One day I will be at liberty to explain everything to you. But, until then, I ask your trust and faith. Surely you nust share my confidence in my character, in my undiminished capabilities?"

Bloedwyn averted her tranquil blue-eyed gaze from Geisen's imploring green eyes, and he slumped in despair, knowing himself lost. She stepped back a few paces and, with voice steeled, made a formal declaration she had evidently rehearsed prior to this moment.

"The Vermeule marchwarden has already communicated the abrogation of our pending matrimonial agreement to your house's governor. I think such an impartial yet decisive move is all for the best, Geisen. We are both young, with many lives before us. It would be senseless to found such a potentially interminable relationship on such shaky footing. Let us both go ahead—separately—into the days to come, with our extinct love a fond memory."

Again, as at the moment of his father's death, Geisen found himself rendered speechless at a crucial juncture, unable to plead his case any further. He watched in stunned disbelief as Bloedwyn turned gracefully around and walked out of his life, her fluttering scaly train still visible for some seconds after the rest of her had vanished.

The cluttered, steamy, noisy kitchens of Stoessl House exhibited an orderly chaos proportionate to the magnitude of the preparations underway. The planned rebirth dinner for the paterfamilias had been hastily converted to a memorial banquet, once the proper, little-used protocols had been found in a metaphorically dusty lobe of the marchwarden's memory. Now scores of miscegenational bestients under the supervision of the lone human chef, Stine Pursiful, scraped, sliced, chopped, diced, cored, deveined, scrubbed, layered, basted, glazed, microwaved, and pressure-treated various foodstuffs, assembling the imported luxury ingredients into the elaborate fare that would furnish out the solemn buffet for family and friends and business connections of the deceased.

Geisen entered the aromatic atmosphere of the kitchens with a scowl on his face and a bitterness in his throat and heart. Pursiful spotted the young man and, with a fair share of courtesy and deference, considering the circumstances, stepped forward to inquire of his needs. But Geisen rudely brushed the slim punctilious chef aside, and stalked toward the shelves that held various MREs. With blunt motions, he began to shovel the nutri-packets into a dusty shoulder bag that had plainly seen many an expedition into Chalk's treasure-filled deserts.

A small timid bestient belonging to one of the muskrat-hyrax clades hopped over to the shelves where Geisen fiercely rummaged. Nearsighted, the be-aproned more-auvian strained on tiptoe to identify something on a higher shelf.

With one heavy foot, Geisen kicked the servant out of his way, sending the creature squeaking and sliding across the slops-strewn floor. But before the man could return to his rough provisioning, he was stopped by a voice familiar as his skin.

"I raised you to show more respect to all the Implicate's creatures than you just exhibited, Gep Stoessl. Or if I did not, then I deserve immediately to visit the Unborn's Lowest Abattoir for my criminal negligence."

Geisen turned, the bile in his craw and soul melting to a habitual affection tinged with many memories of juvenile guilt.

Brindled arms folded across her queerly configured chest, Ailoura the bestient stood a head shorter than Geisen, compact and well-muscled. Her heritage mingled from a thousand feline and quasi-feline strains from a dozen planets, she resembled no single cat species morphed to human status, but rather all cats everywhere, blended and thus ennobled. Rounded ears perched high atop her densely pelted skull. Vertical slitted eyes and her patch of wet leathery nose contrasted with a more-human-seeming mouth and chin. Now anger and disappointment molded her face into a mask almost frightening, her fierce expression magnified by a glint of sharp tooth peeking from beneath a curled lip.

Geisen noted instantly, with a small shock, the newest touches of gray in Ailoura's tortoiseshell fur. These tokens of aging softened his heart even further. He made the second-most-serious conciliatory bow from the Dakini Rituals toward his old nurse. Straightening, Geisen watched with relief as the anger flowed out of her face and stance, to be replaced by concern and solicitude.

"Now," Ailoura demanded, in the same tone with which she had often demanded that little Geisen brush his teeth or do his schoolwork, "what is all this nonsense I hear about your voluntary disinheritance and departure?"

Geisen motioned Ailoura into a secluded corner of the kitchens and revealed everything to her. His account prompted low growls from the bestient that escaped despite her angrily compressed lips. Geisen finished resignedly by saying, "And so, helpless to contest this injustice, I leave now to seek my fortune elsewhere, perhaps even on another world."

Ailoura pondered a moment. "You say that your brother offered you a servant from our house?"

"Yes. But I don't intend to take him up on that promise. Having another mouth to feed would just hinder me."

Placing one mitteny yet deft hand on his chest, Ailoura said, "Take me, Gep Stoessl."

Geisen experienced a moment of confusion. "But Ailoura—your job of raising me is long past. I am very grateful for the loving care you gave unstintingly to a motherless lad, the guidance and direction you imparted, the indulgent playtimes we enjoyed. Your teachings left me with a wise set of principles, an admirable will and optimism, and a firm moral center—despite the evidence of my thoughtless transgression a moment ago. But your guardian duties lie in the past. And besides, why would you want to leave the comforts and security of Stoessl House?"

"Look at me closely, Gep Stoessl. I wear now the tabard of the scullery crew. My luck in finding you here is due only to this very demotion. And from here the slide to utter inutility is swift and short—despite my remaining vigor and craft. Will you leave me here to face my sorry fate? Or will you allow me to cast my fate with that of the boy I raised from kittenhood?"

Geisen thought a moment. "Some companionship would indeed be welcome. And I don't suppose I could find a more intimate ally."

Ailoura grinned. "Or a slyer one."

"Very well. You may accompany me. But on one condition."

"Yes, Gep Stoessl?"

"Cease calling me 'Gep.' Such formalities were once unknown between us."

Ailoura smiled. "Agreed, little Gei-gei."

The man winced. "No need to regress quite that far. Now, let us return to raiding my family's larder."

"Be sure to take some of that fine fish, if you please, Geisen."

No one knew the origin of the tame strangelets that seeded Chalk's strata. But everyone knew of the immense wealth these cloistered anomalies conferred.

Normal matter was composed of quarks in only two flavors: up and down. But strange-flavor quarks also existed, and the exotic substances formed by these strange quarks in combination with the more domestic flavors were, unconfined, as deadly as the more familiar antimatter. Bringing normal matter into contact with a naked strangelet resulted in the conversion of the feedstock into energy. Owning a strangelet was akin to owning a pet black hole, and just as useful for various purposes, such as powering star cruisers.

Humanity could create strangelets, but only at immense cost per unit. And naked strangelets had to be confined in electromagnetic or gravitic bottles during active use. They could also be quarantined for semipermanent storage in stasis fields. Such was the case with the buried strangelets of Chalk.

Small spherical mirrored nodules—"marbles," in the jargon of Chalk's prospectors—could be found in various recent sedimentary layers of the planet's crust, distributed according to no rational plan. Discovery of the marbles had inaugurated the reign of the various Houses on Chalk.

An early scientific expedition from Preceptimax University to the Shulamith Wadi stumbled upon the strangelets initially. Preceptor Fairservis, the curious discoverer of the first marble, had realized he was dealing with a stasis-bound object and had unluckily managed to open it. The quantum genie inside had promptly eaten the hapless fellow who freed it, along with nine-tenths of the expedition, before beginning a sure but slow descent toward the core of Chalk. Luckily, an emergency response team swiftly dispatched by the planetary authorities had managed to activate a new entrapping marble as big as a small city, its lower hemisphere underground, thus trapping the rogue.

After this incident, the formerly disdained deserts of Chalk had experienced a land rush unparalleled in the galaxy. Soon the entire planet was divided into domains—many consisting of noncontiguous properties—each owned by one House or another. Prospecting began in earnest then. But the practice remained more an art than a science, as the marbles remained stealthy to conventional detectors. Intuition, geological knowledge of strata, and sheer luck proved the determining factors in the individual fortunes of the Houses.

How the strangelets—plainly artifactual—came to be buried beneath Chalk's soils and hardpan remained a mystery. No evidence of native intelligent inhabitants existed on the planet prior to the arrival of humanity. Had a cloud of strangelets been swept up out of space as Chalk made her eternal orbits? Perhaps. Or had alien visitors planted the strangelets for unimaginable reasons of their own? An equally plausible theory.

Whatever the obscure history of the strangelets, their current utility was beyond argument.

They made many people rich.

And some people murderous.

In the shadow of the Tasso Escarpments, adjacent to the Glabrous Drifts, Carrabas House sat desolate and melancholy, tenanted only by glass-tailed lizards and stilt-crabs, its poverty-overtaken heirs dispersed anonymously across the galaxy after a series of unwise investments, followed by the unpredictable yet inevitable exhaustion of their marble-bearing properties—a day against which Vomacht Stoessl had more providently hedged his own family's fortunes.

Geisen's zipflyte crunched to a landing on one of the manse's grit-blown terraces, beside a gaping portico. The craft's doors swung open and pilot and passenger emerged. Ailoura now wore a set of utilitarian roughneck's clothing, tailored for her bestient physique and matching the outfit worn by her former charge, right down to the boots. Strapped to her waist was an antique yet lovingly maintained variable sword, its terminal bead currently dull and inactive.

"No one will trouble us here," Geisen said with confidence. "And we'll have a roof of sorts over our heads while we plot our next steps. As I recall from a visit some years ago, the west wing was the least damaged."

As Geisen began to haul supplies—a heater-cum-stove, sleeping bags and pads, water condensers—from their craft, Ailoura inhaled deeply the dry tangy air, her nose wrinkling expressively, then exhaled with zest. "Ah, freedom after so many years! It tastes brave, young Geisen!" Her claws slipped from their sheaths as she flexed her pads. She unclipped her sword and flicked it on, the seemingly untethered bead floating outward from the pommel a meter or so.

"You finish the monkey work. I'll clear the rats from our quarters," promised Ailoura, then bounded off before Geisen could stop her. Watching her unfettered tail disap-

pear down a hall and around a corner, Geisen smiled, re-
calling childhood games of strength and skill where she had
allowed him what he now realized were easy triumphs.

After no small time, Ailoura returned, licking her greasy
lips.

"All ready for our habitation, Geisen-kitten."

"Very good. If the bold warrior will deign to lend a
paw . . . ?"

Soon the pair had established housekeeping in a spacious, weatherproof ground floor room (with several handy
exits), where a single leering window frame was easily covered by a sheet of translucent plastic. After distributing
their goods and sweeping the floor clean of loess drifts,
Geisen and Ailoura took a meal as their reward, the first
of many such rude campfire repasts to come.

As they relaxed afterward, Geisen making notes with his
stylus in a small pocket diary and Ailoura dragging her left
paw continually over one ear, a querulous voice sounded
from thin air.

"Who disturbs my weary peace?"

Instantly on their feet, standing back to back, the new-
comers looked warily about. Ailoura snarled until Geisen
hushed her. Seeing no one, Geisen at last inquired, "Who
speaks?"

"I am the Carrabas marchwarden."

The man and bestient relaxed a trifle. "Impossible," said
Geisen. "How do you derive your energy after all these
years of abandonment and desuetude?"

The marchwarden chuckled with a trace of pride. "Long
ago, without any human consent or prompting, while Carrabas House still flourished, I sunk a thermal tap downward
hundreds of kilometers. The backup energy thus supplied is
not much, compared with my old capacities, but has proved
enough for sheer survival, albeit with much dormancy."

Ailoura hung her quiet sword back on her belt. "How
have you kept sane since then, marchwarden?"

"Who says I have?"

Coming to terms with the semideranged Carrabas marchwarden required delicate negotiations. The protective ma-
jordomo simultaneously resented the trespassers—who did
not share the honored Carrabas family lineage—yet on

some different level welcomed their company and the satisfying chance to perform some of its programmed functions
for them. Alternating ogreish threats with embarrassingly
humble supplications, the marchwarden needed to hear just
the right mix of defiance and thanks from the squatters to
fully come over as their ally. Luckily, Ailoura, employing
diplomatic wiles honed by decades of bestient subservience,
perfectly supplemented Geisen's rather gruff and patroniz-
ing attitude. Eventually, the ghost of Carrabas House accepted them.

"I am afraid I can contribute little enough to your comfort,
Gep Carrabas." During the negotiations, the marchwarden
had somehow self-deludingly concluded that Geisen was
indeed part of the lost lineage. "Some water, certainly,
from my active conduits. But no other necessities such as
heat or food, or any luxuries either. Alas, the days of my
glory are long gone!"

"Are you still in touch with your peers?" asked Ailoura.

"Why, yes. The other Houses have not forgotten me.
Many are sympathetic, though a few are haughty and in-
different."

Geisen shook his head in bemusement. "First I learn that
the protective omniscience of the marchwardens may be
circumvented. Next, that they keep up a private traffic and
society. I begin to wonder who is the master and who is
the servant in our global system."

"Leave these conundrums to the preceptors, Geisen. This
unexpected mode of contact might come in handy for us
some day."

The marchwarden's voice sounded enervated. "Will you
require any more of me? I have overtaxed my energies,
and need to shut down for a time."

"Please restore yourself fully."

Left alone, Geisen and Ailoura simultaneously realized
how late the hour was and how tired they were. They bed-
ded down in warm bodyquilts, and Geisen swiftly drifted
off to sleep to the old tune of Ailoura's drowsy purring.

In the chilly viridian morning, over fish and kava, cat and
man held a war council.

Geisen led with a bold assertion that nonetheless concealed a note of despair and resignation.

"Given your evident hunting prowess, Ailoura, and my knowledge of the land, I estimate that we can take half a dozen sandworms from those unclaimed public territories proved empty of strangelets, during the course of as many months. We'll peddle the skins for enough to get us both off-planet. I understand that lush homesteads are going begging on Nibbriglung. All that the extensive water meadows there require is a thorough desnailing before they're producing golden rice by the bushel—"

Ailoura's green eyes, so like Geisen's own, flashed with cool fire. "Insipidity! Toothlessness!" she hissed. "Turn farmer? Grub among the waterweeds like some *platypus*? Run away from those who killed your sire and cheated you out of your inheritance? I didn't raise such an unimaginative, unambitious coward, did I?"

Geisen sipped his drink to avoid making a hasty affronted rejoinder, then calmly said, "What do you recommend, then? I gave my legally binding promise not to contest any of the unfair terms laid down by my family, in return for freedom from prosecution. What choices does such a renunciation leave me? Shall you and I go live in the shabby slums that slump at the feet of the Houses? Or turn thief and raider and prey upon lonely mining encampments? Or shall we become freelance prospectors? I'd be good at the latter job, true, but bargaining with the Houses concerning hard-won information about their own properties in humiliating, and promises only slim returns. They hold all the high cards, and the supplicant offers only a mere saving of time."

"You're onto a true scent with this last idea. But not quite the paltry scheme you envision. What I propose is that we swindle those who swindled you. We won't gain back your whole patrimony, but you'll surely acquire greater sustaining riches than you would by flensing worms or flailing rice."

"Speak on."

"The first step involves a theft. But after that, only chicanery. To begin, we'll need a small lot of strangelets, enough to salt a claim everyone thought exhausted."

Geisen considered, buffing his raspy chin with his knuckles. "The morality is dubious. Still—I found a smallish deposit of marbles on Stoessl property during my aborted trip, and never managed to report it. They were in a floodplain hard by the Nakhoda Range, newly exposed and ripe for the plucking without any large-scale mining activity that would attract satellite surveillance."

"Perfect! We'll use their own goods to con the ratlings! But once we have this grubstake, we'll need a proxy to deal with the Houses. Your own face and reputation must remain concealed until all deals are sealed airtight. Do you have knowledge of any such suitable foil?"

Geisen began to laugh. "Do I? Only the perfect rogue for the job!"

Ailoura came cleanly to her feet, although she could not repress a small grunt at an arthritic twinge provoked by a night on the hard floor. "Let us collect the strangelets first, and then enlist his help. With luck, we'll be sleeping on feathers and dining off golden plates in a few short weeks."

The sad and spectral voice of the abandoned march-warden sounded. "Good morning, Gep Carrabas. I regret keenly my own serious incapacities as a host. But I have managed to heat up several liters of water for a bath, if such service appeals."

The eccentric caravan of Marco Bozzarias and his mistress Pigafetta had emerged from its minting pools as a top-of-the-line Baba Yaya model of the year 650 PS. Capacious and agile, larded with amenities, the moderately intelligent stilt-walking cabin had been designed to protect its inhabitants from climatic extremes in unswaying comfort while carrying them surefootedly over the roughest terrain. But plainly, for one reason or another (most likely poverty) Bozzarias had neglected the caravan's maintenance over the twenty-five years of its working life.

Raised now for privacy above the sands where Geisen's zipflyte rested, the vehicle-cum-residence canted several degrees, imparting a funhouse quality to its interior. Swellings at its many knee joints indicated a lack of proper nutrients. Additionally, the cabin itself had been patched with so many different materials—plastic, sandworm hide, canvas, chitin—that it more closely resembled a heap of debris than a deliberately designed domicile.

The caravan's owner, contrastingly, boasted an immaculate and stylish appearance. To judge by his handsome, mustachioed looks, the middle-aged Bozzarias was more stage-door idler than cactus hugger, displaying his trim figure proudly beneath crimson ripstop trews and utility vest over bare hirsute chest. Despite this urban promenader's facade, Bozzarias held a respectable record as a freelance prospector, having pinpointed for their owners several strangelet lodes of note, including the fabled Gosnold Pocket. For these services, he had been recompensed by the tightfisted landowners only a nearly invisible percentage of the eventual wealth claimed from the finds. Despite his current friendly grin, it would be impossible for Bozzarias not to harbor decades-worth of spite and jealousy.

Pigafetta, Bozzarias' bestient paramour, was a voluptuous, pink-skinned geisha clad in blue and green silks. Carrying perhaps a tad too much weight—hardly surprising, given her particular gattaca—Pigafetta radiated a slack and greasy carnality utterly at odds with Ailoura's crisp and dry efficiency. When the visitors had entered the cabin, before either of the humans could intervene, Geisen and Bozzarias had been treated to an instant but decisive bloodless catfight that had settled the pecking order between the moreauvians.

Now, while Pigafetta sulked winsomely in canted corner amid her cushions, the furry female victor consulted with the two men around a small table across which lay spilled the stolen strangelets, corralled from rolling by a line of empty liquor bottles.

Bozzarias poked at one of the deceptive marbles with seeming disinterest, while his dark eyes glittered with avarice. "Let me recapitulate. We represent to various buyers that these quantum baubles are merely the camel's nose showing beneath the tent of unconsidered wealth. A newly discovered lode on the Carrabas properties, of which you, Gep Carrabas—" Bozzarias leered at Geisen, "—are the rightful heir. We rook the fools for all we can get, then hie ourselves elsewhere, beyond their injured squawks and retributions. Am I correct in all particulars?"

Ailoura spoke first. "Yes, substantially."

"And what would my share of the take be? To depart forever my cherished Chalk would require a huge stake—"

"Don't try to make your life here sound glamorous or even tolerable, Marco," Geisen said. "Everyone knows you're in debt up to your nose, and haven't had a strike in over a year. It's about time for you to change venues anyway. The days of the freelancer on Chalk are nearly over."

Bozzarias sighed dramatically, picking up a reflective marble and admiring himself in it. "I suppose you speak the truth—as it is commonly perceived. But a man of my talents can carve himself a niche anywhere. And Pigafetta *had* been begging me of late to launch her on a virtual career—"

"In other words," Ailoura interrupted, "you intend to pimp her as a porn star. Well, you'll need to relocate to a mediapoietic world then for sure. May we assume you'll become part of our scheme?"

Bozzarias set the marble down and said, "My pay?"

"Two strangelets from this very stock."

With the speed of a glass-tailed lizard Bozzarias scooped up and pocketed two spheres before the generous offer could be rescinded. "Done! Now, if you two will excuse me, I'll need to rehearse my role before we begin this deception."

Ailoura smiled, a disconcerting sight to those unfamiliar with her tender side. "Not quite so fast, Gep Bozzarias. If you'll just submit a moment—"

Before Bozzarias could protest, Ailoura had sprayed him about the head and shoulders with the contents of a pressurized can conjured from her pack.

"What! Pixie dust! This is a gross insult!"

Geisen adjusted the controls of his pocket diary. On the small screen appeared a jumbled, jittering image of the caravan's interior. As the self-assembling pixie dust cohesed around Bozzarias' eyes and ears, the image stabilized to reflect the prospector's visual point of view. Echoes of their speech emerged from the diary's speaker.

"As you well know," Ailoura advised, "the pixie dust is ineradicable and self-repairing. Only the ciphers we hold can deactivate it. Until then, all you see and hear will be shared with us. We intend to monitor you around the clock. And the diary's input is being shared with the Carrabas marchwarden, who has been told to watch for any traitorous actions on your part. That entity, by the way, is a little deranged, and might leap to conclusions about any actions that even verge on treachery. Oh, you'll also find that your left ear hosts a channel for our remote, ah, verbal advice. It would behoove you to follow our directions, since the dust is quite capable of liquefying your eyeballs upon command."

Seemingly inclined to protest further, Bozzarias suddenly thought better of dissenting. With a dispirited wave and nod, he signaled his acquiescence to their plans, becoming quietly businesslike.

"And to what Houses shall I offer this putative wealth?"

Geisen smiled. "To every House at first—except Stoessl."

"I see. Quite clever."

After Bozzarias had caused his caravan to kneel to the earth, he bade his new partners a desultory good-bye. But at the last minute, as Ailoura was stepping into the zipflyte, Bozzarias snagged Geisen by the sleeve and whispered in his ear.

"I'd trade that rude servant in for a mindless pleasure model, my friend, were I you. She's much too tricky for comfort."

"But, Marco—that's exactly why I cherish her."

Three weeks after first employing the wily Bozzarias in their scam, Geisen and Ailoura sat in their primitive quarters at Carrabas House, huddled nervously around Geisen's diary, awaiting transmission of the meeting they had long anticipated. The diary's screen revealed the familiar landscape around Stoessl House as seen from the windows of the speeding zipflyte carrying their agent to his appointment with Woda, Gitten, and Grafton.

During the past weeks, Ailoura's plot had matured, succeeding beyond their highest expectations.

Representing himself as the agent for a mysteriously returned heir of the long-abandoned Carrabas estate—a fellow who preferred anonymity for the moment—Bozzarias had visited all the biggest and most influential Houses—excluding the Stoessls—with his sample strangelets. A major new find had been described, with its coordinates freely given and inspections invited. The visiting teams of geologists reported what appeared to be a rich new lode, deceived by Geisen's expert saltings. And no single House dared attempt a midnight raid on the unprotected new strike, given the vigilance of all the others.

The cooperative and willing playacting of the Carrabas marchwarden had been essential. First, once its existence was revealed, the discarded entity's very survival became a seven-day wonder, compelling a willing suspension of disbelief in all the lies that followed. Confirming the mystery man as a true Carrabas, the marchwarden also added its jiggered testimony to verify the discovery.

Bozzarias had informed the greedily gaping families that the returned Carrabas scion had no desire to play an active role in mining and selling his stangelets. The whole estate—with many more potential strangelet nodes—would be sold to the highest bidder.

Offers began to pour in, steadily escalating. These included feverish bids from the Stoessls, which were rejected without comment. Finally, after such high-handed treatment, the offended clan demanded to know why they were being excluded from the auction. Bozzarias responded that he would convey that information only in a private meeting.

To this climactic interrogation the wily rogue now flew.

Geisen turned away from the monotonous video on his diary and asked Ailoura a question he had long contemplated but always forborne from voicing.

"Ailoura, what can you tell me of my mother?"

The cat-woman assumed a reflective expression that cloaked more emotions than it revealed. Her whiskers twitched. "Why do you ask such an irrelevant question at this crucial juncture, Gei-gei?"

"I don't know. I've often pondered the matter. Maybe I'm fearful that if our plan explodes in our faces, this might be my final opportunity to learn anything."

Ailoura paused a long while before answering. "I was intimately familiar with the one who bore you. I think her intentions were honorable. I know she loved you dearly. She always wanted to make herself known to you, but circumstances beyond her control did not permit such an honest relationship."

Geisen contemplated this information. Something told him he would get no more from the closemouthed bestient.

To disrupt the solemn mood, Ailoura reached over to ruffle Geisen's hair. "Enough of the useless past. Didn't anyone ever tell you that curiosity killed the cat? Now, pay attention! Our Judas goat has landed—"

*   *   *

Ursine yet doughy, unctuous yet fleering, Grafton
clapped Bozzarias' shoulder heartily and ushered the fop-
pish man to a seat in Vomacht's study. Behind the dead
padrone's desk sat his widow, Woda, all motile maquillage
and mimicked mourning. Her teeth sported a fashionable
gilt. Gitten lounged on the arm of a sofa, plainly bored
and resentful, toying with a handheld hologame like some
sullen adolescent.

After offering drinks—Bozzarias requested and received
the finest vintage of sparkling wine available on Chalk—
Grafton drove straight to the heart of the matter.

"Gep Bozzarias, I demand to know why Stoessl House
has been denied a chance to bid on the Carrabas estate."

Bozzarias drained his glass and dabbed at his lips with
his jabot before replying. "The reason is simple, Gep
Stoessl, yet of such delicacy that you would not have cared
to have me state it before your peers. Thus this private
encounter."

"Go on."

"My employer, Timor Carrabas, you must learn, is a man
of punctilio and politesse. Having abandoned Chalk many
generations ago, Carrabas House still honors and maintains
the old ways prevalent during that golden age. They have
not fallen into the lax and immoral fashions of the present,
and absolutely contemn such behavior."

Grafton stiffened. "To what do you refer? Stoessl House
is guilty of no such infringements on custom."

"That is not how my employer perceives affairs. After
all, what is the very first thing he hears upon returning to
his ancestral homeworld? Disturbing rumors of patricide,
fraternal infighting, and excommunication, all of which em-
anate from Stoessl House and Stoessl House alone. Leery
of stepping beneath the shadow of such a cloud, he could
not ethically undertake any dealings with your clan."

Fuming, Grafton started to rebut these charges, but
Woda intervened. "Gep Bozzarias, all mandated investiga-
tions into the death of my beloved Vomacht resulted in
one uncontested conclusion: pump failure produced a kind
of alien hyperglycemia that drove the Stroonians insane. No
human culpability or intent to harm was ever established."

Bozzarias held his glass up for a refill and obtained one.
"Why, then, were all the bestient witnesses to the incident

terminally disposed of? What motivated the abdication of your youngest scion? Giger, I believe he was named?"

Trying to be helpful, Gitten jumped into the conversation. "Oh, we use up bestients at a frightful rate! If they're not dying from floggings, they're collapsing from overuse in the mines and brothels. Such a flawed product line, these moreauvians. Why, if they were robots, they'd never pass consumer-lab testing. As for Geisen—that's the boy's name—well, he simply got fed up with our civilized lifestyle. He always did prefer the barbaric outback existence. No doubt he's enjoying himself right now, wallowing in some muddy oasis with a sandworm concubine."

Grafton cut off his brother's tittering with a savage glance. "Gep Bozzarias, I'm certain that if your employer were to meet us, he'd find we are worthy of making an offer on his properties. In fact, he could avoid all the fuss and bother of a full-fledged auction, since I'm prepared right now to trump the highest bid he's yet received. Will you convey to him my invitation to enjoy the hospitality of Stoessl House?"

Bozzarias closed his eyes ruminatively, as if harkening to some inner voice of conscience, then answered, "Yes, I can do that much. And with some small encouragement, I would exert all my powers of persuasiveness—"

Woda spoke. "Why, where did this small but heavy bag of Tancredi moonstones come from? It certainly doesn't belong to us. Gep Bozzarias—would you do me the immense favor of tracking down the rightful owner of these misplaced gems?"

Bozzarias stood and bowed, then accepted the bribe. "My pleasure, madame. I can practically guarantee that Stoessl House will soon receive its just reward."

"Sandworm concubine!" Geisen appeared ready to hurl his eavesdropping device to the hard floor, but restrained himself. "How I'd like to smash their lying mouths in!"

Ailoura grinned. "You must show more restraint than that, Geisen, especially when you come face-to-face with the scoundrels. Take consolation from the fact that mere physical retribution would hurt them far less than the loss of money and face we will inflict."

"Still, there's a certain satisfaction in feeling the impact of fist on flesh."

"My kind calls it 'the joy when teeth meet bone,' so I fully comprehend. Just not this time. Understood?"

Geisen impulsively hugged the old cat. "Still teaching me, Ailoura?"

"Until I die, I suppose."

"You are appallingly obese, Geisen. Your form recalls nothing of the slim blade who cut such wide swaths among the girls of the various Houses before his engagement."

"And your polecat coloration, fair Ailoura, along with those tinted lenses and tooth caps, speak not of a bold mouser, but of a scavenger through garbage tips."

Regarding each other with satisfaction, Ailoura and Geisen thus approved of their disguises.

With the aid of Bozzarias, who had purchased for them various sophisticated, semiliving prosthetics, dyes, and off-world clothing, the man and his servant—Timor Carrabas and Hepzibah—resembled no one ever seen before on Chalk. His pasty face rouged, Geisen wobbled as he waddled, breathing stertorously, while the limping Ailoura diffused a moderately repulsive scent calculated to keep the curious at a certain remove.

The Carrabas marchwarden now spoke, a touch of excitement in its artificial voice. "I have just notified my Stoessl House counterpart that you are departing within the hour. You will be expected in time for essences and banquet, with a half hour allotted to freshen up and settle into your guest rooms."

"Very good. Rehearse the rest of the plan for me."

"Once the funds are transferred from Stoessl House to me, I will in turn upload them to the Bourse on Feuilles Mortes under the name of Geisen Stoessl, where they will be immune from attachment. I will then retreat to my soul-canister, readying it for removal by your agent, Bozzarias, who will bring it to the space field—specifically the terminal hosting Gravkosmos Interstellar. Beyond that point, I cannot be of service until I am haptically enabled once more."

"You have the scheme perfectly. Now we thank you, and leave with the promise that we shall talk again in the near future, in a more pleasant place."

"Good-bye, Gep Carrabas, and good luck."

Within a short time the hired zipflyte arrived. (It would

hardly do for the eminent Timor Carrabas to appear in Geisen's battered craft, which had, in point of fact, already been sold to raise additional funds to aid their subterfuge.) After clambering clumsily on board, the schemers settled themselves in the spacious rear seat while the chauffeur—a neat-plumaged and discreet raptor-derived bestient—lifted off and flew at a swift clip toward Stoessl House.

Ailoura's comment about Geisen's attractiveness to his female peers had set an unhealed sore spot within him aching. "Do you imagine, Hepzibah, that other local luminaries might attend this evening's dinner party? I had in mind a certain Gep Bloedwyn Vermeule."

"I suspect she will. The Stoessls and the Vermeules have bonds and alliances dating back centuries."

Geisen mused dreamily. "I wonder if she will be as beautiful and sensitive and angelic as I have heard tell she is."

Ailoura began to hack from deep in her throat. Recovering, she apologized, "Excuse me, Gep Carrabas. Something unpleasant in my throat. No doubt a simple hairball."

Geisen did not look amused. "You cannot deny reports of the lady's beauty, Hepzibah."

"Beauty is as beauty does, master."

The largest ballroom in Stoessl House had been extravagantly bedecked for the arrival of Timor Carrabas. Living luminescent lianas in dozens of neon tones festooned the heavy-beamed rafters. Decorator dust migrated invisibly about the chamber, cohering at random into wallscreens showing various entertaining videos from the mediapoietic worlds. Responsive carpets the texture of moss crept warily along the tessellated floor, consuming any spilled food and drink wasted from the large collation spread out across a servitor-staffed table long as a playing field. (House chef Stine Pursiful oversaw all with a meticulous eye, his upraised ladle serving as baton of command. After some argument among the family members and chef, a buffet had been chosen over a sit-down meal, as being more informal, relaxed, and conducive to easy dealings.) The floor space was thronged with over a hundred gaily caparisoned representatives of the Houses most closely allied to the Stoessls, some dancing in stately pavanes to the music from the throats of the octet of avian bestients perched on their multibranched stand. But despite the many diversions of music, food, drink, and chatter, all eyes had strayed ineluctably to the form of the mysterious Timor Carrabas when he entered, and from time to time thereafter.

Beneath his prosthetics, Geisen now sweated copiously, both from nervousness and the heat. Luckily, his disguising adjuncts quite capably metabolized this betraying moisture before it ever reached his clothing.

The initial meeting with his brothers and stepmother had gone well. Hands were shaken all around without anyone suspecting that the flabby hand of Timor Carrabas concealed a slimmer one that ached to deliver vengeful blows.

Geisen could see immediately that since Vomacht's death, Grafton had easily assumed the role of head of household, with Woda patently the power behind the throne and Gitten content to act the wastrel princeling.

"So, Gep Carrabas," Grafton oleaginously purred, "now you finally perceive with your own eyes that we Stoessls are no monsters. It's never wise to give gossip any credence."

Gitten said, "But gossip is the only kind of talk that makes life worth liv— oof!"

Woda took a second step forward, relieving the painful pressure she had inflicted on her younger son's foot. "Excuse my clumsiness, Gep Carrabas, in my eagerness to enhance my proximity to a living reminder of the fine old ways of Chalk. I'm sure you can teach us much about how our forefathers lived. Despite personal longevity, we have lost the institutional rigor your clan has reputedly preserved."

In his device-modulated, rather fulsome voice, Geisen answered, "I am always happy to share my treasures with others, be they spiritual or material."

Grafton brightened. "This expansiveness bodes well for our later negotiations, Gep Carrabas. I must say that your attitude is not exactly as your servant Bozzarias conveyed."

Geisen made a dismissive wave. "Simply a local hireling who was not truly privy to my thoughts. But he has the virtue of following my bidding without the need to know any of my ulterior motivations." Geisen felt relieved to have planted that line to protect Bozzarias in the nasty wake of the successful conclusion of their thimblerigging. "Here is my real counselor. Hepzibah, step forward."

Ailoura moved within the circle of speakers, her unnaturally flared and pungent striped musteline tail waving perilously close to the humans. "At your service, Gep."

The Stoessls involuntarily cringed away from the unpleasant odor wafting from Ailoura, then restrained their impolite reaction.

"Ah, quite an, ah, impressive moreauvian. Positively, um, redolent of the ribosartor's art. Perhaps your, erm, adviser would care to dine with others of her kind."

"Hepzibah, you are dismissed until I need you."

"As you wish."

Soon Geisen was swept up in a round of introductions to people he had known all his life. Eventually he reached the food, and fell to eating rather too greedily. After weeks spent subsisting on MREs alone, he could hardly restrain himself. And his glutton's disguise allowed all excess. Let the other guests gape at his immoderate behavior. They were constrained by their own greed for his putative fortune from saying a word.

After satisfying his hunger, Geisen finally looked up from his empty plate.

There stood Bloedwyn Vermeule.

Geisen's ex-fiancée had never shone more alluringly. Threaded with invisible flexing pseudo-myofibrils, her long unfettered hair waved in continual delicate movement, as if she were a mermaid underwater. She wore a gown tonight loomed from golden spider silk. Her lips were verdigris, matched by her nails and eye shadow.

Geisen hastily dabbed at his own lips with his napkin, and was mortified to see the clean cloth come away with enough stains to represent a child's immoderate battle with an entire chocolate cake.

"Oh, Gep Carrabas, I hope I am not interrupting your gustatory pleasures."

"Nuh—no, young lady, not at all. I am fully sated. And you are?"

"Gep Bloedwyn Vermeule. You may call me by my first name, if you grant me the same privilege."

"But naturally."

"May I offer an alternative pleasure, Timor, in the form of a dance? Assuming your satiation does not extend to *all* recreations."

"Certainly. If you'll make allowances in advance for my clumsiness."

Bloedwyn allowed the tip of her tongue delicately to traverse her patinaed lips. "As the Dompatta says, 'An earnest rider compensates for a balky steed.'"

This bit of familiar gospel had never sounded so lascivious. Geisen was shocked at this unexpected temptress behavior from his ex-fiancée. But before he could react with real or mock indignation, Bloedwyn had whirled him out onto the floor.

They essayed several complicated dances before Geisen, pleading fatigue, could convince his partner to call a halt to the activity.

"Let us recover ourselves in solitude on the terrace," Bloedwyn said, and conducted Geisen by the arm through a pressure curtain and onto an unlit open-air patio. Alone in the shadows, they took up positions braced against a balustrade. The view of the moon-drenched arroyos below occupied them in silence for a time. Then Bloedwyn spoke huskily.

"You exude a foreign, experienced sensuality, Timor, to which I find myself vulnerable. Perhaps you would indulge my weakness with an assignation tonight, in a private chamber of Stoessl House known to me? After any important business dealings are successfully concluded, of course."

Geisen seethed inwardly, but managed to control his voice. "I am flattered that you find a seasoned fellow of my girth so attractive, Bloedwyn. But I do not wish to cause any intermural incidents. Surely you are affianced to someone, a young lad both bold and wiry, jealous and strong."

"Pah! I do not care for young men, they are all chowderheads! Pawing, puling, insensitive, shallow, and vain, to a man! I was betrothed to one such, but luckily he revealed his true colors and I was able to cast him aside like the churl he proved to be."

Now Geisen felt only miserable self-pity. He could summon no words, and Bloedwyn took his silence for assent. She planted a kiss on his cheek, then whispered directly into his ear. "Here's a map to the boudoir where I'll be waiting. Simply take the east squeezer down three levels, then follow the hot dust." She pressed a slip of paper into his hand, supplementing her message with extra pressure in his palm, then sashayed away like a tainted sylph.

Geisen spent half an hour with his mind roiling before he regained the confidence to return to the party.

Before too long, Grafton corralled him.

"Are you enjoying yourself, Timor? The food agrees? The essences elevate? The ladies are pliant? Haw! But perhaps we should turn our minds to business now, before we both grow too muzzy-headed. After conducting our dull commerce, we can cut loose."

"I am ready. Let me summon my aide."

"That skun— That is, if you absolutely insist. But surely our marchwarden can offer any support services you need. Notarization, citation of past deeds, and so forth."

"No. I rely on Hepzibah implicitly."

Grafton partially suppressed a frown. "Very well, then."

Once Ailoura arrived from the servants' table, the trio headed toward Vomacht's old study. Geisen had to remind himself not to turn down any "unknown" corridor before Grafton himself did.

Seated in the very room where he had been fleeced of his patrimony and threatened with false charges of murder, Geisen listened with half an ear while Grafton outlined the terms of the prospective sale: all the Carrabas properties and whatever wealth of strangelets they contained, in exchange for a sum greater than the Gross Plantetary Product of many smaller worlds.

Ailoura attended more carefully to the contract, even pointing out to Geisen a buried clause that would have made payment contingent on the first month's production from the new fields. After some arguing, the conspirators succeeded in having the objectionable codicil removed. The transfer of funds would be complete and instantaneous.

When Grafton had finally finished explaining the conditions, Geisen roused himself. He found it easy to sound bored with the whole deal, since his elaborate scam, at its moment of triumph, afforded him surprisingly little vengeful pleasure.

"All the details seem perfectly managed, Gep Stoessl, with that one small change of ours included. I have but one question. How do I know that the black sheep of your

House, Geisen, will not contest our agreement? He seems a contrary sort, from what I've heard, and I would hate to be involved in judicial proceedings, should he get a whim in his head."

Grafton settled back in his chair with a broad smile. "Fear not, Timor! That wild hair will get up no one's arse! Geisen has been effectively rendered powerless. As was only proper and correct, I assure you, for he was not a true Stoessl at all."

Geisen's heart skipped a cycle. "Oh? How so?"

"The lad was a chimera! A product of the ribosartors! Old Vomacht was unsatisfied with the vagaries of honest mating that had produced Gitten and myself from the noble stock of our mother. Traditional methods of reproduction had not delivered him a suitable toady. So he resolved to craft a better heir. He used most of his own germ plasm as foundation, but supplemented his nucleotides with dozens of other snippets. Why, that hybrid boy even carried bestient genes. Rat and weasel, I'm willing to bet! Haw! No, Geisen had no place in our family."

"And his mother?"

"Once the egg was crafted and fertilized, Vomacht implanted it in a host bitch. One of our own bestients. I misapprehend her name now, after all these years. Amorica, Orella, something of that nature. I never really paid attention to her fate after she delivered her human whelp. I have more important properties to look after. No doubt she ended up on the offal heap, like all the rest of her kind."

A red curtain drifting across Geisen's vision failed to occlude the shape of the massive aurochs-flaying blade hanging on the wall. One swift leap and it would be in his hands. Then Grafton would know sweet murderous pain, and Geisen's bitter heart would applaud—

Standing beside Geisen, Ailoura let slip the quietest cough.

Geisen looked into her face.

A lone tear crept from the corner of one feline eye.

Geisen gathered himself and stood up, unspeaking.

Grafton grew a trifle alarmed. "Is there anything the matter, Gep Carrabas?"

"No, Gep Stoessl, not at all. Merely that old hurts pain

me, and I would fain relieve them. Let us close our deal. I am content."

The star liner carrying Geisen, Ailoura, and the stasis-bound Carrabas marchwarden to a new life sped through the interstices of the cosmos, powered perhaps by a strangelet mined from Stoessl lands. In one of the lounges, the man and his cat nursed drinks and snacks, admiring the exotic variety of their fellow passengers and reveling in their hard-won liberty and security.

"Where from here—son?" asked Ailoura with a hint of unwonted shyness.

Geisen smiled. "Why, wherever we wish, Mother dear."

"Rowr! A world with plenty of fish, then, for me!"

THE EMPEROR'S REVENGE

by Stanley Schmidt

Stanley Schmidt has contributed numerous stories and articles to original anthologies, edited several anthologies, and
published four novels (all recently rereleased in various digital forms), the nonfiction book *Aliens and Alien Societies:
A Writer's Guide to Creating Extraterrestrial Life-Forms*,
and hundreds of *Analog* editorials. As editor of *Analog*,
he has been nominated twenty-three times for the Hugo
Award for Best Professional Editor. A new novel
(*Argonaut*), a collection of essays (*Which Way to the Future?*), and a story collection (*Generation Gap and Other
Stories*) were recently published. He was Guest of Honor
at BucConeer, the 1998 World Science Fiction Conven-
tion in Baltimore, and has been a Nebula and Hugo
Award nominee for his fiction.

Have you ever wondered what happened after the fairy
tale was finished? Here is a story mixing old-school revenge with cutting-edge technology for a delightful sequel
to one of the most popular fairy tales of all. . . .

(With posthumous apologies to Hans Christian Andersen)

ONCE upon a time, as anybody who has lived in Western
civilization for more than a week knows, an emperor was
royally conned by a couple of itinerant rogues. What hardly
anybody now knows is what happened afterward.

The emperor in question, whom we shall not identify too
specifically except to say that his name was Fred, was not
a happy camper. Sequestered in his chambers (and now
fully and most assuredly dressed) after that dreadful procession, he fumed at his chief adviser, Milton, "It was so *hu-*

miliating! Not only finding out I'd been duped, but finding it out while I was parading down the street stark naked in front of the whole town—and not even knowing I was until it was too late!"

"Actually," Milton said solemnly, though Fred imagined that he was suppressing a titter, "I thought you carried yourself surprisingly well."

"You weren't the one who was naked," the emperor muttered. Then he thought of something else and glared at Milton. "You weren't the one who told me, either, back when it might have done some good. I had to hear it from that infernal little boy, in front of the whole town." He mimicked a shrill child's voice: " 'But he has nothing on!' " Reverting to his own voice, he demanded, "Why did you let things get to that point, Milton? I've always thought of you as 'my honest old minister,' the one man I could trust above all others. So why, when I sent you down to check up on those so-called tailors, did you come back raving about how magnificent the suit they were making me was? You went on and on about the colors and pattern and cut. It sounds suspiciously like you were in on their little conspiracy, to make a fool of me!"

The stooped, white-haired gent cringed. "Oh, never, Your Imperial Majesty! Surely you know I could never do that. But try to put yourself in my shoes . . . so to speak. It's true that I didn't see anything on their loom, and just repeated the lies they told me. But suppose they'd been telling the truth. If their fabrics really were invisible to anyone who was stupid or incompetent, and I came back and told you I couldn't see them, you would have believed *me* stupid and incompetent. Then I would have been out of a job—or worse." He hesitated. "I must say, Your Majesty, that was the most appalling moment of my life. I found *myself* thinking I must be stupid and incompetent, even though I'd never thought myself so and I've always tried to serve you well. But whether I was or not, I couldn't afford to have you think I was. So I *had* to tell you I saw what I was expected to see. After all, even Your Majesty believed them, enough to pay good money for their services—"

"Yes," growled Fred, "and that brings us to another sore point—and maybe, just maybe, a chance for you to redeem yourself. What's being done about getting my money back from those accursed swindlers?"

"Flymme and Flamsteed? They're securely stowed in Your Majesty's deepest dungeon. And several courtly heads are roll—"

"I see. And exactly how does this get me my money back?"

Minister Milton blushed, a startling effect on skin that normally looked like wrinkled white paper. "Well, as Your Majesty knows, the scalawags—Flymme and Flamsteed—stubbornly refused to give you a refund. We hoped some time in the dungeon might give them an incentive to reconsider. I understand the rats and cockroaches can be very persuasive—"

"And have the rats and cockroaches made any progress?"

"Uh, not as much as we'd like, sire. Incredible as it may seem, the scoundrels still insist that they provided exactly what they offered and so they've earned the money. They actually had the impudence to say they can't help it if the court and empire are riddled with stupidity and corruption so that nobody here can appreciate their work. One of them said it must be something in the water, or the very bloodlines of our people. How else, he said, could you account for even that innocent-looking little boy being—"

Fred waved him to silence. "That's more detail than I need," he said. "Spare me. Just get my money back, whatever you have to—"

He cut off abruptly as a fanfare sounded in the corridor without. A big wooden door swung open and a lackey strode in, knelt obsequiously before the emperor, then stood and whispered something to Milton.

Then he stood waiting.

Milton addressed the emperor. "It seems," he said with a slight cough, "there's a visitor in the antechamber who would like a brief audience with Your Imperial Majesty. It seems he . . . uh . . . heard about your recent embarrassment and would like to offer you a way to recover both your money and your respect."

"Well, you know I'd like nothing better," His Majesty grumbled skeptically. "But how does this mysterious visitor propose to achieve this?"

"Well," said Milton, obviously uncomfortable, "it seems

he claims he can *really* do what Flymme and Flamsteed claimed—only better.''

Emperor Fred groaned. "Oh, no, not again! Well, what have I got to loose?" Milton started to say something, but Fred cut him off with a sharp glare. "Don't answer. Just show the *rascal du jour* in and let's see what he has to say."

The newcomer was clearly not from these parts. Fred, seated regally on his throne, watched haughtily along the slope of his own nose as the stranger was escorted in. He was a gangly young man—hardly more than a boy—in an oddly mismatched outfit faintly suggestive of a jester's garb. On his left wrist he wore an odd band of metal, segmented and with one section curiously swollen and capped with some transparent material. Fred had never seen anything like it, but the young man made no attempt to hide it. Fred would have loved to demand that his visitor hand it over for examination, but he decided to play it cool. *Let's see what he has to say,* he reminded himself. *Maybe he'll volunteer something useful—or let something slip.*

The visitor paused in front of the throne and bowed, elaborately but clumsily, as if he'd been taught the correct procedure but hadn't had time to practice. Then he waited.

"You may rise," said His Imperial Majesty. The young man did. "You would be?"

"Spike Poindexter," said the visitor, in a soft, respectful, yet startlingly self-assured voice, with an odd accent. "I'm very grateful to Your Imperial Majesty for granting me—"

"From?" the emperor interrupted.

The visitor broke off. "Beg pardon?"

"Where are you from, Spike Poindexter?"

"Oh." He hesitated, as if undecided which path to follow at a crossroads. Then he said, "MIT. Many centuries in your future."

"Well," said the emperor, "that's an original line, at least. But where are you *really* from?"

"MIT," Poindexter repeated matter-of-factly, "in your far future. My people have learned to travel back and forth in time, just as you travel north or south or east or west."

A nut, thought Fred, though in the idiom of his time and place. He found himself more disappointed than he'd expected; part of him, he realized, had hoped the visitor might actually bring help. Now he abandoned that hope, but found this youth's fanciful babblings amusing enough to humor for a while. "Most interesting," he said. "And how do you do this marvelous deed?"

"It would take far too long to explain," said Poindexter. "One of the drawbacks of the method is that it can only send me back here for a brief period, and then it will snap me back to my own time. My purpose in coming here is to offer you help, and that, too, will take time. I respectfully suggest that Your Imperial Majesty would do better to concentrate on availing yourself of what I offer, and not waste precious time on confusing and unnecessary explanations."

Slick, thought Fred, with grudging admiration. Then he frowned. "Hm-m-m," he said thoughtfully. "So why should you want to travel far into your own past to help us?" His frown deepened and he leaned forward, suddenly wary. "How would you even *know* about us?"

"Your story has come down through the centuries," said Poindexter. The emperor felt his face redden at the thought of becoming a laughingstock not only for his own subjects, but for all posterity. Poindexter added hastily, "Not as history, Your Imperial Majesty, and your name was not mentioned. It was a legend, told and retold till no one remembered just who was actually involved or when or where it happened."

"Well, that's some small comfort. But then how did you know where—and when—to come?"

"It took a lot of research," Poindexter confided. " 'Once upon a time' is pretty vague. But I got intrigued when I heard a comedian retelling your story describe your nonexistent invisible suit as 'a walking SAT test'—"

"A what?" Fred interrupted.

"You don't want to know," said Poindexter, "and you wouldn't believe it if I tried to tell you. Let's just say it's a way to tell how smart somebody is. And I got to thinking, what if you really could build a suit that would measure intelligence that way? The more I thought about it, the more I thought it would make a really neat thesis project—"

"A what?"

"Another thing that's too hard to explain and not worth the trouble. Look, Your Majesty, if you ask me to explain every strange term I use, we're never going to get to the point. How about I just try to explain the really important ones as well as I can?" Fred nodded grudgingly and Poindexter went on, "Well, anyway, I thought I could do it. And where better to prove it than right here where you were hornswoggled? My girlfriend was . . . is? will be? . . . working in history and folklore, and she said myths and legends often have some basis in fact. Her thesis put her onto some leads that gave us a pretty good idea who and when and where you were, and . . . well, here I am."

"Indeed you are." Fred looked him up and down appraisingly. "And now that you're here, exactly what do you propose to do for us? And what do you expect in return?"

"Just the satisfaction of seeing it work, sir—and seeing you get back at those swine. Incidentally, of course, I do expect to get my union card . . . my Ph.D. . . . oh, never mind. That part doesn't concern you."

"Hmph. Your predecessors asked a lot and gave us nothing. You ask for nothing and promise a lot. Sounds just as suspicious to us."

"I can't say as I blame you, sir, but—"

Fred waved him off. "Oh, let's just get on with it. Tell me what you have in mind, and we'll see if we can figure out what the catch is for ourselves."

"Very well, sir. I must warn you that this will be rather complicated, and will include a good many of those hard-to-explain terms. But I feel duty-bound to try. I wouldn't want you to feel that you were buying a pig in a poke."

"Neither would *we*," said the emperor, with a dark hint of warning in his voice.

"Then we're agreed, Your Imperial Majesty." There was a subtle shift in Poindexter's manner, a shift that reminded Fred uncomfortably of Flymme and Flamsteed launching into their sales spiel. "The key to what I propose is not one suit, but a *set* of suits, one for you and one for each of a bunch of other people—including Flymme and Flamsteed. When the right time comes—and it won't be long, because, as I said, my time here is limited—all of you will gather in your grandest banquet hall to mill and swill—er, have a party. We'll call it a 'masked ball.' That way no one will question why all the suits include rather elaborate headgear that covers the wearer's face."

Fred frowned. "Lots of suits? Masks? A party—which, we might add, will cost us more money to put on? This sounds awfully complicated and cumbersome to us. Those scoundrels before you said they just needed to make *one* suit, with nothing special about it except that the stupid couldn't see it—"

"Ah," said Poindexter, with a smug grin, "but what they described wouldn't work. Mine will. Which would you rather have: empty promises of simple magic, or complicated but *real* magic—or rather, science—that you can count on?" Without waiting for an answer, he hurried on, "The kind of thing they promised you exists only in fairy tales, Your Majesty. This is real life.

"Those swindlers claimed they could make you a suit that, all by itself, could look one way to a smart person and completely different to a stupid one. Well, I've read about every science up to the twenty-third century, and I don't know anybody who can do that. But it's not all that difficult to get a similar effect if both the person looking and the one being looked at wear suits, each of which measures and transmits information about its wearer, and a helmet that projects an altered image to *its* wearer on the basis of that information. Given enough interactive computing and image processing capabilities—"

Emperor Fred felt his head swimming, but forced himself to remain outwardly cool. "We presume," he said, "that these are some of the hard-to-explain future terms you warned us about?"

"Er, yes, Your Majesty."

"We would be much obliged if you would try to hold those to a necessary minimum. Simply tell us in plain language what we would do and what would then happen."

"I'll certainly try, Your Majesty." Poindexter paused as if collecting his thoughts—as if he were preparing, perhaps, to translate a tricky thought from one language into another. "Your basic problem with this recent fiasco," he began anew, "was dishonesty. The phony tailors lied about what they could do; the trusted advisers you sent to check up on them—" he nodded slightly toward Milton, who blushed again, "—lied about what they saw. So did everyone else, until that one little boy who didn't know any better than to tell the truth gave everyone else the courage to try it. If you think about it, Your Majesty, a simple lie detector would solve a lot of your problems all by itself.

But Spike Poindexter will give you more. I promised you a way to gauge intelligence, and you shall have that, too, as well as a lie detector.

"Picture yourself at our masked ball, Your Majesty. What you're wearing looks, to the unaided eye, like a plain suit of snugly fitting long underwear, capped with a rather imposing helmet."

The emperor's ears perked up at that, so much so that he momentarily lapsed from correct speech. "Then they won't see me naked this time?"

"Far from it, Your Majesty—though you will surely see some of *them* that way." The emperor's anticipatory grin grew even broader at that thought, and he had to force himself to concentrate as Poindexter went on. "The key to it Your Majesty, is that nobody will be relying on unaided eyes. Everyone will be wearing a mask that covers their eyes, and equipment built into it will project an image onto the inside of the mask. In most cases that image will look exactly like their real surroundings, but the suits are different. Each point on every suit sends a signal that other suits recognize as a particular part of that suit—or, by extension, the wearer's body. And each mask can decide whether to show its wearer that suit as it really is, or—"

Fred was getting dizzy again. "You mean the suits are alive?"

Poindexter smiled amiably. "Not exactly, Your Majesty. But they have built-in computers that can process—"

"Oh, never mind!" Fred interrupted. "So exactly what does who see?"

"That depends on which suit they're wearing and which one they're looking at. With the exception of Your Majesty's special suit, everybody else's takes measurements of its wearer's body. Things like heart rate, blood pressure, skin conductivity, EEG activity—"

"Whoa, whoa, *whoa!*" Poindexter stopped and Fred glared at him. "More of your 'terms,' we assume. Are you going to explain them?"

"I would be happy to try," Poindexter said unctuously, "but due to my time constraints, I fear we'll have to choose between trying to give you a full explanation and getting the job done. I assume you prefer the latter, so let's just say that the suit measures, in a general way, its wearer's mental activity and state of nervousness. The former correlates pretty directly with intelligence and the latter with how honest the wearer is being. If both of those measurements are above a certain level, the wearer passes the test and sees you in the most splendid regalia you can imagine. If he fails, he sees only the aforementioned underwear."

Fred chuckled at the prospect. "And what do *we* see?"

"Well, unlike yours, Your Majesty, the other suits actually do look to the unaided eye like fancy dress—no two alike, and none, of course, comparable in splendor to yours as seen by the wise and virtuous. But to the other masks . . . ah, there's the beauty of it! If they are *not* wise and virtuous—if they flunk the test administered by their suit—they show up in everybody else's mask as bare bodies. And if they lie about how they see Your Majesty, they also turn bright red, rather as your good old minister is doing as I speak."

Fred mulled that over for a moment and broke into a hearty guffaw. "Very good!" he exclaimed, slapping his imperial thigh. "Not only do we get even with Flymme and Flamsteed, but we can use this stuff to check up on everyone around us and learn once and for all who can be trusted and who cannot. That could almost be worth all this extra bother!"

"Now you're getting it," Poindexter said with an enthusiastic nod. "Why buy a mere suit when you can buy a System?" The capital was clearly audible. "You'll be very happy with this, Your Majesty. It's a superb management tool, literally centuries ahead of its time. I might remind Your Imperial Majesty that that's how you intended to use those frauds' magic suit, but what I'm offering you can do so much more—"

"But—" Fred's beaming turned abruptly to a frown as he tried to fit all this together in his mind. "But, how, exactly, does it help us get even with Flymme and Flamsteed?"

"The masked ball," said Poindexter. "You put it on as a regular court festival, with everyone flaunting their most fantastic finery, and you tell Flymme and Flamsteed that they are invited, too—but for them there's a catch. You explain that you have something new that will do what they claimed, but you won't tell them exactly how it works."

"*That* won't be a problem," the emperor mumbled wryly.

"You explain that before the ball is over you will know for sure whether they're telling the truth, as they claim. If they are, you will give them their freedom and write off their debt. But if it proves that they're lying and did in fact swindle you, you will execute them immediately—unless they refund your payments immediately. And then you do it."

"Beautiful!" the emperor breathed, despite a feeling in the back of his mind that there was still something in this that didn't quite fit.

He became aware of Minister Milton tugging at his sleeve. "Ask him," the minister whispered, "about the time limit. And the materials."

At first Fred didn't catch his drift. Then he drew himself up and stared hard at Poindexter. "It seems to us," he said, "that there are two key issues you haven't addressed: materials and labor. You said you can't stay long. So how are you going to make all these fancy suits and masks?"

"Oh, I don't *make* them, Your Imperial Majesty. I grow them, using nanotechnology—"

The emperor glowered. "Another of your newfangled terms you can't explain, I presume?"

"I'm afraid so. Quite routine where I come from, though I'm afraid it will look a lot like magic to you. It works by assembling things at a level too small to see, beginning with a few tubes of tiny 'seeds' that I brought with me."

"Those other two said their work would look like magic," Fred reminded, "and it looked like nothing— because it was. Let us remind you, Spike Poindexter, that if we find you've swindled us, we'll be even angrier than before. There's always room for one more in that dungeon, no matter how full it is. Even the gallows, if it comes to that—"

"It won't," Poindexter assured him hastily, but he looked a bit pale.

"It had better not. Our other question is: where does the material for all these suits come from? Flymme and— Those two whose names should not be mentioned demanded all manner of expensive fibers and precious metals, which I never saw again. Come to think of it, they owe me for all that, too." He looked piercingly at Poindexter. "And

you, we presume, will need far more for your 'System,'
which we expect you'll want us to supply."

"Well, yes," Poindexter said slowly, "I will need rather
a lot of raw material—"

"So how," the emperor exploded, "are you any better
than *them?*"

"I," Poindexter said quietly, "am asking *only* for materials. No labor charges, no profit margin for myself. Zero. I
couldn't take it back even if you gave it to me. As for
materials, I will need a larger *quantity* than they did, but
I'm not fussy about the *quality*. They demanded the finest
silks and gold; all I need, basically, is mass. My nanotools
are very versatile. Bring me mud, table scraps, rocks culled
from your poorest fields, ashes from your fires—stuff you
don't want anyway."

The emperor studied him silently for a minute or so. It
was an interesting proposition, albeit truly bizarre. But . . .
"*Their* proposition was interesting, too," he said finally.
"But we're not as trusting as we once were. Why should
we believe you can actually do any of what you claim?"

"I wouldn't expect you to," said Poindexter, "without
seeing for yourself. I would be more than happy to give
you a demonstration, using only small amounts of material.
If you're satisfied with what you see, we go ahead with the
whole operation. If not, I leave quietly and you're no worse
off than you started." His smile radiated sincerity. "Fair
enough?"

"Fair enough," said Fred. "Let's see what you can do,
and then maybe we can talk business."

"A decision you won't regret, Your Imperial Majesty."
Poindexter beamed confidently. "Let's get to work. We
have a masked ball to plan!"

The demonstration was impressive and thrilling, and Emperor Fred enthusiastically gave the necessary orders to
proceed with his strange visitor's plan. Despite Milton's repeated warnings against being taken in again (no doubt
motivated in part by his desire not to be blamed again),
Fred threw himself into giving Poindexter all the support
he asked for, to make sure the job was done before his
time ran out. Oxcarts full of this and that and all manner

of debris groaned up the dirt road to the outbuilding where Poindexter had set up his headquarters. Lights burned there well into the night, suggesting that work was in full swing—but then, Flymme and Flamsteed had given that impression, too, so Fred sent Milton to look for visible signs of progress.

Milton's reports were glowing, but that, too, had been true when Flymme and Flamsteed were "working." So Fred felt a nagging doubt about whether he was truly getting his money's worth this time, but had trouble working up the nerve to go and see for himself.

He had no trouble at all delegating Milton to deliver his "invitation" to Flymme and Flamsteed, and was only slightly surprised to hear that their initial reaction was derision, bravado, and an expression of doubt about whether they would condescend to accept—as if they had a choice. Meanwhile Fred also delegated Milton (and made sure Flymme and Flamsteed knew about it) to have a thorough search made of the living and working quarters they had occupied before their precipitous fall from grace. Disappointingly, but not too surprisingly, no sign of the missing money and materials was found—which left Fred and Milton to puzzle over where they might have hidden the loot, and how they got it there. With a little thought, it wasn't too hard to imagine ways. With hindsight, it might have been well to keep the "tailors" under closer guard. But then, how could he have done that without dangerously offending them, had they really been the professionals he'd been led to believe?

Rather than stewing too long in those juices, Fred threw himself into preparations for the masked ball, meeting with underlings to figure out the banners and torches and such that would deck the hall. On the third day Poindexter showed up at Fred's chambers for a fitting of the imperial suit—a very palpable suit, even if it did look like underwear. Fred was so relieved and encouraged by being able to see and feel it that he finally nerved himself to go personally to Poindexter's workshop to see how things were going.

It exceeded his wildest expectations. Not only were partially finished garments everywhere, if he stared at any one of them long enough, he could actually see it growing. *This,* he thought, *is truly magic. I was burned once, but this time, I daresay, I'm in capable hands.*

He looked forward with exponentially growing anticipation to The Big Day. And then, in less than a week, it was there.

Emperor Fred surveyed the scene privately before he entered it, hidden behind a screen on a small balcony overlooking the hall. Poindexter's bizarre helmet rested heavily on his head and shoulders, but it interfered not at all with the view. His decorators had done an impressive job with lighting and banners and shields; and his initial impression as he watched guests file in and begin to mingle was that Poindexter, too, had done well. The imperial suit included a special toggle behind his right ear that let him switch between seeing the scene as it was, and as Poindexter's "System" processed it. For now he had it in the "natural" position, and it almost made him jealous to see below him the splendid array of fine colors and textures, feathers and brooches, and quite new kinds of ornament worn by lesser beings among the court. Even their masks were without exception striking and colorful.

It all made him feel rather plain in *his* suit. Not quite naked, as on that terrible earlier day, but close enough to be a little uncomfortable. The emperor's newest clothes were undeniably there, but they were quite plain (just as Poindexter had promised) and fit much closer to his skin than the flowering purple and ermine robes he was used to. He knew from Poindexter's demonstration that to others—or at least *some* others—it would possess a splendor that put even those robes to shame. Still, it was a source of wistful regret that he himself would not be able to appreciate that splendor as they would.

Sighing, he surveyed the crowd once more, trying to judge the right moment to make his own grand entrance—and watching for that of his targets. Still no sign of Flymme and Flamsteed, but Fred gradually grew aware of a subtle change in the crowd below. He sensed a growing abundance of nervous gestures, of some people tittering and surreptitiously pointing at others, and others drawing away from their companions as if wanting to hide and finding no place to do so.

Aha! Fred thought with sudden comprehension, *It must be working!* He touched the toggle behind his ear and gasped in spite of himself as the scene was transformed. A second ago the nervous motions and giggles had made no discernible sense, but now at least a third of the spectacular costumes below vanished entirely, showing their wearers as utterly bare as he himself had been in that ill-fated procession. The emperor let out a regal guffaw loud enough to make several people look up, but he cut it off and covered his mouth before they could see where it came from. *I wonder,* he thought, *how Poindexter knew what they all looked like naked?* Then he realized that he probably didn't. If the magic suits could generate images at will, the nude bodies he saw might be pure guesswork—but nonetheless quite enough to thoroughly embarrass the people as whom they were exhibited, and amuse everyone else.

As seconds passed, Fred saw some of those bodies turning various shades of red, some of them staying that way and others soon returning to normal. Still more surprising was the sizable number of courtiers whose costumes were neither here nor there. He could see them, but they looked vague and smoky or gauzy, and he could see the bodies inside, more or less well as the suits varied between transparency and opacity. *Hmm,* Fred mused, *there's more to duplicity than meets the eye. . . .*

He started concentrating on individuals, trying to memorize whose suits seemed solidly opaque, whose purely transparent, and whose fluctuated, and which exposed bodies spent how much time in what shades of pink. Surely useful information, especially since another special feature of the emperor's new clothes was that all the *masks* were transparent to him, so he could see exactly who was being stupid or smart, honest or treacherous.

Amongst themselves, of course, they could see many of their fellows exposed, literally and figuratively, and the party was rapidly dissolving into chaos. *About time for me to go down and restore order,* thought Fred. Then he saw what he'd really been waiting for: Flymme and Flamsteed coming in through the guests' door, closely followed by two spear-bearing guards—in decidedly diaphanous-looking suits and masks, with decidedly uncomfortable expressions on their faces.

Fred grinned broadly and stood up. *Definitely time for my entrance!* he thought smugly, and with a mostly opaque-costumed Milton following behind, he started down the broad spiral staircase to the grand entry reserved for them alone.

There was a chorused gasp and then a sudden hush as Fred entered the room with measured stride and chin held high. The crowd parted, forming a double row of onlookers flanking his path as he strode unhurriedly across the center of the hall, trying hard not to snicker at their haphazard mixture of fancy dress and undress. Only when he had reached the far end of the rows did he turn and start back the way he had come.

Then he stopped abruptly, swiveling to stare into the face of a hanger-on whom he'd always suspected of habitual perfidy, and who now showed not a trace of a stitch. "Well, Charleston," he said with a calculatedly proud smile, flaunting what Charleston should be seeing, "how do you like it?"

"It's . . . quite magnificent, Your Imperial Majesty," said Charleston, reddening rapidly, from head to toe, as he spoke.

"Thank you very much," beamed the emperor. "How would you describe the color of my mantle?"

"Why, uh, it's . . . indescribable, Your Imperial Majesty. Words could never do it justice."

"Especially if you don't have the slightest idea what it looks like. Right, you old fraud?" The emperor gazed sharply at Charleston. "See us in our chambers tomorrow morning, and we'll have some words you won't forget." He turned to Charleston's long-suffering wife, wondering once more how such a fine woman had ever gotten mixed up with such a cad. "And how about you, my lady? You're looking quite splendid." She was, too, in a full-skirted dress full of intricate floral patterns that never wavered.

"Thank you, Your Imperial Majesty," she said demurely, curtsying. "So are you, if I may say so. And in case my lowly opinion would have any value to you, I'd call it mauve tending toward red. If I may further say, I think the gold and silver filigree perfectly complements your imperial elegance."

His Majesty beamed. "Thank you kindly, my lady." He moved on down the rows, testing one randomly selected victim after another. Mostly the results accorded well with his prior impressions of people he thought he knew, though there were a few surprises— some pleasant, some not— that he'd have to investigate further.

He was particularly pleased to see that Poindexter's attire looked quite stable and substantial—though it was unlikely that he would fail a test he designed.

Fred was beginning to lose interest in his spot checks when he saw his *pièce de résistance* and perked right back up. Breaking his dignified stride, he scurried eagerly over to the two "guests of honor" and sized them up. Flymme and Flamsteed's faces still reminded him of a weasel and a rat, respectively, and he wasn't quite sure what to make of the unsteady opacity of their suits. Did it mean that their intelligence was enough to partially override their nefariousness? (They were, he grudgingly admitted, smart enough to have fooled him— once.) Did it mean that they were honest part of the time? Or that they were such cool and experienced liars that dishonesty did not affect them the same way as others?

"Flymme and Flamsteed," said Fred with a catlike grin, "we're so glad you could come. Are you ready to earn your freedom?"

"One way or another," said Flymme, looking straight into the emperor's eyes without the slightest flinch or excess coloration.

"So it comes down," said Fred, "to a simple question. Are you prepared to admit that you're complete frauds and delivered nothing for all we paid you?"

"We delivered exactly what we promised," Flamsteed said with great dignity. "If your subjects failed to see it, it's because you have surrounded yourself with fools, simpletons, and rascals."

He said it as if he truly meant it and was deeply insulted by the question—but he also turned red as a boiled lobster.

And Fred realized with sudden horror that his bluff had been called and he was not going to get what he wanted. Unless . . .

As he thought the situation through, he repeated the question to Flymme and got the same response. So there it was: he didn't have to release them, but unless he wanted to be seen as a weakling who made threats he couldn't carry out, he did have to execute them—forthwith. And where would that leave him? Rid of them, but still no closer to recouping his losses.

But maybe there was another way to use Poindexter's System. Glancing back to make sure Milton and the guards were attending, trembling a little at the uncertainty of what he was about to try, he said, "We see. Well, gentlemen, it seems we are compelled to end your miserable lives. But it would be rather a shame to interrupt such a nice party to do that, don't you think? So perhaps you'll indulge us if we pass a few of your remaining minutes by asking a few other questions. We are curious as to how you managed to hide our money and the fine materials we supplied you. Is it still in your room?"

"There is nothing hidden!" Flymme and Flamsteed said together—and very redly.

"I see," the emperor said smoothly. "Could it be that some of it is hidden in the room and some of it has been surreptitiously removed?"

"Your Imperial Majesty is talking nonsense!" Flymme objected.

"Are we? How about this? The money is far more compact than the textiles and gold and jewels. It could have been hidden, perhaps, under a floor stone that you loosened and carefully replaced. Our searchers could conceivably have missed such a thing." He stabbed the air between them with an accusing finger. "Is that where the money is?"

The red of both their faces deepened to such an astounding degree that he knew he had hit it. "Very good, gentlemen! Let's pursue this. Is the hiding stone in your workroom or your sleeping quarters?"

No visible change. Evidently the deepness of the red, and perhaps the transparency of the suit, measured the seriousness of the lie. But perhaps an "either-or" question was too ambiguous for even the teller to be sure whether the answer felt like a lie. He would have to rephrase. "Is it in your workroom?"

"No!" the defendants chorused, and their color reverted almost to a calm and normal beige.

Aha! Thought Fred. "Is it in your sleeping quarters?"

The red returned in all its glory, and their bodies began to show through their suits. "Now we're getting somewhere!" Fred exclaimed gleefully. "Is it closer to . . ."

A few more questions narrowed it down to a particular corner. "As soon as we're finished here," Fred told Milton, "you will take guards to their room to pry up all the stones in that corner. We shall look forward to seeing what they find." He thought a moment and added, "In fact, we shall accompany you there ourselves."

He turned back to Flymme and Flamsteed. "Now, about the bulky materials. We know you never went beyond your quarters and your shop and the corridor between them. So evidently at least one of the vendors who delivered goods to you was on the take. Let us guess: they drove away with the material you pretended to use, after paying you for it with a sum well below market price but sufficient to make you comfortably wealthy. Are we correct?"

Ruby-red skin glowing through nearly invisible clothes assured him he was on the right track—and getting the hang of this. "Well, then, let's try a few more questions and see if we can figure out whom we need to arrest. . . ."

And he moved in for the kill.

"You know," he said a few days later, "I think I'm actually going to miss you." He and Poindexter were sitting around in the imperial chambers, waiting for the moment when Poindexter would be snapped back to his own time, which Poindexter said would be sometime in the next couple of hours. "When you first came, I thought you were another Flymme and Flamsteed, and I was in no mood for that. But everything has worked out just fine. Not only did we find all the money under the rock where they were most insistent that it wasn't, but there was a lot more that they got from selling the goods. The merchants who bought them are in Flymme and Flamsteed's old dungeon cell, and Flymme and Flamsteed—well, let's just say they'll never fleece anybody again."

Poindexter looked vaguely uncomfortable. "Well, yes,"

he said with a slight cough. "That's the one part I'm not entirely happy with. Where I come from, the punishment would be considered a bit extreme for—"

"But we're not where you come from," Fred pointed out. "Here, I have to keep my promises, or I'll be seen as too weak to rule." He smiled. "But I don't think that will happen again for quite a while. Everybody was very impressed with the way I proved these rogues' guilt and got everything back. And I still have your System. It is, as you said, quite a management tool."

"Yes, it is. But I should caution Your Imperial Majesty against becoming too dependent on it. It is, as you said, rather clunky—"

"Clunky?"

"Cumbersome. Awkward to use. You don't want to have to stage a masked ball every time you want to judge somebody's fitness for office. Besides, like any equipment, it will eventually break down, and you won't have the means to fix it. So you will have to develop the ability to judge character and size up situations and choose courses of action for yourself." He smiled. "But you know, Your Majesty, I think the System can help you do that. You've already impressed me with the way you found a better use for it than I'd thought of. Maybe you should think of it more as an educational aid."

"Well," said Fred, "that's not exactly what I was hoping for, but I suppose I'll have to try to make the best of it."

"A wise decision," said Poindexter. "By all means keep your suit, Your Majesty, and use it until you don't need it anymore. Don't let it become a crutch, but wear it in good—"

And then, quite abruptly, with a sound like a thunderclap right there in the room, he vanished, leaving Fred on his own.

The Nightingale

by Michelle West

Michelle West is the author of a number of novels, including *The Sacred Hunt* duology and *The Broken Crown, The Uncrowned King, The Shining Court,* and *Sea of Sorrows,* the first four novels of *The Sun Sword* series, all available from DAW Books. She reviews books for the online column *First Contacts,* and less frequently for *The Magazine of Fantasy & Science Fiction.* Other short fiction by her appears in *Knight Fantastic, Familiars, Assassin Fantastic,* and *Villains Victorious.*

Michelle's fiction has always been powerful, filled with images that seem to come almost from beyond the human imagination. Here is another of her moving tales, this one of an android with a singular talent, and its meeting with a woman who possesss what it most desires—

THERE is a pool beneath the fountain adorned by the statue of the Emperor of Teleros. There is always a pool beneath such a statue, although in the Winter Palace, it is a small miracle; Teleros is cold enough in the winter that exposure to the air will kill a man in a few hours.

Great expense is taken, of course, to ensure that only those whose deaths are desired are so exposed, and that happens once a season. The windows above the courtyard are made of colored glassteel, thick as a man's wrist; it distorts nothing, and those who are privileged to receive the Emperor's invitation stand behind the safety of those windows to watch the sport below: a man's death.

Or a woman's. Often a woman's.

There are two seasons here on Asaros, the Emperor's planet of retreat. Summer and Winter. The Summer is not so harsh; it is therefore for the Winter that he comes. He will arrive soon.

I know this because the ships are singing their way across the vacuum. I heard them yesterday, and woke to their song. The great doors of my rooms unlocked, tumbler by tumbler, as the ships sang their complicated harmonies, one after the other. There is no other way to open those doors; I am valued.

I understand this.

My skin is golden, my eyes are sapphire, my hair is the color of snow. My feet are small and delicate, and the Emperor dislikes it when I wear bindings or shoes upon them. This was known, before my birth, and the soles of my feet are much like the glass that keeps warmth in; nothing penetrates them.

My hands are soft, though. My lips are soft. Sometimes they are white, and sometimes they are the color of blood; sometimes, at the Emperor's fancy, they are the blue of death. I wear the clothing he brings me; fashions change more quickly than seasons, ephemeral as the Summer flowers that adorn his rooms. It would not do to have an important servant clothed in something that only the poor would wear—last year's clothing; last year's fashion.

I must change with the times.

I know this. I was trained for it. In the palm of my right hand, the forked branches of lifelines are a conceit, an unchanging pattern. They are sensitive to the movement of ions, the song of electricity, of magnetism.

I should be there, in the room of preparation.

But it is two days, two more days, before the Emperor will arrive at this ghost court, and instead, I chose to visit the frozen surface of a pond.

The water is real.

In the Summer Palace, it dances with breeze, and it its depths, fish swim, cavorting until food arrives. When food is brought, their color heightens, their fins and tails stiffen; they grow fangs and their skin hardens. They fight each other for what falls into the water, and the water itself becomes the color of pale blood.

They were a gift from the ambassador of Dellen. He is long gone, although his people are often represented at

Court; the fish remain. But they change; they bear scars; they die when they are too weak to reach the food offered by the Emperor's servants.

They do not sing.

I step out, upon the surface of the pond; touch the frozen tendrils of what might have once been falling water. The statue is made of something that resembles stone, but unlike stone, it does not weather; it lasts. The features of the Emperor's face are still.

When he is present, they will move; they will mirror his moods; he himself shows nothing.

But the statue's hair is not raven black; the statue's eyes are not brown; the statue's lips are not the pale pink of something that might once have known red. The skin is gray, not bronze.

I touch it; I feel nothing.

I feel nothing at all when I touch the face of anything that is not the Emperor.

No; that is not true. I feel nothing when I touch a face or a body, or anything that is formed in such a way as to affect the appearance of either.

The ships are singing. I have stood there for longer than I had intended; I have lost a day. I linger for only a moment longer, and then I make my way indoors.

The other servants are waking.

They are not like me; they live—and die—in the confines of the Winter Palace. I look at their faces as I enter the doors; they are thin and long. I recognize none of them.

A boy separates himself from his elders and rushes to kneel at my feet. "Lady," he says, "the Emperor is coming."

I nod. "I . . . had word. How long has it been?"

"How long?"

I can see the gleam of perspiration across his pale skin; his dark eyes are wide. "How long has it been since the Emperor has opened the Winter Palace?"

The boy looks over his shoulder.

An old, old man comes to join him. He walks stiffly and slowly; the Winter is unkind to the elderly. But he walks. There are ways to augment the strength of failing legs; those are expensive, and the people of the palace are indentured. They will act upon their infirmity only at the command of the Emperor; it is far more likely that, upon his arrival, he will have them quietly put down.

I do not tell them this. If they know it, they live with the fear, but I have learned, with time, not to invoke that fear.

"Lady," he says. He falls slowly to his knees; I can hear the stretch of his muscles, the wobbling of his breath.

Something about his face is familiar.

This is wrong. I know it is wrong.

There is only one face that should ever be familiar.

"Do I know you?" I ask gently.

I am incapable of speaking any other way.

The old man shakes his head. His face is gleaming in the artificial light of the early dawn.

"Are you certain?"

"I am certain, Lady." He bows his head. "You must come with us; the throne is waiting. It has been waiting for almost a day."

"Yes. A day. Come, then."

He grimaces and turns to the boy. "I am . . . unable to attend you. This is Krysos; he will be your companion."

Krysos.

"Yes. Come. If the throne waits a day longer, the Emperor will know."

Relief. He is relieved. I wonder why.

In the long hall of birds, there is no silence. The air is alive with the flurry of their wings. Bright and gaudy, the parrots cling to branches and squawk in a thousand different languages. The sparrows fly the heights in silence, afraid to sing; above them, white and brown, are the great hunters. There are no ceilings here; the climate in this mile of the palace is controlled in its entirety by orbiting satellites.

The air is warm near the ground; cool near the heights. But it is never too cold; the birds die because of each other, or because of age. Sometimes a combination of both.

The Emperor loves birds. He finds their calls and cries interesting, for he hears song in them when he chooses to listen.

Perhaps once or twice during his retreat he will walk here. He will leave his guards behind; they are not necessary. There is no time, no place, in which the Emperor is defenseless. Only one or two people will attend him. And none of those people will be indentured; he has no need to impress that which he already owns.

The boy by my side is speechless.

His silence would either gratify or annoy the Emperor; it means nothing to me.

Or it should mean nothing. But I am curious.

"Krysos?"

"L-lady?"

"Who is the old man?"

"The old man?" He frowns and then his brows lift. "Caverson?"

The name, too, is familiar. "Did he walk with me, when the Emperor last came?"

The boy's smile is generous, bright. He nods.

"Is he your father?"

"Moons, no! He's my great-grandfather."

"Ah. Did he—did he look like you, when he was young?"

The concept of the old man being young is clearly foreign to him. His brow wrinkles as he thinks; smooths as he pauses. When he is older, those wrinkles will remain no matter how much his expression shifts; they are the lines carved their by time and care; they are real.

My palm aches.

"We must hurry," I tell the boy. But I let him linger perhaps longer than is wise. I know that he will remember what he sees here, not in the way that I remember things, but in the way that the living do: As miracle, as something so bright and so beautiful it fades into the realm of story. Or myth. He will tell his friends, and they will envy him. He will tell his parents, and they will be overjoyed for him. And he will tell his children, and his children will ask him for this story again and again because it is a part of his youth, and because it makes him happy.

"Lady?"

"Is that what I am to be called this time?"

"P-pardon?"

"Am I to be called Lady?"

"Isn't that what you're always called?"

I do not know.

Memory is selective. In the case of the living, the selection process is not clear to me; in my case, it is defined and decided by the Emperor and the throne. "I do not know, Krysos. I think—I think I might once have been called by another name."

The boy's eyes are round. He lifts a hand. "Don't tell me," he whispers. "Don't tell me your name."

"I don't know it."

Relief is palpable.

"Why are you afraid of it?"

He shakes his head. "My great-grandpa told me."

"He told you my name?"

"He told me that your name is only for the Emperor."

Ah. Wisdom. No wise man covets what the Emperor guards. "Thank you, Krysos. May I call you that?"

He nods, tilting his head to one side, staring at me for long enough that blinking causes his eyes to tear.

"What are you looking for, Krysos?"

He hesitates. But my voice is gentle, always gentle. He hears no threat in it.

"Well, uh, I was—well—"

He reaches out involuntarily, and I leap back, rising and falling with perfect grace ten feet from where he stands, lower jaw slack.

"You must not," I tell him, and if I could make my voice severe, if I could layer it with warning or threat of anger, I would. Not because I am angry; I am not.

But to touch me is death, his death.

It has been a very, very long time since the Emperor last chose to grace the palace. I knew it, but I did not understand it until this moment—for his great-grandfather would never have made such a simple mistake.

He blushes, misunderstanding everything. "Sorry," he says, speaking to the tips of his toes. "I just want to know—"

"To know what? Ask, and if it is not forbidden me, I will tell you."

"Are you cold?"

It is not the question I expected.

"Cold?"

"We saw you. Outside. On the ice."

Ah.

"My father was scared. He thought you would freeze. He made my uncles suit up. But my great-grandpa told them to wait for you. He said you'd been there for hours already."

"Your great-grandfather is a wise man." He lift a hand. "I don't know. What do you mean by cold?"

"Cold like ice."

I ask. *Am I cold?*

You are zero degrees. Your temperature is rising.

I turn back to the boy. "Yes," I tell him. "I am cold."

"Should we go back? Should we get a 'suit?"

I smile. "I will not be cold when the Emperor arrives. I do not require warmth; I am cold simply because I did not ask the palace to maintain my temperature at human norm."

"Why not?"

"Because it does not matter. It is not efficient. The Emperor is not here."

He said, "You don't feel the cold."

"I am aware of the cold. It does not kill me."

"Does anything?"

"The Emperor, if he so desires."

He nods. "Same with us," he says quietly.

My hand is throbbing now. "We have to hurry."

He nods again, but still he hesitates. "Do they work? Can you use them?"

"Use them?" For a moment, I am confused. And then I realize what he speaks of. Experimentally, I flex my wings. They feel new. "No."

"Oh."

He accepts the answer until we reach the end of the Aviary, and then he says, "Why not?"

"It's only the illusion of flight that matters," I tell him gently. "Flight itself is forbidden."

He nods at that, too, but for the first time an expression I can't parse changes his features. The Aviary opens its wide doors, and I wait until he has cleared them before I follow.

The hall beyond the Aviary is sparse. It is long, however, and the ceilings are hidden in wells of shadow. As we walk, the lights clear them, cold and distant as stars, but lacking their grace and beauty. He looks up, his head tilted back so far I am surprised he doesn't trip or fall. He is making memories. They will stay with him.

I have walked this hall before. I know it, although I cannot say when. I have seen these lights, these walls, these holographs; I have gazed upon the vistas suggested by the play of plasma along the walls. I do not tell the boy not to touch them as he walks past; if I did, I am not certain he would heed me. He thinks they are windows, and perhaps they are—windows into the memories of the Emperor.

To my eye, they are trapped and unchanging; I see their colors as part of a continuous spectrum of captured light. I say nothing; there is something about the awe in the boy's eyes that I, too, wish to hold in memory.

But my memories are not of my own devising.

Nothing belongs to me.

At the end of the hall is another statue. It is as tall as the ceilings, a man made god; the Emperor. At his right hand is one large chair, its back red and blue, its arms golden. At his left hand, another chair, this in silver, its backing black and gold, the color of the void and the unblinking stars.

It is my chair, and it stands five feet behind the throne of the Emperor.

"We're here," Krysos says, at the same moment I do.

"Now wait," I tell him gently. "But wait here. Do not touch the Emperor's throne. Do not stand in his shadow. And do not touch me until I rise, no matter what you see."

He kneels. "Lady?"

"Yes, Krysos?"

"My great-grandmother says that he once heard you sing."

"Ah."

"Will you sing again?"

"Oh, yes," I tell him softly. "It is for that purpose, and no other, that I was born."

I place my palm on the rest of the chair, and the pain eases instantly. I did not lie to the boy, although I feel I am capable of lying. I do not feel the cold. I do not feel the heat. I have sensors for that; I have a link to this chair, the heart of this palace, this winter citadel. But I wonder if the pain in my hand was cold, and the cessation of pain like human warmth.

The songs start.

I feel them as sensation, a collection of moving waves.

Fashions change in all things. In clothing. In art.

In music.

The Emperor will bring clothing, art, artisans; he will bring new food, new stories, new history. But the music is what he most craves, and it is the music that the ships send me now. Vacuum song, the song of the void.

There are instruments that have been created since I was last awake, and when he arrives, I will know how to play them. Ah; there are new languages as well, new forms of speech, new idioms to mix with the old. Here, hand on chair, I learn them as if they had always belonged to me.

But this time . . . this time something is different.

I am not sure what.

I ask, and the only answer I receive is a subsystem check, a spark of light and electricity, a flood of small nanites.

I hear them as they work; they speak to each other in voices that make no sound. But they find nothing wrong, and they return to their dormant state.

I should be comforted.

The only time I am upset is when something has failed. I know this. But I am not, precisely, upset. Something is different. Something has changed.

I open my mouth.

I sing.

The song itself is new, strange; my voice is like thunder.

And after it is finished, my vision returns; the processes by which the outer world become real once again take the forefront of the system.

I see the boy.

His face is white, his eyes wide, his cheeks hollow and pale. His lips are open.

"Krysos," I tell him gently, "You must never gape like that again. If the Emperor sees you, he will send you out into the cold."

He does not even nod; it's as if the return of my vision has erased some part of his. I have not seen this before. If I could touch him, I would offer him my hand and lead him from this place.

But I do not know why.

* * *

I am not permitted to attend the Emperor upon his arrival. I know that he has arrived; the myth of his return has traveled among this new generation of servants, these men and women born to the customs of cold and isolation.

When they dress and gather, with a mixture of excitement and fear, I find myself wandering back through the colorful, festive halls. My rooms are waiting; the doors are open.

I do not want to enter them. I want to remain with his people, as I have done time and time again. But in this, I have no choice; the palace sings and I step to the beat of its insistent and undeniable song.

My rooms are vast and grand, as befit a woman who might sit in a chair by the Emperor's side. The windows that keep the cold at bay are everywhere; they are colored, yellow and white, gold and silver, blue and bronze; the light they let in is dependent on that color, its rays bending and slanting as they touch my eyes.

There are divans here, chairs, fine tables, a desk which is more than ornamental, although it serves no obvious purpose; there are walls that will come to life when they are touched and their song is sung. There are doors that are hidden from all but the servants granted the hereditary positions that have given them permission to enter.

But there are also cameras, hidden in web of silk and embroidery; there are projectors that, when invoked, will gather light and concentrate it, shaping and chiseling it in just such a way it captures reality.

I sit upon my chair. My hands rest, palms down, although only one is necessary.

Show me.

The walls are rising across the landing pad, glass bending inward as they reach their full height. The wind's voice is bitter and high as they close upon it, trapping it on the outside, where the cold waits.

The ship is small.

Smaller than I remember, it seems to be fashioned of a single piece of gleaming metal out of which flat wings have been teased and pulled. Those wings bear the impression of the star clusters the Emperor owns; the insignia has grown larger and more complex since last I saw it, although the designer has taken care to make, of complexity, a simple, unadorned emblem.

The underside of the ship dilates; light floods the stones into which the Emperor's hundred names have been carved. There are no servants upon the stones; the Emperor has always chosen to maintain the last of his privacy when he arrives at any of his palaces. He will choose the moment of his entrance, the moment of his departure, and he will gather his thoughts as he does so, for every arrival is the beginning of something new, and every departure, an ending, a time to reflect.

But the last time that I recall waking in the Winter Palace, I waited for him just beyond the glass doors; I cast my shadow, and the lights cast his shadow, and when they met, he looked up to see that I was waiting.

And he smiled.

I remember the smile. I remember it, and I feel strange.

All of the guard he chooses to accept he carries upon—and within—his person. No others are necessary.

In his youth, this was not always the case; in his youth, craftsmen made images in his likeness and sent them in his stead, to ascertain the mood of the populace.

Now, the mood of the populace is never in question.

There is not a man upon this world, or any other, that would willingly raise their hand against a god; a god holds the fate of whole worlds in his palm, and on a whim, a god might destroy those worlds with a careless gesture, a careless word.

The cameras are confused by the sudden flare of light from the ship; they adjust their filters, resolving shape and shadow in the harshness of bright white.

And I see, upon the stones, not a single figure, but two.

The Emperor is unmistakable; no matter how he chooses to dress, no matter which fashion he chooses to embrace—or discard—no matter what color his hair, his eyes, I would know him. I am incapable of mistaking him for any other; incapable of *not* knowing him.

But although I was designed for just such adulation, just such riveted attention, such an instant devotion, it is not the figure of the Emperor that catches my eye, that holds my attention; it is the figure of the person beside him.

Smaller, slender in build, her hair is a spill of bronze across her bare, pale shoulders. I cannot see her face; it is so softened by the scatter of light that the lines tell me little. But her eyes are clear; they are large, unblinking, gray as steel. She lifts a hand, or rather, her hand is lifted, and I see—even in the poor light, the ship's haze—that it is lifted by his.

I sit in my rooms, as I have been ordered to sit, the cameras lingering over the still body of the Emperor's vehicle long after he has discarded it.

Understand that I do not love him.

If I am asked—and if the person who chooses to speak so intrusively survives for long enough that the Emperor clearly desires that the question be answered—I will nod regally. If he desires more, I will say, simply, "How could I do otherwise?" And if that answer is not pleasant enough, not musical enough, or not dramatic enough by turns, I will tell the audience that I do, indeed, love the Emperor; that he is my life.

But no one has ever asked me what the word means, and if they did, I would retreat; I would let the palace net take my voice and speak for me in the fashion it thought most suitable for the situation.

Or, if it was appropriate, I would sing. I know songs that speak of love, of a multitude of loves: The love of mother for child; the love of father for son; the love of man for woman, woman for man; the love of a person for their homeland; the love of an artist for his art.

Or a singer for their song, for the truth of a music that comes from voice alone.

Understand, too, that I am not alive.

I have know that I am not alive since the moment I first woke. The man who made me created me to be a thing above the vagaries and misfortunes of the living. Although he himself was old and bowed with the weight of his centuries, he disdained the trappings of mortality; feared them and hated them.

"Life," he said, "knows change; it diminishes beauty; it tarnishes everything." I was to be his gift to the Emperor. To the only man said to transcend life itself with his power and his ability.

I was to be his legacy.

He did not teach me, although he created places within me that might be taught; he did not prepare me for the changing of technology, although he made all concessions to that despised progress when he chose to build me.

Had the Emperor valued beauty, he would have made me beautiful; all of my systems and programs would have captured the changing face of beauty over the passage of time, and using it, would have changed me. Had he valued power, I might have been cunning; I might have built empires merely to show him that I had worth and value.

He valued music.

He valued song.

They became my reason for existence.

But the Emperor has returned to the Winter Palace with a different companion. And although I do not understand why I wish it, I wish that I had never been wakened.

And I wonder how many times he has arrived at this palace when he has chosen not to wake me at all.

When I am at last summoned, it is not the palace that speaks to me. A servant arrives at the door; the boy, Krysos. His face is glowing, red from exposure to cold. He bows, gracefully, the crisp new length of his uniform odd to my eyes. "The Emperor commands your presence in the visitor's hall."

In his arms he carries a bundle of fabric, something that shimmers in the light cast by the room's walls. "You are to wear this," he adds.

I take it from him.

It is blue, the color of the skies beneath which men die. I put it on. It was clearly designed for my use; the back is low; it skirts the edge of my waist, leaves room to expose the folded conceit of wings that are far too delicate to bear my weight in any room save the Emperor's.

This is new to me.

Simple. It bears no insignia, and comes with no jewelry, no circlet, no ring.

The palace net tells me that I require none of these to sing.

I have always known that I am owned.

But until now, I have never felt it so completely as the stigma that it must be to the boy who stands before me.

*   *   *

In the room, the diplomats are gathered. They are many; they number in the hundreds. I pause for a moment; there are four hundred and forty-three. I walk down the stairs and for a moment, a stillness ensues; it is broken almost instantly by men who turn away whispering into their drinks and their conversations.

I have not been given leave to sing. I may speak, but in gatherings such as this, I am mute. I do not know how to approach men of value or power; I do not know how to approach those people who do not bear the Emperor's hidden brand.

It is clear that the men do not recognize me; that they have no concept of my significance. This is unusual. They do not move when I attempt to pass them; it is I who am forced into the dance of manners. But in that dance, I observe them. They are taller than I last remember, and fairer; they speak a language that I belatedly recognize as new. It is the court language; it has been imposed upon those who would keep company with the Emperor, and is heavy with the unspoken, the subtle statement.

Only when I reach the Emperor's side do they still.

He turns to me, and if I had words readied, I lose them to the sight of his eyes. Brown, those eyes absorb all light; his brows raise and gather as I wait for his reaction.

He smiles.

I breathe.

I do not need to breathe. I remember this.

"Lady," he says, taking my hand. He bows and raises it high, and this earns the attention that my entrance did not. "There is someone I wish you to meet."

I wish it, too. And dread it. And I should feel no dread.

The woman who accompanied him on his journey steps into view.

She is wearing a simple blue dress, the color of the sky; its folds touch the ground, obscuring the hint of shoes. The neck of the gown is low, the sleeves trailing, the hems sparkling at some light that is not suggested by the fabric itself.

"Constance," he says, "this is my Lady."

"The songbird?" she whispers.

"That is not what we call her." His correction is laced with affection; she is instantly forgiven the familiarity of the word. Men have died for less in the past.

I bow. I am forced to bow; the subsystems take control of my legs, preserving me from the possibility of his wrath. "I am pleased," I tell her, although I am not, "to make your acquaintance."

But she smiles at me. Her smile is brilliant, tinged with awe and something that I have seen only in the face of the Emperor.

He raises his hands.

Silence falls instantly, like an ice storm, stilling all movement, drawing all attention.

"Ladies," he says. "Gentlemen. You have the singular honor, this day, of being in the presence of the two greatest voices in the whole of my Empire.

"I have brought them together for the first time—for perhaps the only time—to hear the mingling of their voices. This is a historic moment; I beg your indulgence."

And he bows. First, foremost, to her, to this woman he has named. I have no name.

But the smile on her face stiffens instantly, like flowers brought to the side of the winter fountain. "My Lord," she says, bending until she scrapes the ground with her knees, with the simple fall of her dress, "I beg you—for such an occasion, there is need for practice."

His frown fills me with dread.

Dread is a word for the clamoring of nanites, the screaming of subsystems that have been designed solely to please the man who stands before me. The only man who can touch me and survive.

And yet along with dread I feel something else: relief. It will not be long. It will not be long before she is gone; the winter pond is waiting, and the sport of observation demands its due.

But she continues to speak, where my vocal cords would be frozen.

"I beg of you," she says, in a voice so low only he—and I—can hear it. "We must practice. For . . . for this . . . gathering . . . we cannot be less than perfect. Forgive me. Forgive me, my Lord."

Ah, indulgence. His face softens.

He lowers his hand, and after a moment, conversation resumes. I know that it is now focused upon this woman.

"Lady," he says, speaking as gently as I speak, "take Constance to your rooms and give her the chance to practice what you have been taught."

I bow. I would offer her my hand, but he is watching me carefully.

In my rooms, she is quiet.

She looks around at the walls, at the windows; looks up at the cameras that are almost completely hidden. "There is no privacy here, is there?"

I parse the question slowly, and after a moment, I answer. "There is no place in the Winter Palace that is hidden from the Emperor's view. If he chooses, he can watch anything, listen to anything, that occurs."

"Do you know when he is listening?"

It is an odd question. "I know."

"Does he listen now?"

"No." Hesitant, I add, "But if you must speak words that you wish him not to hear, you must not speak them here. Nothing in this room is hidden should he wish to review it."

"Then where?"

I do not understand her. She is becoming agitated; her breath is loud and quick. She is sweating. She approaches me and I take a quick step back. "Do not touch me," I tell her gently. "It will kill you."

"Why?"

"Has he told you nothing?"

Her eyes shutter. "He has told me very little. I am not . . . important . . . in that way."

He intends me to preserve her. The palace whispers his commands, broken into sound and song, up the length of my right arm.

"I was designed to be his, and only his. No one can touch me without preparation and permission. It will kill them."

"How?"

"I secrete a poison, the way you secrete sweat." The explanation is longer. She does not seem to require it.

"What do you mean, you were designed?"

"I am the songbird," I tell her. "He owns me."

"You're not—not real, are you?"

The words sting. I do not like this woman. "I am not human, no." I lift a hand and drop it on the rest of the chair; the noise is louder than I had intended, and she startles. "But I am real."

She falls to the floor again. "Forgive me," she says.

And she begins to weep.

I have seen much in my life. I have seen men reduced to tears in the presence of the Emperor. I have seem them plead and beg. But no one has ever done that for me.

I have often wondered what it is like, to be the Emperor. I now know that of his many powers, his many talents, this is one I do not wish to possess.

I cannot touch her. I would, but it would kill her.

Instead, I send a command to the palace, an override that I have never used. And then I leave my chair to kneel by her side. I am careful to make certain that I am just beyond her reach; people often fail to heed warnings that are delivered gently.

"Constance."

She lifts her face.

"You are here to sing for the Emperor."

She nods.

I know that she will not sing well, not now. A moment ago, this would have pleased me; it does not please me now. I understand neither of these things.

I ask her a question that I had not known I would ask her. "Do you love the Emperor?"

She raises her head slowly, as if I have spoken in a language that is beyond her comprehension. But she does not answer the question. I could ask it again, but it would be unchanged, and her answer, I think, would be the same.

But I wait, and after a moment, she says, "When I met him, I did not know who he was." Just that. She looks down at her hands. Her hands that are adorned with a ring that was once mine. Her skin is not golden; her hands are dark with the sun of a foreign world. I can see the lines across her knuckles, and I know they will deepen with time. If she has time.

"How could you not know who he was?"

"He . . . did not say."

It seems beyond possibility. Everyone knows the Emperor.

"I sing," she says quietly. "I used to sing with a tenor. He was my partner."

I do not ask about him.

"He was not . . . young. His voice was not as powerful as it had been, but he knew better than anyone how to add nuance and emotion to his song. And his emotion drew out mine. I sang . . . with him.

"We were known, upon my world, for our song." She does not smile as she speaks, but her gaze is the distance of memory. "One day, we were asked to sing for a visiting group of dignitaries. He was among them.

"After we had finished our performance, he came to speak with me. He told me—he told me—" She closed her eyes.

I need to know this. I don't know why. "What?"

"That I should not sing with my partner again; that his voice was too rough and too poor a match for my own. I did not know him; he did not wear his insignia. I told him that there was no other man in the world I would sing with."

She closes her eyes. "He . . . disagreed."

Again she retreats, but I understand what has happened, and I do not ask her for an explanation. Who would tell the Emperor that his desire was to be thwarted? That she survives is proof of her voice.

I want to hear her sing.

But this time, I know why.

"When I found out who he was, I felt honored. When I found out that Belavas was dead, I felt . . . lost. I wanted to tell him what he had done to me. I didn't care if he knew; I didn't care if it angered him. I sang. I sang for him, as he commanded."

She bows her head into her hands, curling her shoulders inward. "He asked me to come to his court. To sing for him."

"I accepted his . . . offer." She lifted her head; she was crying. "And I tried. To sing for him. I do not think he was pleased with my voice. I thought he would send me home."

"But he brought you here instead."

"No. He kept me in the palace for five years. Five years. I have had no word from my family. I have sent them no word."

I nod.

She looks up at me. "I cannot sing," she tells me quietly. "Not—not that way. I cannot sing."

"You must sing."

"I know."

Neither of us speak of death.

She wears my ring.

She wears my circlet.

If the Emperor chose to hold court in the long hall, she would—I am certain of it—sit in my chair, her hands impervious to the music of the palace, the subtleties of its voice.

I think I was angry when I first saw her arrive. I think it, but I am not certain; anger is not a subroutine that has ever been invoked before. But if what I felt was anger, what I feel now is different.

"Constance."

She raises her head.

"Why did you ask if I was—if I was the songbird?"

For just a moment, her eyes brighten. "Don't you know?"

"I do not ask questions if I am aware of the answers I seek."

"You are Genevera's lost daughter," she says simply. But in that simplicity, there is some of her earlier smile; I see wonder in her face, awe, the expressions with which I am most familiar. But I see something else as well.

Genevera. The name is familiar. After a moment, I say, "He was my creator."

"Yes. He was that. But more. He was more than that. In his youth, he had the finest voice in the universe." She frowns. "Genevera was my ancestor," she adds. "And the story of your birth has been a part of my family for centuries. It is . . . myth. It is more."

She almost reaches out to touch me, but I step back, avoiding her hand. She lets it fall. I am sorry that she does so. I don't know why. I raise my hand, mimicking her motion, my golden fingers with their static lines spread wide.

"He understood music in a way that the sane cannot. He understood how to make you sing." She shakes her head a moment, clearing her expression of its wide-eyed wonder. "No one understands how it was done. He left no notes.

He left no pictures. He forbid the recording of all parts of the process. When he was done, he brought you to the family hall, and he asked you to sing, and . . ."

"And?"

"Do you not remember?"

"I told you, Constance. I do not ask a question if I know the answer."

She is disappointed now. I see it in the lines of her face, the narrowing of her eyes. What she thought she had found is not what she sees before her.

"You sang," she whispers. "You sang every song that he had ever sung; you sang songs that he had written and had never found the right voice for. You sang songs that had not been sung since the time before the opening of the gateways.

"You were our history," she added. "The history of our music."

"But . . . he gave me to the Emperor."

She lowers her head again. "Yes," she whispers. "Yes, he did. I am so sorry."

I know that it is not of her family's loss that she speaks. She speaks for me. She speaks as if the gifting was somehow a tragedy.

As if I sorrow at some unfathomable loss.

"When the Emperor told me that you were here, I asked him to bring me to you."

"You asked to come here?"

A shadow crosses her face; the play of the room's walls interrupted by something that light cannot alleviate. But she is beginning, I think, to understand me.

"There is only one place that I have ever desired to be," she says softly, "and it is gone now. I will never return. I am sorry, Lady. I am so very tired. I will sing with you. With you, if you will have me.

"But I must rest."

I nod. I ask the palace; the palace confers with the Emperor. For some reason, the Emperor seems well pleased, and assents. "You may rest here, in my rooms, if you will be comfortable here. There are rooms that are readied for you if—"

"No. I will stay here," she tells me, grateful. She rises as the doors to the west slide open, and only when she reaches them do I speak again.

"Constance?"

"Yes?"

"Did Genevera name me?"

She turns and smiles softly. "Yes." And then she is gone.

The Emperor summons me in the morning.

She is still sleeping in my rooms, this Constance, this stranger. I do not use these rooms for sleeping. I require no sleep. When I was . . . newer . . . I used to sit and watch the Emperor, for the Emperor, although augmented and changed, requires sleep as all living things do. He liked that: to be watched in his sleep. I asked him why, but only once, and after I asked, I was no longer allowed to watch him.

Thus I learned that he does not like to be questioned.

"Lady," he says. He sits at his morning table, and there is only one seat beside him. I take it and turn my attention upon his face.

"Understand," he says, touching my face, "that you are my Jewel, you are my glory, my history." He says this as if I am real. "But she is . . . a voice unlike any I have ever heard."

His expression is not pleased. I wait.

"She sang so perfectly; she sang, and for a moment, she was the only voice in the universe. It stilled the other voices. It gave me silence.

"I found her upon one of the Core worlds. I offered her riches and titles and a home beyond anything her world has to offer." Now he is frowning. "She came, but she came in silence. She sang, but her voice was not the voice I heard."

"Perhaps she has aged."

"She has aged very little."

He has not asked me what I think, but I speak. "I think she is like the birds in your Aviary."

"Pardon?"

His voice. I bow my head. "Nothing, my Lord."

After a moment, he chooses to forgive me my lapse. "She has been almost completely silent in my court. In any of my courts. It is only when she heard of you that she was able to sing at all."

"I am here . . . for her?"

"You are here to please me," he says severely. "And it would please me greatly if you could invoke her voice. Make her sing, Lady."

"Yes, my Lord. What priority is to be assigned this task?"

"Any priority necessary."

"Yes, my Lord."

He does not ask me to sing. For the first time in living memory—if my memory is alive at all—he does not ask for *my* voice.

Constance is waiting for me when I return to my rooms. I tell the palace that no one is to observe us; no record is to be kept of what transpires within these walls. When questioned, I repeat the Emperor's phrase in the perfect pitch of his voice; the palace recognizes the nuance of the waves of sound, for my capture is perfect. It complies.

"We will not be observed here," I tell her.

"Truly?"

"Truly."

Her smile is genuine, but it is odd. She rises, naked, from the folds of sheets, dropping them in a pile upon the ground. While she searches for her clothing, I wait. I could wait without breathing, for I wait in just such a fashion in the Aviary.

"Constance," I say, when she has dressed, "what is my name?"

She shakes her head. "I will answer your question," she said, "but first, I wish a favor."

"I am authorized to grant you anything you ask for, if it does not conflict with the safety of the Emperor."

"I want you to sing. For me."

No one but the Emperor has the right to ask me to sing. Only upon the throne he constructed for my use and my instruction am I free to do so, for in singing I acknowledge what has been delivered into my central system. But he has given his tacit permission. "Why?"

"Why?"

"Why do you wish to hear *me* sing? The Emperor says that yours is the voice without parallel. Yours is the voice he desires."

"Sometimes," she says softly, "men do not value what they hold; they value what they cannot hold, what they cannot have."

"But he owns us both."

She loses the warmth of smile. "Yes."

I want her smile to return. "Constance, don't frown. Don't frown, and I will sing for you."

Her smile is strange. She says, "You are so different from what I expected."

"What did you expect?"

"Genevera," she replies. "You are cold, like the air and the ice; you are distant, like the stars. He was such a passionate man."

"You cannot know that."

"No?"

"He was dead long before you were born."

"I know his history."

"History and story, at a great enough distance, are not so dissimilar."

"Maybe. Maybe you are right. But sing for me, Lady, and I will know which of our truths are *the* truth."

"You will know nothing except for the song."

"What other truth is there, for us?"

I begin to sing simple scales. She listens. I display a range that her voice could not possibly capture, and she continues to listen, but her smile is shifting into something intense and personal. I have seen a like expression upon the Emperor's face.

After the scales, I sing the oldest of all my songs.

And her eyes widen. "What is that?" She whispers so softly I am not certain she meant it to be heard.

But I still my song and answer her. "It is Genevera's work."

She nods. "Please."

And I continue.

I cannot say when it happens, but at some point in the song, she joins me. She sings a strong harmony to my melody, taking my notes and blending them with her own until they are almost one.

I could do this on my own. I have been programmed to be an entire chorus.

But her improvisations are not built into my song; they are hers, and they are a reflection of what is mine, of what

is me. I listen to her; I almost forget to sing. Her voice is
so pure, her song so full, I realize that it is I who play
harmony and chorus to her.

And I want to keep singing. When the song is over, I want
it to go on, to continue; I want to *hear* her sing. I have loved
song, if such a word is mine to use, and I realize why the
Emperor chose to keep her: she is song. She *is* music.

I continue to sing when the song reaches its end, segueing
into another of Genevera's early works. She follows me—
or perhaps I follow her—as we tell each other the tale of
the love a man has for his country, for his gift, and for his
family. Such a threefold love is sharp and terrible, filled
with fear and struggle; I know this because her voice falters
several times upon the words that contain it. It is not that
she does not know them; she knows, and she knows them
in a way that I have never known them, who have preserved this song against the ravages of time and history
since my making.

But her voice is a mortal voice; it is contained by vocal
cords, by flesh, by muscle. When this song ends, I stop.

She stares at me, and I, at her.

"You are crying," we say, at the same moment, our
voices distinct and harmonious, a blending of purpose.

But she laughs and I do not. I lift a hand toward her
face and she stills, but she does not draw away.

It is I who jump back.

I lift a hand to my cheeks and I find that she is right:
there is water there, like ice melting in the heat of sun, as
it does when it is brought inside.

"Songbird," she whispers. "I don't care if you touch me."

"I told you—"

"I know. But I don't care."

She is dangerous, then. When she moves, I move more
quickly, avoiding her gaze, avoiding her outstretched palm.

"I care," I tell her.

"Why?"

"Because the Emperor cares."

She tilts her head to one side.

As she does, she exposes the rounded curve of her cheek,
the perfect line of her neck. Her skin is pale.

And I know, as the words die into stillness, that I have
lied. I have lied to her.

I leave her, then. I walk the halls quickly, seeing nothing, hearing her voice, the heights and the depths of it touched in all ways by tragedy and love, by mourning and a fierce, bright hope.

I find the outside, the fountain, the frozen trails of water, and I wait there while my cheeks freeze. Then, with care, I brush what is left of the tears away.

When it is done, I return.

She is waiting for me, dishes of food set upon the low tables in the run room. She kneels before them, touching nothing, and gazes at me when I enter.

"Teach me," I say.

She stares at me, wide-eyed.

"Teach me to sing."

"Can you not hear your own voice, Songbird? Can you not hear the history in it, the touch of Genevera, the desire and the pain with which he worked?"

"I hear sound. I hear notes. I . . . have never heard a voice like yours before."

"It is my voice," she tells me softly. "You have yours."

I frown. I open my lips and I begin to sing, and my voice is a baritone.

Her eyes widen in genuine surprise. Before she can speak, I sing again, and my voice is a child's voice, a lisping, thin voice that contains merely the seeds of greatness. When that ends, I sing in a raucous, rough screech, my hands beating the table in the asynchronous drum of the Northern belts.

She does not join me; she listens, her eyes rounding and narrowing at every change of identity.

And then, when I finish, I begin once more.

I sing with *her* voice. Her voice, its amplitude and vibration a match for what she offered me in our too-brief duet.

She says, "Is that what I sound like?"

"It is what you . . . should sound like. But . . . it does not sound like your song to my ears. And it should. It *should*."

"Songbird," she says, gentle in a way that I have never truly been, "why should your voice be mine? Or anyone else's? Where is *your* voice?"

I must look confused, for she frowns.

"Of the songs you have sung, or the ones that you have not sung, which are your favorites?"

"My favorites?"

"Which are the ones you like best?"

The palace net attempts to speak to me, or through me, and I reject it. Nanites are buzzing. Something is wrong. But although they search, they find nothing. "The Emperor likes the 'Lament of Aegis.' "

"I did not ask you what the Emperor likes." She stands, walks to my side. I almost forget to move away. Almost.

"But what else *is* there? Everything I have learned, everything I have every been asked to sing is what the Emperor desires."

She shakes her head. "Do you know the 'Aria of Halholden'?"

I nod.

"Can you sing the part of Teuaton?"

"Yes."

"Sing it," he says quietly. "Sing it for me."

Only the Emperor has the right to ask me to sing. "From where?"

"The beginning. When he discovers that he has been ordered to betray his adopted country."

I close my eyes. I find the song. It is a man's song, and it is sung by a tenor. "The key?"

"C," she says.

I sing. She listens and when I open my eyes, I see that hers are red and filmed. But she does not weep. Instead, she waits until the end of the solo, and then she begins her reply. I almost stop. I almost forget where I am in the song because I am where *she* is. Her voice is like nothing I have ever heard.

I have never felt envy.

I do not think I feel it now.

But I feel something strange and it grows within me, harbored in silence until I, too, am called to join her. I sing until her voice breaks with the strength of her emotion, and even that breaking is musical, the heart of storm, a terrible desolation.

I am across the room before the note dies. I am in front of her. I am so close I could touch her.

And it is this that breaks the spell of her song. I *want* to touch her.

I have never truly wanted to touch any living being before. It is a terrible feeling.

I lose the song. I find distance, quickly, before hers overpowers us both. I need to breathe. I need to draw air into my lungs, these lungs that were created solely to force air out through nose and mouth in perfect, modulated notes.

She is weeping now. And that, too, is a song.

I bend, I touch the ground because the ground will not pay the price of my desire. And then I push myself up and I turn from the room and I run and I run and I run.

The Emperor is waiting for me. The palace has alerted him.

"Lady," he says, gripping my hands in his and holding them tight, "what has happened?"

I shake my head. "I—I do not know. I am sorry, my Lord, but I—I do not understand."

"Tell me."

"She sang."

His brows rise. "Truly?"

I nod. "She sang for me. With me. She asked me to sing, and I—I know that no one has the right to ask such a thing—but you ordered me—"

"Hush. She has that right. She asked you to sing and she sang for you in return?"

I nod.

He smiles. His teeth are pale and perfect. He draws me into his arms, and I want to pull away; my wings rise before I can bring them under control, flapping ineffectually in the stillness. "This is good," he says.

"No—it is—"

"Hush. Return to her. I wish her to sing for me. I have waited, Lady. I have waited with a patience that the universe has not seen since I was just another powerless politician. I have *waited* and I am almost done with waiting. Make her sing. Make her sing for me. Without her voice, she is of little use."

His voice is what his voice has always been. I know that he means to kill her if she will not give him what he desires, for in death, he will be able to move on.

I have heard this a hundred times. A thousand. I have even, on occasion, felt some regret.

But now, all of my systems are in chaos. I cannot find the thread of their music to guide me; I hear cacophony. I hear something that is wild and terrible, and I feel . . . something.

I do not know what it is. I do not want to know what it is. When he releases me, I bow, and I leave him, having received no answer.

Constance is composed when I return. Her eyes are clear. She is wearing the blue dress that is so like mine, and she is wearing my ring, my circlet. She gazes at herself in a perfect mirror, her back, her wingless back, toward me. But the mirror announces my presence, and she turns away from what she sees.

Because he will not listen, I speak to her. "I am sorry . . . for leaving . . . like that."

"You were summoned?"

"No. No—I—I—"

She does not look alarmed. She approaches me, and I realize that I have seen such an approach before, between the people who gather by the Emperor's side. I draw back. "No. You mustn't."

And she stops, waiting for me, her breath so quiet it might not be there at all. I see myself in her in that moment, myself, in the Aviary, waiting for the flapping of panicked wings to still.

"I have upset you."

"I—I—something is wrong. I don't know what it is. I can't think—I—my subsystems are not responding. Am I breaking down?"

She shakes her head.

"My breath is wrong—I could not sing like this—I—"

"You are afraid," she says.

The words are strange. "I? Afraid?"

She nods.

And when she does, I realize that she is right, this descendant of my father, this woman whose voice is perfect. I am afraid. "But how can I be afraid? Does fear not come from something? Is it not felt for something?"

She nods again.

I turn away from her. I would leave her here, but the Emperor's words repeat themselves again and again. "Come with me," I tell her, without looking back.

She gathers her skirts, for her skirts are meant for display and not movement, and she follows me like a shadow. I am aware that my skirts are likewise cumbersome, and I gather them in handfuls the same way.

I lead her to the Aviary.

His permission was implicit. I do not ask explicitly. The palace accepts this act of subterfuge, for the Emperor's desire is clear and it is all-encompassing. If I can coax song from her voice, he will forgive everything.

As the doors open into this pretense of the outer world, she freezes as if Winter reigned. But it is warm. "Come," I tell her. "I wish to show you something."

"What?"

"His birds."

She reaches for my hand and then lets hers fall away. I do not even have to warn her, and I linger by her side, just a little too close for her safety. Do I want to kill her?

No. No. No.

But what I want *will* kill her. I do not understand it. He did not explain.

She looks up at birds in flight; at hawk and sparrow, at eagle, and then, down the long mile, the jeweled plumage of parakeet, parrot, bird of paradise.

"Does he collect all birds?" She whispers.

"Not all. There are no flightless birds here. If they cannot soar, he does not keep them."

"What becomes of them?"

"They die."

She says nothing, searching the blue of the sky, the distance of trees, the height of crags. "They don't live in cages," she says at last.

"They are not aware of their cages. It is not the same thing."

She turns to face me. "Are you?"

"Am I?"

"Aware of yours?"

I have no answer to give her. The answer I should have given has been lost to confusion and chaos.

I sing here, and she stares at me oddly, her voice silent.

The birds sing back as I move, for they are familiar with me now, the only flightless creature that he has chosen to gift with the Aviary.

She says, after a time has passed, "Thank you."

"Pardon?"

"Thank you."

"I am sorry, Constance, but I do not understand these words."

"Thank you for singing . . . his song." Her eyes are red again. "It was forbidden me. Did you know?"

"No."

She lowers her face into her hands, her lined hands, her changing hands. I see heat in them, glowing across a spectrum that her eyes cannot see.

"You sing well," she says faintly. "When I closed my eyes, I could almost forget that you weren't him."

"Constance—"

"Did you understand the song?"

"Yes. It is about—"

"No, not the words. Did you understand it?"

"Song is a collection of phrases, of sound waves, of pitch. It is a knitting of disparate notes, a collage of continuous breath." Before she can speak, I add, "No. But I understand that song is much more than that to you, and I want—"

I do not know what I want. I turn to her.

She says, "I will not sing for him again."

"But you must!"

Her eyes widen.

I can only speak gently. That was programmed into my vocal cords. I can only *speak* gently. But my song has no such limitations placed upon it, and I realize that, without melody, without notes, I have sung what must be sung.

"Songbird," she whispers. "I would sing for him for the rest of my life if he could bring back my master." She bows her head. "But I have tried. I have tried, and in the wasteland of his court, I cannot find the heart of the songs I once loved."

"But you said that you did sing when you came to court."

"Yes. I did. Because when I came to court, I hated him. I hated him. Do you understand? Hate was my song. Anger. The terrible desire for vengeance.

"It sustained me for years."

She bowed her head. "Do you know why he desires music?"

"It is necessary."

"Yes. Yes, for him, it is necessary. It is only in music that he hears what others are, what they can be; only in music that he forgets what he is. What he became in order to rule the galaxy." Her eyes are burning now. Her voice is vibrating. She is singing, I know she is singing.

"Then hate him," I tell her, gentle again. "Hate him for as long as you live. But sing."

She says, "Hate is a fire."

I do not understand. She looks at me oddly, and says, her gentleness a mirror of my own, or perhaps the substance to which I am simply mirror.

"Hate is a fire," she whispers. "It burns and burns. But after a time, like fire without oxygen to maintain it, it dwindles and dims. There is no fire left," she adds, touching her heart. "There is nothing at all here. I sing, and he knows that my song is gone."

"But you sang for me."

"Yes."

"Then sing for me. Sing for me, where he can hear you, and he will be content."

She closes her eyes. Opens them. "Do you love the Emperor?" she asks me.

And because her voice is a song, I answer with song. "No."

"But you sing for him."

"Song is all that I am. And if not for him, there is nothing to invoke it."

"Sing for me," she says. "Here, in this place. Sing for me."

"Which song?"

"Any song?"

"But I—"

"Sing any song that you want to sing."

I shake my head. "I . . . do not have . . . a favorite song."

She reaches out and her fingers stop a hair's breadth from the gold of my skin.

"You have sung the song I best loved as an adult. Let me sing you a song that I loved as a child in the hall of Genevera."

She begins. Her voice is soft; it has none of the dizzying

height or power that defined it in my rooms. But I listen, enthralled, my subsystems racing to record what I cannot faithfully reproduce.

It is a cradle song. A song a mother sings for her child, or a father for his. It is a song not meant for a voice so fine, so perfect, so powerful as her own; a common song, a thing that demands so narrow a range that even an old and broken voice might carry it and make it sound tuneful.

And I am transfixed by it. I do not know what my subsystems are doing. I listen. I listen and I hear it, suddenly, in another voice, a voice so distant that I have never recalled it until this moment.

When it is over, I stare at her.

"May I keep this song?"

"If you can remember it, yes. It was a gift."

I bow. I take her to my rooms.

In the morning, the Emperor summons us both.

He does not choose to speak through the palace net; he sends a servant. He sends the boy.

The boy bows proudly. He is so young. I was never this young, but my systems recognize youth in both its awkwardness and its fragile beauty.

"Krysos," I tell him, gently, "we will go to the Emperor. But I bid you, I ask you, to carry a message."

"To who?"

"To your great-grandfather."

He nods.

"Tell him—tell them all—to dress for the Winter."

He does not understand the message. But he is in awe of me, of the golden possession, of the Lady of this gilded cage. I know he will do what I have asked.

I do not know if it will do any good.

Constance waits for me.

And as we walk, I speak.

"Please. Please, Constance, sing. I will sing the song of your choice."

"There in only one song I desire."

The palace whispers. "Not that song. Any other song. Any one but that."

And she smiles. She looks old, although she is not old. Her eyes are not narrowed, but they are an odd shape.

"I am glad," she says, "that I have had the privilege of listening to you sing. I felt . . . for a moment . . . that I was home." She bows her head.

I, who have never been harsh, find harshness now. "He will kill you if you refuse."

"I know." She looks up at me, and I realize that she is not tall. "Tell him—tell him that some birds cannot sing in cages."

She will die.

The Emperor's life is defined by the things he puts in cages, no matter how large those cages are.

"Genevera knew this," she said quietly. "He knew it. Understand that he created you because he thought that you could sing in a cage, and be content; that the Emperor's voices might be stilled in a way that did not cull the music from the galaxy over which he presides." She watches my expression, and after a moment, she speaks again.

"I am not the first singer that he has taken from her home," she says quietly. "In the beginning, he was a patron of the arts, and of those, he best loved music. He loved the drama of it, the love and the loss; he was transfixed by what he *could not* himself do.

"In Genevera's time, his family—our family—was a songhouse of great fame and note. Genevera's daughters were known throughout the galaxy for their voices, and his granddaughters inherited that talent. His sons were tenors without parallel.

"He loved them fiercely and drove them mercilessly, because he thought by so doing, he might increase their worthiness in the eyes of the Emperor.

"And he did. Genevera was revered. His daughters and his sons were taken, one by one, to sit at the Emperor's side.

"And by the side of the eternal ruler, they sang; they were heard, far and wide, by dignitaries from the league of planets, and they were admired. Their fame spread.

"But the Emperor, even then, had no time for the trivialities of life. None of Genevera's children were allowed to bear children until their voices had lost all power, and when that had happened, conception was difficult. Artificial means kept the family line going, but the children of that artifice were . . . lessened. They did not grow up in the songhouse;

they were not raised on music. It was not their first memory, their first love, their last act at the end of the day.

"And Genevera realized that he had doomed his house.

"And so, with the help of technicians whose power I do not understand, he created you. You were his gift.

"And you were our salvation.

"I heard of you when I was growing up. I did not understand how powerful a gift you were, how much you had done to protect us, until the Emperor came.

"But I understand it now. I thank you, Songbird. If I do not sing, it does not matter; my sisters will sing. My brothers."

"They will never be your equal."

"Not to the Emperor's ear, no. But they will be more. They will be free."

She is going to die.

I cannot stop her. I realize that I cannot stop her. But I beg her anyway. I am practical. I know that the Emperor will be displeased with me if I fail to invoke the song he desires, and it is my duty—and my existence—to serve him. But it is not for that reason that I wish her to sing.

If she is a bird, and she is in a cage, might it not be my cage? Might we not share it, and song?

The doors to the Emperor's audience chamber open before us. He is seated upon the ceremonial throne in the long hall. People are gathered beneath both chair and statue, and they speak among themselves until we enter the room.

He rises.

"Ladies," he says. "Gentlemen."

They stop.

I close my eyes. Had he chosen to speak to us in any other room, there is some chance that I might preserve her life—but not here. Not here. Not even I could survive publicly humiliating my Lord.

And what would death be, for me? Would it be sleep?

I listen as he introduces us.

I listen as he tells the most important men and women of this decade, this year, this hour, that he will grace them with an entertainment. There is menace in that word.

And I listen as Constance turns to the Emperor, kneels,

and bows her head in perfect silence. She does not even have to say the words.

I turn to him. I lift my wings, unfurling them until they stretch out, and out, twenty feet from tip to tip. It is only when they are fully extended that I understand why I have done this; I am shielding her from the strangers who even now are whispering, placing their bets.

I have hated nothing in my life, if life is what I have, and I do not know if what I feel now is hate.

"Very well," the Emperor says, in the softest of voices. He does not need to shout; the palace magnifies his tones into stately, icy dignity. Everyone, highborn and low, short-lived and long, hears his words. "If you will not serve in the fashion for which you were chosen, we will choose a different entertainment.

"Come," he says, raising his voice. The men and women converge upon the doors that swing wide like vultures. Even vultures exist in the Aviary, and I have never thought them ugly until this moment; they will forever be scarred by my experience this day.

Guards come to lift her to her feet. They are his guards. They are real.

I rise my hands before their exposed faces and they halt instantly.

"What is this, Lady?" the Emperor says. His voice is cold.

"It is my gift," I tell him gently. "It is my gift to you, my Lord."

And speaking thus, I walk to where Constance kneels, and as I have desired these past days, I take her in my arms. I touch her.

She looks up at me, slowly.

Meets my eyes. Sees that my hands are around her. I hesitate for just another moment, and then I reach up and brush her dark hair from where it has fallen across her forehead. I want to see her eyes.

She does not scream or struggle.

This will displease the Emperor, for he has decided upon spectacle. Indeed, I hear the palace; I hear the clamor in my own body; they are at war, now.

"Come, Constance," I tell her. "I will take you to my . . . favorite place."

The men and women are already moving toward the exquisitely colored glass that lines the observation hall. Unless the Emperor orders them to do otherwise, the guards will not intervene, for my touch is death, and I *will* touch them.

For her, I sing. I sing quietly. I sing the song that she loved as a child.

The poison will not kill her before the cold does. I linger in the warmth a moment. I cannot produce heat. I cannot protect her.

I carry her. She weighs exactly fifty-five point two kilograms. Her heart is racing. Her body is attempting to undermine the toxins. She is augmented. I had not realized that. She will survive for a while yet.

As we walk, I begin to sing a different song in a voice that was forbidden to her. A man's voice. A dead man's voice.

I feel the palace net now; it is strong.

But it is not as strong as my song. I do not know why this is so, but it is so, and I am grateful for this mercy.

As I sing, she begins to sing. The poison has not silenced her. The air will slowly fade; her ability to draw it will weaken.

But while it is still strong, she begins to sing her aria, and I, mine, and our voices, two voices, are one. I do not look up at the audience. I am aware of it. I am aware of where it is.

The beauty of these windows is that they are permeable; if they were not, sound would not travel through them. Spectacle without sound is like song without sound; of what use are a dying man's pleas if they cannot be heard, if they can only be guessed at by people so jaded they have a poverty of imagination with which to guild a death?

And yet.

And yet they are silent as we sing.

Her voice is strong. It is not as loud as it was when she first sang with me, but there is something about the voice that is so achingly pure, so terribly beautiful, that I am almost paralyzed by it.

I carry her. I feel the cold of the outside air as it rushes into the lock between the palace and its glacial garden.

This is my place.

I sing. I sing and she sings and when the last note fades, I surrender it to her shaking voice.

The cold takes her limbs. Her face turns red as blood rushes outward to the extremities it cannot warm; it turns pale as blood retreats in an attempt to maintain the central system.

She lifts her hand. Her hand shakes, but she struggles anyway, and this time, I do not tell her to stop. She touches my cheek. I am certain that I am as cold as ice to the touch, and I wonder if she feels me at all as anything other than death, part of her death.

"Maria," she says softly.

I meet her eyes; I say nothing. "You were Maria. You were his last daughter. Sing," she says. "Sing the songs he taught you. Sing the songs he wrote just for your keeping." Except that she does not say this; the words are broken by the shuddering of her jaw. She is cold, and she clings to me, clinging to the life that she could not find song to preserve.

I am weeping.

She is not. She is fading, and I—who have held no one but the Emperor—hold her as if her loss is the only fear I have ever known.

Because it is. I understand it now; the clamoring of the subsystems, the terrible chaos, the noise that is not song.

I hold her, and I sing all the songs that she has asked for. I sing them loudly. I sing them sweetly. I sing as I have never sung before, pitching my waves of sound as if they were weapons.

As if.

The windows shatter.

One by one, they shatter. Proof against the cold, they shiver and splinter and break, shards of colored light, a frozen, cracking spectrum. Rain.

The cold strikes them all.

All except the Emperor, except the man I was created to serve.

He stands among his followers, his hands behind his back. I sing now, and the song that I sing is unlike any I have ever sung, although he knows it; he knows every song I have ever learned. And why should he not? Every song I have ever learned is his.

I must have a heart. I must have a heart like Constance's; it has fled the shelter of her body, freezing like glass.

And he watches, his eyes wide; listens, oblivious now to the voices of the screaming throng that realizes only now that there is no safety to be found in time as warmth rushes out in clouds of condensing air.

Only the servants will remember this, if the Emperor allows them to live. They are dressed for the cold. They wear their 'suits. They witness.

And the Emperor weeps.

"A gift," he says, and the palace carries his voice to me, his songbird, his caged creature.

"Ah, a gift. Songbird, Lady."

I weep, too.

Constance, I weep.

I will sing for him. I am his, and I am loyal, and I obey him.

I will sing, and I will sleep, and I will wake again, and he will call me because you have taught me a truth about music that I could never have learned if I could not hold you now: I have a heart.

How long will it sustain me?

HE DIED THAT DAY, IN THIRTY YEARS

by Wil McCarthy

We have it on good authority that Wil McCarthy is the best guy ever. He not only walks on water, but has been known to bathe in it. He is also an aerospace engineer, novelist, journalist, and science writer. His various publishing credits include 1998 *New York Times* Notable Book *Bloom,* and Amazon.com "Best of Y2K" SF novel *The Collapsium.*

This particular story emerged from an interest in the mechanisms of memory and consciousness, and a healthy preoccupation with love, sex, food, and death.

MONDAY through Friday, Jeremy spent his daylight hours in a stuffy, windowless cubicle. Plenty of twilight hours, too—working "Chinese overtime" at seventy-five percent pay, crunching numbers and contemplating the *raison d'être* of his servitude: the ownership of a house. Not a big one or a fancy one, just a simple tract home on the outskirts of Southampton, in a not-too-dingy neighborhood twenty miles from the ocean and fully seventy miles from his native London.

Just barely affordable, he'd told himself, but like a ship sailing through northern fogs, he'd espied mortgage payments peeking out above the waters of his finances, never guessing they might prove the merest tips of a single monstrous iceberg that held insurance, utilities, maintenance, repairs, lawn chemicals, and every other conceivable thing in its vast, frozen bulk. Never guessing that a hidden spur could tear his hull lengthwise at any moment, filling his holds with the chill waters of bankruptcy.

The alternative, of course, was to cut his losses and dash back to the flats that had previously housed him. Throwing away his blood and sweat, just handing it off, serflike, to some absentee landlord. And sharing walls, yes, like sharing the back side of his shirt with some sweaty stranger. Even buying an apartment wouldn't fix that, and anyway he was damned if he'd own a piece of real estate that didn't touch the ground. If the building burned down, he'd be left with, what? Deed to a volume of empty air?

No. Call it a character flaw, but he needed an actual house around him, owned and operated by him, so at night he could look up sleepily at the ceiling and know that it was *his* ceiling, held up by *his* walls and standing on his own little piece of the Earth. His kingdom. But as his mother would say, nothing worth having came any way but dear; for his double sins of greed and pride, he paid. Did he ever! These sins are exactly the thing that killed him.

His savings dwindled, his credit card bills swelled, and then his pipes gave out and there was nothing for it but to call in a plumber who charged, it seemed, by the millisecond. When finally it became clear that it might be his destiny to *lose* the house, and his credit rating along with it, he moped around a bit and then took a weekend job to bring in extra money.

Tending bar was, he found, just exactly like being at a party. Unfortunately, it was the sort of loud, smoky party attended by people who liked a drink first thing on Friday evening and then didn't draw a sober breath until Sunday at the earliest, and he was the one washing their glasses and wiping up their spills, and a captive audience for all the stupid stories that no one else wanted to hear, and he didn't get to go home with some pretty girl when he got tired of it. He didn't even get to go home *alone,* not until the hour had come, the place had cleared out and he'd scrubbed his sinks and counters down with cleansing solution and left it all to dry for the next day.

His lawn took on a rough, unshaven look, the hedges along it growing wild as mop heads, but fortunately it became a rare enough thing for him to see his home in daylight that the sight rarely intruded, and the irony of *that* certainly wasn't lost on him.

Then one Friday evening, a pretty girl did come and sit by him, and she didn't drink herself stupid or tell him any stories about her week while he washed and stacked the glasses. Instead, she ordered a Coke, rooted around in her purse, filed her nails for a bit, and then turned and asked him if he was happy.

"I beg your pardon?" he replied, not really sure he'd understood the question.

"Are you *happy?*" she repeated, giving him a sort of vague, half-knowing smile. "It's just that I never see you here during the week, and you don't quite seem like the sort of person who tends bar. So I thought maybe it wasn't by choice."

Jeremy set down his rag, waved a hand through the coils of smoke hanging in the air. "By choice? Why; does anyone do this by choice?"

"Well, of course. It's a position of respect, of dignity. You're trusted with significant sums of money, and with stock and equipment worth many times more than that. People come to you with their problems, and when somebody picks a fight and you tell them to break it up, they listen to you. It's like being a fire chief or an office manager or something."

"*He's* the office manager," Jeremy said, jerking a thumb at the door behind him. "And I've never broken up a fight in my life. Can I freshen that for you?"

"Thanks, yes."

He went back to washing glasses, until a gaggle of drinkers boiled up from the restaurant floor with fresh orders, and the pair at the end of the bar decided they needed another round, and that touched off another series that kept him jumping for a good ten minutes. But when he'd finished, the young woman was still there, jutting up like a rock in river as patrons swirled about her, calling and laughing and singing along with the radio.

"It's nice to stay busy," she observed. "Makes the time go."

"Does it?" Jeremy asked shortly. But he felt a smile rising, felt it break the surface.

"There, now, that's not so bad, is it?" What her voice

lacked in finish it made up for in sincerity. This was, he thought, a grocer's daughter, or perhaps even a barman's. Not a good girl, per se, judging by the short black skirt and less-than-missionary blouse she'd chosen to wear, but then again who dressed like a saint on Friday night? He'd dated his share of gentlemen's ladies, and there really wasn't much to remember them by.

"I'm Jeremy," he said, wiping a hand dry and then offering it to her.

"Alice," she said, taking it. And then she did a thing he'd heard about but never actually seen done: she raised their joined hands to her mouth, and gently nibbled the end of his middle finger. He had absolutely no idea what to say to that, and evidently neither did she—in another moment they were both laughing, alone together in a bubble, a pocket universe into which the barroom hubbub scarcely seemed able to penetrate.

This is what killed him.

Jeremy's business, by the way, was in the mathematics of fate. It worked like this: turbulent phenomena were fine and predictable over short spans of time, but ugly and messy and random in the long run. Even the most detailed weather simulations, for example, were useless past about five days, because you knew your starting conditions with only finite precision. Even the tiniest errors would grow over time, and if you twiddled your guesses one way, the long-range forecast might be one thing, and if you twiddled them ever so slightly in the other way, it might yield something entirely different.

But from this sea of infinite possibility there arose a kind of meta-order, occasional reefs of near certainty jutting up from the deeps. The weather would fluctuate, right enough, but winter would come along eventually, and spring after it, and sometimes you could say with 95 percent confidence that on an afternoon twenty-six days hence, it would be snowing hard in Bonn. So, far from vanishing the concept of destiny, twenty-first century mathematics had enshrined and legitimized it—in a world of turbulence, there were still some things you could count on.

It mattered very little that Jeremy's training was in marine meteorology while his actual work was in finance. The numbers didn't care about abstractions like that. If only human society were so forgiving!

The woman's eyes, he noted, were brown.

"A Newcastle, please," someone said later, a moment or an hour, breaking the spell. The two of them shared a regretful look before the receding tide pulled Jeremy away. After that he was busy for the rest of the night, never sharing another word with her, but she watched him as he worked, cast little smiles and funny faces at him now and then, and somehow that was enough. Their acquaintance-ship grew. When closing time came, he half expected her to come straight home with him, and was oddly pleased to receive instead nothing more than a business card and a peck on the cheek.

"Come 'round and see me tomorrow," she said, not sultrily or coquettishly but in a simple way that indicated her hope that he really would.

"Count on it," he told her, thinking maybe this weekend job thing wasn't so bad after all.

Watching the unselfconscious, high-heeled swivel of her buttocks as she walked away, he felt a stab of passion rather more intense and possessive and smugly self-satisfied than he had any right to. *Jesus, Jer, it's not like you fucked her right there on the bar.* The image that came to him then was sharp, vivid with sensory detail: soft pinkness against the wood, her breath coming out in grunts and gasps. And most of all, the taste of sweat. God, yes.

"Alice Frane, Designer," the card said in delicate letters. It gave an address, a telephone number, an e-mail, and smelled faintly but distinctly of her.

He wandered home in a fog.

In the morning he awoke, having slept well and deeply, dreaming of nothing. He admired his calm as he downed morning stimulants, arranged breakfast, showered. Only when he'd begun to dress did he give up and have a wank, throwing himself back on the bed and imagining, once more, Alice's body writhing beneath his. Not on the bar this time, but on the blasted, hellish surface of the planet Venus, the yellow air hot against their skins, bodies rising and sinking in puddles of molten lead. *Stop! Don't! Save it!* a part of him was screaming. *We might need this!* But the rest of him just laughed at the idea. Plenty more where that came from.

After he really did get dressed, he felt calm enough to pick up the phone and dial the number on the card. Alice Frane, Designer.

"Hello?" a voice said after the second ring. Her voice? Maybe.

"Is Alice there?" he asked.

"Oh. Is this Jeremy?"

"Yes."

"She's at services right now. Can you come around at eleven?"

"Eleven? Well, yes. Of course. But . . . May I ask whom I'm speaking with?"

"This is her answering machine," the voice said.

Well, well. Software like that cost several times what Jeremy earned in a month. This "designing" must pay pretty well, assuming the voice didn't belong to a sister or roommate or even Alice herself, having him on.

"Is there a message?" the voice inquired patiently.

"No. Uh, yes. I mean, I'll be there. Can you give directions?"

"Uh, huh. Where are you coming from?"

The directions that followed were clear and succinct, and he was even warned to avoid the construction on such-and-such street, and encouraged to take advantage of the much lighter traffic on so-and-so. It wasn't a sister, he decided. Or if it was, she had a taxi dispatcher's workstation bolted to her nightstand.

He thanked the voice and rang off.

When he arrived at the specified address, he thought at first that there must be some mistake. Too nice. Much too nice. Fancy answering machines were one thing, but nobody with the wherewithal to live *here* would be dropping into seedy little pubs to pick up on the barmen. The building's software seemed to be expecting him, though; the pedestrian gate was exceedingly polite.

Did he feel a stab of house envy? Not really, he decided. Four walls and a roof, that was the thing. If he did somehow own a place like this, he'd probably swap it for a place like his current, and set up the excess in a trust to pay the property taxes in perpetuity. But it would be nice, being able to afford it.

Alice's front door was made of real wood, and he'd only knocked once before it opened wide to reveal . . . Well, Alice herself was the first thing he noticed—dressed now in a fine Sunday jumper, for all that today was Saturday. Floral print on white with a matching jacket over the top. Behind her was another surprise, though: the house, rather than being posh inside, appeared all but empty, one giant interior space whose vastness was broken only by some cluttered tables up against the far wall.

"Hello," Alice said, sounding pleased.

"Hi."

"Won't you come in?"

He smiled. "Dying to, actually."

Inside, he saw the space was not quite as barren as he'd thought. Off to one side was a kitchen; off to the other, a bedroom set, and in the distance an automobile, sitting before a large, automatic carport door. White floor, white ceiling . . . only the interior walls were lacking. But the central area, the living room if you will, looked more like an unusually spacious laboratory than anything else. He saw two computerlike devices, a rack of small, marked bottles, some standing glassware, other objects less identifiable.

"I've got a kettle on," she offered as she ushered him in, closing the door behind him.

"That'd be great, thanks."

She showed him to a seat at the kitchen table, busied herself with the clink of cups and saucers.

"Nice place you have here," he said. "Kind of, uh, surprising."

"People always say that." She smiled and handed him a cup, then picked up her own and sipped from it. He glanced at his own, sniffed it. Not tea but coffee, pale with added milk. Fiercely sweet when he sipped it.

"It was . . . a pleasure," he attempted, "meeting you last night. I'm glad you invited me over."

"Really, Jeremy?" She turned, faced him fully, her expression suddenly earnest. "Did you feel it, too?"

"Feel it?"

"That sense, that destiny. Like we'd known each other already. Oh, listen to me, putting the cart before . . . I don't even know your last name."

"It's Hobb."

"Hobb." She sampled it, nodding. "Do you believe in love at first sight, Jeremy Hobb?"

His heart fluttered. Love? That was a big word. "First sight," too, for that matter. His first glimpse of her hadn't been anything all that remarkable. And yet . . .

Without warning, she dropped to her knees in front of him, placing a hand on each of his thighs. Her eyes sparkled. His heart fluttered again.

"Do you feel the chemistry?" she demanded, leaning forward, her face upturned, red-painted lips mere inches from his crotch. "Do you feel a particular longing, a particular hunger? To be with me? Not just to be with someone, not with me just because I'm conveniently here. Do. You. Want. Me?"

"Yes," Jeremy admitted. "You. Not just anyone. We made a . . . connection last night, and I wanted to know more. It's why I'm here."

"Not just for the hope of sex?"

Um . . .

"I'd be lying if I said that weren't part of it," he said truthfully.

"But not all?"

"No. Definitely not."

"Good," she said, relaxing visibly. Her hand dove into a jacket pocket, came back holding something. A pill, red. She held it out to him.

"Er," he commented.

"Trust me, Jeremy Hobb. If you feel what you say, take the pill for me."

"It's . . ."

"Not birth control," she said. "It's a psychoactive. Designed by me. I want you to have it."

"None for you?"

"No, no, that would ruin the effect."

Jeremy, being very much a creature of the times, did take drugs at parties, sometimes without asking what they were. This request was not so completely out of line. But usually there were lots of other people taking them as well—safety in numbers, as it were—so it wasn't all that much in line, either.

But then again, what did Alice Frane, Designer, stand to gain by poisoning him? His worldly riches? Hardly.

He took the pill, washing it down with a swallow of the too-sweet coffee, and wondered what, exactly, she had in mind. The pill seemed to dissolve in his throat, rising vapor-like into his sinuses.

This is not what killed him.

"How long until this takes effect?" he asked.

She smiled, rubbing her face against his inner thigh. "It should be nearly instantaneous. From the nasal and bronchial mucosa straight to the blood-brain barrier. It—"

"Stop that, please," he said, moving his leg.

She pulled away a bit. "Why? What's wrong?"

He pulled back, scooting his chair a bit. Feeling something a little off. Wondering, now, why he'd let her give him the pill. A desire to please? To *be* pleased, no matter what the cost? Not bright. She wasn't even all that pretty, not really.

"Jeremy, what's wrong?" she repeated.

He sighed, scooting his chair farther back, looking at her there on her knees, trying fumblingly to arouse him, to coax some promise of love out of him. Giving him drugs for it! Suddenly, he was glad things hadn't got any farther than this. The thought of waking up in this woman's bed was, actually, not that pleasant. He'd probably come to his senses just in time.

"I . . . don't think this is a very good idea, you and I," he said, as gently as he could manage under the circumstances. "I mean, you're very nice, but I don't know that we're really one another's type, if you see what I mean."

"You don't love me, then?"

To her credit, she didn't betray any signs of deep hurt or embarrassment. Well, good. Better that she salvage her dignity. Better that this be over with.

"No," he said, "I'm afraid I don't."

"No sense of connection? No special bond?"

He shook his head. "No, Alice. I'm sorry. I should have—"

"Do you even like me?"

His reflex was to answer yes, to spare her feelings, but it seemed he owed her something more than that. He couldn't blame her for getting the wrong idea, after all. Not after the way he'd come here, the way he'd spoken to her . . . Really, if her feelings got hurt, it was largely his own fault. And that wasn't something he wanted.

"I have no dislike for you," he said honestly. "I think we could, for example, be friends. If that's what you want."

She lifted her head, smiling with a curious wickedness. "You have no idea," she said, "how happy I am to hear that."

"Excuse me?"

Rising to her feet, she dusted her knees off with a swipe and then held a hand out to him. "Alice Frane, Designer. What you've ingested is an oxytocin antagonist, a chemical designed to block the brain's response to . . . call it infatuation. The early stages of love."

He blinked. "What?"

"I've been working on it for months, and you have no idea how hard it is to find a suitable test subject in this town. The dosage is tiny, by the way. You should be fine in a minute."

Oxytocin antagonist? thought Jeremy. *Test subject? What the hell was she talking about?*

"I apologize for the deception," she said, holding her hand out closer to him and waving it slightly, a nonverbal demand that he shake it. "It's necessary that the subject's romantic interest be genuine. We can induce it chemically, but then the spatial distribution inside the brain is all wrong, which is another way of saying there are side effects. To get a proper test, we need all the variables constant, wouldn't you say?"

Jeremy took the hand, shook and released it, then wondered why he'd done it. Something very confused in his brain, in his feelings. Not so much the confusion of ambivalence or ignorance as that of a sharp blow to the head. Although he *was* feeling damned ignorant as well. And ambivalent.

"How're you doing?" Alice asked, now sounding genuinely, if slightly, concerned. "You look . . ."

"Confused," he said. "Angry. You tricked me."

"Yes," she admitted.

He rose unsteadily from the chair. "I'm getting out of here."

She shrugged. "I don't blame you, actually, but let me give you something for your trouble before you go. You don't imagine I'm quite *that* callous, do you?"

Well . . . Before he could answer, she'd turned, snatched something off the counter. A check register—the paper kind. She took up a pen, scribbled quickly. Tore off a sheet.

"Here. Please."

He took it from her, again before he'd really thought it through. The hell of it was, he did want to please her. To be liked by her. He looked: her writing, barely legible, had made the check out to him. For much more money than he'd been prepared to see, a sum slightly more than he made in a weekend at the pub.

"Not bad for a minute's work, eh?"

He stared at the check for a moment, then flipped it over. Found a notice to the effect that endorsement was required for deposit, and constituted a release of the payer from any further obligation, financial or otherwise, for services rendered.

"What is this?" he asked, his brain rising finally, turgidly, up out of the fog. "What kind of racket are you running?"

"No racket," she said, surprised, not quite defensive.

"You're a *drug* designer."

"Mood designer, yes. What did you think?"

What did he think? That she'd liked him, wanted him in some way? It had seemed a reasonable hypothesis at the time. Now he'd fallen in love with her in an evening, fallen out in ten seconds, and fallen . . . what, back in love again? Just as she was giving him this really, particularly good reason to despise her? It was too much, too many feelings at once. Contradictory feelings that, far from canceling one another out, seemed to crash together like incoming and outflowing waves, sending up towers of spray.

"It doesn't matter what I thought," he said with what struck him as a pathetic sort of dignity.

"Were there side effects?"

"Yes," he said. Then: "None of your business, actually. I think I'll take the hush money, and hush. Now if you'll excuse me . . ."

"It isn't hush money," she said, standing straighter, not quite barring his way, cup and saucer clinking in her hands. "What I've done is perfectly ethical. This is a licensed pharmogenia, you came here voluntarily, took the enhancement voluntarily . . . You haven't been harmed in any way."

"You lied to me," he pointed out curtly.

"Did not either! When did I lie?"

He felt his face grow hot. Hotter, actually—he'd been blushing for quite some time, now. He spoke slowly: "You pretended to like me. To be romantically interested. On what planet is that considered ethical?"

She quirked her brows together, looking honestly puzzled. "Who said I wasn't interested? I needed a genuine attraction, somebody charming and witty and available, somebody with enough sense to see the same things in me. I was so happy to find you there last night, hopping around with that towel on your arm, playacting. More like a barman than any real one I've ever seen."

She stopped, examined her nails for a moment, met his eyes again.

"I *do* believe in love at first sight, Jeremy Hobb. The marriages ruined by it, the kingdoms toppled . . . What would the world give for a cure? Mood design is the art and science of liberation, the decoupling of human spirit from the engines of biological imperative."

He shook his head, perplexed, once more at a loss. "You want a world without love?"

"Oh," she said, "God, no." And she leaned forward and kissed him on the lips.

That was what killed him.

The rest of their conversation went like this: he had a perfect right to be angry—she certainly would be if their situations were reversed—but she hoped he would let her make it up to him. They could spend the day together. He didn't know about that. Well, how about this: she knew he needed the money. He virtually *radiated* debtor's anxiety. If he'd agree to sample two more substances for her, she would see him well compensated, and get to spend time with him besides. He *really* didn't know about that. What did she take him for? But she named a figure, shockingly high, and he crumpled.

"They're a bit more . . . experimental," she admitted. "We can't be completely sure of the effects. I need someone intelligent enough to articulate the experiences clearly."

That would be, a part of him insisted, a really exception-ally bad idea. Whether she liked him or not—and he wasn't at all convinced that she did, that she wasn't just leading him on for her own purposes—it was pretty obvious that his relative poverty, his double sins of greed and pride, had been a large part of what had drawn her to him. Intelligent, yes. Alone, yes. Ready to fall in love on a moment's notice, and vulnerable to . . . financial persuasion.

But the *money,* countered another part of him. Eleven point two house payments! Enough to really dig himself out, to quit the pub, quit the overtime, to stay dug out on a long-term basis. That was not a small thing, not a thing he could easily walk away from and live with himself after-ward.

And a third part of him: God help the underdamped system. Chaos would have its way with any variable not sufficiently anchored by stabilizing influences. His work took fate for granted, a gift from the gods, but what, really, built up those islands of gelid near-certainty? Sinks and sources—features existing on a larger scale, mathematically speaking, than the perturbations that sought to disrupt them. What ocean liner was ever capsized by a three-foot wave? What nation drowned beneath the flood of a single minor river?

Base axiom of the financial fractanalyst: the occurrence of islands could not be controlled; the seizing and holding of them could.

Unhappily, he observed: "You know which buttons to push."

"Well, I *hope* so," Alice said. And then she smiled and dropped her eyes, suddenly shy.

Had he doubted her beauty? Had he really?

The first pill she gave him was blue, washed down with a hot sip of freshened coffee, fiercely sweet.

"How long for this to take effect?"

"I'm guessing about an hour."

"But you don't know?"

"Not really. Are there any immediate effects?"

He paused, sniffed, thought for a moment. "A slight diz-ziness. And . . . is that garlic I smell?"

"Garlic," she said, writing that down in a little paper no-tepad. "Interesting. I wanted an olfactory telltale, but interpretation can be so subjective. The smell—" she winked, "—is in your head. How's the dizziness? Still there? Maybe you should sit."

They'd been leaning side by side against the kitchen counter, their hips almost touching.

"I think I will," he agreed, moving away and taking his seat. What was going on in his brain? What was she doing to him now? The light-headed feeling was slight, passing already, but the sense of foreboding persisted. As well it should: this was not a smart thing to be doing. Not something he could, for example, easily explain to his mother.

Alice, still standing, loomed over him. Inspecting. "How do you feel?"

"Unwise," he said.

She laughed. "Fair enough. The love snuffer should be just about dissipated by now, I think. Are you . . . repelled by me?"

Repelled? She tossed her hair, and he felt himself grow hard at the sight. She licked her lips and the erection became painful, straining against clothing, straining against the skin that contained it.

"That's not a word I would choose," he offered guardedly, wary that this might be some new trick. "Why, have you given me some sort of aphrodisiac?"

"No, something quite different. Whatever emotion you're feeling now comes directly from your own heart." She leaned closer, placed a finger on the edge of his jaw, traced downward. Touch of feathers: tingly, electric. "Is there a spark in your heart, Jeremy? A trace of desire?"

"Maybe," he allowed. But his voice betrayed him, trembling, cracking.

"Well, come on, then," she said, and her hands moved to the closures of the jumper and pulled them apart, revealing white brassiere lace underneath. She found a hook and parted that as well. Her breasts, pushed together by taut fabric, seemed to grope for him, pink nipples like blind, soft eyes.

He could have resisted, he would later think. He could have walked away. He was not, after all, some mindless rutting machine. But even his hands were hungry for her, and who was he to refuse them?

In another moment she was in his lap, jacket discarded, floral-print jumper peeled to the waist. Brassiere still clinging to the shoulders, open and welcoming, framing the bob and swell of her. Light taste of sweat on her skin, nipples hardening beneath his tongue.

"Oh," she said.

He lifted her, carried her, legs wrapping around his waist. The bed wasn't far at all.

She resisted, at first, when he tried to relieve her of those last bits of clothing. No words exchanged, but reproach clear in her manner: please me and we'll see. He did his best, and minutes or hours later she was peeling the jumper off herself, rolling to the side, disentangling her legs. She kicked the fabric away, clad now only in pink cotton underpants. He kissed them, deep, wanting, pressing the heat of his breath through to her. Then he pulled them down off her and she said nothing, wordlessly approving. He traced the rise and fall of her knee, the sharp curve of ankle as he slipped them off and away.

Her pubic hair was soft and brown, exactly the color of her eyes. He went for his own shirt buttons, undid one, found her hands there stopping him. Reproachful: please me and we'll see. Dying to, actually. She tasted exactly as he imagined.

How many times did she shudder beneath his ministrations? Soon it was one continuous shudder, one steady, panting moan, until finally, wordlessly, she willed him to stop. Enough; he'd proved his sincerity, could take what he wanted of her. It was she, this time, who unfastened his buttons.

It was he who stopped her—the dizziness back again, the smell of garlic. Stronger this time.

"Something's happening," he said.

She sat up, suddenly alert. "Garlic?"

"Garlic," he agreed. "It's back."

Her smile was mischievous, almost cruel. "Unfortunate timing for you, I'm afraid. I'd better dress."

She took a moment to wipe his mouth with a clean corner of sheet.

Disappointed: "Stop it. Dress? Why?"

"You'll see."

He didn't much like the sound of that, but he rolled off

the bed and stood, watching her reach for panties, bra,
jumper. The act of dressing was itself maddeningly erotic.
Soon she was on her feet, slipping back into her shoes and
urging him into the kitchen. Her jacket lay where it had
fallen; she retrieved it.

Unhappily, he took his seat. Dizziness and garlic stronger
than ever, overpowering.

"What's happening to me?"

"We'll see," she said, handing him the cup and saucer
again.

Something surged through the insides of his skull, not so
much a pain as a pressure. Alarming. But then the garlic
smell was fading, the nausea and dizziness shrinking away.

"How do you feel?" she asked.

"Better. What happened?"

She shrugged. "You tell me."

Shaking a little, he took a sip of his coffee. Stone cold.
He dropped the cup, watched it spin, fall, shatter.

"How long before it takes effect?" he asked, his voice
swimming out from between his lips with underwater
slowness.

"You're just coming out of it now," she said. "What's
the last thing you remember?"

"Taking the pill," he said, slowly but without hesitation.
"And then a smell."

"Garlic?"

"That's right."

"And then a feeling of light-headedness?"

He thought about that. "Yes, I think. A little."

"And are there any unusual sensations right now?"

He thought again, taking quick stock of himself. "I'm
sweaty," he said. "And my . . . testicles are a bit sore."

That certainly brought an unclinical smile to her lips.
"Normal," she assured him, "under the circumstances.
Anything else?"

"Well, um . . . I seem to have broken my cup. Only I
don't remember it happening."

"You've lost a little time."

He nodded unhappily. "I thought maybe I had. How awful.
Is that the effect? Is that what's supposed to happen?"

"More or less," she said, nodding and smiling. "It's a
memory drug, but the details are . . . complicated. You

know, why don't you let me explain it to you over, say, a continental lunch?"

Hesitation. "I haven't brought much money."

"Oh, please," she said, flipping a hand at him, annoyed at the implied insult. "My treat. Believe me, you've earned an afternoon on the town."

The way she said this somehow struck him as nakedly erotic. God, but she was beautiful, and he couldn't shake the sense, somehow, that their relationship was already an intimate one. He even fancied he could taste, vividly, the musk of her on his lips.

The restaurant she took him to was quiet, dim, cool. Filled with discreet niches which seemed to swallow patrons whole, leaving no verbal or auditory trace of their presence.

The pill she gave him to ingest was green, translucent, tasteless. Slick going down, rising up again as vapor.

"What will this one do?"

She paused for a guilty moment, then seemed to decide he had a right to know. "Right frontal inhibitor, to suppress your filters, for heightened sensitivity. If I've got it tuned for the proper stimulus pathways, it should . . . enhance your dining experience. I call it 'Gourmand.' "

"That doesn't sound so bad," he said.

"No. But I may be skewing the results by providing an *a priori* description. Autohypnosis can be as powerful as any mood alteration I've ever cooked up. But what the hell, it's been a brilliantly successful day. Let's live a little."

"You make it sound almost like we're partners," he observed, taking a sip from his water. Frowning.

"You have no idea how much you've helped, and I do mean to make it up to you. I hope you're hungry."

"Famished, actually."

They studied menus, discussed them a little, closed them. A waiter appeared, as if from nowhere.

"Cassoulet, please," Alice said. "And a glass of red wine."

A vintage and year were suggested and agreed to. The waiter turned.

"And for sir?"

"Escargot," Jeremy instructed, "lightly sauteed. Green salad with buttermilk, hold tomato. Trout with almonds, medium well, slice of dark rye on the side. Glass of Coke, vodka chaser, and a fresh glass of water; this came out of the tap. If you haven't got anything bottled, at least put a lime in it to cover that awful mustiness."

"Very good, sir. Very perceptive. Cook will be pleased."

"No doubt."

The waiter retreated, amused.

"I don't know how you usually order," Alice observed.

Distractedly: "Neither do I. Not like that, I suppose. Same knowledge, different inclination."

"How are you feeling?"

"Hungry."

Their drinks arrived. The glass of water, its sides sweaty with condensation, sported a thin wheel of lime on its rim. Jeremy took the glass, raised it, sipped experimentally. Better, much better. Tasting more of water than of pipe. But he dropped the lime in anyway, for flavor. The Coke was better: biting, sharp, bubbles carrying the essence of it deeper into the tongue the way Coke bubbles always had. The vodka was excellent.

He realized Alice was speaking: ". . . more generalized inhibitor, but there'd have been too many alternate pathways for breakdown. The mood designer always strives for specificity of effect."

"That's nice," he said.

"About the memory drug you had this afternoon," she began.

He sipped the vodka again, savoring the deep, almost oily texture of it, the clean ethanol aroma, the taste like buttered steam.

"Yes?"

"I'm thinking of calling it 'Finals Week.' Once I get the dosage and decay times worked out, I'm shooting for a latency of about twelve hours per pill. Take you through the days you'd rather not experience."

He finished the vodka, let it dissipate a little before drinking from the Coke. Why wasn't there bread here? What kind of restaurant didn't bring bread?

"I'm not sure I understand," he said.

She smiled self-consciously. "Of course not, I'm sorry. What, exactly, was your experience of that enhancement?"

"The blue pill? Not much. I took it, and suddenly my

cup was on the floor." Instant coffee, heavily sweetened and creamed. Bleah. Maybe he'd get a cup of the real thing after eating. Probably he would, yes.

"Your experiences of any particular moment form an electrochemical signature," she said, "which can be captured almost like a photograph can be captured."

"Okay."

His salad arrived. Lifting a fork, he stabbed a crisp leaf and raised it, dripping, to his lips. Eh. The dressing a bit sour, a bit salty for some reason. Adequate, but far from optimal.

"Memories from that point forward," Alice went on when the waiter had gone, "can be tagged. When the decay point arrives, the tags are deleted, along with all associated memory, and the original snapshot is restored. The world is full of amnesia narcotics, but usually they just interrupt the memory process on a continuous basis, which leads to confusion and erratic behavior. The subject can't remember things from one moment to the next, and while subjective chronology is disrupted as a result, there's still generally some sense of time having passed. And of course there are side effects like euphoria and suggestibility that distort the personality further.

"What I'm after is more like the 'Skip' button on a CD player, simply jumping ahead to a point in the future without any delay or confusion. The perfect cure for impatience! You say that *was* your experience?"

Around a mouthful of cress: "I guess so. Why 'Finals Week,' though?"

She shrugged. "Just a thought. I always hated times like that in school, all the work and the stress, and I don't know what I'd have paid for the chance to skip over it all. And colleges are a lucrative market."

He paused, stopped eating for a moment. "How much time did I lose this afternoon?"

"About an hour."

"An hour? God. And I was conscious during that time? What was I doing? In the kitchen the whole time?"

"Well, most of it," she said, coloring slightly in the candlelight.

"But aware? Talking? Behaving normally?"

"Well, yes. I mean, within my ability to judge."

"Your invention is useless, then."

She blinked, her face drawing down. Not liking that. "Useless how?"

"Think about it," he said. "You take the pill, maybe wash it down with a nice woodruff-tinctured May wine. Sit back, wait for your exam or whatever it is to be over. But it isn't over. You're still there, living through it, and you say to yourself, 'What a gyp! What a robbery! I'm the unlucky one!' "

"Unlucky?" She was shaking her head, not quite grasping his point.

"Unlucky," he repeated. "For practical purposes, you've been split into two people: one who takes the final exam, and one who doesn't. And if you're still sitting there right after you take the pill, if you haven't skipped ahead, then you're the one who's stuck with the exam you were trying to avoid! And, you take another sip of your wine, savoring, mulling it over the tongue a bit, and contemplate the fact that for your trouble, for sitting down and taking the test like a good little girl, you get killed. Erased! And the other you, the lazy bitch who stuck you with the chores, skips off with the credit! Think about it: you take the pill, and suddenly you're saying 'Oh, my God, I'm the one that gets erased!' "

He leaned closer, wiping a smudge of buttermilk dressing off his chin. "If somebody did that to me, I'd want to get back at them. Not take the exam at all, for starters. Maybe go off and have a little party, too, with the credit cards. Buy a decent meal, smoke a cherrywood pipe, then sit around drinking French roast until the ax falls. That's what I'd do."

"But that's ridiculous," Alice protested, partly amused and partly, he thought, irate that a putative employee should criticize her this way. "It's *you* who gave you the enhancement. You'd only be hurting yourself."

"I'd be hurting the bastard that killed me."

"Nobody killed you. You'd wake up with a little hole in your memory and a whole lot of consequences to pay."

"No, *he'd* have the consequences to pay. I'd just be a temporary storage file spooled off by his brain and then deleted. If identity is the continuity of memory, and if my memories will never reach him, then I'm not a part of him, and he has no right to command or abuse me. No more than a twin brother has."

"But there's only one of you," she said, as if correcting an obvious error. "One body, one brain, and in the end, one memory."

"In the end, yes. After the temporary is gone. Imagine that it's a physical copy, rather than a . . . mental ghost, if you will. Imagine that you've taken a *Star Trek* transporter beam and made a perfect duplicate of yourself. She has all your thoughts and memories, she's exactly like you in every way, except that she's programmed to turn to dust at the end of twelve hours. And you expect her to spend those twelve hours doing chores for you and then peacefully going off to die. How do you feel about the morality of that?"

"That would be wrong, obviously, but it's not the same thing."

"How would you feel if you *were* the duplicate? Would you do the chores?"

"Of course not. But it's not the same thing. Drugs don't create copies of you. At worst, they delete small pieces of the original. That's all."

"If I'm the piece that's going to be deleted, how is that different? In what way is that better for me?"

The waiter reappeared, setting a basket of dinner rolls down on the table. "Everything all right?" he asked, eyeing the two of them uncertainly.

"Fine," Jeremy told him. "Is there butter for these?"

"On your left, sir."

"Ah. Great."

Alice unfurled a hand partway, subtly inviting the waiter to remain a moment longer. "Garçon," she said, "if you'd ingested a drug which, in twelve hours' time, would erase your memory of those twelve hours, would you behave irresponsibly?"

The man twitched under her gaze, caught between the conflicting goals of pleasing the customer and remaining, as was his job, invisible. "Er," he replied, "well, no."

"If you had chores to do, would you do them?"

"Of course."

"Would you view yourself as any sort of temporary creature, doomed to die when the drug wore off?"

Uncertainty in his manner; would this conversation affect his tip? Would his supervisors approve if they overheard? "I . . . don't think so, Miss. Should I?"

"No, of course not. Thank you."

"Will there be anything else?"

"No. Thanks."

"Thank you," he corrected, and slipped politely, if gratefully, back into the shadows.

"You see?" Alice said, turning, her smile vaguely triumphant.

Jeremy, tucking away the last of a bitter, sandy-tasting roll, snorted. After a rigorous proof like that, what was there to say? Alice wasn't so much a scientist, he realized, as an elaborate sort of dope pusher. He wondered about her training—what sort of school had she gone to, exactly?

A muffled voice drifted over from a nearby table, its owner unseen: "I'm with you, buddy. Nobody sets me up, deletes me, and then gets away with it, even if it's *me* that does it. I'd maybe take that drug for something really bad, if I had to shoot my dog or something, but never for an exam. Now will you please lower your voices?"

Alice sighed and said, more quietly, "It takes all kinds, I suppose. This is useful information: people who think the way you do would never be interested. I doubt the percentage is all that high, though."

"Have you ever taken it yourself?" he asked.

She shook her head.

"Might think differently if you did. Take the pill, find you haven't skipped yet, find out you *are* the skip . . ."

There was nothing, it seemed, to say to that, and anyway the waiter returned a minute later with their food.

"The kitchen staff would all take the exam, Miss," he said, a bit tentatively, as he moved the plates from tray to table. "I asked them for you."

"Really." Alice's eyes glittered at him. "That was very thoughtful."

"They also said, ah, that they wouldn't take the drug, Miss. Not for that. Maybe for something more . . . dreadful."

"Really."

Oops. The waiter clearly knew right away that he'd overstepped himself, that he'd brought displeasure to the table.

"I . . . may have asked the question wrong," he said. "Do enjoy your meals."

He took his tray and departed.

The aromas of the food drove all else from Jeremy's mind. He set to it with conviction, recoiled, set to it again.

"How is it?" Alice asked distantly, watching him eat but now only partly interested.

"The snails?" he grunted, making faces. "Like shit. Literally. Bird droppings in their food supply. The trout's not much better; he's overcooked the skin, undercooked the meat, and the nonstick coating must be wearing out in the bottom of his pan, because he's used that spray stuff on it. I can taste it from three feet away."

She flipped her hair and smiled at him peculiarly, the way a lover might, after a quarrel that had petered out unsatisfactorily. "Hyperacuity," she said, popping a spoonful of cassoulet into her mouth. "I'll remember to reduce the dosage a bit next time."

Back at Alice's house, back in what passed, more or less, for his right mind, Jeremy refused a third pill. "You said two," he explained carefully. "I'm entitled to another check. The big one, as we agreed."

"As we agreed," she said grumpily, taking up her checkbook and scribbling. "You can't tell me it's been such a horrific experience, though."

He held his hands up. "I never said it was. But I can really use this money, as I think you're aware, and I'm not interested in dancing for it any more than I have to. I've house payments to make. Why, what is it? The pill, I mean."

"Finals Week again," she said hopefully. "I thought I'd go for a longer gap this time."

"Ah, no," he said, emphatically but with, he thought, reasonably good humor. "I thought we went over that. I'd never have taken it the first time if I'd known what it was. I mean, really, you couldn't pay me enough."

A sly smile slid onto her face, clicking firmly into place. "You're still here, Jeremy. We're still talking. You are willing to be persuaded. You're *asking* to be persuaded."

"I'm not," he said.

"You are," she insisted, stepping forward. "You haven't

walked out or told me to bugger off yet. You still want something. But it isn't money—we've already solved that problem. So what other problem is there, that you'd like me to solve for you?"

She cocked a hip suggestively.

"No," he said. "Good-bye, Alice."

"Just a Sunday," she said. "An empty, do-nothing day. Your . . . duplicate . . . won't be stuck with some unpleasant chore, he'll be making love with me, all day long."

"And forgetting about it afterward? No thanks."

"I didn't say he'd be the only one," she said, her voice more confident now. "You get your share as well. Effective immediately."

Her hands moved to the closures of the jumper and pulled them apart, revealing white brassiere lace underneath. She found a hook and parted that as well. Her breasts, pushed together by taut fabric, seemed to reach for him, pink nipples looking out like blind, soft eyes.

He could have resisted, he would later think. He could have walked away. He was not, after all, some mindless rutting animal. But his eyes and hands and loins were hungry for her, and who was he, really, to refuse them?

Afterward she gave him a pill. Garlic, vertigo, then nothing. Every sensation perfectly normal. Was this, he thought, feasting his eyes on her unclothed-at-last body, what fate felt like? Going through the motions of life, seeking small pleasures where he could but knowing full well that his continuity, his chain of memory, his *life,* would end in less than a day?

He thought about hopping up, grabbing his credit card, running out and spending it to the limit. Punishing himself, his other self, for this slow execution. But what purpose would that serve? In what way would that improve his final hours? Better to stay here and rut.

He looked at her, face now peaceful in repose. She'd played him well, got just what she wanted out of him. Bought him off with beads and trinkets, cast a spell, something. The hell of it was, he was still glad he'd met her, still glad to be in her arms now. He would slay dragons for her, he realized. Battle armies, fulfill quests. How tragic for him.

"How are you?" she asked, watching him watch her.

"Brilliant," he muttered. "Everything is going just brilliantly."

"And are you still you?" A slight smile accompanied the question.

"I feel like me, yes, obviously," he said, piecing the words together slowly, trying to place in her mind the very obvious ideas looming in his. "But when this thing wears off, what I'm feeling now won't matter. At present, I'm the me that doesn't get to continue."

"And the . . . other you? The original, who you think you're a copy or a fragment of?"

Jeremy shrugged. "He's done me an injustice, yes. All right; if you prefer, I've done myself an injustice, but either way, the experience of this conversation will not be integrated into the person we both call Jeremy Hobb. So I fail to see how I, the person having the conversation, can be the same person he is. No matter how similar we are, no matter that we share the same body. Mathematically speaking, we're separate entities."

"Love," she chided, "you've got a split personality."

"I suppose I have, yes. Temporarily."

"Need something to take your mind off it?"

"Hmm."

"Wondering what my lips can accomplish that the rest of me hasn't?"

"Hmm. Maybe." She moved. "Probably." Moved again. He sighed. "Almost certainly, yes."

He spent the night with her, only belatedly realizing he'd forgotten to call the pub and quit. Bad form; they'd be angry, withhold his pay. Well, let them.

In the morning she made him breakfast, made him a man several times, made him lunch. They listened to music through a lazy afternoon, and then finally ordered delivery of a Chinese dinner.

"Shouldn't I be forgetting about now?" he asked, finally, over moo goo gai pan growing cold in its container.

"I'd've thought so," she agreed. "Well before now. I'd like to take some measurements, if it's all right."

He sighed. "I've denied you nothing else, Alice. By all means, have your way."

She either missed or—more likely—chose to ignore the

irony in his tone. A cap was fitted over his head, connected
by wires to a thing like a computer. Blood and urine samples were collected. Colored lights were shined, one by one,
into his eyes.

"That should be enough," she said finally. "I'll run some
simulations, see if I can figure out what's happened. There's
nothing much for you to do but go home and wait."

"Just like that?" he asked.

"Like what?"

"Kicking me out, sending me home. Already?"

She clucked, reproachful. "What did you think, love, that
you could just move in? I didn't say I wouldn't call."

After I'm erased, he thought, and flashed her a grimace.
"No, of course. You need your results."

"Partly," she said, "yes. But not entirely. I think you
know I'm a bit sweet on you. Come on, it's probably safer
if I drive you home."

Home. *His* home, standing on his own little piece of the
planet. That for which he had sacrificed . . . what? Not the
continuity of his life—that was sold even cheaper. It was
hard to believe, he reflected, just how much damage the
right woman could do. Better to have loved and lost your
mind, then never to have lost your mind at all?

Well, no sense crying about it now. One trick he'd always
been proud of was the ability to put himself to sleep, no
matter what. He invoked that magic now, grimly determined, fully expecting not to wake up as himself.

But he did.

Morning stimulants, shower, breakfast, a quick peek at
the newspaper, and then it was time for work. Work! Financial fractanalysis! The idea struck him as more than a
little absurd: spending eight hours crunching numbers in a
windowless cubicle, and him a dead man at any moment.
A man who, at any moment, would have a doppelgänger
beamed into his body straight from Saturday evening.
Straight from Alice Frane's bed. What a shock.

God, what *had* he been thinking? Should he stay home? Call
in sick? Anxious, wanting answers, he called Alice instead.

"Found anything?" he asked her, in the most offhand
tone he could muster.

"Maybe," she said guardedly, sounding not quite prepared to be speaking with him. "I . . . hope not. Are you home? Can I come over?"

"Um . . . Well, yes. Why, though?"

"We need to talk."

Oh. Need-to-talk news was never good. Why go to all the trouble of having her over? Telephones were perfect in that you could hang up whenever you'd heard enough. Which mightn't be long at all.

"Just tell me now," he said, the words like ash in his mouth.

"I may . . ." she began, then stalled.

"Go on."

"I need to know something about you. Whether you believe in an afterlife."

He tried a laugh. "That's not a very encouraging question, Alice."

"Do you?"

"Believe in heaven? No."

"Then you're in trouble. I may have miscalculated the gap. I mean, obviously I miscalculated, but . . . I'd assumed a more or less linear growth of decay time as a function of dosage, but it looks like it might actually be exponential. Meaning we're talking about a much longer latent period than what we thought."

Icy waves broke over him, chilled him, numbed him. "How much longer?"

"A lot."

Pounding his fist on the table, "Dammit, Alice, how much longer?"

"Three hundred years," she said.

Three. Hundred. Years. A nervous giggle escaped him. "What? Am I supposed to be worried? Three hundred years from now, secure in my grave, I'll forget everything?"

"Jeremy," she said, "there's more. Listen to me: The erasure can occur prematurely if the decay process is short-circuited."

"By?"

"By certain . . . irreversible chemical reactions in the brain. Reactions which occur during, um, death."

"Ah." A kind of calm settled over him.

"I can make this up to you, Jeremy, I really can."

"Really," he said. "Kiss cock until you're blue in the face, is that it? Buy me off with sex and dinners?"

A pause. "Something like that."

He felt his forehead: clammy, wet. Whence this fear?
What had he lost? Alice's question was very perceptive; if
he believed in heaven, he lost nothing. A moment's forget-
fulness, and then paradise. But the atheist's heaven, nothing
more than the realization of death, a quick moment to com-
pose one's thoughts, to assess one's memories . . . That
moment, that final reconciliation, would never come.

"I didn't have to tell you this," Alice said when his silence had gone on too long. "If I didn't care what happened
to you, I could have just said everything was fine. Didn't
work, okay, you won't be forgetting. You'd never have
known to complain. Not until . . ."

"No, not until."

"I didn't have to tell you," she repeated.

"True," he said, conceding the point. "Your candor is
appreciated. Really."

"I don't think there's anything legally actionable here,"
she added quickly. "Even if you could prove it, what would
you be proving? Your life won't be shortened one second,
and when the end comes, it'll be like dying in your sleep,
never knowing anything had happened."

"No," he said coldly, "it won't be like that at all."

And then, suddenly, the proverbial lighthouse beam
winked on over his head, and he saw what it would be like.
He began to laugh.

"Jeremy? Jeremy, are you all right?"

"I'm fine," he said, meaning it. "And you know what? I
think you *should* come over. If you've a guilty conscience
to assuage, who am I to leave you suffering?"

Her breath, huffing softly in the telephone mouthpiece,
filled him with images; her mouth on him, his mouth on
her, the involuntary grunt of her voice as they lay twined
together, spinning out wave after wave of pleasure. But
these sounds were different: the huffing of an animal, suddenly afraid, suddenly realizing it might be in danger. Preparing its fight or flight.

"If you work with me," she said carefully, "there's every
chance we can find a solution. Induce you early."

Induce him early? What a laugh! Kill him early, she
might as well say. If he—if the fragile memories that com-

prised him—had to be erased, why should it be one second, one instant earlier than necessary?

"I'm not angry," he said gently. "You're right, it's really not so bad. Not for me."

And she must have caught his meaning then, because the exhalation of her breathing slid aside into uneasy laughter. Not *him* who would suffer, no, but that other, very familiar person who had sold him out for a roll in the hay. For *that* Jeremy Hobb it would be a warm cuddle, the popping of a pill, and then . . . what, the smell of garlic and then straight into the arms of the reaper? The thought was terrifying: to skip not a day, not a week, but every future moment except the last! What worse fate was there than to become, all at once, an old man gasping on his deathbed, all the intervening hours and days and years forgotten? With that moment of reckoning there, the awful realization that he'd traded himself away, the realization that life had burned away in an instant, that there would be no more?

But for *this* version, for the temporary person now inhabiting this flesh, there was nothing but an indefinite postponement of the erasure he dreaded, an opportunity to steal back the future he otherwise lacked. And what was so dreadful about that?

"Forget it, Alice," Jeremy Hobb said, laughing harder, the river of his joy slopping up over its banks to threaten the entire landscape. "You've cured my split personality. And you know? It serves the son of a bitch right."

And that, dear friends, was what killed him.

EROS AND AGAPE AMONG THE ASTEROIDS

by Scott Edelman

Scott Edelman has been the Editor-in-Chief of *Science Fiction Weekly* (www.scifi.com/sfw/), the Internet magazine of news, reviews, and interviews, since October 2000. Prior to this, he was the creator and editor of the award-winning *Science Fiction Age* magazine from 1991 to 2000. He was also the editor of *Sci-Fi Entertainment*, the official magazine of the Sci-Fi Channel, for four years, and has also edited other SF media magazines such as *Sci-Fi Universe* and *Sci-Fi Flix*. He was the founding editor of *Rampage*, a magazine devoted to covering the field of professional wrestling, and for a time edited *Satellite Orbit*, the leading entertainment guide for C-band satellite owners. He has been a Hugo Award finalist for Best Editor on four occasions. His short fiction has appeared in *The Mammoth Book of Awesome Comic Fantasy*, *Moon Shots*, *Mars Probes*, *Treachery and Treason*, *MetaHorror*, *Tales of the Wandering Jew*, and others. Upcoming appearances include stories in *Crossroads: Southern Stories of the Fantastic* and *Absolute Magnitude*.

For as long as there have been storytellers, there have been those who have tried to define that most elusive of emotions, love. Here, Scott Edelman gives us a far future take on it like no other.

L ATE one night, Expeditor First Class Meryl, who could dance across the asteroids as effortlessly as dirt-bound men skipped from one paving stone to the next, paid what he feared could very well be one final visit to the Belt Boss. All was silent on the asteroid of governance, a place that out of hope and memory they had learned to call Earth. All seemed to be asleep save the dying bureaucrat—none could divine the cause of this sudden onset of illness, and none could contemplate a cure—and the messenger who came to comfort her.

The Belt Boss lifted her white eyebrows when Expeditor First Class Meryl entered her chambers. A smile, quivering and slow, crept across her features, but then, all of the Belt Boss' movements were now quivering and slow. Thousands of colored lights on the walls, blinking like stars seen through an atmosphere, told them that all went well around the Belt this night. And all was going well, except for the fact that Expeditor First Class Meryl had to visit the Belt Boss in such a state, with death fast approaching.

Meryl had noticed that with each passing week, the Belt Boss needed less sleep, as if she was shrugging off one deathlike state for another, and he felt that he should help fill those haunted hours. She had lost the power to find rest in dreams. Others knew that, Meryl would swear it, and yet only he came to her side to fill her nights with something other than loneliness and regret. Though Meryl knew that loneliness could not be numbered, its agonies immune to measurement, these sad, final hours had taught him one thing: There was no one more alone than a dying Belt Boss.

"So you come to me still," she said. Beneath the annoyed tone there was both pride and pleasure. "Why do you bother? The others probably think you more of a fool than they think me."

"You know why I come. I come because I cannot find it in myself not to come."

"That is your nature. And that is good. Would that the others felt so. Exeter weaves a dance of death about me, and instead of coming to pay his final respects to a dead woman, he plants spies, taps the comm links, and spends his days and nights testing the weather of politics. Are you sure you do not feel yourself to be wasting your time here, Meryl?"

"I do not."

And so they talked, as they'd done each night for weeks, of the things that concerned them. They talked of the bal-

ance of a life lived on such a tiny ecosystem, and how
wearying it could become, but also how beautiful. They
talked of Earth, not this one that had been carved from
airless stone, but the one neither would likely see again.
They talked—yet again—of the miracle that allowed him
to be the first to stumble on the ancient alien artifact that
bound itself to him with its technology that made him capable of doing what he did, with the Belt Boss insisting that
his find was destiny, and Meryl equally as insistent that it
was only luck, and pure dumb luck at that. They talked of
how they missed true days and nights, rather than those
that space had forced them to invent, and how glad they
were that they at least existed somewhere, and how lifetimes had their days and nights as well—a topic that
seemed to give the Belt Boss no trouble, but which Meryl
felt most uncomfortable discussing.

And as all conversations tend, when the participants are
giddy with talk and lack of sleep and waking dreams, they
talked of love.

The Belt Boss sighed. Her lips moved as if she was chew-
ing something bitter, and trying to decide whether she
would swallow it to save face or spit it out as she really
wished. She looked away from the Expeditor First Class,
and cocked her head, and when she spoke, it was with an
unapologetic suddenness.

"I have told this to none save my own soul, Meryl," said
the Belt Boss. "And even there I have had trouble speaking
the truth. At four-score years and two, with most of those
days spent in the confines of this room, I still do not know
the meaning of love. No, no—do not be embarrassed by
this revelation, Meryl. I have done nothing, or rather, been
guilty by inaction of anything of which to be ashamed. A
Belt Boss must think more of ruling than of love. The years
pass by, years of the Belt always coming before herself,
and though she allows herself to know something of men,
she allows herself to know naught of love."

Meryl cleared his throat, suddenly finding it difficult to
speak. He knew her far too well. Managing the tens of
thousands who lived and died on these hurtling rocks, ruling a country that consisted not of landmass but of a ragged
necklace of beads hung about the neck of an uninhabitable
world below, these things left little time for friendship. Keep-

ing the oxygen farms pollinating, the space grooves unimpeded, the nuclear chords vibrating, took a level of dedication that left time for little else. And that required level of obsession with the job ill-served her as the end neared. People who looked at the Belt Boss never saw the person behind the authority, but only the power of the position, and when the promise of future favors faded, supplicants stopped visiting, and the comm stopped chirping. But she was not alone in her loneliness.

"Belt Bosses are not the only ones afflicted so," he finally said.

"As I thought."

The room fell silent once more as the two eyed each other, and Meryl grew anxious in that silence. He nodded and requested permission to leave.

"Not yet," said the Belt Boss. "Stay with me but a little while longer."

The Belt Boss had always needed him. Hers was the brain that kept civilized the community that had over the centuries sprung up circling the unforgiving planet below; his were the eyes and ears that helped her do so. But this need seemed different.

Expeditor First Class Meryl tried to banish the choking quiet with more conversation, but to each subject he introduced, the Belt Boss would give no response, and would simply lie back, propped up by pillows, watching Meryl squirm in his seat. Meryl finally abandoned his attempts, as the Belt Boss evidently wanted to have no more discourse on the algae fields, or the plasma conduits, or the difficulty of carving out new asteroid caverns at a rate to keep pace with their growing population, and the chambers were silent once more.

"I would like to send you on a quest," the Belt Boss said abruptly, ending the silence with a thought Meryl recognized as having been beneath the surface during all their verbal parrying. "You know that the Physician Master Class has told me that I have but a short time to live, and what my senses tell me of myself agree with what I have been told. I am soon to exit this world, but before I go, I must unravel one last puzzle. I must know what love is like. I have experienced all but this. Meryl, I can travel no longer, and I want you to be my eyes and ears on this, as you have been my eyes and ears on so much else. I need you to journey to each Master around the Belt and ask all of these wise men and women what they know of love, and then come back and share with me your findings before I die. Will you do this for me, Meryl?"

"You know I will," said Expeditor First Class Meryl, stunned. This talk of love! Death was hard enough to stomach, but the delusion that *this* topic could know boundaries was even more difficult to bear. Still, Expeditor First Class Meryl knew without a doubt what his actions would be in response to what the Belt Boss bade him do, and so his promise sprang to his lips. "Whatever you ask."

"Go now," said the Belt Boss, suddenly tired. "I will program the navigation codes so none will be able to see your travels or map your progress. Until you return, you will be invisible. And when you have discovered love, come back to me and show me where it lies."

Meryl could think of nothing more to say, and backed away from the Belt Boss, who was deep asleep before he had even left the room. When the iris was fully closed behind him, Exeter, who coveted the title of Belt Boss in a more unseemly manner than most, appeared at his side.

"The Belt Boss, she is, ah, doing well, eh?" said Exeter. Meryl did not like the thought of him lingering so close to her cavern.

"Not as well as she once was," said Meryl. "But then— who is? It is so good of you to ask after her health."

"You have been visiting her a great deal these days," said Exeter. "Far more often than the parameters of your job would require."

"She seeks my counsel during this trying time. I had not realized anyone would consider that anything worth taking note of."

"You'd be surprised at what people take notice of, Expeditor First Class," said Exeter, reaching out to touch the medallion that hung about Meryl's neck. "Be careful how you plan your days. Be careful of your loyalties. Remember—the Belt orbits about the planet below, and not around any one of us."

"I am always careful," Meryl said, and to show Exeter that he did not feel he had to be so with him, he turned and moved away to the iris of the outer lock. Exeter would not dare follow him there, knowing what Meryl was about to do. There was only so much envy that some people could stand.

Meryl smiled to see the clumsy pods arrayed within. The bulbous drones were the method of transport that everyone else on the Belt but he was forced to use. He was, yes, no matter how the Belt Boss wished to perceive it, lucky.

What if he had not been the one wrestling ore planetside when the alien device was blasted free during their mining? What if it had therefore adapted to someone else instead of him? Then Meryl would have remained a Miner all his life and never been an Expeditor, let alone an Expeditor First Class, and certainly never have met the Belt Boss. He felt overwhelmed with gratitude, as he always was the moment before activation.

He thumbed the medallion that hung at his neck, and the air shimmered about him. A field, microns thick, suddenly separated him from the stagnant, metallic air of the lock. He signaled the puter to open the lock door.

Nothing ahead of him but free space, he ran past the docking bay. Protected by a subatomic film he did not understand, he leaped toward the frigid wasteland of sky. Sometimes, as he built momentum, it was as if the stars wanted him, and he often found it difficult to hold back from launching himself out of the well of gravity coursing from the planet below. But he never made that greatest leap of all, never did more than merely think of it, because doing this one thing exceedingly well had made him invaluable to the Belt Boss, and that made him happy. His bound took him the several thousand kilometers to the next asteroid in an instant, as if he had folded time and space. He did not know how he did it, only that he could. The alien technologies had only been able to give him so much.

This first rock up from Earth was barren—none were allowed to live so close to the center of it all—and so he skipped farther up the line. The Belt Boss wanted answers from the Masters, and so Meryl hopped from rock to rock until he approached the asteroid of the Astronomer Master Class.

He came to rest lightly near an igloo of rough stone. He was tempted to rap his knuckles against the wall, but with one such as the Astronomer Master Class, Meryl knew that was not necessary. The vibrations of Meryl's approach alone were enough to upset the man's instruments and send him scurrying to investigate.

After a moment, Meryl sensed through the soles of his boots a vibration not of his own making. The entire dome lifted slowly open as if attached to the ground by a hinge. A small, circular window, flush with the asteroid surface, was revealed underneath. Meryl could see the Astronomer distorted through the glass, a wizened old man with skin like that of an asteroid's surface.

"Who is that who's come so far to bother me?" he transmitted, blinking in the starlight. "It's almost time for me to begin my watch. I've no time for visitors, not now, not when there's so much to be done. Who's that out there?"

Meryl took a step nearer the window, and the Astronomer squinted as if just beginning to see him.

"It's Expeditor First Class Meryl, on a mission for the Belt Boss. Don't you recognize me? Who else do you know who can pay a visit to you on foot?"

"On foot or in a pod, an interruption is still an interruption. Not even the Belt Boss can stop the motion of the stars. If we must talk now, come in quickly. We'll have but a short time for conversation before the Belt brings us to the proper slice of sky for the stars. We'll converse as I prepare. But afterward, only silence, for watching the stars is a holy act."

The dome slammed down around Meryl, and he could hear the rhythmic cycling of the air pumps. In another moment, the window at his feet slid back. He climbed down a ladder into the darkness, and when his feet touched a rough floor, he staggered for a moment, bumping against something hard and cool.

"Do not move!" shouted the Astronomer Master Class from somewhere in the darkness, now a warm voice rather than just a digitized transmission. "Let your eyes adjust before you take a step. The instruments of man are not the only tools which must be prepared for the watching of the stars. There are also the instruments of God. Let your eyes be welcomed by the dark."

Soon Meryl could see, though not as well as he had seen outside. Though he imagined that perhaps the Astronomer Master Class suffered no distress, from years of living here.

Meryl watched as the man scurried quickly about the huge circular room, checking mathematical calculations that floated before him as if on invisible sheets, and fiddling with dials that adjusted minutely the direction in which the huge telescopic instruments that filled the room pointed. Then it was back to the calculations again, on and on, back and forth, without stop. The Astronomer Master Class noted Meryl's gaze following him about the room.

"So you can see already. You have better eyes than most. So tell me what the Belt Boss desires." The Astronomer Master Class did not cease in his actions as he talked, nor as he waited for Meryl's reply, continuing his preparations.

"The Belt Boss desires to know of love," said Meryl, feeling foolish even as he broached the subject. "She wants your opinion on the matter. She has sent me out to speak with all of the Masters. You are the first."

The expression of the Astronomer Master Class was unreadable in the dim light.

"Love? Ask an astronomer of love? Might as well ask a soldier of peace. I can tell you nothing about love. I have lived here most of my life, alone, watching the skies ever since I apprenticed to the last Astronomer Master Class. I can't see that I would know anything unknown by the Belt Boss."

"Let the Belt Boss decide."

The old man paused in thought, and sat.

"If you wish. Though I truly can give you no advice. Nothing I know of love is witty enough to be made into an epigram, nor wise enough for another to emblazon over his mantel to live by. So let me instead just tell you a story, and may the Belt Boss get from it what she will.

"Once there was a boy in love with a star."

Meryl nodded, hoping that this would yield the Belt Boss what she thought she needed.

"It was his star, he thought, and no one else's," continued the Astronomer. "He first saw it high above on the very first night he was allowed to step out onto an asteroid's surface alone. That it was out of reach he did not learn until he tried to caress it, jumping as high as he could, and it was not until his legs were aching from the strain and could leap no more and his skin was raw from scratching against the inside of his suit when falling and could bleed no more that he was content to sit quietly and look at it. By the time he was ready to quit attempting to embrace his star and content himself with merely gazing at it, his oxygen was running low and he had to bid farewell to his beloved star.

"In his memory it was perfect, a thing above and beyond anything he had ever known. That following day was filled with disdain, for as he compared all about him with what he had seen during the previous day's excursion, he found himself unable to contend with their inanities. His parents thought him feverish, and so called a doctor, who put him to bed. He did not mind. The world inside his asteroid held nothing for him anymore. When his parents finally fell asleep, he sneaked form his bedroom to the monitor and winked at his beloved star, and then he slipped into his suit and ran to a place where he could commune with his star without the intruding presence of humanity.

"The heavens seemed the right place for it, he thought, as perfection had no place in a flawed world. He would go to it, he decided that night, and not make it come to him. His dreams that next day, as he slept in the bed where his parents once more placed him thinking him sick, were concerned with uniting himself with his star. He dreamed of sprouting wings and flying there. He dreamed of taking one of the pods he had seen the grown-ups use to move from asteroid to asteroid and blasting himself to the roof of the universe. He had dozens of fitful dreams that day, all of them on the topic of uniting himself with his love.

"That night, as his parents retired to dreams of their own, primarily ones of fear for their son's health, their son woke and once more escaped from his room to keep his vigil. If anything, as he gazed at his star, his love was stronger. Peacefully content, he fell asleep on his back, the beauty of his star stealing any discomfort. His father found him that way the next morning. When awakened and questioned by his father, he did not want to tell him what he had been doing, until he realized that if he did not tell his father the truth his suit would be locked away and he would never see his star again. His father nodded and grunted as the boy told him how he had found a star he loved, a star that none had seen before, a star that only he would ever know. His father listened and then led him home, where a

wave of his hand brought a map alive to float before them.
A map of the stars. The boy froze as his father made it
spin, and then pointed at a pinprick that represented a star.

"His star.

"The boy shouted and screamed and ran from the room,
and collapsed, fatigued, as far from his cavern as he
could run.

"And when he next opened his eyes, he saw his star,
only it was not his star anymore. It belonged to the world.
Others now knew it. It did not seem quite so perfect anymore. He looked at it for hours, trying to find in himself
the love he'd had for it before, but he could not. He rose
and went home, leaving the star still high in the darkness
behind him.

"His parents smiled at him, knowing how boys will be,
and he smiled back at them, a smile of hate. At that instant
in his life, he decided that he would find himself another
star to love.

"Only this time, he would tell no one."

The Astronomer Master Class paused. Meryl waited,
dizzy. When next the Astronomer spoke, his voice was
thick.

"Enough of this. Come. Let's look at the stars."

The Astronomer Master Class sprang to his instruments
again, leaving Meryl to ponder what he had heard. Had he
heard truth and fact? Or was he listening to allegory? Had
there been such a boy? Was that boy the Astronomer Master Class himself? Or was it all just a lie to fulfill the Belt
Boss' request? Meryl could not sort this out, but hoped
that the Belt Boss would be able to gain something from it.

"I'm afraid that I have no time to look at the stars," said
Meryl. "The Belt Boss, she is . . ."

"I know," said the Astronomer Master Class, who let
him climb to the surface once more, where he turned his
back to the planet below, and contrary to what he had just
told the Master, did pause to look at the stars. He could
reach them, he knew it, all he had to do was point the way
and he would be taken there by an invention of aliens long
dead. He wanted desperately to make the great voyage, but
not when there was one who still needed him, not when
there was one who . . .

Meryl pushed it out of his head and then thrust himself

off the asteroid face and bounded across three barren rocks until he came to the next Master.

Inside his scooped-out cavern, the Teacher Master Class addressed an invisible audience that watched his hologram across the Belt. Meryl interrupted the man and explained the nature of his quest.

The Teacher Master Class snapped his fingers, dismissing his class, and the mathematical equations that glowed in the air around them vanished. With a sweep of his hand, he drew a large circle, three meters tall, the full height of the room. Then he delicately drew another circle beside it, so small that it was almost not a circle, but a dot.

"This," he said, pointing at the smaller circle, "is what we can know."

Then he passed his hands through the air in a great arc describing the great circle within which he stood.

"And this is what is knowable."

He put his hands behind him, and bowed his head.

"I want to tell you about one of my students," he said, lifting his head. Meryl could see that the man's eyes were moist. "I want to tell you about my *best* student. Or who I supposed at the time was my best student."

Meryl sensed from the tone of his tale that this was not the first time he'd shared it. This was a ritual that the Teacher Master Class had gone through many, many times before.

"My student was in love with learning. I mean this not in the way a scholar is in love with learning for the love of manipulating facts in search of the truth. Nor the way a student will revel in learning in search of high grades. No, the boy loved learning for itself, loved the very process of learning. A literal thrill would course through his body each time he soaked up something new. He loved to learn and could not live without it.

"His parents were poor, unable to afford schooling in those days before the holosystem finally made it inexpensive for all. They begged me to accept him. I asked to see him alone before I made my decision. His parents waited outside this very room while I spoke to the boy in here.

"The lad told me that he was thirteen years old, but he certainly did not look it. He was thin, with long, scraggly hair over a prominent forehead, and if I'd had to guess his age I would have thought him a tall eleven. I asked him a few questions about the basics of mathematics, but he knew nothing. He could not read. I asked him what he thought made him suitable to join my class. He blushed and turned away when I asked him this question.

" 'Come, you must tell me,' I said.

"He looked back at me, smiling.

" 'I just enjoy to learn,' he said. 'That's all. Ask my parents.'

" 'You just enjoy *learning*,' I'd said, correcting him, and when I told him so, a slight shiver passed through his body, and he thanked me.

"I spoke to his parents. It turned out that he was quite a helpful lad in their Belt-scavenging business. They only had to show him something once for him to know it forever. I was surprised that they would part with such a valuable helper, if indeed he could do all they said he could, but they both wanted what was best for their son. He was their hope. Pity.

"I agreed to take him. I was dubious at first because of what little he knew in the academic way before coming to me. But he picked up the basics quickly and I could see that he was an incredibly fast learner.

"After his first month in my class, I began to notice a strange change coming over him. It appeared to me as if his forehead had grown. I did not know to what to ascribe it, and so I ascribed it to an illusion. I thought perhaps it was the result of cutting his hair short in the style of the rest of the boys that had made his head seem so much larger. But I was wrong. It was, impossibly, the knowledge up there that had made his head so big. Whereas with the other boys the nanobots merely aided in their retention of knowledge, with this one, something quite different had happened. With this one, the nanobots were responding to build him a better brain commensurate with all he had learned.

"By the middle of his first term, I noticed that his head had grown to the size of a watermelon, and he had to carry it about in his hands, as his neck could not support it all alone. He had to duck to fit inside his transport pod. His parents never complained, for they believed it was best for him. They believed that he would have what they had not;

he might even become Belt Boss someday. He stayed after school to get extra assignments from me, he hungered for knowledge so, but still I did not see where it would lead. I was a blind scholar. I appreciated his enthusiasm, and aided in every way I could his thirst for knowledge.

"As we studied the maps and he ingested the new worlds the explorers of the Belt had discovered, his head grew to larger proportions. As I got deeper into the mysteries of the Earth we have all agreed to leave behind, his head became like a perfect sphere that threatened to rival the moons. And when we discussed the history of our new kingdom, it was as if within the brain he had hidden history entire.

"The nanobots continued to replicate, continued to build him greater storage capacity until he could no longer fit his head through my door. He would sit outside during class, watching me through the viewports. And the more he learned from me, the larger still his head grew.

"Eventually, he came to me with complaints. His head ached all the time. I advised him to take his studies more slowly, that he had forever in which to learn.

" 'Forever is not long enough to learn it all,' he said to me, sighing.

"His headaches grew worse, and I fear that I was not wise enough to do what I had to do. I could not bear to bar him from my class, for he was the best of my many students. His presence there came to be the only thing that made teaching worthwhile.

"One day, class began without him, and I was in the middle of lecturing on the War of the Inner Belt when the boy's father landed outside the classroom.

" 'Teacher, you must come quickly,' he demanded. 'My son is dying.'

"I dismissed the class, and rushed to the scavenger's asteroid. He warned me to be in control of my emotions, and then led me to his cavern. I was shocked by what I saw there. The boy's head had grown to fill almost the entire room, from wall to wall, from floor to ceiling. Sticking out from under his gigantic head were spindly pairs of arms and legs, as if in his growth his head had swallowed all the rest of his body. He opened the tent-sail lids of his eyes and I could hear the whirring of the nanos as he peered at us. He greeted me, and I begged to know what had happened. He gestured then with one of his withered hands at a stack of disks close by the entrance.

"I recognized the disks at once. They were the school's master encyclopedia containing all recorded wisdom. The lad confessed that, growing impatient with the rate at which he was acquiring knowledge, he had borrowed the set and hidden it in his pod (having first talked one of the other boys into doing the actual physical work of pilfering it from my library, since he himself could no longer enter it). Arriving home from school the previous day, he proceeded to spend the entire evening reading it as it flickered by on his puter, until he swooned from the pain. He did not wake until I found him there.

"He had lost consciousness, he told me, halfway through the final disk, and because his own head now blocked the screen from him, he wanted me to read it to him. I refused. Any more knowledge and the boy would surely die. I realized that then.

" 'What will we do with you, what will we do?' I said, shaking my head and leaving for the docking bay. I tried to think of a way to save my student. While my mind roamed, looking for a solution to his problem, I felt a tremendous explosion, and rushed back to the family living area.

"It was as I feared. Inside the cavern, there was only blood and splintered circuits. The mother, who had been coming after me at the time of the explosion, told me what had happened. When I had left, refusing the boy's request to aid him in what I knew would be his death, the boy pleaded with his father, and his father gave in. Even though he knew the boy would die, he wanted him to die happily.

"I sometimes picture that man, squeezed in beside his son, slowly picking out the words from the screen as best as he could, not getting any sense out of the syllables himself as he tried to please his son. He knew his son was dying, but did he know that he would go in quite that way? I must admit that I had no such clue. Did the father know that he would be taken with his son? Sometimes I wonder. Sacrificing that way, there was real love."

The Teacher Master Class composed himself. Meryl slipped away and left the Teacher Master Class to resume his holoclass. Meryl should have been teary-eyed from the Teacher's story, but he felt strangely distant. Would all the Masters speak to him in veiled riddles, offering him metaphors as their messages? He'd expected to hear of more personal matters, rather than fables about others.

But that's the way it proved to be for most of his journey skipping from asteroid to asteroid, talking with the other Masters of the Belt. The Mathematician Master Class had no private passions to share, but instead told a tale of how numbers could not help but breed, which is what led them to stretch toward infinity. The Explorer Master Class gave no hint of unrequited love, but talked only of his own love for the unknown. The Writer Master Class explained how the letter u so loved the letter q that it tried to follow it everywhere. It wasn't until he reached the habitat of the Xenobiologist Master Class, a most unlikely Master from which to learn of humanity, that Meryl first heard what he considered to be matters of consequence.

The asteroid of the Xenobiologist Master Class was on the far side of the planet from Earth. Meryl was astonished to realize that he had already danced halfway around a world, and he wondered what it would be like to keep on going farther and farther away from the center of his universe, but he could not bear to leave the Belt Boss behind with her quest unfulfilled. A cylindrical room rode them through the asteroid like an elevator, until they were at its heart.

"I'm sorry that my wife won't be able to join us," said the Xenobiologist Master Class, once they were alone together, and Meryl had explained his mission.

"Love," said the Xenobiologist Master Class softly. "I'm still trying to figure that one out for myself, you know. In my numberless years out among the stars, I have met thirty-one different sorts of aliens. There have been sixteen humanoids, ten animallike creatures who exhibit human intelligence, three machine races who were programmed for intelligence aeons past and who have since achieved full sentience, and two races who have no forms at all, but are alive in free-floating intelligences. And all of them—*all* of them—are as confused by the concept of love as we are."

"I don't think that's the sort of answer I should bring back to the Belt Boss."

"No, I suppose not. Then let me tell you, as truthfully as I am able, about one man, and one, well, one woman."

At last, thought Meryl. *At last we come to reality.*

"He was a trader in artifacts, exploring out among the distant stars. As a result, he had cause to travel the galaxy far beyond the limits accepted by the rest of our race. So he was able to see the effects of love in others than just those like ourselves. He confronted species with customs far different than our own. Why, in one, the aggressor actually served up part of his own body to the pursued for sustenance, in order to prove the seriousness of his intent. In another, two actually meld their intelligences into one.

"The methods differed, but the madness always remained the same.

"Our trader was a single man, and the stars did not give him many opportunities to change this station. He rarely saw another of his own race. And then, on a distant planetoid not one of his species had ever visited, he unexpectedly met an alien who was also far from her own home planet. She as also about as far from his idealized dream lover, the one perfect thing he had sought in an imperfect world, as was possible. Her form was inhuman, with eight snaking protuberances that acted as the arms and legs of her short, squat body; her skin was rough like rock, with growths that blossomed and then fell off at a touch. But her soul, ah, her soul was all too human.

"And though he never thought the act would occur to him, he fell in love. He was as overwhelmed by his emotions as a schoolboy. The strength of that ardor was amazing to him, and with that strength he won her over. She told him, or rather, signed to him, because what they had existed beyond translation, that she had never known such love, never been the target of such a passion.

"Bound by love, they traveled the galaxy together and alone, far from civilization, and there was no impediment to this affliction of the heart until on their travels they needed to return to the Centrum to restock supplies and sell their wares. And there, at last in contact with others, all whom they met flung themselves at the feet of the trader's beloved—not that they could really be called feet—declaring an undying love, just as the trader himself had done. The species of the enthralled did not matter. Neither did the gender. At first, our lovers tried to deny it, but as the numbers of the afflicted grew, they had to admit to themselves one horrible fact.

"They realized that these men, these women, these other aliens, could not help it. Because his beloved—or what he thought of as his beloved—released alien pheromones that were irresistible to any but her own species. It was only the fact that her race rarely traveled off its homeworld that prevented this from being known. He could not help but be smitten, nor could they. That was the effect she had. And he began to worry—what did that mean for his own love? Was it real? Or was it brought about solely by alien body chemistry?

"For a great while he tortured himself with this.

"It could very well be that he was a hostage to love, having no choice whatsoever in the matter. But what if he would have fallen in love with her anyway, and this scientific curiosity was a great coincidence?

"As for the female, think how she must have felt as the chosen recipient of such love. To discover that when they were together, that when she had intermingled with any other race, love was not an emotion, but rather an allergic reaction! What comfort could ever be found in such a love?"

The Xenobiologist Master Class fell silent then.

"What did they decide?" prompted Meryl. "Are they together still?"

"They were greatly disturbed by this confluence at first, and thought of ways to test their love. At first, he donned a space suit at all times he was with her, to see whether he would still feel that love if he did not have the sense of her self in his nose. That indeed gave them troubled times, but they could not perceive whether this was due to the falloff in pheromones, or simply the stress such a barrier would cause to any couple. Then, for a while, he made her wear overpowering perfumes, to see if he could still love her in spite of noxious odors, and when this, too, caused problems, they could not for sure say why. Could you love someone so adorned? There is more than enough stress in any relationship without deliberately introducing more.

"And so, they finally decided—"

"Yes?" asked Meryl.

"They finally decided that it did not matter. Their love was irrational, brought on by random causes, not subject even to their own whims. But isn't that what all love is? How is that different from what the rest of the sentient beings in the universe feel? And so to protect their love they decided to live in such way that she would see no more of others, so that her alien scent could embolden none but him, but also, that he would seek a new profession, and travel no more, so that he would see no others of her race, so that his love would not be torn in two by desire. And, I must say, they lived happily ever after."

"Never knowing if their love was real?" asked Meryl.

"If their love was not real," said the Xenobiologist Master Class, "then no love ever was."

Meryl nodded. This at last gave Meryl much to ponder, and would surely do the same for the Belt Boss.

"I am sorry that I could not have met your wife," he said.

"So am I," said the Xenobiologist Master Class. "So am I. Believe me—you would have loved her."

As Meryl continued on his journey, he was glad to have finally heard something of worth, for the Engineer Master Class, the Geologist Master Class, and even the Psychologist Master Class were useless, spinning metaphors akin to those to which he gave ear during his first stops. The Physician Master Class told him of the way germs used love to spread throughout the universe, but that was of no help to a human trying to figure it all out. The Historian Master Class (who was the least help of all) offered no wisdom of his own, but wasted Meryl's time by demanding that he repeat all the stories he had heard for his own files.

Totally confused, having in weeks circled a Belt that would have taken months in a pod, Expeditor First Class Meryl approached the asteroid of Earth from the opposite direction which he had left. Meryl thought of all that he had heard as he bounded toward his home. He weighed the evidence as he skipped back, trying to make unified sense out of the contradictions, but he was unsuccessful. He had no idea what to tell the Belt Boss, other than that on this one subject, even the Masters fell silent.

Exhausted, Meryl went to his chambers to freshen up before he visited the Belt Boss. He asked the puter to recap all that had occurred since his futile quest began. To his horror, he discovered that the Belt Boss had died in his absence, finally succumbing to her mysterious weakness. He fell upon his cot in shock and sorrow, and after an untimed slumber felt hands upon himself. He was being summoned for an audience with the Belt Boss.

Meryl was confused for a moment, for he knew the Belt Boss was dead, but as he awakened, he remembered that though he had known but one, the Belt was never without a Belt Boss for long; there were limitless volunteers for the job. It was the new Belt Boss who wanted to see him. As he made his way along a familiar path through the corridors, two guards walked before him, and two behind, and he saw fear in their eyes, an emotion Meryl had not often seen in others when his Belt Boss had been alive. He could not imagine why this would be so, but he did not have to imagine long.

As he passed the irises that led to the caverns of other Expeditors, he saw there occasional circles of blinking black lights, apparently placed at random. But soon he recognized a pattern, for the doorways so decorated marked those who had been loyal to the previous Belt Boss. He was stunned, for the ceremonial patterns meant that they were no longer among the living. Could it be that it was only his absence during the tumultuous transfer of power that had kept him alive?

As Meryl was ushered in before the new Belt Boss, he was not surprised to see the grim features of Exeter in the familiar chair, surrounded by the blinking lights that had once framed another. No matter that they told him all was well along the Belt, Meryl knew that things could never be well again, for in the man's eyes Meryl saw that his suspicions were true—Exeter was indeed brutal enough to dispatch any who might be perceived as a threat to him.

"You have been gone from Earth a long time, Expeditor. Too long, and at a strange and difficult time. It seems odd to us that you would leave the side of the Belt Boss in her dying moments. Odd, and some might think, almost a treasonous thing."

Meryl's face flamed as he explained the mission on which the Belt Boss had sent him. As he began to speak of his journey and the many stories he had been told, a smile broke out on the Belt Boss' lips.

"Stop, Expeditor, tell us no more." The Belt Boss just barely suppressed his laughter. "It was obviously just a senile wish on the part of the former Belt Boss that sent you away. I do not think you yet understand how lucky you were that she did this. Let us speak of it no more, and let no mention of it be made to anyone else. I will allow you to continue to use that gift of yours. I, too, will be needing eyes and ears of my own."

The Belt Boss waved impatiently, excusing Meryl, and in the man's eyes he saw, and in the seeing, knew—Exeter had been more than just a witness to the weakening of the former Belt Boss. He had been a catalyst. Dazed, the Expeditor First Class backed out of the cavern which he had last seen inhabited by another Belt Boss.

Overcome by the weight of his luck, he wandered through the corridors to his chambers, where he repacked what he had just hours before returned to his shelves. He had the computer show him an image of the Belt Boss he had known for so long, the Belt Boss who had with her quest given him a gift greater than any love, and afterward, gazed for one last time at his room. Then, shaking with tears of joy and tears of sadness, he made his way once more to the outer lock which would lead him from Earth.

This time, thanks to a love he'd dared not admit until now, it would be forever.

THE CONTROL DEVICE

by Fiona Patton

Fiona Patton was born in Calgary, Alberta in 1962 and grew up in the United States. In 1975 she returned to Canada, and after several jobs that had nothing to do with each other, including carnival ride operator and electrician, moved to seventy-five acres of scrubland in rural Ontario with her partner, four cats of various sizes, and one tiny little dog. Her first book, *The Stone Prince,* was published by DAW Books in 1997. This was followed by *The Painter Knight* in 1998, *The Granite Shield* in 1999, and *The Golden Sword* in 2001, also by DAW. She is currently working on her next novel.

One of the Fiona's recurring themes, at least in her short fiction, is that of the honor and loyalty of the professional soldier. Here, however, she takes a different view of a warrior and who he is loyal to when there is no one left to serve. See if you can guess which fairy tale this is based on, and no, it's not from the Brothers Grimm.

THE Empire had fallen. That was the first thing Imperial Flight Lieutenant Trevor Halen remembered when he regained consciousness. Not his injuries, not the battle his squadron had just fought and lost, not the final burning, cometlike ride to the planet below, or even the standard "Where am I?" He knew where he was. He was hanging upside down from his safety harness, one leg wedged in the half open cockpit of his small, dying fighter.

Blood dripped from his face and hands to spatter against the crumpled metal beneath him, and reaching out, he managed to brush a hand against one twisted wingtip. A thin thread of energy—all that was left of the fighter's power supply—trickled through the filaments of his palm contact. Memories flooded over him: the intoxicating taste of raw energy tingling up his arms as he gripped the controls for the first time, the heady sense of speed and invincibility as he shot toward the enemy, one of a thousand young skirmish-fighter pilots, the elite of the Empire, who, for too short a time, had ruled the skies, and the deep, peaceful silence of space echoing back to him through circuits and nerve cells.

The trickle of power slowed, then stilled. He dropped his hand.

The Empire had fallen.

Station Cx-7, in orbit around Tol-Llamris, the Emperor's own home world, had been the last Imperial holdout. Halen's squadron had faced off against an enemy ten times their number to give His Majesty's transport ship a chance to escape the system. When the revolutionaries had finally broken through their defenses and hit the transport with a concentrated barrage that had vaporized it instantly, the skirmish-fighters were down to less than a half a dozen. Halen had three enemy ships on his own tail when the station itself suddenly exploded in a blinding flash. In the second before the energy waves sent his tiny fighter careening into the atmosphere, before his head hit the controls with a crack that even his flight helmet couldn't cushion, and before his ship, receiving no response from its pilot, switched to emergency auto, dumping its armaments as it blazed toward the planet below, he realized that everyone he'd ever known, family, friends, everyone, was gone, wiped out in a instant. He never sensed his fighter activate the damaged pilot eject before plowing, nose first, into a jumble of rocks and trees—it hadn't exactly worked anyway.

The Empire had fallen.

Closing his eyes, Halen let the darkness rush over him again on a wave of dizziness and guilt.

The sound of distant gunfire jerked him back to his senses with a curse a few moments later. The *newly liberated* citizens of Tol-Llamris would have tracked his descent to this place. If he didn't want to be shot on sight, he had to get out of there. Bracing his back against the harness, he placed his left foot on the fused canopy rim and, ignor-

ing the stab of pain that shot across his right ankle, he
pushed. The rim moved no more than a fraction of a centimeter, then jammed again.

"C'mon," he snarled, kicking at it in frustration. "Let . . .
go!"

Both rim and harness gave way at the same time.

Halen hit the ground hard. The breath knocked out of
him, he stared dazedly up through the trees, watching the
long trails of station debris burning their own paths through
the atmosphere toward him.

Everyone . . .

"Stop it."

Shaking his head roughly enough to cause a nasty head-
ache to dance across his temples, he forced himself to
stand. "Fall apart later," he ordered. "Right now, get out
of the nice Imperial flight suit with the target on it, okay?"

Leaving one bloody handprint on the fighter's side, he
struggled out of the bulky helmet and coveralls, then reluctantly stripped off his rank insignia, staring down at the
bright, blood-spotted bits of metal for a long time. The
Emperor himself had pinned these on his collar three years
and a lifetime ago.

The Elite of the Empire . . .

He closed his fist over them.

Most Imperial pilots began their training at age sixteen,
receiving their wings and their commissions two years later,
but those small enough and fast enough to pilot the diminu-
tive skirmish-fighters took to the skies at age fourteen, only
moving up to the larger and heavier mesh-fighters when
they grew too big to fit into the tiny cockpits. Small for his
age, at seventeen Halen had expected to serve at least another six months with his squadron. Now it looked like he
might be grounded forever.

The sound of gunfire grew closer, and with a jerk, he
flung the insignia into the underbrush, then stared down at
his dark blue uniform in disgust.

"Yeah, that's so much better. Now you're just an Imperial officer in a pair of flight boots."

*"So pick a direction that won't drop you into a nest of
people who want to kill you,"* his mind countered.

He gave a scornful laugh. "Right. How about up?"

"How about west?"

"Why west?"

"Because the gunfire's coming from the east."

"Yeah, okay, whatever." With a grimace, he slowly began to make his way over the rocks.

Through sheer luck he managed to find what looked like a service road a few minutes later. He limped along it, flinching at the unfamiliar sensation of gravel under his boots and jumping at every sound. Tall, shaggy trees loomed over him, dappling his face with drifting shadows and whispering strange, organic secrets in his ears. He shuddered.

Once on leave, he and his cousin Dolen had taken a half hour tour of the ancient forests of Phainar. Urged on by a crowd of station-born mechanics, they'd left the security of the hover pod to place their hands on the rough bark of a huge plantlike . . . something. They'd felt nothing. Whatever the "ground-nuts" might say, to the station-born and ship-born, organics had no discernible energy and so no life.

"But they sure are noisy."

Straining to hear over the whispering in the trees, he caught the more familiar mechanical whine of a web-trap an instant too late. There was a flash of light, and a sharp blow to his chest as he was knocked off his feet by a violent electrical discharge. His palm contacts absorbed much of it but, already injured, his body could not absorb the rest. The last thing he thought before the energy webbing snapped up to entangle him was that he hadn't believed he'd get caught so quickly.

He regained consciousness for the second time in as many hours to find a tall, dark-haired man going through his pockets. The man's clothes were bulky and nondescript, the heavy stubble on his cheeks suggesting he'd been living rough for a while, but he held a complex control device—probably for the webbing—in one hand and had a nasty looking blaster in a holster at his side. He brought the weapon up when he noticed Halen staring at him.

The young pilot tried an experimental glare.

"Find anything you could use?" he asked with cold politeness.

The man straightened. "No, but then I only just started

looking. I figured you'd be out for at least another ten minutes." He gave him a mirthless smile. "Citizen Jen Bern, Independent Contractor. And you'd be?"

Calling up as much bravado as he could muster, Halen just sneered at him.

Bern chuckled. "Nice manners." Cocking his head to one side he looked him up and down. "Imperial something obviously, but Imperial what, eh? You'd save me a lot of trouble if you'd just tell me." He waggled the blaster, but Halen just glared silently back at him. "No? Well then let's see, there's blood all over your face but not on your clothes. That wouldn't be your little Imperial fighter all smashed up two kilometers east of here, would it?"

Halen kept his expression blank. "No."

"The reason I ask is that with no pilot it's open salvage."

A muscle jumped in Halen's jaw.

"Of course, with it being an *Imperial fighter,* it's probably the Revolutionary Council's salvage anyway."

Halen shrugged.

"No interest at all?"

"No."

"Hm. Well, if you didn't crash that little fighter, what are you doing out here?"

"What are *you* doing out here?"

"Me? I'm holding a gun on a smart-mouth Imperial whose hanging from a giant spiderweb and I'm trying to decide whether to give him over to the Revolutionary Council for execution or just save myself the trouble and kill him now. What do you think I should do?"

"You could let him go."

"You know, it's funny but I'm actually considering that. See, I have this little problem that you just might be able to help me with. As you were hanging there I had a chance to get a good look at you. You're kind of a scrawny little bugger, aren't you? You're what, about one point six meters tall and around forty kilos?"

"Maybe."

"Too small for an Imperial ground trooper, I'm thinking. They usually recruit the hulking, protruding brow ridge type for that duty."

Halen couldn't keep a smirk from flicking across his face and Bern smiled back.

"Now, the revolutionaries have been killing those bastards for weeks," he continued. "And, quite frankly, I can see why. They don't know when to quit fighting and listen to reason. I'm hoping you do."

"Maybe."

"Good boy. So, like I was saying, a scrawny kid with no weapons and no body armor, just a pretty Imperial uniform has to be either some kind of adjutant—in which case the Revolutionary Council would pay a reasonably good reward for what's in his head—or he's one of those mysterious little skirmish-fighter pilots we've heard so many rumors about. Now, with a crashed skirmish-fighter back there, I'm betting it's my second choice.

"So, my question is this: are you one of those 'do or die for the Empire,' kind of skirmish-fighter pilots or just a boy on the wrong side of the war?"

Halen looked up, his eyes dark. "What does it matter? The war's over."

"It matters because you lost. How long do you suppose you'll last on your feet? Two, maybe three hours at most, before you get your brains blown out. So do you want to die before you've learned to shave, or do you want the means to stay alive and buy a decent razor?"

Halen's eyes narrowed.

"What would I have to do?"

Bern jerked his head. "Back there a ways is a storage bunker, one that served the Imperial Palace no less—which is about a dozen kilometers west of here and just crawling with revolutionaries, by the way. The thing is, with all the fighting and killing to keep them occupied, the Revolutionary Council hasn't found this bunker yet." He held up one finger. "Yet. But I have. My problem is, the door took a little more damage than I thought it would when I tried to open it and it jammed partially open. I can't get in. I'm too big, but you . . ." he smiled, ". . . should be just about the right size. You go in . . ."

"And loot the place for you?"

"Not at all. Far be it from me to help myself to revolutionary spoils. However, when it's mine, that's different. I had a small data recorder taken from me by some snotty little Imperial technocrat before the fall. Now he's dead, and my property's in there. What you loot for yourself is your own business; there's clothing, supplies, tools, everything you'd need to set yourself up as a civilian mechanic or something equally invisible. I just want my data recorder. Do we have a deal?"

Staring up at the trails of blazing debris still falling from the sky, Halen took a deep breath. "Yeah, we have a deal."

Bern held up the web control. "Then I guess I'd better know your name."

"Halen. Imperial Flight Lieutenant Trevor Halen," he added when Bern raised one eyebrow.

"Nice to meet you, Trevor." Bern hit the release button and Halen fell forward to hit the ground with a grunt of pain. "The bunker's this way."

They walked for a few hundred yards—Halen uncomfortably conscious of the weapon in the other man's hand—until they broke into a small clearing. In the rocks he could see a camp, camouflaged by netting, and a line of small stealth generators to one side of an underground bunker. The blast door was irised almost completely closed, patterns of char and damage etched across its face. Scattered about were the remains of various explosive devices. Halen turned an incredulous look on the older man.

"You tried to blast your way into an Imperial storage bunker?"

Bern shrugged. "I almost made it."

"Yeah, almost." He approached the door cautiously. "So everything you've tried has already gone off, right?"

"As far as I know."

"Great." Halen peered cautiously into the darkness, then began to strip off his uniform tunic. "So where do you figure this data recorder of yours is?"

"In one of three storage rooms on Sub-Level One. The first room holds personnel supplies, clothes, bedding, rations, and the like, for the Palace support staff. The recorder might be there, but I doubt it. The room will come equipped with a copper tug-drone. That's how you'll know you're in the right room. You can program it to search the storage compartments for you."

Halen turned. "Wait a minute, tug-drone? Aren't they programmed to guard their assigned property against theft?"

"Of course, but I'll give you a device that will control it. Just punch in the tug-drone's access code and it'll obey whatever command you send it."

"So where do I find its access code?"

"On the back of its neck."

"Oh."

"The second room holds tools and small mechanical parts, things like that. Again, if you want anything, just help yourself, but remember, it has to fit through the iris. This room comes equipped with a silver tug-drone. Again just punch in its access code the same as with the copper one."

"Silver and copper tug-drones?"

Bern shrugged. "Hey, he was *your* Emperor. You people never questioned his decadence before. Why should you start now?"

Halen snapped his teeth together, but indicated that the man should continue.

"Likely this is where my data recorder ended up, but again, maybe not. They got pretty sloppy toward the end there. Too eager to make a run for it, I guess."

He glanced slyly at Halen to gauge his reaction, but the young Imperial just met his gaze with a blank expression.

"The third and final room," the man continued "comes with a *golden* tug-drone. This is the room where the money is."

"Money? Imperial money?"

The man leaned forward. "Imperial booty: gems, precious metals, and intricate machinery from across the galaxy used to pay the Emperor's favorites. Take what you like, use it, sell it, whatever, I don't care, just get me my data recorder."

"So, what makes it so important?"

The man raised the blaster, touching the barrel almost gently to Halen's temple.

"It's important because it's mine and I want it."

Halen backed up a step. "Fine, whatever. You got this control device?"

Bern handed it over as well as a small headset. "Keep me informed of your progress."

Clipping it in place, Halen headed for the iris.

"And, boy?"

Halen glanced back.

"Like I said, this bunker supplied the support staff at the palace. There are no weapons stored here, so don't even bother wasting our time looking for one. I have the only gun you need to worry about."

Halen cast him a withering look before turning back toward the bunker.

The entrance was dark after the bright sunshine outside and the iris opening much higher than he'd expected. Halen hit the floor hard and lay stunned for a moment as various injuries made themselves known again.

"This is getting really thin," he muttered.

"WHAT?" The sudden crackle in his ear made him jump.

"Son of a . . . !"

Adjusting the receiver to a lower setting, Halen pressed his fingers against his temples. "Nothing. I'm inside," he answered after a moment.

"I figured that when your feet disappeared. Why didn't you report in?"

"Because I was too busy falling on my head."

"You should look where you're going."

"Yeah, well, it's dark."

"So find the controls for the lights."

"Right." Struggling to his feet, Halen brushed his hand against the charred remains of the door controls.

"You mean besides the ones you've already fried?"

"Obviously. Follow the entrance corridor. You should find another doorway and another set of controls."

Halen limped along the wall, one hand groping out in front of him until he fetched up against a door. Fumbling about, he found its control panel and pressed his palm against it. The hallway came alive with the comforting thrum of renewed power.

His headset crackled.

"What's happening?"

His eyes watering in the sudden glare, Halen shrugged. "I found the lights."

"And the door controls?"

"Them, too."

With one command, the door irised open, lights slowly illuminating the long narrow passageway beyond.

"I'm in . . ." He scanned the doorway. "Corridor P-11."

"Good. You should see a line of doors along both walls."

"Yeah."

"You want the fourth door on the right."

"Okay."

"Now turn left. Follow this corridor for two more doors until you get to one marked 'stairs.' "

"Got it."

"Go through. Go down."

If not for the endless stream of commands, Halen would have lost himself in the maze of corridors, but finally he stood before a door marked "Personnel Storage Facility: Sub-Level One."

The room was sparse. Closed storage bins marched along two walls, and crouched in the center, under a tightly closed iris, was a huge gleaming copper tug-drone, its round, dark opticals the size of his fighter's view screen. Halen approached it cautiously.

"Back of the neck, huh?"

Using one thigh as a step, Halen clambered up its body, feeling his injured leg protest the movement. Reaching back, he felt for the raised access code and brushed his fingers against a small control screen. Not bothering to use Bern's device, he slapped his palm against it.

"Hey, beautiful, time for your wake-up call."

The tug-drone leaped to its feet.

"Boy? BOY!"

Lights spun about in front of his eyes. Groggily, he raised himself up on one elbow.

"What?"

"What happened?"

"Um . . ." Halen glanced up at the tug-drone towering over him, its huge opticals glowing with bright red energy. So far, it hadn't pointed any of its various, nasty looking built-in weaponry at him, but he still sat up very carefully.

"Nothing," he answered.

"Your nothings seem to come with a lot of cursing."

"Yeah, well, the thing just took me by surprise."

"Did it attack you?"

"Not exactly."

"The device should have given you total control over it."

'Yeah, well maybe next time I'll use it," he muttered under his breath.

"Say again."

"Nothing."

"Did you punch in the access code correctly?"

"I don't know. I'll . . . try again."

Gingerly he got to his feet. Pulling out Bern's device, he approached the tug-drone once more.

It took less than a minute for the machine to inform him that the data recorder was not in the first room. It took Halen a lot longer than that to find everything he wanted; the bin nearest the door contained dried field rations and he spent a long time just stuffing his face before Bern's impatient voice sent him back to his task. After rifling the lower bins, he commanded the tug-drone to lift him up so he could reach the ones nearest the ceiling. Used to the tight quarters of his skirmish-fighter, Halen didn't even flinch as the machine's great hands wrapped about his waist, but it was still a strange feeling to be airborne in such a manner. He found a pair of nondescript coveralls and a jacket that would do although none of the boots were small enough to fit him. With a sigh, he reached for the next bin.

Inside he found a complete selection of medical supplies. Using the tug-drone's opticals as a mirror, he managed to wipe most of the blood from his face and hands, spraying skin graft directly into the wide, but shallow, cut above his hairline and across the various cuts and scrapes on his arms and legs. There were two large wraparound bruises across his right knee and ankle, which were already swelling alarmingly, and he grimaced as he taped and stuffed his foot back into his flight boot. If it was broken, it was broken. There was nothing he could do about it now. He gave himself a quick anti-inflammatory shot and a painkiller, then the medical kit went into a duffel bag and Halen commanded the tug-drone back to its place beneath the iris and made for the far door.

The second room was identical to the first except for the much larger silver tug-drone crouched in the center of the room under an identical closed iris. Its opticals were the size of a warship's view ports and glowed a deep green when, keeping a respectful distance, Halen activated it with Bern's control device.

Their search was also identical. Halen used the tug-drone to look for the data recorder to no avail and then to get himself outfitted. Bern's idea of a mechanic was a good one, so he collected a number of tools and small parts, reluctantly dumping some of his rations to make room in the duffel bag then, with a now jaunty wave at the silver tug-drone, he headed into the third and final room.

He wasn't sure what he was expecting to see, jewels and gold bars piled to the ceiling maybe from the way Bern talked, but the last room was identical to the first two with the same double line of storage bins marching along the walls. A bright golden tug-drone, even bigger than the copper and silver ones put together, crouched in the center of the room under another even larger iris, its opticals as big as the view ports on a space station.

Ignoring it for a moment, Halen poked into a few bins first, marveling silently at the number of intricate devices he found. In one he found an energy reserve and upgrade for his palm contacts and installed them gleefully. *"No weapons, huh?"* he thought to himself as he felt the reserves tingle up his arms. *"What do you know about Imperial weapons, anyway?"* The Emperor'd had some of the smartest people with the nastiest minds in the galaxy coming up with weapon designs for him.

"Sure, but he still lost," his mind pointed out caustically.

"We were outnumbered."

"Is that really going to be your excuse?"

"Shut up." Heading for the opposite wall of bins, Halen pushed the argument away.

He was so absorbed in his search that Bern had to contact him twice—his voice growing more and more agitated—before Halen activated the tug-drone, its eyes glowing with a brilliant blue light. When commanded, it immediately crossed to a high bin and pulled down a small, plain data recorder. Halen spent a moment trying to operate it, but even on pressing his palm contact against the tiny activation screen, the thing remained stubbornly dark and finally he stuffed it in his pocket. It was nothing to him if it was broken. Turning, he began to gather up handfuls of portable riches, pulling yet more food and all the machine parts from the duffel bag in order to fill it, too. Then, slinging the heavy bag over his shoulder, he made his way back through the three rooms.

He was panting by the time he reached the entrance, his right leg aching like it was on fire. Stuffing the bag through the iris, he jumped as Bern's face suddenly appeared on the other side.

"Where's my data recorder?"

"In my pocket."

"Give it to me."

"I'm sure. Help me out first."

Bern glared at him for a moment, then shrugged.

Getting out was a lot easier than getting in. Once Halen's head and shoulders had cleared the iris, Bern caught him by the coveralls and pulled him free, then dropped him to the ground. He held his hand out."

"My recorder?"

Halen tossed it over, then got stiffly to his feet.

"It looks brok . . ."

The shot cut him off in mid-sentence. Two bolts from Bern's blaster slammed into his palm contacts, knocking him over backward, and before he could react, the upgrade shot them back out again. The older man had barely enough time to register surprise before they hit him squarely between the eyes.

His body shaking with aftershocks, Halen picked himself up gingerly and limped over to stare down at the charred ruins of Bern's face.

"I have the only gun you have to worry about," he echoed with a sneer. "Yeah, and you had the only gun *you* had to worry about too, ground-nut."

After helping himself to the data recorder, the web-trap, and the blaster, he dragged Bern's body into the bushes, then glanced about the clearing. With all the blood and brain matter splattered around, the bunker probably wouldn't remain hidden much longer, but at least he could set up the netting and the stealth generators; he might want to come back here sometime. That accomplished, he then shouldered the duffel bag, and made his limping way back to the road.

He reached Venko, the Palace support town, just before dusk. The streets were full of jubilant citizens and Halen joined in, attaching himself to a group of apprentice mechanics bent on drinking themselves into a celebratory stupor. By the time a company of revolutionary ground troops arrived to enforce the curfew at midnight, they were all on a first name basis. The party moved indoors and Halen bought the first of a dozen rounds of the strong local liquor. By dawn he had just enough sense left to find a room in a nearby hotel, web-trap the door, and collapse in the vicinity of the bed.

The celebrations lasted for weeks. Halen quickly became a favorite with the local youths as he seemed to have an inexhaustible supply of money. None of his new friends were ever sober enough to ask him where it came from and avoiding the suspicion of the actual revolutionaries was easy. The officers and the Revolutionary Council never came near the small, cheap bars they frequented and the ground troops were more interested in ferreting out disguised Imperial bureaucrats than in harassing drunken teenagers vomiting in the town square. As for himself, Halen couldn't think of a better future than one addled by drink, so wherever there was a party he could be found, throwing his money around, and trying to forget he'd ever lived a life of speed and reflexes.

But one day, when he'd crawled out of bed just after noon, he was appalled to find that he'd run out of money, the few small bits of machinery left wouldn't buy him a single drink, never mind outfit him for the gala event happening that night. The Revolutionary Council had declared the Imperial Palace cleared of all classified material and had invited the citizens of Tol-Llamris to come and view the first jewel in the new government's crown. Everyone was going to be there.

"Everyone except me."

Rubbing at the soft line of hair along his jaw, Halen stared morosely out the window. He could return to the bunker, but there was no guarantee that it hadn't already been discovered. He might get there only to walk straight into a nest of revolutionaries with no good reason for being there. Then he'd really miss the party. Rifling through his duffel bag to see if there was anything left he could sell, he pulled out Bern's data recorder.

"Oh, right. I forgot all about you." He squinted down at it. "So, what little secrets do you hold?"

None of the buttons turned out to be the power button. Pushing them at random did little good, neither did keying it with his palm contact, but finally he managed to press a shallow indentation in the bottom and the case broke open to reveal a tiny control device, ringed with buttons so small they were difficult to focus on. At the top was a small view screen. Halen touched it experimentally with the tip of his little finger, and it lit up at once with a series of program and command codes. Halen nodded.

"Okay, if you can be programmed, let's hope you can be programmed with something useful. Let's see, I need money, so . . ."

He keyed in the access code for the golden tug-drone, then paused as he was about to press the command button.

"You'd come straight through the roof, if this works, wouldn't you? I'd better get outside."

Suddenly feeling more energized than he had for weeks, he reached for his pants.

He walked about a half kilometer into the trees around town before he reached a clearing that might do. By that time he'd had his fill of buzzing insects and tangled, feet-tripping underbrush. With a deep breath, he hit the control button.

The golden tug-drone powered down into the clearing almost silently less than a minute later, its massive blue opticals glowing with life. Halen grinned up at it.

"Hi, there. Have I got a mission for you."

The party that night was the wildest he'd ever been to. Drunken revelers roamed the Palace grounds, laughing, fighting, drinking, and marveling at the riches carefully displayed behind ropes and armed revolutionary guards. Halen allowed himself to be swept along in their midst, weaving through the opulent rooms and gardens with a dozen friends, making all the right noises, but inside he was cold. He'd seen it before when there was nothing between himself and the wealth of an Empire except a single oath sworn to its leader. However, when they reached the Emperor's private hangar, he let out an involuntary gasp.

Beneath a tightly closed iris was the most beautiful fighter he'd ever seen. Small and streamlined, it glowed with a pure white luminescence in the hangar's low lighting. Fine threads of gold, silver, and copper trim flowed along its length, accenting the perfection of its wings and the smooth oval of its darkened canopy. Halen could feel his hands twitching with the need to touch it. He took one step forward and came up short against an energy barrier.

The duty guard laughed at his pained expression.

"That's as far as you get, citizen."

Fetching up behind him, his friends grinned.

"A beauty, isn't it?" Kerzen, nephew to the new Deputy Mayor asked with a laugh.

Halen made himself nod. "Yeah."

One of the younger boys inched forward. "What is it?"

Before Halen could say anything, Kerzen shrugged with the studied arrogance of someone with access to exclusive and classified knowledge.

"The Emperor's personal mesh-fighter. Customized, of course," he bragged as if it were his own. "Fully loaded, fully armored. My uncle said the Emperor buzzed the town once and you never heard it till it was gone, it was that fast."

Halen felt his throat go dry.

"Whose is it now?" the other youth asked.

"The Council's. My uncle says they're trying to decide what to do with it."

"You mean, who gets to fly it?"

"Well, sure. It can't be just anyone, you know. They say the controls are so sensitive that one false move and splat! It'll probably just sit in its hangar forever. Nobody here's good enough to fly it, are they?"

Without taking his eyes off the beautiful ship, Halen felt himself tense.

"No. Nobody here."

*   *   *

Three days passed. Halen itched to try his hand at the little fighter's controls, but he didn't dare visit the hangar again. The ship was guarded day and night by special revolutionary troops; there'd already been attempts to steal it by a few of Tol-Llamris' less than patriotic citizens and every last one of them had been shot.

Pacing the length of his hotel room, he tossed the control device from one hand to another in frustration.

"I don't care how well it's guarded," he growled at his reflection in the hotel window. "I want it." About to fling the control-device onto the bed, he suddenly stopped, his eyes widening.

The golden tug-drone powered down into the clearing, drawing the beautiful ship behind it as easily as if it were hauling Halen's old skirmish-fighter. It set it down gently, then stood to one side as the ex-Imperial pilot approached the ship in reverent awe.

It was even more perfect up close; sleek and smooth, without so much as a speck of dust to mar its gleaming white surface. When he placed his palms against one side, he could feel the latent power thrumming deep within it. He closed his eyes, reaching for its core program, trying to awaken it with touch alone, but the ship remained stubbornly dormant, its access code unknown.

He stood there for over an hour pressed against the ship then, with real reluctance, directed the tug-drone to take it up. Making his own way back to town, the limp which had almost disappeared thanks to the services of a very expensive doctor, now grew more pronounced than ever. When he finally reached his hotel room, it was dark. Slumped in a chair by the window, he stared in weary defeat at the Palace lights sparkling in the distance. If he couldn't get the fighter's access code, couldn't fly it. If he couldn't fly it, there was no point in tormenting himself by just drooling over it. Catching up his jacket, he headed for the door. And if there was no point in drooling over it, he might as well drink himself into a stupor so he would stop thinking about it.

The next day, when he managed to drag himself out of bed around noon, the streets were abuzz with news. Someone had lifted the Council's prize ship right out of its hangar, delivering a nasty electric shock to the guard on duty, then returned it undamaged. The revolutionary flight mechanics had been over every centimeter of its hull, checking and rechecking it for fingerprints, DNA strands, anything to help them identify the thief, but had turned up nothing. It was as clean as the day it was made.

In the midst of his friends, Halen marveled with the rest, although not at the thief's audacity, but rather at his own abject stupidity at having spent all that time practically making love to it without once worrying that he might get caught. Swallowing rather too much beer at once, he wondered who'd cleaned the hull, the tug-drone or the ship itself.

The thought that it might be the ship replaced most of his anxiety with excitement. If it was the ship, then that meant that somewhere, deep inside, it had felt him and responded to him. And if it had responded to him, that meant it had accepted him, and if it had accepted him, then it was meant to be his. He had to try again. Two revolutionary soldiers passed their table, casting him a longer look than usual, and he felt himself pale.

"Right," he muttered between clenched teeth as he tried not to check if they were still staring at him. "Don't be a complete moron, Trev. They'll have traps and surveillance cameras all over it by now."

"What?"

Halen snapped his head around to meet Kerzen's curious gaze.

"Huh?"

"You said something."

"Just that . . . they'll have traps and surveillance cameras all over the ship by now," he repeated. "So the thief will probably never come back."

"Well, he won't if he knows what's good for him."

"Yeah, if he does."

Halen lasted another three days. Then, desperate to see the ship again, he sent the golden tug-drone off to the Palace once more.

This time, having convinced himself that the ship itself wouldn't let him get caught, he climbed up and sat with his legs stretched out across one wing and his back pressed up against the ship's side. Palms down, he bent all his concentration toward reaching its core program, but again it eluded him. His mind filled with schemes to find its access code, schemes to break into the Palace himself, or send the tug-drones in to tear the place apart looking for it, schemes to hold the Revolutionary Council, the Mayor, the entire town, hostage if he had to, until they gave it to him. But eventually, with dark storm clouds gathering overhead, he gave up for the day and commanded the tug-drone to take it home again.

The next day the talk was once again all about the daring thief who continued to outwit the Revolutionary Council and its guards. This time the flight mechanics had programmed the ship's onboard computer to record its journey, but when checked, it had somehow logged touchdowns in over two dozen clearings in the nearby woods plus several public areas around Venko and even in the Palace itself. Again, there was no sign of human tampering.

Holding court in their favorite tavern, Kerzen told them that the hangar had been closed off to the public, that it was surrounded by guards and a ring of hair-trigger laser defenses, that the ship itself had been chained to the hangar floor and the iris had been welded shut. The Council was determined to catch whoever had made a fool of them and starting today there would be curfews, checkpoints, and extra patrols until the thief was caught. But, he added with a grin, betting on the street was two to one that the thief would try again, and four to one that he'd get away with it.

Halen listened to all this silently, the thought of his beautiful little mesh-fighter locked in its hangar—as much a prisoner on this world as he was—strengthening his resolve. He would try again. He would find that access code and the two of them would fly away from this place forever and nothing would ever ground them again.

He set out an hour later, slipping past the checkpoint on the edge of town and heading into the woods at a run.

This time when the tug-drone set the little fighter down—with no sign of damage from the chain or the welded iris—

Halen clambered over every square centimeter of it, searching for any clue to its access code or even a latch or a lock he could pry open. There was nothing: no markings, no numbers, no panels or handles, nothing. Hours passed. Finally, he admitted defeat. Jumping to the ground, he frowned up at its opaquely impassive canopy.

"Okay, if I can't fly you out of here, I'll carry you out." Placing one palm against its side, he fumbled in his pocket for the control device.

The trickle of energy from a pinpoint hole in its power line warned him of the trap an instant too late as a ring of ground troops exploded from the underbrush. Before he could react, the closest one leaped forward and hit him across the temple with the butt of his rifle. Halen went down in a burst of bright red stars.

The trial was nothing more than a formality and coming, as it did, after his interrogation, Halen didn't remember much of it anyway. Later, crouched in a tiny cell under the town hall, he held one arm tight against what was probably a couple of broken ribs and tried to ignore the jailer who'd decided it was his duty to keep Halen informed of the scaffold's progress.

Halen had blinked uncomprehendingly at him at first.

The man had snickered. "What? You figured we'd shoot you? Hardly. You're not the first techno-pumped little fighter brat we've executed, not by half. There'll be no blast-rifle bolts for you, boy, just a plain old-fashioned rope around your neck and then you're jerked into the air. Not so fast that your neck breaks or anything, it'll be slow so you choke for a really long time; your face goes all purple and your tongue and your eyes pop outta your head. You might even mess yourself, how does that sound?"

Despite the blood and bruising on his face, Halen had shot the man a look of withering contempt, but now, staring out the barred, ground level window toward the rapidly filling town square, he felt suddenly more afraid than he cared to admit.

He snapped his teeth together. Whatever happened, he wasn't going to show that to any of them. He was an Impe-

rial fighter pilot, one of the Emperor's elite, and he would
act like one, however his body might betray him on the
scaffold.

A moment later, his thoughts were interrupted by the
sight of one of his younger drinking companions hurrying
down the street. Not looking where he was going, he
tripped on a loose bit of pavement, and went down, sprawl-
ing, before Halen's window.

The ex-pilot shook his head.

"What's your hurry, Vernon?" he asked in as conversa-
tional a tone as he could manage through the swelling of
his lower jaw.

The boy's eyes widened, then his face grew pale as he
recognized who was speaking to him.

"Uh, nothing," he stammered.

"Trying to get a good seat?"

The boy sat up, his eyes downcast, and said nothing.

"There's no hurry, you know, they won't start without
me. I'm the main event." Halen cocked his head to one
side, a sudden thought making his heart race. Vernon was
a weasely little guy who never had enough money to pay
for his own drinks. He hung around, saying whatever he
thought the others wanted to hear and hoping to be included in a round or two. He was greedy and cowardly but,
although he'd bailed just as quickly as the others, Halen
couldn't really bring himself to despise him. He took a
step forward.

"It won't be for another couple of hours yet, Vernon,"
he said, pleased that his voice remained so calm. "And
you'd never get a decent seat anyway. So how'd you like
to make a small fortune instead?"

A look of fear flashed across Vernon's face.

"I can't help you escape or anything, Trev," he whispered, "they'll kill me, too, for sure."

"I'm not asking you to help me escape," Halen assured
him in his quietest voice, praying the other boy wouldn't
bolt. "I just need a small favor." He put a catch in his voice.
"I wanted to record a good-bye message to my mother, but
my data recorder's in my jacket pocket and they've got my
jacket upstairs."

"And you want me to break in and get it?"

Bern's face flashed through Halen's mind, but he thrust it aside.

"It'd be nothing for you, Vernon, you're small and quick enough. You'd be in and out in a second."

"I dunno, Trev . . ."

"There's no one there, Vernon. All the guards are watching the scaffold go up." He caught and held the other boy's gaze. "I tell you what, my hotel key is in my pocket, too. Do this and I'll give you the access code for the key. All my stuff'll be yours. You've seen the kind of money I've got. I'll leave it all to you, if you just let me record my message." He gripped the bars, making his knuckles go white. "You'd do that for me, wouldn't you, Vernon? You'll let me say good-bye?"

Slowly, the other boy nodded.

The exchange was made just before the guards came for him. Halen gave him the access code and Vernon took off like a terrified rabbit seconds before the door opened. Then, with his arms bound tightly behind him, Halen was led outside.

It seemed like the entire town had come to see him hanged. Halen didn't bother to look for his friends, but he knew they'd be there, hidden in the crowd, as eager as anyone to see an Imperial swing, but also scared that he'd say something before his death that might implicate them in something, in anything. Kerzen especially must be pissing himself with fear.

Halen smiled inwardly. Kerzen and all the rest would soon have a lot more than that to worry about. He mounted the steps of the primitive looking wooden scaffold, then turned to face the Revolutionary Council.

Forty hard-bitten men and women, the soldiers who had brought down an Empire, stared back at him, barely concealed hatred gleaming in their eyes. Armed soldiers surrounded their makeshift grandstand, more stood to either side of the scaffold and still more flanked the crowd. They were taking no chances. As if anyone would be so suicidal as to help him, he thought bitterly.

The executioner came forward to ask him the traditionally stupid question, and he made his request in as pathetic a voice as he could muster. For a second he feared they wouldn't grant it, then the oldest of the Councillors nodded. The bounds around his arms were cut and, after the executioner had examined the data recorder, he handed it back.

"One minute."

It was all Halen needed.

Pressing the tiny indentation, he allowed the case to fall to the ground, then hit the memory button. The three codes he'd punched in earlier and one unfamiliar code lit up across the screen.

The white mesh-fighter arrived first. Streaking across the sky almost silently, it dropped down beside the scaffold, scattering people as it came. Halen stared at it, open mouthed like the rest, cursing himself for never once realizing that was what Bern had been after all along. But seconds later he forgot all about the mesh-fighter as the three huge tug-drones came hurtling toward the square. Halen threw himself down the scaffold steps as he shouted a single word into the control device.

"FIRE!"

Most of the civilians managed to find cover, but all forty Revolutionary Councillors and every guard carrying a weapon lay dead when Halen finally called the tug-drones off. Standing beside his new fighter, he glared darkly at the cowering crowds. For half a moment, he considered setting the tug-drones loose on them as well, but then he just turned and laid one hand gently against the mesh-fighter's side.

There was the faintest tingle of energy against his palm and the canopy slid soundlessly open. Halen almost started crying with relief.

With the silver and gold tug-drones covering the crowds, Halen commanded the copper tug-drone to lift him toward the cockpit. Its great fingers closed about his waist, sending pain radiating across his ribs, but as soon as he took hold of the rim and drew himself into the soft, formfitting leather interior, the pain eased. As the canopy slid closed, he heard the crowd give one involuntary murmur of appreciation. He smiled. The thief had won after all. Taking hold of the controls, he commanded the mesh-fighter into the sky.

It rose as silently as it had descended, the three tug-drones powering along behind it. The revolutionaries would soon regroup and come after him, but he had a head start and a small but powerful mechanical army at his back. He should make it through all right.

The Empire had fallen, but Flight Lieutenant Trevor Halen had not fallen with it. Whatever happened, now at least he was no longer grounded and alone. Speaking a single soft command, man and fighter hurtled upward through the atmosphere and out toward the cool comfort of open space.

THE LAST INVASION OF IRELAND

by Richard Garfinkle

Richard Garfinkle won the Compton Crook Award in 1997 for his first novel, *Celestial Matters,* which was outlandishly set in a universe conforming to the cosmology of the classical Greeks. His second novel, *All of an Instant,* was published in November 1999. An avid student of mathematics, history, and religion, he lives in Chicago with his wife and children.

While not based on a fairy tale per se, Richard's story is a wonderful imagining of what might have happened when the legends of ancient times got their hands on the magic of technology.

"STAND straight, you sorry pack of changelings. Listen hard! I'm here to teach you to be Fairies! Learn and you might survive out there. If not—well, the hills and rivers are full of bodies and a few more Elf-wannabes ain't gonna choke 'em any more."

Sergeant Keough's voice was hard and even as he repeated the same speech he'd given on the first of each month for the last four years, the same words he had shouted at me and my squad when we came to Angus' sidhe the day the Invasion came to Ireland. They're all dead but me now, all of those first Fairy Knights: Warren burned down by the Outlandish in the pullout from Belfast, Sarah broken and flashing out her final glamour in the fourth assault on the Irish Sea, the others as well bleeding their golden Fey-lives out in human red.

Everyone thinks I'm lucky, that I survived on pure clover-fortune. They don't know what I know, and I haven't the guts to tell them.

Keough's latest batch of recruits had precious few sons and daughters of Erin among them. Most were refugees, the meager tattered remnants who made it here from the seven conquered continents of Earth. The scientists and officers from foreign lands had been taken by the Good Folk, brought within the mist-shrouded, holo-glamour-haunted hills to aid humanity's cause. The rest of the survivors, the ones who weren't important enough to be billeted within the walls of the sidhes, were left outside to try and survive if they could or to join the Fairy army and get a little protection for their relatives.

"This is your ELF-shot," Keough said, holding up one of the silvered gloves with the circular antennae on the fingertips. "It can disrupt an Outlandish's sense of balance as well as tearing up some of the circuitry in their battle suits. Every shot that hits is a shot that hurts. Remember, they can't make any more armor, so if five of you die to take down one suit, that's five good lives paid for our advantage."

Advantage. Keough still sounded as if he believed the war could be won by force of elfin arms.

"Captain!" Keough was calling to me, waving me over, a break in his routine. I came, and he saluted.

"Recruits, this is Captain Sean Kincaid, first of the Fairy Knights. If you learn well and go brave out there, you just might join his Fairy Raid and hit the enemy hard."

The glamour on Angus' sidhe shifted, projecting now a rowan-wooded hillock patchworked with rings of giant mushrooms and sounding with high, piping music that disorients the Outlandish. My Faerie-Sight visor flicked through the registered patterns of illusion until it matched the projected image. As always, the reality, the hard steel and stone bunker, was grim and dull compared to the legendary image cast forth.

Keough saluted again, dismissing me with apparent respect, the way drill sergeants through the ages have always been able to send off the soldiers they've taught, no matter how high their rank.

And I did have to go. My Raid was waiting for me. The Good Folk in the sidhes had perfected the final weapon against the enemy.

Ten years ago the Outlandish had come to Earth in their fleet of ragtag spaceships. They had been spotted by our orbiting telescopes, and the news had spread all over the Earth. Aliens, real aliens. The hopeful had wondered what gifts they were bringing. Beaten, battered, poverty-filled Ireland had too many hopefuls then. I remember my Gran cursing out the Prime Minister, warning him about what outsiders with gifts had done to our nation in the past.

The first close observations of the Outlandish flotilla had turned people's attitudes around. The ships were so battered and war-bruised that it looked like the Outlandish were refugees. Then some of Earth became compassionate, hoping to help them. Gran railed at them, too. Poor Gran, how I need your advice now.

The Outlandish didn't bother to talk or ask for help. They just attacked, hitting the major countries first: China, the US, India, Australia.

Ireland, beaten down in war after war, hadn't been worth their bother until everyone else had been conquered. The Outlandish didn't understand that a nation invaded over and over learns to fight back even if the entire rest of the world has fallen.

We had fought them, blooded our ground, lost our brothers and sisters, lost our humanity, and we had held them to slow progress while the final weapon was devised, not shot nor glamour nor enchantment, but poison. We Knights were too be given lots of Faerie Food seeds to sow in the ground and dump in the rivers.

After that . . . well, the Good Folk talked glowingly about victory and finally bringing down the Outlandish. The few remaining humans lapped up this talk. The Outlandish had taken over all the Earth except Erin, and now the chance to defeat them had come forth from the secret places of the sidhes. It was glib, convincing speech with just enough blarney to set church bells ringing in my head.

I knew what the Good Folk were up to, conniving Fairy Lords, dancing their entrancements, but I didn't have the heart to tell the rest of the Fairy troops.

They didn't have my background. My family—some of

them skittering back across a couple of thousand years—
my family had been bards. We had known the songs and
stories and passed them on. I was brought up on the tales
of the invasions. I had learned that the Fir Bolg had lived
in Erin first. Then the Fomor had come and taken the land
from them, driving the Fir Bolg into the sea. Then the
Tuatha De Danaan had come and made war with the
Fomor, then made peace then war again under Lugh, Master of All Arts, who was half De Danaan and half Fomor.
I knew the stories of the Fomor's defeat and the dominion
of the De Danaan, pure and perfect rulers and stewards of
Erin, a god-perfected land. Then the Sons of Mile, the humans, had come and defeated the Tuatha De Danaan. Only
in Erin had mortals conquered their gods, driven them underground into the original sidhes, the real Fairy hills, not
the man-made, steel-hardened, ELF-shielded barrows of
the Good Folk.

But the De Danaan weren't beaten down just because
they were pushed under the hills. They had ways of fighting
back, of winning a place in Erin.

The Good Folk were copying those ways. Everyone knew
it, all the Fairy troops, all the refugees. It made sense to
the romance within soldiers' hearts and displaced souls.
Methods that had worked well in the ancient stories could
work now, if brought up to date with modern human technology and the secrets of the Outlandish bought with many
lives all across the world.

"This is a Pixie-LED." Koeugh's voice was barely audible over the sounds of Flying Steeds screaming into run-
ways after battles in the air. Captain Haramura, best Lance
of the De Dannan Archers, popped the canopy from his
steed, Yellow Shaft, and shook his fist toward me, his
marker of victory. I shook back, sparking fireworks of con-
gratulation from my personal glamour. It was a salute of
praise, but also a shelter for my face so he couldn't see the
falseness of my smile. Haramura and I were old soldiers
here and I didn't want to see him betrayed, the air-horse
shot out from under him.

"It will confuse the radar and ladar imaging systems of
the enemy," Koeugh went on after saluting Haramura,
"making the Outlandish see troops where there aren't any."

Clever hardware, all very clever. But I knew that there

were other, more useful weapons still in storage, waiting for the Ogma-committee to give them Fairy names and stories, Good Folk propaganda.

My ancestors were bards, and they didn't stop being bards just because Ireland converted from the old religion to Christianity. I had monks in my ancestry, some from the time before that was a social embarrassment and a few from after, by-blows of the monasteries and nunneries. In private my family had been proud even of them; they added more color to the songs of our history.

The most color came from Brother Michael back in the fourteenth century. He was the source of legend and scandal so broad that there were stories accusing him of witchcraft as well as others claiming he was a saint. Two-Faced Mickey we called him in family tales that were both more saintly and more sinful than the stories the public knew. One time he and a red-haired lass were seen wrestling on the top of a hill. He claimed she was the devil in disguise and he was keeping her from blighting all the villages around his monastery. Others had a different explanation, and Mickey's story changed a few times in the telling: devil, witch, Fairy, he was never too clear. But the truth didn't matter, the stories did. Mickey had spurred us on, keeping the bardic traditions no matter what the religion or the politics. Why was he poking his nose into my thoughts now, when the stories were about to go against us?

Mickey fed me a few reminders of our other monastic ancestors. Some had been simple chroniclers who with too much devotion to the truth laid down the simple and terrible facts of their lives. They had recorded the later invasions, those of humans by humans, the Danes, then the English come a-conquering.

Under the English Troubles my family had updated bardic attitudes and skills, becoming writers of republican songs, makers of newspaper stories and international press releases. We had struggled hard, and one of my forebears had been speechwriter to the Prime Minister when a reunited Ireland raised its flag at last and spat one final time at the islands to our east.

But our independence didn't last long. When the EU collapsed in civil war and the French invaded our shores with a savagery that even the English had never matched,

my great-grandmother had served as leader of covert intelligence for the Irish Underground. Gran had been a wonderful spinner of tales. She had had the French secret police
running after their own tails, hunting attacks that never
came, missing those that did. When the French were cast
off, Gran was given a medal and a job as top spy. I still
have that Blarney-Stone-stamped medal in the one-kilo
pack that held all the personal possessions a Fairy Knight
was permitted.

Gran, I couldn't have figured it out without you. If you'd
lived would they have made you one of the Good Folk,
given you a shot at immortality—or would they have
pushed you outside, afraid of what you would do to their
sidhes?

She'd always been good at catching me in lies. Inspired
by Two-Faced Mickey I had learned to be a great liar as a
boy. I'd think my fabrications through and spin them
clearly, telling tales well enough to fool most adults. I'd got
away with a lot, but not when Gran was around. She'd
always get me, and make me undo whatever impishness I
had perpetrated.

I asked her once, with an eight-year-old's resentment of
being outclevered, "How d'ye know, Gran?"

"I'll tell you, Sean, because the secret won't help you lie
to me, but it may stop you from being fooled by others.
It's easy to tell when someone's handing you a story. You
know how?"

I could tell she was waiting for me to say yes, just so she
could catch me one more time. So I told the truth. "No,
Gran. How?"

"Stories are too pat. They fit. Everything connects. Even
the loose dangly bits are meant to tease and get the mind
going in the direction the teller wants. Real events aren't
like that. They don't hold together, don't make sense. They
just are."

And that's how I knew what the Good Folk were up to.
They were spinning a tale around us, making a glamour out
of the war. A bedtime story that would lull their soldiers to
sleep, no matter how alert to enemy action they seemed.

My three dozen Fairy Knights assembled in a briefing
hollow, under a makeshift bunker protected by a portable
holo-glamour that made it seem just another stand of trees.

These were my picked Fairies, veterans all in their holo-glamour latticed armor, bright silver, tall and wondrous in their Faerie lord appearance. They carried their ELF-shot and their Pixie-LEDS and their Gae Bolga guns. O'Rourke and Williams (my only English-born soldier but now as Irish as the rest of us) were fieldstripping our Spear of Lugh, making sure the hardening would hold under the EMP generators, so that the weapon could strike and re-turn while disrupting Outlandish ECM. They looked up and saluted as I came in, joining the rest.

"Captain?" Williams said, his war-bitten forty-year-old face shade-showing through the eternal youth of his Elf-lord haughtiness. "Is this really the last battle?"

"It is, old son," I said, keeping my own appearance shrouded in glory.

My Elves hungrily gathered to hear my words. I had inspired them before and I would do so again today, even if this was the last day we would truly fight.

"All right, Fairies," I said. "The Good Folk have en-trusted us with the first wave of Faerie Food. We need to plant it in the ground, and most of all we need to reach the rivers. Once the Food's out to sea it'll infect the algae and make its way up the food chain. The scientists of the Good Folk estimate it'll be only three years until there isn't any nourishment on Earth that the Outlandish can eat."

I told it just the way the Good Folk wanted, and my Fairy Knights ate it up, food for their minds, savory and sweet, but with no *foison*, no real nutrition to it. *Foison* was what the Faerie Food would take out of the ecosystem, and that was what the Good Folk had taken out of their own words.

And it worked on my troops. They had fought a war of illusion and deception for years, but they could still be tricked by their own leaders.

"Form up," I said. "Silent Raid, as the wind that passes and chills."

We bundled up, seven squads of five Fairies, our holo-glamours linked together, cameras pointing in all directions. Our Fairy Armor read the terrain and projected it back. The cooling systems pumped out a breeze at the ambient temperature. We set out as if there were nothing and no one here, apart from the slight defects in appearance, sound, and chill, that hinted at Fairy Presence. Such hints were vital. They could raise hackles on a human's back, set the beasts a-howling and the birds a-fluttering, and leave the Outlandish slapping their tails on the ground in confusion.

Out we marched, invisible except to each other. On our Raid we went. Beyond the outer perimeter of the camp that lay in the shadow of Angus' sidhe were the bombed and blasted ever war-torn fields of Erin. Like the wind that pushed back the ships of Mile we went forth to do the Good Folk's bidding.

Outlandish patrols were everywhere, the "click-clack-click" sound of their battle-armored troop leaders melding with the "hiss-slap" as their double-tailed infantry hit the ground. They were afraid. It had been a pleasant surprise to discover that they could fear, and over the years we had taught them so much fear that they now fired weapons at shadows and threw explosives into the wind. But fear wouldn't win the war for us. There were just too many of the Outlandish.

Their ships, which hadn't appeared large enough to bear many soldiers, had carried a huge cargo of embryos or eggs or something like that. I never understood the science of their breeding and didn't have the time or teachers to learn it. However the Outlandish had done it, from their small vessels they had poured forth in their hundreds of millions.

The Good Folk had taken in all the researchers they could find to crack the Outlandish technology and make weapons to fight this unending onslaught. The sidhes were overstuffed with what Williams called boffins. I wondered what would happen to them when the war was over. The sidhes couldn't hold that many people for long, and the more deeply entrenched of the Good Folk were likely to want space to live and a chance to have children in safety.

The children of the Good Folk, that was who we were fighting for. That was why we were battling in Elf-array. None of the other soldiers knew it, only me.

What could I say? How could I tell my Knights that we were living out a fairy tale so the Good Folk could tell their yet-to-be-borns how the great and noble Fairy Knights had given their lives for the safety of those who lived in sidhes?

No doubt the little ones would snuggle down happily, thinking of us keeping the Outlandish at bay, how under their divine and immortal parents we had defeated their enemies.

Immortal. No one else knew about that either. But I had seen the Cauldron of Rebirth where bodies could be grown around revivified brains, stolen technology adapted from the Outlandish incubators. The Outlandish didn't use it to keep their leaders alive, just to quickly grow their troops. But the Good Folk had found old uses for this new technology.

"Found, found, found! Outlandish patrol, four klicks west," Patricia Minkowski said into my ear-receiver. Patty was, as far as I knew, the last Pole left alive. She fit in very well with us Irish, having also grown up in a much invaded land.

"LED them off," I said, ordering her and her subpatrol away. "Hunt them up and down. Call the Spear of Lugh down on them if you have to, but keep them from the Shannon."

Off the five of them went, casting off invisibility like a gossamer cloak to reveal their forms awful, beautiful, and terrible, Elfin warriors in gold and silver with sound of thunder and glance of fire. Harp song followed them, songs to bring tears, and sleep, and fear to the Outlandish. Mingled light of Sun and Moon and X-ray bursts flared forth from them. The Outlandish would flee in fear until they had gathered enough of their comrades to risk a charge against my knights. But by then my Fairy Knights would be moonbeams and shadows again. Soon thereafter, they would flare and flash in a different place. They would lead the enemy up and down.

While we, in secret, did witch-work upon the blasted heaths of Erin. Thh-pok, Thh-pok, the Faerie Food seeds went into the ground.

Radio distance away, I could hear the screams and confusion of the enemy. The patrol was good and clever, but soon a big enough swarm of Outlandish would come and iron out where they were, separating the appearance of Elves from human reality. I weighed the lives of my patrol against our mission and galled myself with the choice I had to make, the Good Folk's choice.

"Hunt them up and down, Patricia," I radioed. "Go with

broom before. Call down Yellow Shaft and Red Javelin from the Flying Steeds. Buy us enough time to reach the Shannon."

"Found, found, found and all around," Patricia radioed back. Then the bombs fell, the fires flashed, and the fay-killing iron of the Outlandish circled my poor knights. But my Elf-soldiers had done their work. We had reached the holy waters of the Shannon.

It would be an excellent tale the Good Folk would be telling their little kiddies, a safe-making story, a "don't worry dear yes the nasty Outlandish are still there but our brave Knights made sure they couldn't hurt us," story.

That was what none of the other Fairies had figured out. The Faerie Food couldn't just be left out there to kill off the Outlandish. It would take too long, and once they knew they were dying, the Outlandish ships would take revenge on the planet. If they couldn't have the Earth, no one else would have it either.

No, I knew what was going to happen. It had happened before when the Sons of Mile had conquered Erin. They had taken the land, but the Tuatha De Danaan had withdrawn their blessings so nothing could grow, no rain could come, no fish be caught—until, cap in hand, the Sons of Mile had come to the sidhes of the Tuatha De Danaan and bargained with them, made them their gods in return for their blessings, rain and crops in return for safe dwelling in the sidhes.

The Good Folk were going to do the same thing. They would give the Earth outside their sidhes to the Outlandish and in return the Outlandish would serve them or starve.

But there wasn't much room in the sidhes and we Faerie Knights and the refugees who hadn't been useful enough to be inducted into the Good Folk would be left outside for the Outlandish to revenge themselves upon.

What could I tell my poor fey troops? This plan was the only way to save any of humanity, even if it was only the Good Folk and their wee ones.

And we outside would become a fairy tale for those inside the man-made hollow hills.

"Seed the seas," I ordered and my remaining Knights and I sprayed poison pellets into the waters that had given life to our ancestors. We had made the story of the Good Folk come true.

Now what could we do but lie down and die?

"Stand up and lie, Sean." Gran's voice echoed through my head, a ghostly telling, a breath of inspiration from a real fairy queen. "Make up your own tale. Steal, cheat, deceive. You want to be an Elf, be an Elf!"

And a farther back ghost echoed Gran. Two-Faced Mickey, Saint and Sinner, called to me across the centuries. "Two sides to a story make a better tale, Sean, lad. Better to kill and kiss the devil."

The idea came, clear and bright, a beautiful, graceful, mean, and sneaky idea. The Good Folk wanted fairy tales.

Well, we would give them one!

"Boys and girls," I said. "Our mission's done. There'll be no more half-true orders from the Good Folk. Time you heard it all."

So I told them the truth. We were running as I did so, the crackle of our radios amidst the radiation adding a static music to my story. The Outlandish were gathering, clustering around the Shannon seeking to find out what we had done, to learn their fate, but we were long gone. Over the noises of earth and alien I told my Fairy Knights all about the Good Folk and their plan, and how we were supposed to fade into the storybooks, closed up on night tables under the hills.

"But we're going to make a different story from their Seelie comfort-tale," I said. "We're going to be Unseelie. We're going to troop and raid and steal what we need from the Outlandish and the sidhes if we have to. We'll get as many recruits from the camps as we can, and as much hardware as we can take.

"We shan't hurt the Good Folk—they're still the last of humanity and, no matter how elfin we become, we've got to remember that they are Children of Mile just like us. But they'll all learn, Good Folk and Outlandish together, that there's another kind of fairy tale than the happy-ever-after. There's the kind that makes you hide in your bed and hang up crosses, ring church bells, scatter iron about, and, oh, yes, leave out bowls of milk and porridge if you want to be safe.

"The Good Folk are teaching the Outlandish our stories, and we're going to slip a few of our own into their grim fairy books."

In the elf-light under a stone monument as old as the Fir Bolg we gathered.

"Captain," William said, pulling all the BBC English he could into his native Yorkshire voice. "How can we live out here? People can't survive on stories."

"You're wrong, Sergeant," I said. "We've been frightening the Outlandish for years. We can stay safe amid their fear."

"We've been dying for years, as well, Captain Kincaid," Williams said raising the formality. "Even though they're scared of us."

"Only because we were fighting them. We're raiders now, old son. Raiders like your Viking ancestors who took Britain from the Celts and sacked and settled Dublin. The Good Folk have won the war. We don't have to fight it anymore. All we need to do is survive and make them fear us."

"Fear?" Corporal O'Rourke licked the word across his teeth, letting long moon-silver fangs grow from its sound.

"Fear." Williams bounced the word on the ground and watched it fly high like a raven prophesying doom. "A good basis for spinning a yarn."

"And what a yarn it'll be," I said. Two disembodied heads appeared near my shoulders, one taken from a photograph, the other from a self-drawing in a monk's chronicle. Gran and Two-Faced Mickey and I smiled our triple smile, mean upon mean upon mean.

My Knights kicked off the iron chains of despair, grinned their soldiers' grins and holomorphed their bright faces into long and shadowy seemings. Horns grew out of my helmet and my appearance became hot like death chasing. The sounds of hounds came from my speakers and the roar and whimper of captured ghosts bawled forth from my troops.

Patricia Minkowski and the three Knights remaining from her patrol limped into camp, loping like kelpies out of the swamps and river, battered but alive.

"I heard," Patricia said, and she became tall and willowy with hair like weeds, teeth green like patinaed copper, and a belt of screaming heads around her waist. Beautiful. We rose up and howled like Redcaps charging down from the hills, like the blast of winter that freezes hearts, like the passage of a witch that curdles milk.

We will hunt you up and down.

The Rade is coming. Lock your doors, hide under your hills.

The goblins will get you if you don't watch out.

Trick or treat.

Sleep tight, my little changelings.

NANITE, STAR BRIGHT

by *Tanya Huff*

Tanya Huff lives and writes in rural Ontario with her partner, four cats, and an unintentional chihuahua. After sixteen fantasies, she wrote her first space opera, *Valor's Choice*, the sequel to which, *The Better Part of Valor*, is just out from DAW. Currently she is working on the third novel in her *Keeper* series, which began with *Summon the Keeper* and *The Second Summoning*. In her spare time she gardens and complains about the weather.

Tanya Huff writes fantasy and science fiction stories that could compare to fairy tales; tight tales that pack a maximum punch in a minimum space. The following story is no different, as we fade in on her take of a very overworked craftswoman, and the unusual help that comes into her shop.

L OST in the intricate depths of a subatomic filter, Ely Shoemaker remained oblivious to the dark shadow that fell suddenly over her workbench. Then something clamped down hard on her left shoulder.

"God damn it, Christine, I'm working!" Grabbing for the edge of the counter with one hand and shoving up her faceplate with the other, she whirled around and came face-to-face with absolutely the last person she wanted to see.

"Where the hell's my tachometer?"

Unable to stop herself, Ely glanced toward one of the repair shop's crowded shelves.

Jean Perault followed her gaze. His lip curled. "Yesterday, you said it'd be fixed no later than 17:30 today! It's later, Shoemaker. It's a whole half hour later, and my tach still isn't fixed!"

"It's just the backup . . ."

"Yeah, it's the backup, but that's not the point. Point is, you said you'd have it fixed. And you don't."

"I meant to." She shook free of his grip and resisted the urge to jump off the stool onto his foot. Unfortunately, Perault was a shift boss at the fuel station and she couldn't afford to piss him off. Or at least piss him off any more than he was already. "I was going to do it this morning; I got it apart, but I had an idea of how to fix my scrubber."

"Your scrubber?" He leaned around her and stared at the piece of machinery on the counter. "You're not still working on that piece of junk, are you?"

"It's not a piece of junk. If we can get the contaminants out of the gas at the source . . ."

". . . we won't need to refine on station, we won't have to handle the waste gases, and we won't run the risk of another Red Tuesday. I've heard it all before, Shoemaker, but that doesn't change the fact that both the mag field and the electrical activity are too bloody strong to overcome with something small enough to fit into the pipelines."

Ely opened her mouth, but Perault cut her off before she could actually say anything.

"And, yeah, if you could get it to work, the company'd pay you a small fortune for it, but you're missing the point."

"Which is?"

"Which is, my tach was supposed to be fixed today!"

"Look, Jean, I'm really sorry." Hands spread, she tried a conciliatory smile. "You're right. I shouldn't be messing around with this and ignoring paying customers. I'll fix your tach this evening and you can pick it up tomorrow on your way in to work. You weren't going to install it until tomorrow morning anyway."

"That's not the point . . ."

"I know."

Perault stared at her for a long moment. "Well, only because I don't have a choice . . . First thing, tomorrow though—0600. We've got a ship in at 0630 and I want to be there, with my backup tachometer, when they arrive."

"You will be."

"I'd better be." He stomped toward the hatch, paused

with one foot out in the corridor, and turned. "If I'm not, and my crew ends up sitting around with their thumbs up their collective ass because we've had a breakdown with no backup part, you're covering the costs even if that means you have to sell every piece of junk in here for scrap."

"Switch to decaf," Ely muttered as the hatch slammed shut behind him. "It's just a goddamned backup tachometer."

"Which you promised to have fixed this afternoon."

She pivoted slowly on the stool as Christine came through the hatch that connected their living quarters to the shop. "How long were you there?"

"Long enough. I was on my way in to get you for supper when Perault arrived. He has a point, Ely."

"I know." Slipping off the scope, she laid it on the counter beside the scrubber. "I really did mean to fix it."

"So I heard," Christine slid her arms around Ely's waist and rubbed her cheek against her shoulder. "Fix it after dinner."

"Please tell me it's not textured protein patties again."

"All right."

"Oh, God, it is, isn't it?"

"It is, but looking at the bright side, there's not very many of them."

"Christine."

"We can't afford anything else. We still owe the company for those three weeks I was sick."

"Damned bloodsuckers . . ."

"Blood we could pay them." Leaning back, Christine rubbed thumb and forefinger together and added with a resigned sigh, "It's cash we're short of."

"Who isn't?" Ely snorted. "If I could just get this scrubber working, we'd be so far ahead you could get sick every month if you wanted."

"Sick every month?" One corner of her mouth curled up. "You really know how to sweet talk a girl. Now, come to . . ."

The hatch into the shop swung open and both women turned to watch as an old man carrying a battered plastic crate stumbled over the lip. He staggered forward three steps, sideways one, and would have toppled had Ely not raced around the counter and grabbed his arm.

"Careful, Joe. Here, let me take the box. It looks heavy." It was heavy. She managed to get it to the counter but only just. "Damn, Joe. What've you got in here, rocks?"

The old rockhound cackled at the joke—either not caring or not remembering it was the same joke every time he showed up. "Got good stuff in there, Ely. Good stuff."

"You think so? Well, let me have a look, then . . ."

Dr. Joseph Grim, Ph.D., had once been one of the company's best geologists. He'd been responsible for three top finds and a number of smaller ones—skipping around the edge of the asteroid belt from ore to ore, from bonus to bonus. When his luck ran out, it ran out in a big way. Certain he was on the way to his next big find, he ordered his pilot deeper into the belt than anyone had ever gone. No one knew why his pilot had agreed; no one would ever know. The ship crashed on one of the bigger rocks, the four-man crew died instantly leaving only Dr. Grim. When his air ran out, unable to remove the tanks, he hooked himself up to each corpse in turn. When that air ran out, he used the equipment he had on board to pull oxygen from the ice on the rock. By the time the company found him, he was pretty much insane.

He used his savings to buy a small ship and go back to the belt.

He wouldn't tell anyone what he was looking for.

When his savings were gone, he began selling the things he found.

Mostly, he found debris swept up by the belt. The flotsam and jetsam of five centuries of space travel.

Mostly he found junk.

This trip was no different.

Piece of nozzle and hose from a hydroponics setup. Chunk of burned and broken tube lining. Ely set them down on the growing pile. *Something that looks like an old distributor cap.* The last thing in the crate was about thirty centimeters long and maybe half that around in the center. The ends tapered to blunt points and it looked as if a number of things had been broken off it over the years. *And I have no idea what this is. Or what it's made of.* It was the color of old brass and the metal felt greasy. Hefting it, she was willing to bet it was probably hollow, or honeycombed. Not solid, anyway.

She set it on the top of the pile and looked up to find both Joe and Christine staring at her.

The old man rubbed his hands together. "Good stuff, eh?"

"Same as always, Joe."

Christine rolled her eyes.

When Ely made her first offer, Joe's lower lip went out. Translation; he didn't have enough to pay his docking fee. At her second offer, his lip went in but his brows drew down. He was calculating what he'd have to do without. When she made her third offer, he smiled.

And a damn good thing too. Ely thumbprinted the transfer on his grubby disk. *'Cause that's already ten times what this crap is worth.* But she couldn't leave him sucking vacuum, and once or twice he'd actually had something she could use.

"When was the last time you ate, Joe?"

He turned to peer up at Christine. "Ate?"

"You've been forgetting again, haven't you?"

He shrugged, clearly having already forgotten the question. "Maybe?"

"Come on." She slipped his arm through hers. "You might as well join us for dinner although it's just textured protein."

His smile had all the pure joy of a child promised a treat. "I like textured protein."

"You would," Ely muttered taking his other arm.

"Because I'm crazy?"

"That'd be my best guess."

Ely returned to the shop after dinner, pulled the pieces of Perault's tachometer out of the mess on the shelf, and set them on the counter. She could fix it in an hour, maybe less, and then she could spend the time until power-down working on her scrubber. Fixing odds and ends was *not* going to get them out of the hole they were in.

Reaching past the pile of Joe's junk—her junk now—her elbow hit the oval *thing*. Steadying it turned into lifting it, turned into examining it, turned into discovering no more about it than she'd seen earlier. Intrigued, she slipped on her scope and dropped the faceplate.

At high resolution, it became quite obvious that the thing had been damaged. Stubby ends, no more than three or four molecules wide and a dozen high stuck up along opposite sides of the long axis.

Which gave her an idea . . .

Power-down caught her deep within her scrubber.

Perault's tachometer was still in pieces.

"It's all right. Don't panic." In the dim light of the emergency exit sign over the shop door, she set the scope carefully aside. "I set the alarm for five. It's fixed when he's here at six. No problem."

Pulled from a dream where she was attempting to open a jammed door with a heavy drill, Ely woke to find Christine's head on her pillow and Christine snoring into her ear. By the time she got her to roll over, she was wide awake.

It feels like it's the middle of the night.

Heaving herself up onto one elbow, she peered at the clock.

0552.

"Oh, crap!"

"What is it?" Christine muttered sleepily.

"The alarm didn't go off."

"Shoemaker's wives go barefoot."

"What? Never mind." She dragged a pair of overalls on, combed her hands through her hair, and ran for the shop. Maybe Perault would be late.

He arrived seconds after she did.

"Look, Jean, I can explain . . ."

"I don't want explanations, I want my tachometer." A long arm snaked out and snatched it off the counter. "Looks okay," he grunted reluctantly.

It looked better than okay. It looked new.

Frowning, Ely replayed the previous evening in her head. No question about it, she had definitely left the tachometer in pieces on the counter.

"Hey, you even filled in the gouge that moron McGregor put in it during the disconnect. Now, you didn't have to do that."

"I, uh . . ." Ely shrugged. "You know."

"You do good work, Shoemaker. When you finally get your head out of your ass long enough to do it." His brows dipped in and he held out his free hand. "Your disk. I haven't got all morning."

"Right." She passed it over, watched as he thumbprinted

the transfer, and took it back all without saying another word. There didn't seem to be anything she could say.

"It was fixed?"

"Yes."

"And you didn't fix it?"

"That's right."

Christine stared at the place on the workbench where the tachometer had spent the night and shook her head. "It had to be one of your friends playing a joke on you. Maybe Dave. That's the kind of thing he'd think was funny."

"Yeah, but Dave's night shift this week. He couldn't have got away to do it. And no one wanders around this part of the station after power-down. No one with half a brain anyway."

"Which doesn't exclude a number of your friends from the maintenance crews. I suggest you make some calls." Kissing her quickly, Christine headed for the door. "I'll be done by 1630. It's your turn to make dinner."

Ely waved absently in the general direction of her wife's back. "Yeah, sure. Whatever." She pulled a vacuum pump off the shelf, disassembled it, and stared at the pieces. They remained pieces.

Suddenly restless, she went back into their tiny kitchenette, stared at the empty coffee canister, tried to remember the last time there'd been anything in it, and couldn't. It had been ages since they could afford even the chicory stuff and since they grew the chicory on station, that was saying something.

Fixing odds and ends wouldn't clear their debts, but it would, at least, buy them some coffee.

Back in the repair shop the vacuum pump still hadn't fixed itself.

"Okay. Fine. Be that way."

The seals were shot, but then it was always the seals on vacuum pumps. She had another four on the shelves with the same problem. By 1530 that afternoon, she'd fixed all but one of them. The fifth, the largest pump, had been left running even after the pressure had begun to fall and the whole thing had seized into one solid mass.

"Replacing the seals is the least of your problems," Ely

muttered, pushing it aside. Fixing it would mean a tidy bit of change to cover parts and labor—but gods, where to start? She'd have to drill out two of the heat sink boots and one gasket cover would have to be cut off. She had the gasket cover in stock, but the boots, she'd have to make.

"So I might just as well deliver the pumps that *are* fixed and leave this until tomorrow." Besides, she'd never got around to making those calls and at this hour most of her friends off the old maintenance crew would be at Sam's Bar.

"You were supposed to make dinner."

"Sorry." Ely crossed the shop with one hand behind her back trying to judge Christine's mood from her expression. Twenty years of practice had made her no better at it than she'd been when they first met. As usual, Christine wasn't giving anything away. "For what it's worth, no one was anywhere near here last night after power-down. I asked around, then I stopped by security on the way back and had Janet check the logs."

"Did you tell her why?"

Curiosity had overcome any earlier pique over the uncooked dinner. Ely breathed a mostly metaphorical sigh of relief. "Did I tell her that someone snuck in and fixed a tachometer? Not likely. She'd think I was drunk. I told her I thought I heard someone trying to jimmy the hatch."

Christine frowned and unfolded her arms. "What kind of idiot would try to rob us?"

"Funny, that's what Janet said. I bought us something."

"Ely."

"No, it's okay. Perault's transfer covered what I paid Joe and I fixed those four small pumps today so . . ." She brought her hand out, the small bag balanced on the palm. The smell was unmistakable.

"That's real coffee."

"Yes, it is."

"Ely, that stuff costs five times what the chicory costs!"

"But it's ten times better."

"Our debt . . ."

"Won't look so intimidating once we're highly caffeinated."

"You think?" Christine sighed again, but this time she

smiled as she did it. "Come on, I'll reheat your protein patty."

Next morning, Ely hooked her stool up to the workbench, set her mug down, and discovered the big vacuum pump had been repaired during the night. Not only repaired; it tested at a higher efficiency than it had been originally rated for. Stranger still, a chunk of Joe's broken tube lining was missing.

"What do you mean, missing?" Christine demanded.

"I mean, not here." Ely held up the remaining chunk. "Look at that clean edge. Something's cut a piece of it off."

"Something?"

"Probably the same something that fixed the pump. "

"Let's hope."

"You're taking this very calmly."

Christine shrugged. "Why shouldn't I? So far, the *something* has been very helpful."

"Well, yeah, but . . ."

"Look, I'm going to be late for work. If you want to have security go over the shop, be my guest, but I personally don't think we should look a gift . . ." She paused, searching for a word and surrendering without finding one. ". . . gift in the mouth. Or am I wrong in assuming the transfer for the pump will be a sizable one?"

"Relatively," Ely admitted, turning the pump on its side and staring at the bottom.

"Glad to hear it."

When Ely looked up, Christine was smiling. "We're dumping and cleaning the D-bank yeast tanks today, so I'll be home when I get here."

"Right. Bye." The smile hadn't been because she liked the thought of clean tanks. She'd been smiling because of the transfer for the pump. She hadn't smiled like that because of Ely for a long time. Not even the coffee had made her smile like that.

"Okay, fine. If that's the way you want it."

Twisting her hair up and securing it with a bit of wire, Ely pulled down a broken grappling arm removed from one of the exterior cleaning bots and, shoving her scrubber to the far end of the bench, she went to work replacing a joint. When she stopped for lunch, she threw a rag over the scrubber because even at the end of the bench it was too great a temptation.

By power-down, she'd received three more transfers for repairs and could barely keep her eyes open. Leaving the parts of a compressor scattered over the bench, she went to bed.

When she stumbled into the shop at 0630 the parts had been reassembled and the casing shone.

"Okay, now you're just showing off."

But the payment, added to all the others, meant they might actually have enough in the account to pay their bills at the end of the month.

And because she refused to be shown up by an invisible mechanic, she spent the day fixing a rotor that had been sitting forgotten on an upper shelf for nearly four months.

That night, she left three sprinkler heads from hydroponics sitting on the workbench in a row.

They were fixed by morning. Another piece had been taken out of the tube lining.

"Ely, what are you doing?"

"I'm building a sort of curtain."

"A what?"

"Something to hide behind that'll keep me from reading on standard sensors."

"Okay." Christine rubbed her forehead wearily and sighed. "Why?"

Ely ran power into the thermal screen, frowned, and disconnected the coupling. "So I can find out who's been sneaking in here at night."

"Station security . . ."

"Can be got around; you know that as well as I do. No, if we want to catch whoever's doing this, we'll have to do it ourselves."

"Do we want to catch them?"

She'd been thinking about that all afternoon. "Yeah. We do. Whoever's doing this has their own agenda, and I'm not going to keep following it blindly."

Shaking her head, Christine walked past and into their

quarters, throwing back a tired, "Maybe they're helping out of the kindness of their hearts."

"Right," Ely snorted. "Or maybe it's elves."

Half a dozen elves in greasy overalls danced across the top of the workbench. They were singing, in a jolly sort of way, although the words made no sense. Just as Ely knew she was about to understand, and knowing it was vitally important she understand, she woke up.

Wondering where she was, she lifted her head out of a puddle of drool, and peered around. *Oh, right. I'm behind the "curtain."* And then, redundantly, *I must've fallen asleep.*

The emergency exit light over the hatch lit the area enough for eyes adapted to the darkness to see the workbench and the broken temperature gauge lying on it. There was no one in the shop.

Ely checked her watch. Two thirteen. Three hours and thirteen minutes since power-down and there was no one in the shop. Had they been keeping her under surveillance? Did they know she was there? Maybe the temperature gauge wasn't enough of a challenge. *Whatever. At three, I'm packing it in and . . .*

The click was just on the edge of audible.

Ely froze. The sound had come from much closer than the hatch.

Another click. A little louder.

The temperature gauge began to sparkle. At first Ely thought her eyes were playing tricks on her, that the sparkle was no more than the random specks of color and light everyone saw when staring into the dark, but the specks weren't random or colored. They were white and making definite patterns on the gauge, and the more she looked, the easier they were to see.

Then a small clump moved off to the pile of Joe's junk still on the end of the bench and settled on a coil of corroded copper wire. They brightened, flashed blue for an instant, and returned to the gauge.

No more than ten minuets later, the whole sparkling mass rose up into the air and moved back to the pile of junk, landing on the oval sphere, thinning, and finally disappearing.

* * *

"So you're saying, tiny lights came out of this . . . thing and fixed the temperature gauge."

"Not only fixed it, they fabricated a new piece for it out of this old copper wire." Ely was so excited she almost bounced. Waiting until power-up at five when she could actually see what had been done had been the longest three and a half hours of her life. "See the shiny bit?"

"I see it."

"And here, in the gauge."

Christine stared at the shiny copper amidst the incomprehensible bits. "Okay." She looked up and managed to catch her wife's eye. "So what are they?"

"They've got to be some kind of nanotech."

"You can't see nanotech, El. I mean, isn't that kind of what the nano part means?"

Ely grinned. "You can't see carbon molecules either, but get enough of them together and you can see the lump of coal."

"Okay, granted, but nanotech's been illegal since the meltdown of '37 when those ore processors went out of control."

"I know." Ely lifted the oval sphere, one hand stroking it possessively. "But what if someone just tossed this bunch into space instead of destroying them?"

"Then they broke the law," Christine reminded her. "You have to turn them in."

"What? No. First, do you know what the penalty is for getting caught using nanotech—which I've been doing for almost a week now—and second, these have clearly been programmed to do repairs and I'm not giving them up."

Arms folded, Christine exhaled wearily. "Ely . . ."

"I said, no. Think about it for a minute, Chris. This is our chance to get out of debt. It's like being able to hire a precision mechanic to do all the crappy, time-consuming stuff and not only not having to pay *them* but not having to pay for the energy they use either."

"Which is?"

"I don't know, but probably hydrogen just like the big boys use, only they pull theirs out of the atmosphere instead of your friendly neighborhood gas giant." She set down the oval and caught up both of Christine's hands. "They fixed three sprinkler heads in one night and on two of them they had to fabricate a new actuator nut. Do you know how long that would take me on the lathe? Those things are so damned old no two are the same size. So forget about the debt for a minute, think of how it'll feel to pay off all of our bills at the end of the month and have enough left over to stock up on real food."

Still not entirely convinced, Christine shook her head. "We can't forget the debt."

"Okay, so we throw in a box of patties every month and put what we save on the debt. We'll be free and clear by the end of the year. Sweetie, you know the company hates to spend money on this station—bunch of cheap, suit-wearing bastards—so I can get as much repair work as I can do and with these little guys helping, I can do three times as much."

"The problem isn't getting the work. There's always been lots of work, *that's* why you decided to go into business for yourself. The problem is not getting it done." Turning her head, Christine looked pointedly at the scrubber still under the rag at the end of the bench. "You have a tendency to get distracted."

It took a major effort of will, but Ely stopped herself from mirroring Christine's movement. "I worked on the scrubber so much because I knew I could work my ass off doing repairs and it wouldn't make any difference. But that's changed."

"Changed?"

"By the nanites."

"If we get caught with them . . ." But her tone had become speculation rather than protest and Ely knew she'd won.

"We won't."

"Promise me."

"I promise."

"Okay."

The second week after Joe's visit—which was how Ely had begun to think of time passing—was pretty much a repeat of the first. Pretty much. Word got around that Ely

Shoemaker had finally got her head back together and was doing the kind of work everyone knew she *could* do. As a result, for every repair that went out, two or three came in.

There didn't seem to be anything the nanites couldn't fix or fabricate as long as they had the raw materials close at hand. They never left the bench and although Ely used her scope on the oval almost daily, she couldn't find the way they went in and out.

"What's that?"

Ely flipped up her faceplate and took the mug of coffee with a smile of thanks. "That, my darling, is part of the broken guts of a proximity buoy."

"That satellites that help guide ships into the fueling bays?"

"None other."

"Okay, call me an alarmist, but shouldn't it be out there guiding ships?"

"And it will be tomorrow morning,." Ely grinned. "I mean, I could work on it for the next two or three days, but I think I'll fix a couple of vacuum pumps and leave it for the staff."

Next morning, not only was the buoy still in pieces but two small titanium components were missing.

"What the hell are you guys up to?" Moving the oval to the center of the bench, Ely flipped down her faceplate. It looked much the same as it had except the tiny stubs along both sides of the long axis were definitely longer. The first two had, in fact, been joined by an intricate lacework of metal.

Well, it doesn't take a rocket scientist . . .

She was looking at the missing titanium.

Instead of fixing the buoy, they'd found what they needed and had begun making repairs.

"Which they've been programmed to do. Make repairs . . ."

Except that suggested the oval sphere was more than just a container for nanotech.

Was it a home?

A ship?

A ship, Ely decided. Her instincts were usually bang on about mechanical things.

And if it was a ship, not a container, then whatever was inside couldn't be nanotech.

Little tiny aliens?

Elves?

No. She banished that image and decided to stick with little tiny aliens.

So. Once they completed their repairs; what then? Would they be willing to stick around as unpaid labor? Probably not. The easiest solution? Keep them away from titanium 6/6/2 and nothing had to change.

Ely pulled off her scope and sat staring at down at her hands. Using illegal nanotech to get out of debt was one thing, but to know what an alien lifeform needed and then to keep them from it . . . The whole thing stank of slavery.

"How much?"

"Aerospace grade titanium doesn't grow on trees."

Ely frowned. The only trees she'd ever seen were the fruit trees espaliered in hydroponics. "What the hell does that mean?"

"It means, you ignorant vacuum sucker, that it's not just lying around to be picked up by all and sundry. It's difficult to extract, it's hard to work, it's . . ."

". . . a part of every satellite, in most of the gas mining equipment and all of the heat exchangers. There's a lot of it around!"

"And there's a lot of uses for it." The company acquisitions clerk, looked blandly up at her over steepled fingers. "More uses than available alloy. Which makes it very, very expensive."

"I only need a hundred grams," Ely snarled. She'd extrapolated the amount needed for total repairs from the amount already covered by the satellite components. "I don't want to sheathe the whole fucking station in it!"

"Good. Because I can get you a hundred grams; it's just going to cost you."

It was just going to cost her everything she'd made over the last two weeks.

"You've got to be kidding." Christine took four jerky steps away, and four back, her hands cutting words out of the air. "You break the law using this nanotech to get us out of debt and now you want us to go further into debt so it—they—can repair their ship and fly away?"

"Yes."

"Why?"

Ely sighed. This hadn't been going at all well. "I'm not positive they're nanotech."

"You were positive when you convinced me it would be a good idea to break the law." She leaned forward, brows drawn in. "You *convinced* me, Ely. And *now* you've changed your mind?"

"Well, yeah, sort of. I still don't want to turn them in. I want to let them go free."

"Because they might not be nanotech?"

"Yeah . . ."

"Because they might be little tiny aliens?"

"Or elves." Ely tried a smile but Christine wasn't amused.

"If they're aliens, then where did they come from?"

"I don't know." Ely rubbed her thumb over the end of the sphere. "We'll probably never know."

"Well, we certainly won't know if you spend everything we have on a going-away present for them."

"Your salary . . ."

"Won't cover the bills."

"I'll work harder, I promise."

Christine stared at her for a long moment. "Fine. Here, in case you've forgotten . . ." Lips pressed into a thin line, she wound her wedding ring up off her finger. "Titanium. Only common alloy but they might as well have this, too." Tossing it down onto the workbench where it rolled into Joe's pile of junk, she spun on one heel and stomped into the living quarters.

"Chris . . ."

The hatch slammed.

"Oh, yeah, that went well."

Power-down found Ely behind her curtain, a hundred grams of titanium 6/6/2 sitting beside the oval sphere on the bench. This time, when she heard the first click, she was staring at the sphere. She couldn't see a hatch . . .

You know, a smart woman would be wearing her scope.

. . . but she could see a sparkling line arc out of the upper curve and descend to the titanium. The tiny lights froze for a moment, the first time she'd seen them motionless, and then they exploded outward, weaving wild patterns above the bench. It was silly to extrapolate emotion from a thousand points of light but Ely thought she'd never seen anything look so happy.

No, not happy. Happy didn't have the intensity.

Joyous.

She fell asleep around three and woke up when the power came back on.

The oval sphere, two bands of slate-gray lacework along each side, hovered about fifteen centimeters above the workbench. As Ely approached, it settled slowly down to the scarred surface.

Old friends in the maintenance crew were curious about why she needed to space something out one of the small bot air locks. She had to exchange a promise to tell the full story for the new codes. They wouldn't believe the story, but it would be safe enough to tell as soon as the little guys got away.

They show up when you're down on your luck, I mean really down on your luck, and they make things better. Why? Well, they were programmed to fix things, weren't they?

She didn't need to be told which security camera was currently off-line; fixing it was on the day's to-do list.

Once she got the air lock's inner hatch open, Ely carefully lifted the sphere out of her toolbox. She thought she could feel it vibrating against her fingers, but it was probably imagination. When she set it in the lock, it rose and pivoted along its center axis.

She'd clearly put it in backward. "Sorry."

"So am I."

When her heart started beating, when she could move again, Ely turned, wide-eyed, toward Christine.

"You're doing the right thing . . . and don't say, *I know*, because that's really irritating when someone's trying to apologize."

"Okay. How did you find me?"

"I went to the bar. Dave told me." Christine leaned forward and peered into the lock. "It's pretty."

They closed the inner hatch together, dogged it down, waited for the pressure to equalize, then, holding Christine's hand, Ely opened the outer hatch.

The ship, if ship it was, hovered for a moment longer, sparkled briefly, and was gone.

                              *   *   *

The repair shop felt empty when they returned to it.

Dropping onto her stool, Ely shoved the piece of buoy out of the way and laid her head on her arms. Then she lifted her head and turned the buoy back toward her. "Okay, I guess they only needed ninety-four grams. They've replaced the titanium components."

"Did they finish the repair?"

"Looks like it."

"Nice they showed a *litte* gratitude," Christine muttered, rummaging around in the junk for her wedding ring.

"Yeah, nice." Which was when it hit her. Slowly, barely breathing, Ely turned toward the scrubber and pulled off the rag.

It looked exactly the way it had when she'd stopped working on it. Virtue, it appeared, was its own reward.

"Thank god. They didn't use my ring."

The ring sparkled in the light as Christine held it up and Ely frowned. The ring had a matte finish. It shouldn't be sparkling. "Let me see that." Settling the scope on her head, she flipped down the faceplate. Under high magnification it became obvious that the micronic oxide layer of the titanium had been electronically thickened to create different refractive effects. All the colors of the rainbow danced across both the inner and the outer curve of the band.

"What's wrong with my ring?"

"Nothing's wrong. They left us a message."

"A message. What does it say?"

All the colors of the rainbow . . .

. . . forming a complete set of schematic diagrams.

If they'd built the scrubber for her, how could she have built a second? Or a third? Or sold the patent to the company for the small fortune it would bring?

"It says, *and they lived happily ever after.*"

THE PRINCESS AND THE ACCOUNTANT

by Robert E. Rogoff

If the name Robert E. Rogoff seems familiar to you, but you can't figure out why, maybe it's because you've seen his contributions to virtual Internet communities, including The Well, Usenet, and SFF Net. You might remember his 'zines, such as *The Height Report*, a sociological journal, published on demand from digital inventory as long ago as 1994. On the other hand, it's entirely possible that you actually have read some of his stories, which so far have tended to be short, quirky, and humorous—not unlike the man himself. Even if you haven't read his work in *Aberrations* or *Crank!*, you might have at least seen his name on the cover of *Galaxy* a number of times.

Although common men in simple professions often got their due in fairy tales (the brave little tailor comes to mind), we think it's a safe bet that no one ever thought of the following occupation as a mold for a hero, at least, until now.

ONCE upon a time on a planet somewhere in the Milky Way Galaxy, there lived a pragmatic, dependable man named Ralph Glorp. Ralph worked as an accountant for the Royal Distribution Agency. He was charged with smoothing out the fluctuating cycles of the kingdom's economy.

One day, he entered the office of his supervisor, Shirley Lumula.

Shirley Lumula was a wise woman of indeterminate age, with a broad body and a mind to match. Lumula had a keen eye for nuance, and was by nature an astute observer of people, places, and things. She sensed something amiss in Ralph's bearing, and said so.

"I sense something amiss in your bearing," said Lumula, looking up from her desk. "What troubles you?" she asked.

Ralph looked around the room. Ripped-open snack packages and dishes crusted with caked gobs of food cluttered the tops of Lumula's mismatched office furniture like fossil shells of extinct marine animals. Datasheets were scattered all over the place, like small scraps of used clothing. Some of the sheets were turned off, some were carelessly left turned on, and some even blinked random strings of nonsensical alphanumeric characters, signaling that they were broken.

Ralph had never understood how an administrator could work amidst such haphazard clutter. His own office had always been neatly ordered, as befit a pragmatic, reliable accountant who was charged with smoothing out the fluctuating cycles of the kingdom's economy.

Ralph sighed. "I've decided to quit my job," he said.

Upon hearing Ralph's statement, Lumula ducked backward, as if to avoid being hit. She blinked her large blue eyes five or six times, momentarily stunned into silence. "You've been working here for three centuries," she said, "and you've always seemed content before. "What makes you want to quit? And why now?"

Ralph could feel heat flow into his face as he blushed a deep red. He stared at his shoes for a moment, then grinned modestly. He reached into his hip pocket and pulled out a crumpled datasheet. Nervously, Ralph smoothed out the sheet's wrinkles as he placed it on the desk. Quickened by the room's full-spectrum lighting, the sheet bloomed into a full-page illustration of a beautiful woman, jewel-bedecked and attired in a brocade gown.

"You have a picture of the Princess," commented Lumula. "So?"

Ralph cleared his throat. He took a breath. "I'm going to the Royal Palace to marry her," he said. "As you can see by her picture, she's the most beautiful woman in the universe."

Lumula sighed. "When designing a person's genome," she told Ralph, "physical beauty is often used as a substitute for other redeeming qualities."

"Well, she's the Princess!" exclaimed Ralph. "And that makes her redeeming enough for me!"

Lumula cocked her head and tapped a finger on the desk-top several times. "You realize, of course, that from where I sit, what you intend to do seems quite foolish. Do you honestly believe that out of all the possible suitors in the universe, the Princess would want to marry you? Do you think the King would want you as a son-in-law? Royal marriages are made out of political expediency—I can't see much of that in getting married to an accountant with a middle-class genome."

"Well . . ." Ralph hesitated for a bit. He had never been particularly adventurous or romantic. Until recently, he had been more than content with the pragmatic, dependable life for which his mind and body seemed so perfectly designed. Something about Ralph had now changed.

What had changed? Maybe something had gone wrong with his hormones, or with his genes. Maybe something in the environment had influenced his neurological processes. Or maybe the change had been planned, engineered right into his genome in such a way as to make his newfound romanticism kick in after his biological clock had ticked enough tocks.

Whatever the reason, Ralph knew one thing. It was his destiny to marry the Princess.

Lumula sat back in her chair, steepling her fingers. "She's the Princess, and you're an accountant."

Ralph cleared his throat and stood as tall as his middle-class body could. "Yes," he said, "that's true."

Lumula blinked her large eyes. "So what's going on here, do you think?"

"I don't think," said Ralph. "I know. I know it's my destiny to marry her."

"Your destiny?" asked Lumula. She shook her head. "Now I've heard everything! Well, be that as it may, I hope you weren't thinking of leaving immediately, were you? Although there's a waiting list for most jobs, nobody is standing in line for yours."

"I'm sure you'll find a replacement for me soon. Working here is challenging and rewarding—the Royal Distribution Agency is vital to the kingdom's economy! Without us, who would figure the percentage of goods and services to take from the people who produced them? Who would plan how to divide those goods and services among the whole population, according to social standing?"

"No need to lecture me on the importance of the RDA, Ralph. If I didn't like it here, I'd go jack into the Supernet to vegetate for a few hundred years, as do most people without hobbies such as jobs." Lumula tapped the desk some more. "Come on, Ralph, what's going on? Have you developed an infatuation with this woman? Why not just cyber-socialize with an artificial life form? Design it to impersonate her."

"This is no schoolboy crush! My love for the Princess is both passionate and mature."

Lumula sat forward in her chair and folded her arms on the desk. Her brow wrinkled with thought. "Do you feel true love, and not merely lust? Love is forever, but lust is right now. If you actually love her—not just lust after her—then there's no reason to leave so soon. You'll be able to stay until I hire a suitable replacement."

Ralph awkwardly waggled his head in an exaggerated manner he thought displayed pride. "What I feel is true love, and this love has been building for many years. Now its time has finally come. My destiny cannot be denied. I must leave—right now!"

Lumula sat back, examined her fingernails, looked up again, and said, "Very well. If this is your destiny, then it cannot be denied. I release you from your job. Best wishes."

And so, Ralph set forth on his journey.

On his way out of the building, a security guard stopped him. The security guard was a compact woman with a face the color of sand. She asked Ralph what he was up to, leaving the building so early in the day.

"I'm going to the Palace, to marry the Princess," explained Ralph, flourishing the datasheet with the photo. "She's the most beautiful woman in the universe."

"Sure seems to be, judging from this picture," said the guard. "But what business do you have going and marrying her?"

Ralph waggled his head. "It is my destiny," he said.

"Well," said the security guard, "we sure can't deny destiny, can we?"

And with that, the security guard buzzed Ralph out. Ralph strapped on his solar-powered in-line skates and struck out for the Palace.

Cutting through peaceful grassland punctuated with scattered tree copses and thickets, the road to the Palace was wide open—a flat band of smoothness crested by a pair of rails that had once been used by automated vehicle traffic. The road extended to the horizon, to the very limit of vision, an optimistic reminder to Ralph that his vistas had now expanded.

Ralph was cruising along when suddenly a Police soldier jumped out at him from behind a billboard and pulled him over.

The helmeted man hopped off his skateboard and crouched in a fighting stance. He was dressed from neck to toe in a matte-black uniform. His eyes hid behind mirrorized goggles that shone cold like ice. "Hold it right there!" he commanded. He had a scratchy tenor voice that seemed incredibly loud contrasted with the quiet of the prairie setting. "What purpose have you for using this highway? Don't you know it leads to the King's Palace?"

"Of c–course—of course I know that," explained Ralph, his hands trembling. He noticed he was hunched over and was clenching his fists. He willed himself to relax, cleared his throat, and straightened up. "I'm going to the Palace," he said, "to marry the Princess. She's the most beautiful woman in the whole universe."

"I see," said the Police soldier, a wry grin betraying his bemusement. "Why?" he asked.

"Because it is my destiny," said Ralph.

"Destiny, huh?" muttered the Police soldier, almost to himself. "How do you like that?" The Police soldier paused a moment in thought, and then said: "Destiny cannot be denied. You may pass."

Ralph sighed with relief and persevered.

On the horizon, Ralph could make out a small, glowing dot, flickering like a distant flame. It was the Palace, which, as he knew from his datasheet research, played a continuous light show across its outer walls during peacetime.

Without warning, a large shape loomed before him, impeding his progress. Startled, Ralph realized that an indentured warfighter was aiming a projectile weapon at him. The tall, stocky man wore a sharp dress uniform of orange and black, the colors of the aristocracy.

"State your name and purpose, stranger!" he yelled.

"My name is Ralph Glorp," said Ralph. Ralph's confidence had grown since his last challenge, and his demeanor showed it. "I'm going to the Palace to marry the Princess." He spoke firmly. "She's the most beautiful woman in the whole universe."

"Interesting. Why are you doing this?" asked the indentured warfighter.

"Because it is my destiny."

"Destiny cannot be denied," said the indentured warfighter, flashing Ralph the formal salute reserved for members of the aristocracy. "You may pass."

A few moments later, a one-man hovercraft swung to a stop in Ralph's path with a whoosh and a dull thud as it settled to the ground. Ralph had to brake quickly to avoid a collision. Out of the craft jumped a lanky man wearing a news cam on his head like an overenthusiastic hat. He was a journalist. The journalist stuck a microphone in Ralph's face and asked, "Is it true you're gong to the Palace to marry the Princess?"

"That's right," said Ralph into the camera, smoothly. "And you can tell your viewers that she's the most beautiful woman in the whole universe!"

"Thank you, Ralph Glorp!" said the journalist, zooming in for a few close-ups. He closed his report with a wry commentary about destiny, clambered back aboard his hovercraft, and zoomed away with a swoosh.

Ralph drew nearer his destination. He chanced upon a tourist snapping pictures. The tourist wore his hair long and sported a full beard, as the men did in the cold land of Snowdrift.

"Hey!" cried the tourist in his Snowdrift accent. He wiped a trickle of sweat from his face with a shirtsleeve. "You're dot guy on da news!"

"That's right," boasted Ralph, beaming proudly.

The tourist laughed, elated at his good fortune to meet a celebrity. "I understand you're going to da Palace to marry da Princess."

"Yes," said Ralph. That's what I'm going to do, all right."

"I also understand she's da most beautiful woman on da whole planet!"

"Yes. Although that may be somewhat of an understatement."

"Cool!" said the tourist. "You're one lucky fellow."

"That I am," said Ralph.

"You know, destiny cannot be denied. Would you mind posing for a few snapshots?"

"Not at all, but I'm surprised tourists can get permission to roam around taking pictures so close to the Palace."

The tourist chuckled. "Who says anyone gave me permission?"

Ralph quickly looked over his shoulder. No Police soldiers were around. Relieved, he turned back to the tourist. "That's a nice camera you have there," he said.

The tourist smiled. "Yes, it cost me a lot of money."

"Money?"

"In Snowdrift, we exchange symbolic tokens of value called money."

"Ah, yes—money. As someone who loves our great Royal Distribution System, I must tell you: money sounds like a bizarre and ridiculous concept. But then, Snowdrift is a distant and mysterious land. You have all manner of unique customs there, don't you? Is it true Snowdrift women bear their children live, right out of their bodies?"

The tourist looked away and sighed. "Dot fad is losing popularity dese days," he said quietly.

"What a relief!" exclaimed Ralph.

The tourist finished taking his pictures and bid Ralph farewell. Ralph powered up his skates and proceeded.

Not much later, Ralph came upon a field of grain waving lazily in the breeze. A large threshing machine cut a swath through the field, noisily harvesting the crops with flaying arms as it wheeled itself along.

Seated in a chair positioned next to the field was a tenant farmer. She looked up, noticing Ralph, and set her drink on the end table next to her chair. She whistled and called out, "Stop, you ridiculous machine!" The large, whirring robot gasped and shuddered to a standstill. The tenant farmer seemed to think something was hilarious. She chortled as she rose, and with a big grin, waved to Ralph.

Ralph slowed down until his skates were barely moving him along. He could smell the acrid scent of fertilized soil.

The tenant farmer walked over, so Ralph stopped to see what she wanted. She was a head taller than Ralph. Beneath her coveralls, her body was well-toned. "I thought I recognized you!" she said, wide-eyed with awe. "You're the guy!"

"Right!" said Ralph.

"She's the most beautiful woman in the whole damn universe!"

"Right," said Ralph.

"Destiny cannot be denied!"

"Right."

The tenant farmer moved closer to Ralph. She put one of her large hands on his shoulder and grasped the front of his shirt with the other. She pulled his face right up to hers and looked deep into his eyes. She was so close that Ralph could feel warm puffs of her breath on his skin. Her breath smelled of alcohol. "I'm no princess," she said, "but you know, farmer women enjoy the company of famous men, too. Care to join me for a drink?"

Ralph cleared his throat. "Maybe another time," he said, unsuccessfully trying to wriggle free.

The tenant farmer let loose a long sigh, all over Ralph's face. "Okay," she said, releasing Ralph. "But you don't know what you're missing."

Ralph sighed, brushed himself off, and said good-bye.

He was about to leave when a sharp object poked him between the shoulder blades. "Halt!" cried an official-sounding voice. Ralph slowly turned around. He looked up to meet the direct gaze of an Elite Lightning Goon, dressed in sleek, strength-augmenting battle armor that gleamed in the sunlight. The Elite Lightning Goon drew back with a start. Quickly, he shouldered the plasma rifle with which he had been prodding Ralph a moment earlier. "Oops," the man said sheepishly. "Sorry, Mister Glorp. You should always remember to wear your orange and black out here. You may pass, of course. Destiny cannot be denied." The Elite Lightning Goon saluted.

The tenant farmer, who had been standing nearby, walked over to the Elite Lightning Goon and said, "Hi there, good-looking. I love a man in strength-augmenting battle armor."

Ralph shook his head and set forth again.

As he approached the Palace, Ralph's eyes widened at the brilliant orange pulses of light cascading across the slick black Palace walls like neurotransmitters coursing through the synapses of a dreaming child.

At long last, Ralph found himself standing at the drawbridge to the King's Palace. He cupped his hands around his mouth and shouted: "Hello there!"

A palace guard, leafing through a news sheet to pass the time, recognized Ralph immediately from his picture, featured prominently on the latest download's page one. The palace guard scrambled to lower the drawbridge. "Say there, Mister Glorp," said the palace guard as Ralph entered the castle gates, "I've never seen the Princess myself. But the sheet says she's the most beautiful woman in the whole universe! You must be one hell of a great guy!"

Ralph merely smiled, then started up the wide staircase that led to the throne room.

Groups of orange-and-black-clad aristocrats bowed courteously as Ralph passed them. A servant girl of tender years giggled as Ralph strode the length of the diamond-walled room to a large, elaborate chair—the throne, where sat the King.

"Your Majesty!" chorused a page, hoarsely. "Announcing his Eminent Respectedness, Mister Ralph Glorp! Mister Glorp comes calling upon Your Majesty's lovely daughter, The Most Beautiful Woman in the Whole Universe."

"Approach the throne," said the King. His voice boomed mellifluously. "I have been expecting you."

As Ralph drew nearer, he noted the family resemblance between the handsome King and his beautiful daughter. He again considered Lumula's idea that beauty was a substitute for other redeeming qualities. The royal family selected only the choicest quality genes. Lumula's idea was surely wrong. "Your Majesty," said Ralph, "as a loyal accountant lo these past three centuries, I request the hand of your daughter in marriage."

The King looked around. Wearing news cams, journalists thronged the room. A hush fell upon them and the other privileged personages gathered to witness this historic mo-

ment. Dignitaries from lands as far away as Snowdrift
craned their necks for a better view.

The King slowly rose to his feet. After a suitably dramatic period had elapsed, he looked at Ralph and said,
"Ralph Glorp, I mean you no disrespect, but you are not
worthy of the hand of my daughter. I have had my experts
examine your genome, and your specs are basically those
of a middle-class accountant. I regret to inform you that
marriage to my daughter is not in the genes."

"I mean you no disrespect either," replied Ralph, "but
I have come too far to be turned away now. I have come
to marry your daughter."

The King turned his head and squinted one eye. "You
are certainly spirited for a mere accountant! Alas, spirited
is not enough. You may leave now."

Ralph stood tall and waggled his head. "I am sorry, Your
Majesty, but that is unacceptable. I need to see the Princess—
right now!"

The King placed his hands on his knees and snorted.
"Right now? Right now! You want to marry my daughter,
yet you demand to see her right now? Love is eternal. Lust
is right now. You are wearing my patience thin, accountant." The King turned and bellowed, "Goons! Remove
this accountant from the Palace—right now!"

In a flash, Ralph found himself being lifted and carried
away by two Elite Lightning Goons. Ralph looked back
and cried, "DESTINY CANNOT BE DENIED!"

The Elite Lightning Goons broke stride and looked back
as well. The King ducked backward, as if to avoid being
hit. He blinked five or six times, momentarily stunned
into silence.

The Palace staff, the aristocrats, the dignitaries and journalists, the massive gathered audience—all of them gasped
as one.

Finally, the King quirked an eyebrow and broke into a
wry smile. "Yes," he said, "you are correct: destiny cannot
be denied. However, as it always has been, your destiny is
to be an accountant."

And so with that, Ralph returned to his job at the Royal
Distribution Agency, and his pragmatic, dependable ways.

"Has this foolish escapade taught you anything?" asked
Shirley Lumula.

"Certainly," said Ralph.

"And what's that?" asked Lumula.

Ralph cleared his throat. He looked down at his shoes. Then he said: "I should have had that drink with the tenant farmer."

DANCING IN THE ASHES

by Richard E. Friesen

This story—Rick Friesen's first professional sale—began
with comments by David Brin. Brin volunteers at a junior
high, and was astounded that the thirteen and fourteen year
old girls he met there wanted to go back and live in the
Middle Ages. Friesen's story is drawn from the less familiar
Tattercoats version of the fairy tale. "The most popular
modern version," Friesen says, "came from France, where
they took out two of the balls and added the fairy god-
mother. In the process, they removed any initiative, courage,
perseverance, and intelligence shown by Cinderella."

"PARDON me, ma'am," Ally said to the woman with
a fur coat and gold jewelry. She'd only been there
an hour—long enough to walk to town from the grove
where her mother's dimensional portal dropped her.

The woman glanced at her and motioned to the man
following. He stepped up and hit Ally across the arm with
a riding crop. He aimed a second blow at her head, but
she danced away. He gave chase. She spun out from under
his next blow and slipped on a pile of manure. He kicked
her in the side. She tried to crawl away from the pain—
against the wall, under the mud, away.

The blows ceased, and she looked up. The man said
something. She understood most of it. The implant with
her mother's dictionary supplied the rest; "Learn not to
address your betters without permission." He walked away.

Ally laid her head back on the ground and tried to
breathe. Her ribs cried out against even that. Biting her lip,
she fought to regain control. Instead she cried.

A rat came over and sniffed her leg. Another joined it. Ally blinked, having never seen a rat, save in a pet store, A third one sniffed her hair. She screamed and jumped up.

Then she stood, breathing hard, as the rats vanished. People walked by. Her bruised arms and side throbbed. After a bit she flexed her arms and legs. Nothing broken. Nothing clean either. Mud caked everything from her matted hair to her canvas high-tops.

Her shivers competed for attention with her growling stomach. It wasn't terribly cold—just wet and miserable.

With few choices, she gritted her teeth and took a step closer to the street. She tried again. "Pardon me . . ."

No one paid the slightest heed, but she kept trying. The third man raised a mahogany walking stick. She ran.

In an alley, she stopped and sank to the ground with a whimper. Holding her bruised ribs, she rocked herself for comfort and to ward off the chill.

They could understand her—at least she understood them. Her mother had studied this place the year before she died. She'd even spent hours and hours teaching Ally the language. Ally knew enough to get by. She'd done something wrong.

She got up and walked out of town, back to where she'd arrived. Not that it would help. She couldn't go back. She just needed a chance to think. What was she going to do?

Her stomach growled again.

She looked back toward the quaint medieval city and the palace beyond, then sat down to eat the sandwich she'd packed. Even the raisins and granola bars wouldn't last long.

To avoid thinking for a bit more, she fished one of the little metal cases from her pocket. Opening it in the palm of her hand, she reached inside to pull out her mother's black starlight gown. She set the nutcase down—as her mother said, only a nut would believe what she'd done by rearranging the dimensional strings. Ally held the dress at arm's length and danced around the clearing. She imagined dancing with her prince.

She could sell the gowns. No one here would have seen anything like them. She could sell the Swiss Army knife and the matches, too, but for how much? And using them might be better than selling. She needed more information. She needed to know the language better, and the culture, and why they were trying to beat her.

During the slow, hopeless walk back to town she purged her soul. Step into a new world and people would hand you boundless feasts and deep red wine. Right. A prince would just happen by and sweep her off her feet. Stupid. Castles and banners and men fighting for her honor. Hogwash. Dared she hope for a warm fire and stew rather than bread, milk rather than water?

The women's shelter, even the horrid foster home—where intellectual activity amounted to watching game shows—had been better than that.

By the time she made it back, she had a plan. A simple plan—find a way to survive while she learned the language Then find a way to move up.

Passing through the city gates, she stayed to the side, out of everyone's way. At a market, she found a corner to huddle in and study the passersby.

Most people dressed in simple, dull colors and unadorned woolens. A few, however, like the ones who'd beaten her, walked with grace and power. People made way for those. Then there were the ones in between—nice clothes, neat, respected not feared.

The combined stenches of rotting food, manure, and sweat ceased bothering her. The drizzle stopped. Her damp, dirty clothes still stuck to her skin, but she felt warmer. No one noticed her. She tried to make herself invisible to the ubiquitous flies, dogs, and rats, too.

She saw a stray dog approach a heavyset woman out shopping. The woman smiled and petted the dog. She even offered it a tidbit. Ally sat up straight. Nice to a dog, nice to a beggar?

The woman arrived at a mansion and headed around back. The thought of knocking on the door, even the back door, banished Ally's chill in fear and trembling. She hurried to catch up. Dancing around the corner, she leaped a stone bench.

"Gracious!" the woman said as Ally knelt in front of her.

She'd rehearsed her speech. "Please, ma'am, I need help."

The woman took in Ally's muddy and torn clothes. "Well, I should say so."

"Is there anything you can give me? Food? Clothes? I would gladly do anything you ask."

"Oh, child!" The woman slumped. "I fear you are beyond me. I am but a kitchen servant. What useful things can I tell the steward you offer?"

Ally paused for translation, then opened her mouth, and closed it again. She could work with computers. She could dance. Then it came to her. She could sew. That would be useful here. "I can . . ." She could sew with a machine. Ally shook her head and looked at the ground. "Nothing."

Folding her arms, the woman stared hard at Ally for a moment, then shook her head. "Well, now. Shelling peas and carrying the ash bucket should not be beyond you. A child can do so much. For such chores I can provide a corner to sleep in, scraps from the table, and rags to wear. No more. The Lady can hardly argue about that little."

Ally blinked a moment as she translated the words she didn't know. Then she beamed. "Oh, that would be, um, most . . . welcome, ma'am!"

Her only reaction to Ally's halting speech was a wariness that crept over her eyes. Aloud she said, "And you can just stop that. I'm no 'ma'am.' I'm Matilda."

"Yes, Matilda."

Matilda reached behind her and took a wooden bucket from a peg. "Draw water, and we'll see to cleaning you."

Ally cranked the bucket up and poured it into the one Matilda had given her. Then she stripped and washed off the mud and grime in the frigid water. Matilda returned with a rough, threadbare woolen dress, stockings, shoes, and a scarf. Ally kept her own underwear and rescued her nutcases. She shuddered and shook from the cold water, so Matilda went back for a tattered shawl.

Matilda shook her head. "Leastways as dressed as a beggar. It's time we should be working." She handed Ally a bowl. "Go pick some peas from the garden."

Turning to look at the garden, Ally saw a dozens of varieties. Nothing looked like a pea. She was useless. "Matilda."

"Yes?"

"Which ones are the . . . peas?"

Matilda blinked at her, again reassessing her generosity. "Where were you grown, child?"

Ally looked at her feet. "Far away."

Nodding, Matilda took her on a tour of cabbage, various beans, squash, peas, carrots, and more. She told Ally how to judge ripeness and how to pick them. Ally just hoped she remembered it all.

When they had enough peas, they started back for the house, and Ally stopped. Even so near the palace, odors of excrement and rot filled the air, mixing with the flowers' perfume. The garden stank more than the market—especially near the tiny wooden shack. The mansion, however, seemed elegant and well kept. "Matilda, who . . . lives here?"

"The Lady Aristide and her two daughters own this property. The lady is the widow of Baron Aristide. This was the only property he owned when he died, so she must needs rent it to the poorer nobility and wealthier merchants who require residence near the palace."

Ally translated, then wanted to ask if a baroness running an inn was scandalous. She couldn't find the words in time, so she said the other needful thing. "Matilda, I need to . . . relieve myself." Ally held out the bowl.

Matilda nodded, taking the peas. "Be quick. We have supper to prepare."

Ally went back to the little shack and found a board with a hole in it placed over a pit. She'd guessed right. It stank. Holding her nose, she sat down. She dreamed then of indoor toilets, of running water, and clean, smooth seats, but most of all, a fresh pine smell.

When she'd finished, she looked around. "Hey! Where's the toilet paper?"

With the warm spring breeze blowing through the open windows, Ally twirled into an empty room at the front of the manse. The servants laughed at her when she practiced her steps, but she never ceased. For the entire fall and winter she had practiced those and her litany—running water, electric lights, heat. Oh, blessed heat. Indoor toilets. No horse shit.

Another carriage rolling up outside distracted her. Ally peeked out the window. The new arrivals waited behind four others, with no sign of a stableman or a porter to carry luggage. Her chance had come.

She finished cleaning the last of the winter ashes from the fireplace as quickly as she could and rushed back to her little spot in the gap behind the kitchen hearth. She was ready. She'd moved all her belongings to one nutcase. The other waited empty. She splashed water on her face from the cistern by the back door, and wiped off as much grime as she could.

Walking back through the house, she rehearsed her speech. The porters had uniforms, they got paid. She'd spent her weeks learning the language, now she just needed a chance.

Brendan the Steward stood at the center of a maelstrom. 'The Duchess of Harnel and her daughter are here. What room are they in?" "The butcher only had one side of beef. We need three." "The carriage house is full." "Where are the clean sheets? I need clean sheets!" To each request he gave a calm and reasoned answer. "The string quartet will be here soon. Serve tea in the great hall until they arrive and the sheets are done. The duchess and her daughter go in the violet suite. Park them on the lawn, just put them in neat rows. Lamb will do, and goose. The beef is for the King's guests. Just serve it all with style."

Ally waited for a small break in the storm, stepping forward only when he had a moment to rub his brow. "Sir? Excuse me, sir. But if you have a uniform, I could help carry bags. I would be good at it."

Brendan turned to look, then backhanded her across the cheek. She cried out and fell. "You are a scull. You shall remember your place, or you shall no longer serve this house." He kicked her in the stomach. Ally doubled up in pain, drawing her knees to her chest.

Ally held still, eyes shut, until she heard his footsteps. He muttered, "Next she'll be wanting to go to the ball!"

Ally crawled over to the wall and pulled herself up. Then she stumbled back to her mat in the kitchen and her place behind the hearth. The dark little space had cobwebs and a wooden floor, with dust everywhere. It smelled of mildew and rats. She huddled against the wall in the shadows, weeping. She'd just wanted to help!

What a stupid girl she was. How could she think coming

here would solve her problems? The problems that started when her father had taken her out for dinner and dancing. She never passed up a chance to dance. And it all seemed so innocent.

Ally had whirled in time with the music and imagined she was dancing with her prince. But when the song ended, she'd looked up into her father's eyes. "Thanks, Daddy." She gave him a hug, and he kissed her cheek.

"The pleasure's mine, Allison. It's a joy to watch you dance. I am so glad you came on this date with me."

Ally shuddered and stepped away from him as they walked over to their table. They'd been going on Dad-and-daughter dates since she was four. Now, eleven years later, and a year after her mother died, it felt wrong. She searched his face for answers, for reassurance. Smiling, he pulled her chair out.

She willed herself to relax. There's nothing wrong. He's my father, and I love him.

"You are so graceful. All the lessons and practicing were worth it."

"I want to be able to dance for my prince, when I find him."

Her father shook his head. "Princes come in all sizes and shapes. Most don't wear crowns."

The waiter brought desert before she could answer. They spent the next few minutes absorbed in raspberry sorbet.

When he started to say something, Ally rose. "Let's dance." She didn't want to hear it. She wanted to be safe in his strong arms. She wanted to be his little girl.

Three nights earlier she'd snuggled against him while watching TV. He'd put his arm around her and stroked her hair. The way he used to touch Mom's hair. It was nothing. It had to be nothing. She'd moved to the other end of the couch.

Out on the floor, he took her hand and led them into the simple waltz. He'd improved since they started dancing together. Now he maintained his dance space. As they floated around the room, he said, "I haven't enjoyed myself this much since I was dating your mother. And I did promise her, when she was dying, that I'd never be with a woman of less intelligence or beauty. She said I was being silly, but I meant it. It will keep her memory alive."

Ally missed a step and tripped over her foot. Her father caught her. "Is something wrong?"

She extricated herself and resumed the dance. "I'm fine. I just . . . I need to use the bathroom."

He looked puzzled. "Okay. I'll wait at the table. We'll do the next dance."

Only her years of dancing kept her knees from buckling as she walked to the women's room. Inside, she found a stall and collapsed. She shuddered and moaned as tears ran down her face. It couldn't be. It couldn't be. But she knew better. He'd said it himself, many times. The last time was when he'd stroked her hair that way, "You're as smart and beautiful as your mother." Her Nobel Prize–winning mother.

She'd known for weeks, but she loved him and couldn't admit it to herself. She was on a date with her own father, and she'd agreed to come. Ally retched into the toilet.

When she'd recovered enough to stand, she went out to wash her face. She looked at herself in the mirror. "What am I going to do?"

She took a deep breath to clear her head. One thing at a time. First get out of the bathroom before he came looking for her. She stepped over and pulled the door open a crack. He wasn't waiting outside. Creeping into the dim corridor, she peered around the corner toward the tables and the dance floor. Then she dashed out the front door and into the night.

A nightmare of women's shelters, Social Services, and foster homes followed. Her father had sued to get her back, and the lawyers had made it seem like she'd imagined it. She'd needed a prince to rescue her, but he hadn't come. She'd dreamed of him, dreamed of dancing the night away. Anything to get away from the horror of her life.

Then it occurred to her she could go find her prince. She knew where he lived—in that town with smoke rising from chimneys and the palace standing sentinel over all. She'd seen it in her mother's lab, where she opened the dimensional strings to look at other universes.

Her father had told her two other labs had managed to

look between the strings. None had sent probes like her mother and her team.

The rest had been easy—sneak back home to gather things she'd need, use her mother's access codes to get into her lab, and come here.

The portable return units could be tracked from the lab—it only made sense if they were going to get back. Thus she couldn't take one. Of course, that also made it hard to prove she had gone—the first human to do so. Regardless, she had no way back.

With her knees pulled to her chest, Ally recited her litany over and over, "Disinfectant, sterile bandages, antibiotics."

That's how Matilda found her. "Oh, child! Tell Matilda what happened."

"I just asked him if I could help."

"Who? Brendan? Oh, child. The likes of us, we're below him. He'll not speak to me but for orders."

Ally sat up. "Below him? But . . ." All the little clues fell into place—like the beating when she first arrived and how the servants treated each other. She should have seen it from the language. She rocked back and forth, swearing. "I'm just a scullion, but if I work very hard, and learn the things you know, you might sponsor me as a kitchen servant, a downstairs maid."

Matilda brightened. "Yes! I just might."

"And being a chambermaid upstairs?"

"Oh, no, child. Sculls can not become chambermaids."

She hid her face against her knees. Her nutcases and her brains didn't matter. She'd been classified. "I'm too far from home. Much too far." For asking to help, she could have lost even her lowly place. She had to get away, but getting away would cost money. Or her body.

For a few minutes neither spoke. Ally's mind drifted until she examined her little hideaway again. "So why don't you use this closet?"

" 'Tisn't a closet. The King's grandfather built the palace, and this. They say he used to visit Lady Aristide's great-aunt."

Ally smiled. "Some things never change."

"Best we finish our work."

"Yes." Ally rolled to her knees and got up. Her stomach muscles protested, which reminded her of Brendan's kick.

Then she remembered what he'd said. A ball. All these women had come for a ball.

Silk and satin filled the air, sending scents of perfumes and powders winging down the hall. Light from the oil lamps danced across the tapestries and stone walls, the flames tossed in the wake of scurrying servants and frantic young ladies.

Ally, wearing dirty rags, bounced, twirling, down the servants' stair. Unseen and unheard, she'd carried water for baths while the ladies supped. She'd mopped the dining room while they bathed. She had cleaned, fetched, and carried for other maids. Now, while the chambermaids dressed the women, young and old, in their finest gowns, Ally headed for the kitchen and the scraps she called supper. She found half-eaten crusts, day-old vegetables, bones with tough meat still clinging to them—food even the servants would not eat. Food fit for a scull.

Thus, as the carriages whisked the ladies into the night, the servants made their weary way to the kitchen for a bite before bed. Ally, quiet as a mouse, climbed the stairs again.

In one room she found a cold bath and washed herself for the first time in weeks. After drying off, she opened the first nutcase, retrieving her sparse makeup and the first gown. She eschewed the heavy powders and perfumes, not caring in the slightest about current fashions. Her hair she left straight and simple, adorned with a white flower from the garden. She slipped into her custom-fit shoes and donned the starlight dress. As a precaution, she packed her rags into a nutcase.

She slipped down the main stairs and out the front door. The crisp night air steeled her resolve. With luck far greater than she'd had since she arrived, she would find a prince and escape. Even with no prince and no escape, she could dance.

Less than half a mile separated Lady Aristide's manor from the palace gate. On the way over she passed several other mansions and the servants' entrance to the palace. The walk gave her time to fret about many things—taxis, bicycles, skates, scooters, and whether they would let her in. After all, she had no invitation.

Thinking about her dismal failures as a beggar, and the

way Brendan treated her, she decided to act like a noble—
arrogant and rude.

Two guards flanked the open gate. The stone wall around
the gardens stood a bare six feet, serving for privacy rather
than defense. Even from the outside, Ally could see lanterns in the trees, lighting the grounds like Christmas. Music
echoed over the wall, drawing her close. Before the guards
noticed her, Ally stopped and lifted her head high.

She approached like the queen herself—purposeful in
step, haughty in demeanor. She still expected them to stop
her and ask to see her invitation.

They didn't even look at her.

Inside she sighed, paused a moment to collect herself and
crossed the grounds to the palace. Every window blazed.
A servant led her past marble statues, ten-foot high tapestries and oil paintings. The light flickered, sending shadows
leaping like living things. Soot covered the ceiling. Even
with all the lamps, to Ally it seemed dim.

They arrived at double doors carved with resplendent
knights. More servants opened these. Music and light spilled
out, assaulting Ally's senses. She smiled at the figures on
the hardwood floor inside. The men wore doublets, hose,
and soft leather boots. The women in full skirts and tight
corsets teetered through sedate dances.

As Ally stepped into the room, those nearest turned to
look. Women standing against the walls stared. Men on the
dance floor watched over their partner's shoulders. Ally's
gown was not quite so full, her waist not quite so slender
as the other women's. On the other hand, her black dress
glimmered as if it held the light of a thousand stars.

Attempting to avoid the mistakes she'd made when she
arrived, Ally slid to one side of the door and stood to
watch. She could do the dances. The dances looked easy.

To check on the etiquette for waiting, Ally scanned those
not dancing. Then she blinked and looked again. They
ranged in age from fourteen to forty, with not a man evident. Ally surveyed the room again. Every man present
had a dance partner.

A gaggle of girls around Ally's age converged on the
corner near her. ". . . two years and he isn't married!"
one said.

"Mayhap we should have brought our brothers."

The others laughed.

"A younger one spoke up, "Mayhap we should chase his father, since his mother so dotes on him."

"I daresay our luck would be better, if you but prefer bastards."

"And looking at his son, ugly ones at that!"

"I *like* his looks!"

"It matters not how he looks, he could have any one of us for a smile."

"And all of us, were the price sufficiently steep."

They hid their laughs and dismayed squeals behind their hands as a well-dressed man walked by headed toward Ally. "Good even, milady." He bowed to her. "I seem to be remiss in my duties, as I don't recognize your house."

Ally blinked. She'd expected him to ask her to dance. Her house? Oh. Her name. She hadn't thought of that. No one at Lady Aristide's knew her surname, though. "I am Lady Skye."

"Thank you, milady." He bowed again. "Permit me to wish you luck this evening." With that he walked away, writing something on a card in his hand.

Luck? He knew. He knew she didn't belong. Why else would she need luck? She wanted to just slide back out the door. Then the song ended and the dancers scattered, with most of the men choosing new partners. As she wondered if any of them would choose her, Lady Aristide walked by, then stopped. "I beg pardon for my failing memory, but it seems we have met."

Ally shook her head, and had trouble finding her voice. "Um, uh, it seems unlikely."

With a tiny shrug, Lady Aristide walked away. Ally just had time to take a breath and consider flight when a man appeared at her shoulder. She tried not to be disappointed. He stood only as tall as she did, his nose protruded like a beak, his hair followed no plan, and his round face tended toward fat. Still, his deep brown eyes seemed to search her soul. "Would you care to dance, Lady Skye?" He did not bow.

"Certainly, kind sir." Ally gave a very small curtsy.

He smiled and led her out onto the floor. As the music began, he led her through one of the sedate, dignified dances she'd seen the others do. He danced well enough, but Ally noticed the easy steps, the simplicity, and his lack of passion.

"Skye is a family I am not familiar with. Did you choose your attire to accentuate your name?"

"My father had this dress made for my mother. I expect he did have our name in mind. It had not occurred to me."

"Your father has impeccable taste."

"Perhaps too much so."

The man raised an eyebrow, but Ally did not elaborate, so he changed the topic. "Are you enjoying my ball?"

Ally sighed and looked around at the other dancers. "I had . . . hoped for more."

He returned a crooked smile. "Oh? Am I so disappointing?"

"What? No! I meant, well, not you . . . the dancing!"

For a moment he seemed puzzled. "You wish something more difficult, perhaps challenging?"

"Yes."

He inclined his head. "My lady has but to ask." He swung her out to arm's length, then twirled her back into a dip. As rusty as she was, he led so well that she followed through every turn and spin and step without missing a step.

It was all she had ever imagined, except in her dreams he stood taller, more handsome. Even so, the room swirled around her in time with the music. No one mattered but the man in her arms, until the music stopped and she found herself standing toe-to-toe with him in a circle of onlookers. He gave her a genuine smile. "My lady, that was delightful!"

"Oh, my, yes."

"Would you care for some refreshment?"

"I would."

As they left the floor, a servant appeared. "Wine, my lady?"

Ally started to shake her head—she wanted water. She had, however, tried that months earlier, and added clean water, fruit juice, and refrigerators to her litany. Not to mention Imodium. "Please."

As the servant left, a woman walked over—wearing the second best dress in the room. The man who'd taken her name followed a step behind. Ally's dance partner inclined his head to the woman. "Hello, Mother. May I present the Lady Skye."

Unsure who this woman might be, Ally nodded, too.

The woman raised an eyebrow and spoke to her son. "A most interesting turn." She smiled. "Were I appropriately attired, I would provide Lady Skye with competition."

Ally's dance partner smiled, too, and his eyes sparkled. "My lady has but to ask."

The intimacy brought a sour taste to Ally's mouth. What had this woman done to her son? Ally clenched her fists, wanting to punch out her lights.

His mother said, "Another time, then. Is your father so detained elsewhere that he cannot come to your ball?"

"I believe he was seeing to Pippert."

"Ah, yes. Duty before duty." She smiled at Ally, and walked away.

Her partner turned to the servant with the list. "Harwell, leave us. My dance partner has been chosen this night." The man bowed and departed.

Ally took a sip of the fruity red. "If I'm not too forward, who is this Pippert?"

"Merely a servant who forgot his place. After tonight, merely a prisoner, of no concern to anyone." Her partner gazed into his goblet and swirled the wine, but did not drink.

Ally stared at his hand and concentrated on breathing. Slow and easy. He didn't know. He wasn't going to send her to prison. She tried not to think about damp, infested dungeons.

He misread her silence and smiled. "Your pardon, my lady, but mere minutes ago I had contemplated becoming thoroughly inebriated."

Ally shook away the visions of rats and gruel. "Why? Weren't you enjoying the dance?"

"Not even moderately. You see all these women?" He gestured toward everyone else. Ally looked around the room again. Three quarters of the females present were watching her—or him. "They all wish to become my bride. I am but a piece of meat in a butcher's window."

She stared at him. He'd said, "my ball." Ally took another drink to cover her discomfiture. If slaves who forgot their place went to prison, at least she could dance. She took a long breath and let go of her hopes of escaping to the palace. "Don't worry. I came to dance. I don't plan to marry anyone."

"Truly?"

"Truly." She willed herself to believe it.

"Then dance we shall." He led her back to the floor.

Ally put a hand on his shoulder. The music led them into a slow, graceful turn—difficult in its subtlety and precision. Ally marveled at how well he maintained his dance space, and the little cues he gave for the next move. Not even her teachers could compare.

When the dance finished, he took her out into the gardens. Ally, strolling with hands behind her back, took a deep breath. The trees and flowers, together with the lanterns, purged the city's foul odors from the air. "This is the first time I've enjoyed myself since I arrived."

"Oh? And why is that?"

She gave him a tight smile. "Survival. I only wish I could go home."

"Why can you not?"

Shaking her head, she stretched out her arms and turned a melancholy circle—no lights, no cars, no planes. "It's too far. From here, way too far. And . . ." And her father waited. "And I think you should explain."

"I am at your command. What do you not comprehend?"

Ally walked back over to him, thinking about sculls. "Somehow I doubt you will ever be at my command. I want to know who you are, why this ball, and why those ladies in there."

He raised an eyebrow. "You came to my ball and have no idea who I am?"

Ally shrugged, "I'm rather new here, and out of touch."

He smiled. "I am Crown Prince Desmond Arthur Nicholas. Two years ago I completed my training for the knighthood. My next task was to find a bride and ensure the succession. So far, I have failed. My parents have become . . . desperate." He glanced back at the ballroom and the waiting women. "My father gave an open invitation. Any woman well enough attired might attend."

Desmond? Whoever heard of a prince named Desmond? The women thought his mother doted? They had more chance getting the king away from her? She turned and looked at the ballroom. "I appear to have rained on their parade."

"Milady?"

Chuckling, she turned back and looked in his eyes. This was her handsome prince? And she his scull. "I am not a suitor. You would not find me suitable. I came here to dance."

Desmond blinked. Then he laughed. "Marvelous. If dance you wish, dance we shall." He led her back inside, to continue her dream. But the music and the steps were the only thing right. Her dream did not have prisons or sculls, beatings or ash buckets. In her dreams she could always go home.

"This truly means nothing to you?" He twirled her.

"I came to dance, and you just happen to be the best dancer here, Your Highness."

"Most refreshing." As if to prove her praise, he started a complex quickstep Ally struggled to match. "Not only am I the prize in a grand competition, but the selfsame women find me most intimidating, *especially* when I dance."

She surprised him with a step for him to copy. "My father taught me people are who they are, regardless of their parents."

Desmond nodded. "A wise man. Being born a prince does not make me princely."

"Nor does it make my father wise."

Desmond twirled her away from him, then followed, sliding in a most unprincely fashion to stop at her feet as the music ended. "My pardon for resurrecting old wounds, and my thanks for another glorious dance." He kissed her fingers.

Harwell came over and whispered in Desmond's ear. Desmond looked over to the door and nodded. "Lady Skye, would you excuse me for a moment? Whether my birth makes me worthy or not, it does require I bid certain guests farewell."

As Desmond walked toward the door, Ally saw Lady Aristide among those leaving. When she returned, the servants would assist removing gowns, makeup, and coifs. Those servants would look for their scull.

Ally turned and walked the other way. At a side entrance she asked a servant where the bathroom might be. She bit her lip to hold back tears.

In the curtained alcove, she pulled the nutcase from her pocket. When she removed the star gown, she held it up and bit her lip again. Closing her eyes, she stuffed it into the case.

Hoping Desmond gave lengthy farewells, she dressed and slipped out. Invisible in her rags, Ally walked past retainers and ladies, servants and guards. She reached the servants' entrance to the palace and walked past the sentries, eyes averted. Just then she wanted nothing more than to go back to her real life, with no nobility, no servants, and no guards. She wanted a warm bath, a Diet Pepsi, and a car to take her home.

Two days later, Ally walked up the stairs again. Carrying more water. For another bath. Not a single woman had left. The news had come as everyone packed the day after the ball—the king had ordered another. The talk amongst the ladies, and the servants, reverberated with one thing—the mysterious, dancing Lady Skye.

The rumors and whispers brought a frown to Ally's face, but her heart and her feet refused to bow to the visions of dungeons in her head. She danced through the maze of servants and cooks preparing supper in the kitchen. She whirled down an empty hall, practicing her footwork. She leaped from stair to stair up and down. After all, only dancing made her life bearable.

Realizing that, she stopped in her tracks. Bearable enough to risk prison?

"Greetings, Lady Skye." The servant at the door bowed.

Ally blinked. He knew her by sight? That did not reassure her. She smoothed her slinky moon dress. The gray satin dress reflected a pale white light, blurring the line between dress and room. She shimmered.

Standing on the threshold, Ally tried not to laugh. Where before the dance had been graceful, with appearance the highest concern, now difficulty and skill—or lack of both—became paramount. She saw more botched turns, more trodden feet, and more missteps than in any basic class. Ally smiled even wider when she saw Prince Desmond out amongst them. With skilled and graceful steps he evaded his partner's feet.

Ally's arrival rippled through the room. It echoed off the far wall and brought Desmond's mother. Concentrating on the dancing and trying to deduce the correct steps, Ally didn't notice the queen until she stepped up beside her. Startled, Ally turned and curtsied. "I beg your pardon, um, Your Highness, for not recognizing you the other night."

The queen smiled, "We forgive you. Desmond tells me you are interested only in dancing, not becoming a princess."

She did want to be a princess. She didn't dare. "Mostly I want to go home."

The queen gazed at Ally a moment, as if trying to penetrate her game. "I do not, in truth, wish to give him up. The requirements of state, however . . ." The queen let her bitterness trail off unspoken.

Spiders crawled up and down Ally's back—keep him how? Ally asked about the bitterness instead. "Do you love his father? Is he a good king?"

The queen's gaze returned to Ally. "A good king? That is for others to decide. It matters not if I love him, for the kingdom is his wife, and I his mistress."

Before Ally could answer, the song ended and Prince Desmond approached. He nodded to his mother, kissed Ally's hand, and smiled. "I am most relieved to see you."

Ally smiled, too. "I'm glad you had another ball. Shall we show them how it's done?"

His eyes sparkled. "By all means." He took her in his arms, and led her onto the floor. Desmond and Ally paused to catch the beat, then lit a fire across the room.

Ally's dress reflected Desmond's crimson surcoat. Dancers scattered like chaff. Poor reflections indeed.

"Why did you vanish from the ball, without allowing me to bid you good night?"

Ally smiled and shrugged, "It was late. I had to go home."

"Ah, and where is your home?"

The music conspired for her to turn her back, and she

lost her smile. "I misspoke," she said over her shoulder, "I went to the place where I now live. Home is a long, long way from here."

Desmond spun her around, swung her feet off the ground, and set her down facing him. He smiled. After two more times through, Desmond spun her again. She whirled and finished with a bow as the music ended.

The servants waited with wine. Desmond took a sip. "Tell me about your home far away."

Ally walked out into the garden. Desmond followed. How could she explain telephones, airplanes, computers, dimensional transporters, and electric lights? "I lived in a fairy tale. Food stayed fresh for weeks, we flew through the air to all parts of the world, the glass in our windows, was crystal clear, and hot water came from a pipe in the wall."

Desmond laughed. "Lady Skye, such stories! How is it possible to believe them?"

Ally offered him a tight grin, and considered how such things would sound in this world. "Simply because one cannot imagine something, does not mean it can't exist."

Desmond blinked, smile fading. "True. So, I should believe what you say on its face?"

Shaking her head, Ally took Desmond's arm and led him back toward the dance floor. "No. If you did, the entire palace would think you'd gone insane. Even so, it's true."

As they stepped amidst the whirling arms and legs, Desmond looked into her eyes. He began to smile. Then, during a series of quick turns—back to front and front to back—he said, "Lady Skye, may I have your hand in marriage?"

Ally missed a step. She imagined showing up for the wedding rehearsal in her rags—the looks on their faces, and the cell they threw her in. "Prince Desmond, you would not want me as a wife, let alone a princess."

"Lady, you wound me." His lips smiled. His eyes did not.

"My Prince, if I were going to marry anyone here, it would be you. What I truly want is to go home. I came to your ball to dance with you, and you alone. Let that be enough." *Oh, let it be enough.*

For a moment he just danced, but his eyes never wavered from hers. "My lady, if that is the sum of what you can offer, then I must accept it, for tonight."

Ally smiled at the promise of another ball, even if it

meant pursuit. She squashed the hope in her heart. He was, after all, a prince. Trying to marry him would mean prison. The evening dissolved into music, turns, and quicksteps.

When Lady Aristide moved toward the door, Prince Desmond did not go to say good night. Ally almost panicked. Then the song ended, and she excused herself to go to the bathroom. As before, she changed into her rags.

Stepping to the curtain on the alcove, Ally peered into the dim corridor. Then she closed her eyes. Oh, God. What was she going to do? Leaning against the far wall stood Prince Desmond.

She took a long breath, imagining the beating she would get. With little choice, she put her gown back on and stepped out.

Desmond offered his arm. "Shall we return to the ball?"

Threading her arm through his, Ally shook her head. "No. Take me for a walk along the balcony." On the other side of the ballroom, the one closer to Lady Aristide's, the ground dropped away somewhat, leaving the patio several feet off the ground. So far, she'd had no reason to go out there. Now, she had no idea what good it would do.

Desmond pointed out the fine marble, the detailed carving, and the marvelous artwork spaced along the rail. Ally scanned the garden for a way out.

She didn't see it at first because some lanterns had blown out in the tree. Her eyes rested on the darkness. A large evergreen stood with a larger willow behind it. One willow branch extended over the wall.

She looked for a route. Then she heard Desmond say her name. "What?"

"My pardon, Lady Skye, you appear distracted. I was merely pointing out the fresco inside the ballroom itself. If this is of no interest . . ."

Ally smiled. "Forgive me. Please continue."

"I would rather dance with you once again." The orchestra started another song, and Prince Desmond turned to listen to the first strains.

"Good night, Fair Prince." Ally vaulted the rail.

She landed and fell onto her hands. Without looking back, she got up and ran—away from the willow tree. At a hedge by a fountain she doubled back. She glimpsed Prince Desmond on the balcony, mouth open.

She skirted an open area with numerous lanterns. The shadows concealed her all the way to the evergreen. Slipping behind it, she thought about changing, but if Desmond caught her there, she wanted to be in the dress.

Taking a deep breath, she hiked up her skirts, then climbed the willow. It had good low branches and leaves to hide her. In the crook of two major boughs she stopped to change—a perilous adventure teetering between tearing the dress and falling.

Back in her rags, nutcase in the pouch tied at her waist, she shinnied out the long branch and over the wall. With each move she added to her long litany. Due process, freedom of speech, democracy, no cruel or unusual punishments.

Lying cheek on the bark, she looked to make sure no one would see her, especially not the guards. A carriage went by, then she put her hand around the limb and lowered herself until she hung above the street. It still looked too far.

She let go.

Ally winced as she fell to her hands and knees. On the other hand, no one would notice skinned knees, scraped hands, and sore feet on a scull.

Ally flitted up the stairs. Carrying more water. For another bath. She didn't spill a drop. After the second ball, expecting the third, no one had even begun to pack. How long could this go on?

This time, however, she would have a way out. The night before, after everyone went to bed, she had taken a lantern into her closet that wasn't and followed it to the palace. She'd had time to recite the entire litany.

When the servants opened the door to the ballroom, Ally paused to smile at the dancers again. Even more tried to emulate her. A few had done their hair or makeup like hers. This time, Prince Desmond had his timing down. He stood just inside the door, hands behind his back, smiling.

He took a moment to glance at the bright yellow sun dress before its brilliance forced his eyes up. Prince Desmond inclined his head. "Greetings, Lady Skye. You are as beautiful as ever. Would you care to dance?"

"Always." She took his arm, and he led her onto the

floor. The music transported them into a world defined by each other's feet, arms, and bodies.

On their first break, after four dances, Desmond drank some wine and lost his smile somewhere in the crystal. "Lady Skye, pardon my directness, but why have you continued to run from me?"

"Don't apologize. I wish I could give you a direct answer. I am not what I appear."

He smiled. "You appear to be the most intriguing woman I have met in my short life."

Blushing, Ally kept her head up and looked in his eyes. She remembered the beatings, the prisoner. "If you saw me somewhere else, well, you would not see me."

Desmond reached out to touch her cheek. "Were that so, I would not be worthy of you."

Ally blinked and stared. Not worthy? He couldn't know. He amazed her just the same. "Dance with me," she whispered.

"My lady has but to ask."

Desmond took her in his arms. For the first time she noticed his hand on her waist—not a dancer's hand, a man's.

Desmond sighed as they walked alone through the garden— alone save for a half dozen servants. Ally smiled, unable to resist teasing him. "You want to kiss me, don't you?"

He blushed, but he also smiled. "Most assuredly. I am also loath for this night to end."

"Me, too. Will you have a fourth ball?"

With a small frown he looked off into the distance again. "Not soon, I think. Our treasury is not unlimited."

Ally stopped and turned away from him, closing her eyes. She remembered life before the dances, the life of a scull, and did not want to return to it.

For a moment he said nothing, then stepped up beside her. "Lady Skye, forgive me. I do not wish to cause you grief."

Ally shook her head and waved off his apology. She sighed, and looked at his face. "No, no. No need. It is simply that for most, your kingdom is not a pleasant place to live."

"For that I am sorry also." He turned then, and paced

behind her. "However, it has occurred to me I am not without resources. I would provide ships, horses, and men to take you to your far home, if that were to bring you happiness."

Ally stared at Desmond for a moment, then ran to a bench, threw her arms over the back, and wept.

After a moment she heard Desmond walk over. She ignored him. He stood near, and silent. Finally he drew her into his arms. She held on for dear life and cried for her lost home.

When the sobs subsided and she wiped her eyes, Prince Desmond asked, "What have I done to cause you such distress?"

Smiling sadly, Ally touched his cheek. "Not every sadness is your fault." Then she took a deep breath, ran a hand through her hair, and sat. "Dear Prince, you make me wish I were a princess. Your offer is astounding, and, unfortunately, useless. All your horses and men, ships and gold could not get me home."

He sat beside her. "Pardon me, my lady, I fail to understand."

Ally nodded, "I know. My father and mother are both wizards. Remember? I lived in a fairy tale. I might as well be from the moon."

Desmond blinked, then looked up at the silver crescent. "Well, it is in the sky."

For a moment Ally just stared at him. Then she giggled, and laughed. Her smile restored, Ally took a delicious breath. "Thank you."

"You are most welcome, my lady." He rose and offered his hand. "Shall we?"

Hand in hand they strolled past flowers and fountains that reflected leafy shadows and starlight. Ally savored every sensation, knowing she would never return.

As they stepped inside, Harwell appeared. Ally decided he must be the chamberlain or something. When Prince Desmond turned to speak with him, Ally bit her lip and walked away.

She almost made it to the corner, and the door deeper into the palace. Desmond cried out, "Lady Skye!"

Ally turned to face him as the music died and all eyes

watched. "Good-bye, My Prince. I will miss you." She fled into the palace. She stumbled. Tears blurred her sight.

Trotting down the corridor, she turned away from the entrance, away from the garden, and away from the wall. After checking for guards and princes, she scurried across an open foyer, and lost her shoe.

Ally stopped and hopped back to get it. She almost stepped in the tar. He'd put tar on the floor! To catch her. How had he known?

Before she could wiggle the shoe out, she heard voices. She had to reach the tunnel before anyone saw her.

She found the corridor with the old residences. At the end of the hall, she saw the massive grandfather clock. Voices echoed behind her as she pulled it away from the wall. Slipping through the crack, she dragged it shut, sealing herself in darkness.

Ally pulled the flashlight from her pocket. Batteries. Lightbulbs. On the second step, her bare foot landed on a sharp rock. She swore, then laughed. "Oh, Desmond."

Dirt, grime, and grease covered her—even when she washed, Ally couldn't get clean. She finished pouring the ice-cold water over her skin and tried to dry off with the rough towel. Her clothes stuck to her damp body as she dressed. She relished the ground-in dirt that made a mockery of her ablutions. After all, it was her dirt, in her clothes, in her place.

She shuffled into the kitchen to find scraps for breakfast. Maybe someday she could aspire to be a kitchen servant like Matilda. Then, after a decade of saving money she could escape this place. If she still remembered how.

An electric current ran through the house—the whispers assaulted her. "The prince is here. The prince . . . the prince . . . the prince."

Ally stopped, and her head came up. If he noticed her . . . but he wouldn't. It would end the fantasy, and she could get on with life, a scull, the servant of servants. So be it. Forever and ever, amen.

Or he would, and he'd throw her in prison for impersonating a princess.

Striding to the front of the house, she considered finding

a tea service or wine bottle. Instead she swept up the ash bucket and brush. Let him see the true Ally.

In the parlor, Desmond paced. Harwell tried to follow. A half dozen guards stood nearby. Lady Aristide had not appeared. Harwell said, "Are you certain she is in this house, my lord?"

Desmond snorted. "We had every exit from the palace covered. I never dreamed she'd try that tunnel, so I only put tar on the floor there. This is no ordinary woman, Harwell."

Ally stood, mouth open. Every exit? She should have known.

A servant brought a tray with tea, and Ally considered the risk in showing her face. She'd come this far . . .

Practicing her best invisibility, Ally shuffled through the room to the servants' exit. There she turned to push the door open with her back. Desmond looked at her, and relaxed.

Without reacting, Ally dropped her eyes and went through the door. There she stopped.

"Your Grace," a new voice said. Lady Aristide made her entrance. Ally imagined the deep curtsy. "To what do we owe this honor?"

"Fair Lady Aristide, I do believe Lady Skye is hiding in your manor."

"Your Highness, I assure you . . ."

"Lady Aristide, she is here. I have seen her. She was also most correct about me. Not a week past she could have walked by me in the street or in this room and I would have failed to see her at all. I fear I am not worthy of her."

Ally shook her head—he *had* seen her. She stepped back into the room. "I disagree, Your Highness."

Desmond turned a dazzling smile on her, while Lady Aristide frowned. "What are you doing here?"

"I came to get my shoe back."

Lady Aristide scowled and motioned for Brendan. Desmond snapped his fingers. Lady Aristide and Brendan froze as Harwell placed the missing shoe in the prince's hand.

Desmond knelt at Ally's feet. She kicked off her grimy slipper and allowed the prince to put on her shoe. He rose and took her hand. "I begin to understand," he said. "At times a mirror is not so easy to look in as a window."

"Most of us never see a true reflection."

"Lady Skye . . ."

Ally held up a hand. "I am not a lady, I am a scull, and my name is Allison. Allison Skye."

Desmond smiled, mocking himself. "Very well. But you are not truly a scull. Both your parents are wizards."

She shook her head. "Here I am a scull. Only at home is it different. I am not a princess."

Desmond glanced at Lady Aristide, then at Harwell and Brendan. He straightened his shoulders and looked Ally in the eye. "I say your actions have proved otherwise. Allison Skye, will you marry me?"

The entire room gasped. Ally chuckled. She hadn't believed he'd still ask. Her heart melted. She loved him.

As she started to reply, the door opened and the queen walked in.

Everyone knelt except Desmond. And Ally. The queen walked over to Desmond and rested a hand on his arm, as a lover would. "So you have found her. Not, perhaps, what we expected." She circled Ally, appraising her attire and cleanliness.

Desmond nodded, no longer smiling. "I expect the court will find her scandalous, but that may prove beneficial."

The queen nodded, looking in her son's eyes. "I take it she is not truly a scull."

Ally tried to find a reasonable way to ask if she'd seduced her son. Then the queen said, "I find I approve." She put her hand back on Desmond's arm. "Have you decided, my son?"

Desmond nodded, then clasped Ally's hand between his. "I ask again. Allison Skye, will you marry me?"

Ally looked into his deep, thoughtful eyes. If she could be happy here, it would be with this man. If.

A voice across the room said, "I believe I have a better offer. Much better." Rising from a chair in the shadows, her father smiled.

How had he found her? She could go home, eat ice cream, take a hot shower! But he would . . . She would have to run away again.

Desmond looked at her father, then back at Ally. "Who is that man?"

"My father," Ally said, in a little-girl voice.

The queen snapped her head toward Ally. "Child, what has he done to you?"

The stern authority in the queen's voice drew Ally's gaze. She looked in the queen's deep brown eyes, so like Desmond's. Here was her chance. That chance restored her. Straightening up and setting her jaw, Ally said, "He tried to seduce me."

The queen's eyes never left Ally, but her mouth grew taut. "Arrest him."

Ally's gaze jumped to her father. If he'd brought a gun . . .

As the guards closed in, he yelled, "You can't do this to me. Do you know who I am?"

Ally laughed, "Here, you're no one."

He dived for the chair. He didn't make it. A guard slammed him to the ground and dragged him back to the queen. Beneath the chair lay a burlap sack.

Ally dashed over and pulled it out. Beneath his clothes she found the portable return unit. Not running away, he could leave tracks. She could go home. Cradling the unit in her arms, she rose, and came face-to-face with Desmond. "What . . ."

"This? It's my way home." Then Ally saw Desmond's heart break. She sank into the chair. She would never see him again. How could she leave her true love, her prince, for a Diet Pepsi? And air-conditioning, and the Bill of Rights, cars, disinfectant, refrigerators, microwaves, mirrors, TV, computers, electricity, doctors, medicine, airplanes.

If she went home, she would live to a hundred. Here she would die at fifty, or thirty, or nineteen. So would Desmond. She didn't want him to die. "Would you . . ."

He raised a hand. "Do not ask. For if you did, I would break all the vows I have made to my father and my country."

She stood and set the unit on the chair behind her. "Then I will . . ."

Desmond shook his head. "No. If you truly live in that fairy tale as you say, knowing of a certainty you could return home, you would never be happy here. As I love you, I must bid you go."

"I could visit."

"I must take a wife."

"Every word you say makes me love you more. How can I leave you this way?"

"How can you stay?"

"He's right, you know. We can't stay. Now let's go home," her father said.

Ally picked up the portable unit and walked over to where the guards held her father. "I'm leaving you here."

"Here? Totally out of the question."

Ally smirked. "Over the years, try to reflect on how badly you screwed up."

She turned back to Desmond, but her father said, "How will you explain my absence?"

"If no one's there, I won't have to. If there is." Ally shrugged. "But he was right behind me. His hand on my shoulder."

The queen raised an eyebrow. "Young woman, your departure will bring a sad day to our kingdom, but Desmond and I understand sacrifice."

The king had not even come to the balls. Ally blinked back tears and, unable to speak, bowed to the queen. Then she walked back to Desmond and swallowed the lump in her throat. "I will go, but I will leave you a gift beyond price, if you can but tame him." She turned and gestured to her father. Even with crude tools he could make pipes, toilets, gas burners, steam engines. "A wizard."

"Milady, you said . . ."

"He designed my dresses."

Desmond glanced at her father and raised an eyebrow so like his mother. "A pale substitute."

Ally nodded, then kissed him for the first and only time. His arms held her tight, his body warm against hers.

She pulled away. "Good-bye, Fair Prince."

"Fare well, Allison Skye, and think of me."

She brushed a tear from his eye, "I will. I surely will."

Ally left the inn with the memory of his lips on hers and hot tears on her cheeks. Wearing her dancing shoes, she walked down the road and into a fairy tale.

SLEEPING BEAUTY

by Bruce Holland Rogers

Bruce Holland Rogers' fairy tales have appeared in *The North American Review*, *Realms of Fantasy*, and a variety of original anthologies. He is a two-time winner of the Nebula Award, and the author of dozens of short stories, one of which was recently adapted as a Showtime original motion picture. He also has a nonfiction book, *Word Work: Surviving and Thriving as a Writer*, due out in 2002.

Quoth Bruce, "One major difference between science fiction and fairy tales: In fairy tales, the world does not change. The princess can fall asleep for a hundred years and wake up to a world that she knows. In science fiction, enough change occurs in a hundred years to make the world strange to those who awaken in it."

ONCE upon a time, when the sun was getting tired, there was a captain whose fondest wish was to take his crew and passengers away from the solar system of their ancestors to settle on a planet of some other star. So he set out in his ship, the *Good Hope*—which was bigger than the palaces of most kings—to find a suitable world.

It takes a very long time to travel between the stars. If not for the Stillness, every person on the ship would have died of old age long before the ship arrived at the nearest star. But inside of the Still Cells, the captain and crew and passengers made the journey as if frozen in time. Nothing moved in them but the inspection bots that crawled slowly through their Still molecules, detecting and repairing any changes that came with the passing centuries.

While everyone slept, a machine called the Ai ran the ship. The Ai controlled the scoop and engines. If the ship hit a bit of dust that pitted the hull, the Ai sent bots to make repairs. Halfway through the journey, it reversed the engines to slow the giant ship. And when the ship was much closer to the star, it was the Ai that inspected the system to see if there might be a world suitable for people.

At that first star, two planets were barren and airless. Four planets were massive and gassy and too far away. The barren planets might have been made suitable by crashing comets into them, but this star had no Oort cloud. There were no comets to use. Since no planet of this first star could be made suitable for people, the Ai searched for another young star of solar mass and calculated a vector path for reaching it. The Ai steered the ship to this second candidate star. All the while, the captain, crew, and passengers were Still.

From a distance, the second star's wobble looked promising to the Ai. There was a planet of the right mass and period to be Earthlike, but after journeying for centuries, the Ai drew near enough to see that the planet was not a single planet at all, but a binary pairing of irregular bodies in a belt of much smaller objects. This was not at all what the captain and his people needed, so the Ai searched for a third star.

And so the journey went for a long, long time. One promising star after another proved to have no Earthlike planet. But the Ai was patient. Century after century after millennium, it searched. All the while, the captain, crew, and passengers were Still.

Back on Earth, things were changing. People had made bots and Ais that were more and more clever. Humans could merge their thoughts with the thoughts of Ais. They could take bots up into their bodies and reshape themselves at will. With each passing year, the minds and bodies of what once had been humans changed more and more. With each passing year, humans could more and more shape the world around them by wishing something different and commanding it to be so. With energy and bots, they could build or become almost anything.

These trans-humans learned a new way of traveling, too. They could transmit data across synchronous quantum state gates and use that data to assemble copies. A bot-laden Ai-augmented human could transmit his or her profile from

Earth to a distant state gate and create an instant twin. Trans-humans built faster and faster ships to erect gates deeper and deeper in space.

While the ship bearing the captain and crew plodded from one yellow star to another at half the speed of light, the web of gates grew outward from Earth like a super nova shock wave. Human space expanded and overtook the sleeping ship without even noticing that the ship was there.

The next time that the Ai looked at a promising yellow star, it woke the captain and his crew. "We are approaching this star from above the orbital plane. There are intelligent life-forms in this system," it said.

The captain could see that this was true. Visible structures rose from the surface of all the rocky planets, even the inner two worlds that had almost no atmosphere. Objects that might have been machines or might have been armored animals orbited the gas giants. Artifacts shaped like eggs or hoops or towers drifted through the interplanetary space. At the captain's command, the ship's Ai radiated patterned bursts from X-ray to microwave to announce their presence and show that the ship carried intelligent creatures.

In this system, there dwelled six trans-humans, each living on a planet of its own. The trans-human on the third planet searched through human history, analyzed the relevant data, and was the first to reply to the Ai's communication. "Welcome, *Good Hope*," it said. "Are you having a pleasant journey?" In the hours that followed, other trans-humans chimed in with greetings of their own.

Now the captain was very much surprised to be greeted in his own language. He was even more surprised to learn that the artifact builders in this system were human, or at least were descended from humans. Thousands of years had passed while the captain had been in Stillness. He felt as if he were waking to a dream. And not a happy dream, not at all. Each planet of this system belonged to a different trans-human, who saw the planet as an extension of itself. They would no more offer a place on their worlds to the people of the *Good Hope* than a fine lady would invite lice to live in her hair. Even if one or two of the worlds were suitable for a colony, those worlds weren't available. Any other stellar system the *Good Hope* might go to would be just as full since trans-humanity was spreading through the galaxy faster than the *Good Hope* could travel. It seemed that the fondest hope of captain and crew would not be realized. They would never have a world of their own.

The trans-humans, however, took pity on the captain. They agreed that he and his people should have a world of their own, and as quick as thought, they began to devise one. They gated bots and reefs to the system's outer reaches. The tiny bots fed on heat from the reef reactors and assembled dust from the Oort cloud into a hollow sphere. The world they built was like a hollow planet with its atmosphere inside. The bots built stones and mountains, pools and oceans, sandy deserts and loamy plains. In the center of this sphere burned a zero-point reef, a sun to this inside-out world.

The captain might have been sad. His crew and passengers were not to be pioneers for humanity, establishing a hopeful outpost for the dying sun they had left behind. The humanity they had left behind had not only saved itself, but had outgrown them. The captain might have felt that he and his people were, instead of bold pioneers, the ones truly left behind. But he chose instead to celebrate his good fortune. He had launched his ship toward an uncertain fate, yet he had brought his crew and passengers to a new world that they could settle and make their own.

The *Good Hope*'s crew and passengers entered their new world. They began to use their own primitive bots and germ cells from the Earth to shape and cultivate their new home. Soon grasses waved on the hollow world's plains. Newly invented fishes swam in the seas.

With a grateful heart, the captain invited each of the six trans-humans to come to the new world in person and celebrate what they had made. Until now, the people of *Good Hope* had not actually seen their benefactors. One by one, the six arrived, each more astonishing than the one before. The trans-human from the first planet was scaled like a fish, and like a fish it did not blink its four diamond-lensed eyes. Though it had four arms like a Hindu god, it had no mouth, no nose, no ears that anyone could see, and it rode across the vacuum on the outside of its little craft. But a cloud of bots around it vibrated the air so that it could speak.

The trans-human of the second planet was as big as a

whale, but at the front of its bulk was a face—tiny in comparison to the body—not all that different from the faces of the *Good Hope* people. Indeed, the captain could talk face-to-face with this trans-human and imagine that a person of his own size had fallen into an ocean of flesh, floating so that only her face showed.

The master of the third planet appeared to be as much a plant as an animal. The trans-human of the fourth world was shaped like a manta ray and never left the ship it wore like a suit of armor. The fifth was nearly as big as the great whale-sized being, but it bristled with silvery hairs or wires. The tiny sixth trans-human, no bigger than a terrier, arrived unnoticed, riding in the silvery bristles of the fifth.

Now there was also a seventh trans-human that arrived, a spidery, crabby, mechanical thing that gleamed golden when it entered the new human habitat. This being had lived for a long time on the other side of the Oort cloud. None of the other trans-humans had thought to mention its existence since it hardly ever communicated with them. They had not even known with certainty that it had not met with some accident. They would not have missed it. It was selfish and unfriendly.

The people of *Good Hope,* expecting six trans-humans and seeing six, did not suspect that anything might be amiss. But the tiny master of the sixth world, seeing its unfriendly neighbor arrive, decided not to announce itself and remained hidden in the silvery bristles.

The crew and passengers had debated long and hard about what gesture of gratitude they might make to the trans-humans. Through their gates, the trans-humans could communicate instantly with all of trans-humanity. With their advanced bots and reef reactors, they had godlike powers over matter. What experience could the crew give them that the trans-humans could not access from human history? What physical gift could they bestow that the trans-humans could not make for themselves?

After the captain made a welcoming speech, the humans gave their benefactors the gifts they had settled on. They played music of their own invention. They sang a grateful song. And they presented the trans-humans with artifacts from their ship. While the trans-humans could have manufactured duplicates of the dishes, tools, or instruments that the humans gave them, these particular items were from Earth, ancestral home to all.

It was hard to tell precisely what the trans-humans thought of their gifts. They were so different from the humans in their shape and manner that the *Good Hope* people could not detect their emotions. However, all but the golden one said some sort of thank you.

Then the biggest trans-human, the one with the human face, said that it was programming a cloud of bots and releasing them into the atmosphere. These bots would enter human bodies and keep them in good order. As long as the people of *Good Hope* did not meet with any accident, they would live as long as their zero-point artificial sun burned in the center of their world, and that would be for a very long time.

The scaly master of the first world then released some bots into the soil. These bots would analyze and maintain human populations, halting reproduction if the humans began to strain their finite resources.

A third trans-human gave a gift of improved memory, so that the people of *Good Hope* might remember their lifetimes even as they spanned many thousands of years. A fourth introduced speedy, random evolution, so that their ecosystem would always be in a state of interesting, challenging flux. The fifth introduced bots that would build up beautiful inorganic structures from the soil and then dismantle them, making random sculpture gardens here and there and everywhere.

But the golden trans-human did not announce the nature of its gift. It threw down the bowl it had been given and squirted a cloud into the air. "You were not invited here," it said. "The Oort cloud and all that is in it belongs to me." Then it left.

The trans-humans that had given their gifts backed away and extended various probes to sample the aerosol of bots that the golden one had left behind. The humans backed away, too. The ground beneath the bot cloud was turning gray. One by one, the trans-humans jettisoned their sampling elements and hurried away, all except for the one that had hidden in the silver bristles of its larger companion. That one hopped down to sample those bots, too, and at last it told the captain, "These bots are like cancer on a planetary scale. They are designed to hunt complexity and simplify it. They are designed to reproduce without limit. They are very well made." Now the jettisoned probes of the other trans-humans were turning gray and crumbling as if made of sand.

"Can you construct immunity bots against them?" asked the captain.

"I do not think so. The others left because they are afraid."

"And you are not afraid?"

"I am only a partial copy of myself," said the trans-human. One of its feet was turning gray. "I am expendable." Then it ejected an aerosol. "These bots will slow the infection, but they will not stop it. I expect that there is a solution, but I may not have enough time to discover it."

"Then what are we to do?" wondered the captain.

The trans-human hissed another aerosol. "These bots will induce stasis." It shifted its weight as its gray leg dissolved. "I am gating information to the rest of myself. I will think about this." Grayness spread along its body. "When I have a solution, I will reverse the stasis." Then it crumbled into gray ash.

The captain noticed that the toe of his right boot had turned gray. He kicked, and the grayness crumbled. Part of his foot was missing. He felt no pain. The captain wondered what stasis was, but at that very moment the stasis bots began to operate and the captain was blind and deaf and dumb. Stasis was like Stillness, the realized, and it was working from the outside in. Molecule by molecule, cell by cell, he was being frozen in time. He had time enough to think that the stasis bots must be smaller than the gray infection bots, because they had dispersed much faster. Or perhaps they were motile. Then stasis narrowed his thoughts. He was thirsty. He was breathing. He was.

Then it was as if he was not. He was Still.

Stasis froze the gray infection. One by one, it froze the people who had come from the *Good Hope*. It froze the air, the grass. It froze the water surface in mid-wave, then froze the depths. Stasis crept through the shell of the world and froze the *Good Hope* and minimal crew still docked outside. Only the zero-point reactor in the center of the hollow world went on as before, burning like a sun and powering the stasis bots.

Of the trans-humans who had fled the infection, only one carried any of the infection with it as it fled. Unfortunately, it was the trans-human from the inmost planet. As the infection spread on that first planet, a few bots were blown outward on the solar wind. With time, they landed on each of the other worlds. One by one, the trans-humans used their gates to consult all of trans-humanity for a solution to the plague. One by one, they succumbed to it. They did not protect themselves with stasis, not even the trans-human that, through its copy, had brought stasis to the hollow world. Each trans-human thought that it could devise a solution to the infection. And each one was wrong.

All of the six worlds were dead and gray.

The trans-human of the Oort cloud disappeared as well. Perhaps it had finally succumbed to some accident. Perhaps even it could not adapt to the gray infection of its making. Perhaps it continued to change, as trans-humans tended to do, and became something even less human. Perhaps it went away.

The hollow world continued its slow orbit of the star. Time passed. The star evolved, pulsing as it burned heavier and heavier elements. At last it collapsed, exploded, died, and cooled, a dark star with a dark companion.

Far, far away, there lived a trans-human called The Thaen. It had a massive head covered with sensory organs for the full spectrum of radiation, and very little body beyond its modest propulsion system. The Thaen thought it strange that life was so rare in the galaxy. Stranger still, *intelligent* life was, as far as anyone could tell, unique. It had arisen only on Earth. The Others that humans had long expected to encounter among the stars were nowhere to be found. But anther galaxy might have at least one intelligent species of its own, and The Thaen would have liked nothing better than to meet it.

So it was that The Thaen modified itself for a long journey in deep space. With an enlarged body to hold a reactor reef, it set out on a trip through the intergalactic void. It arrived at Andromeda just behind the automated ships that other trans-humans had launched. Already the gates carried by these ships had produced copies of other trans-humans. And what strange beings they were.

The Thaen of course knew that time dilation would slow its subjective time. It knew that a long time would have passed for trans-humanity by the time The Thaen arrived at Andromeda. Even so, it was surprised by how different the trans-humans emerging from the gate were from The Thaen itself. Trans-humanity had continued to evolve and change. These *trans*-trans-humans were small, quick, and adaptive. They were as gregarious as The Thaen's generations had been solitary. They were as uniform as The Thaen's cohort had been diverse. They spread like fire through the Andromeda Galaxy, building social colonies on planets and in the void.

The Thaen traveled across the width and breadth of Andromeda, but the only intelligent life-forms it encountered were these spreading descendants of its own kind. However, they might as well have been the aliens it sought. They were so different from The Thaen that it found them difficult to communicate with. They understood its language easily enough—they could all link to the data of the gate, but The Thaen found the manner of their thinking strange and the nuances of their language bizarre. And even though all the technological history of the trans-trans-humans was accessible to The Thaen through the gate, The Thaen found developments in recent centuries hard to fathom. An energy beyond zero-point had been discovered and exploited. It was called metaspatial architecture, but though The Thaen grew its brains to try to understand it, it grasped this new science only tenuously.

But The Thaen didn't need to tap metaspatial architecture in order to continue its search for alien intelligence. It set out for another galaxy. It arrived to find that galaxy populated by a web of bots and organisms that filled the interstellar space like the filaments of mold. The Thaen first took this bot-and-flesh structure for the desired alien. But then The Thaen found a gate. The Thaen connected and learned that this web was of human descent. When The Thaen queried, the organism or organisms—it might have been one mind or a multitude—did not respond. It was not interested in The Thaen.

Through the gate, The Thaen could see that post-humanity had made great conceptual leaps while The Thaen had come from Andromeda. Post-humanity no longer needed to cross space to spread itself from galaxy to galaxy. Instead, it transcended space. Post-humanity was everywhere now, and everywhere it was engaged in some undertaking, some creation that The Thaen, no matter how it tried, could not understand.

The Thaen had never found any intelligence that was not human. But it had encountered alien intelligence, nevertheless, because everything that had once been human was now alien to The Thaen. Connection through the gates brought The Thaen no closer to these minds that it could not understand, minds that would not respond to it. The Thaen was alone.

"Are there none like me left in the universe?" it asked through a gate. And in the data it glimpsed the static, hollow world of the *Good Hope*. The hollow world still orbited the corpse of its star.

Long did The Thaen travel to return to the galaxy of its birth. By the time it found the hollow world, the shape of the universe had begun to change. Light did not always follow the shape of space-time, or what The Thaen expected the shape of space-time to be. Stars that should have gone on burning for aeons winked out. Post-humanity was responsible, but The Thaen could not guess what they/it were/was doing, or why.

The zero-point reef still powered the hollow wold's artificial sun. The captain and his people were still frozen as they had been for millions of years. The Thaen deactivated the gray infection by manipulating its metaspatial architecture. The stasis bots shut themselves down. The hollow world woke up.

The captain and his people needed no explanation. They knew at once that The Thaen had saved them from the gray infection. They sang their grateful song to The Thaen. Though they were primitive creatures, the captain and his people were the closest The Thaen had to its own kind. It loved them. In their way, they loved it.

So it was that the pioneers who had set out to make a place for humanity indeed made one, though it was not as they had imagined. And The Thaen that had set out to find the Alien had found it, though it was not as The Thaen had imagined.

The universe continued to change. It was being engineered into something else. All of its rules were being altered by post-humanity's descendants, and when the captain or The Thaen peered out at space, they could not understand what was happening there. Space was no longer dark, but glowed blue. New suns sparked to life, but their spectra varied wildly from moment to moment.

But the captain's people and The Thaen lived happily ever after in their hollow world as long as there remained a universe to live in.

JULIE E. CZERNEDA

"One of the fastest-rising stars of the new millennium"—Robert J. Sawyer

Web Shifters
☐ **BEHOLDER'S EYE (Book #1)**   0-88677-818-2—$6.99

☐ **CHANGING VISION (Book #2)**   0-88677-815-8—$6.99
It had been over fifty years since Esen-alit-Quar had revealed herself to the human Paul Ragem. In that time they had built a new life together out on the Fringe. But a simple vacation trip will plunge them into the heart of a diplomatic nightmare—and threaten to expose both Es and Paul to the hunters who had never been convinced of their destruction.

The Trade Pact Universe
☐ **A THOUSAND WORDS FOR STRANGER (Book #1)**
                                    0-88677-769-0—$6.99

☐ **TIES OF POWER (Book #2)**   0-88677-850-6—$6.99

OTHERLAND

TAD WILLIAMS

In many ways it is humankind's most stunning achievement. This most exclusive of places is also one of the world's best kept secrets, created and controlled by The Grail Brotherhood, a private cartel made up of the world's most powerful and ruthless individuals. Surrounded by secrecy, it is home to the wildest of dreams and darkest of nightmares. Incredible amounts of money have been lavished on it. The best minds of two generations have labored to build it. And somehow, bit by bit, it is claming the Earth's most valuable resource— its children.